MATTHEW HUGHES

TO HELL AND BACK
Costume Not Included

**ANGRY
ROBOT**

ANGRY ROBOT
A member of the Osprey Group

Lace Market House,
54-56 High Pavement,
Nottingham,
NG1 1HW, UK

www.angryrobotbooks.com
Cape town

An Angry Robot paperback original 2012

Cover art by Tom Gauld.
Set in Meridien by THL Design.

Distributed in the United States by Random House, Inc., New York.

ISBN 978-0-85766-139-5
eBook ISBN 978-0-85766-140-1

Printed in the United States of America

9 8 7 6 5 4 3 2

COSTUME NOT INCLUDED

ONE

"I thought you weren't speaking to me," Chesney Arnstruther said into the phone.

"I'm not speaking to you," said his mother. "I'm telling you something for your own good, is what I'm doing."

Chesney took the phone from his ear and looked again at the display screen; the call was coming from the country estate of the Reverend Billy Lee Hardacre. He tried to counterattack. "Are you living with him?" he said.

"I'm proud to be assisting him in his great work," Letitia Arnstruther said.

But Chesney had been raised by one of the most accomplished interrogators of the age – his mother could have offered master classes to Torquemada's top cadre – and he knew an evasion when he heard one. "Are you living with him?" he said again, then dropped the big one: "In sin?"

"He is a great man," she said. "A prophet. An angel of the Lord comes to him."

"I know," said Chesney, "I was there."

"There in body," said his mother, and now Chesney could hear the sound of tables being turned, "but not in spirit."

"I've had plenty of 'being there in spirit'," the young man said. "Great sulfurous heaps of it. I've been to Hell and back, and more than once. Now I just want a nice, quiet life as a crimefighter."

"After all that Billy Lee has done for you," she said. Chesney sighed. She was always at her best when working the guilt. And, of course, she never missed one of his sighs; now she bored in with the precision of a sadistic dental surgeon going for the deep nerve. "He got you the deal that you're so enamored of – and your little demon, too."

"Mother," Chesney said. The single word carried the sound that a sentient sandcastle would have made as the first ripples of the irresistible incoming tide undercut its proud ramparts.

"He's on in five minutes. Watch him. Hear what he has to say."

"Aw…"

"Don't you 'aw' me, young man. Tell me you'll watch the program."

Chesney made a sound that he imagined Russian circus bears made when they were poked to dance yet another encore.

"Chesney!" The ripple had become a rip tide.

"All right. But I'm not buying in," he said. "That's for sure certain."

"The reverend knows best," she said. "He's got the angel of the–"

But Chesney had hung up. He was less awed by the angel – technically, a high-ranking Throne – than his mother was. He'd seen God's messenger at work and wasn't all that impressed. A smooth-voiced bureaucrat was Chesney's take on the heavenly visitor, and no use at all when the situation came to a real crisis.

It had all happened little more than a month ago. Chesney, a mild-mannered auditor at Paxton Life and Casualty, a modest-sized insurance company in the Midwest, had accidentally caused Hell to go on strike. With the seven deadly sins on hiatus, the world had rapidly ground to a halt. Without greed, lust, vanity and the rest of the panoply of mortal iniquity, people had stopped working, competing, wooing, consuming – indeed, all the activities that made life what it was, even if, theologically speaking, that was what it wasn't supposed to be.

Chesney had turned to his mother for help. Letitia Arnstruther, a ferocious church lady who could have given the Plymouth Rock puritans a one-lap lead and still beaten them through the strait and narrow gate, took him to the Reverend Billy Lee Hardacre, former labor negotiator, best-selling novelist and currently a television preacher of Nielsen-busting prowess.

Hardacre had advanced a theory: that creation was a book that God was writing, and that Chesney and everybody else were characters in the unwinding tale. The point of the divine literary effort? The preacher's answer was that sometimes you read a text to learn something; but to learn some things, the best way was to *write* a book. God, according to Billy Lee, was writing us in order to learn about good and evil.

There had been a negotiation. Chesney had been there. So had the Throne, Heaven's delegate. And so had Lucifer, whose infernal domain had been brought to a standstill. The details of the settlement did not concern Chesney; what mattered to him was that he came out of the crisis with his soul still intact and no one's property but his own, and that he got what he had always dreamed of – in his spare time he was now a costumed crimefighter, assisted by a weasel-headed, sabertooth-fanged demon named Xaphan, whose most recent earthly assignments had placed him first on the quarterdeck of a notorious seventeenth-century pirate, and then in the inner cabal of Al Capone's Chicago mob.

Not part of the negotiation, but a no less welcome antidote to Chesney's previously celibate existence, Chesney had acquired his first ever girlfriend. Melda McCann was brave enough to have followed Chesney literally into Hell, where she had been prepared, if necessary, to give Satan himself a squirt of the pepper spray she never left home without. Fortunately, that necessity had not arisen and now Melda was his more or less constant companion. She even knew of his crimefighting avocation and its demonic adjunct: more than knew; she approved.

Chesney suspected that Melda had initially been strongly drawn to the idea of dating a celebrity, but he was also sure that she had come to like him for himself. He had, she had told him, "qualities." Chesney's own view of himself was colored by a lifetime of coming to terms with the reality that he was not like other people. The therapists who had worked with him as a child had diagnosed him as "suffering from "high-functioning autism," according to the assessment they had given his mother, and which Chesney had read with the assistance of the public library's medical reference shelf. As Chesney saw things, the world presented itself to him as an obscure, murky landscape in which, here and there, were pools of pure, undiluted light.

Numbers were pools of light to Chesney. They sang to him, as he had once told his employer's daughter, Poppy Paxton, with whom he had thought himself in love, until he came to know her better. Comix occupied another pool of light, especially the adventures of the *Freedom Five* and his favorite: Malc Turner, a UPS delivery man who, after handling a strange package from a parallel dimension, became *The Driver*, scourge of criminals and terrorists.

To these islands of illumination, Chesney had now added two more: crimefighting and what passed between him and Melda in the privacy of their bedrooms. Much to the young man's relief, it had turned out that the contents of all of the many instruction books he had read on the techniques of intimacy had coalesced at some level of his unusually structured psyche to augment a hitherto undeveloped talent for the arts of love.

It also hadn't hurt his chances that nature, or divine providence, had made up for the oddness of his mental equipment by granting him an extra portion in the size of his genitive organ. Chesney had had no idea he was well outside the middle of the bell curve when it came to both length and girth. The only other penises he'd ever seen belonged to performers in the pornographic videos he used to rent before Melda came along. Based on what he'd seen, he was just average.

His exceptional grasp of technique he put down to his unusual ability to remember details even while grasping complete gestalts. Melda had waved away his offered explanation, being a woman to whom deeds spoke for themselves. "Hoo, boy!" she had said, after their first exploration of his abilities, "You don't look the type, but…" And then she had switched to a nonverbal mode of expression that, Chesney was pleased to agree, said all that needed to be said.

Chesney was looking forward to another nonverbal colloquy with Melda McCann this afternoon. It was a summer Sunday. Before her advent into his life, the day would have found him in the park near his apartment, eating a fiery chili dog and watching athletic young women in spandex and sports bras running on the path that followed the river. Today, Melda was coming to his place, bringing a picnic lunch they would go and eat in the park before heading back upstairs to satisfy a different appetite. Afterwards, they would laze around the place until evening, when Chesney would summon up his demon, put on his masked costume, and go out to fight crime.

But first – he gritted his teeth at the thought – he

must do what he had told his mother he would do. He picked up the television's remote and pressed buttons. The screen came to life, showing a commercial for a set of "handwoven mini-tapestries" depicting "great scenes from the Holy Scriptures." The camera did not linger too long on any one image, but Chesney nonetheless gained a clear impression of the goods being offered. Adam and Eve were rendered in a color-scheme reminiscent of *The Simpsons*, and the apple looked like a misshapen cell phone being fought over by a couple of teenage mall rats. Moses parting the Red Sea might have been a traffic cop diverting pedestrians from a street with a burst water main.

"Just three payments of twenty-nine, ninety-nine, and these magnificent wall hangings are yours to keep and treasure," said an oily-voiced off-screen narrator as a 1-800 number flashed repeatedly in bright colors across the center of the screen. In small print below, Chesney saw that the "magnificent wall hangings" actually measured only two feet by two-and-a-half.

The commercial ended, the screen going momentarily black, leaving only the retinal imprint of the flashing telephone number. The cable station briefly identified itself – *The Word and Nothing but the Word* read a display card decorated with sunlit clouds and a long, straight trumpet – then the screen went black again. Now a choir began to sing Handel's *Hallelujah Chorus*, with backup from electric guitar and bass. The screen erupted into light, a brilliant starburst of white and gold.

This is new, Chesney thought. He double-checked to make sure he had the right channel. Billy Lee Hardacre's weekly program, *The New New Tabernacle of the Air,* had always before opened with the sound of a pulsing heartbeat and a black screen. The first visual should have been a long shot of the preacher seated at a desk on a darkened stage, a single spotlight illuminating his silver-haired leonine head bent over a sheaf of papers. He would look up, the image would switch to a close-up, and he would begin his gravel-voiced jeremiad against the evils of the week that had been.

But now the starburst lingered, a four-pointed star whose downward-pointing lowest projection lengthened and kept on lengthening, so that the image evoked both a crucifix and the star that was supposed to have lured three Persian magi across Mesopotamia to Bethlehem. And then came a little special-effects image manipulation: Billy Lee appeared to step through the starburst from the darkness behind, his hands raised, arms outspread, his contact lens-enhanced blue eyes brilliant beneath the swept-back pompadour of shining hair.

The sounds of choir and guitars faded away. In the silence that followed, the preacher lowered his arms, looked straight into the camera and said, "He is coming!"

Chesney groaned. It was a little groan, half suppressed – as if his mother, though miles away, might hear him. "No," he said, more to himself than to the man on the television, "I'm not."

The Reverend Billy Lee, broadcasting live from a highly automated studio a few miles from his walled estate, ninety minutes by car south of the city where Chesney lived, did not hear the young man's groan or his denial. And Hardacre would not have changed his message even if he could have heard the defiance. He was, as he was now telling the television audience, the bearer of a message from on high.

"I am the forerunner," he said, his eyes shining, his square-jawed, broad-browed face set in an expression of exalted expectation. "I am the harbinger. I am the messenger who brings the word. And the word is: he is coming. A prophet, the bearer of a new gospel, a gospel for our times. He is coming."

The camera angle changed, and the preacher turned to meet it. "I have met him. He has crossed my threshold, sat at my table, broken bread with me." Now the well-modulated voice fell to a breathy whisper. "And he was attended," Hardacre said, "by an angel of the Lord."

"That's not how it happened," Chesney said. "The angel was there to see *you*."

The man on the television was pressing on. The glow had faded from his face – camera trickery, Chesney thought – as the preacher began to talk about the world and its current state. He talked about violence in places where violence was not unexpected, about greed and venery in the usual locations, about pride and envy. He cited examples of humanity's lack of humanity, of hunger and want amidst gluttony and excess, of blood for blood and hate for hate.

"But all this," he said, turning to a new camera angle, one which brought the glow back to his visage and the gleam back into his eyes, "all this will soon come to an end. We will turn a page, begin a new chapter, create a new story – a good news story – to ring down the ages to come.

"The moment is almost at hand, it marches toward us with every tick of the clock. He is coming. The prophet is coming. And all shall be made new."

As he was speaking these last lines, an image appeared on a curtain hung behind the preacher. A rear-projected image that moved as the draped cloth rippled in a faint breeze – probably, thought Chesney, generated by a fan on the floor. The image was as of a halo of light surrounding the dark silhouette of a man's head and shoulders. The head was small and round, the shoulders none too wide. Chesney recognized the outline shapes: they were based on his own unprepossessing anatomy – in fact, they were photoshopped from a picture his mother had taken of him, in her back yard, on his twenty-fourth birthday.

"No!" he said, and he would have said it just as loudly, even if his mother had been in the same room, even if she had been wearing her most severe frown, a down-turning of the mouth's corners that made her lips resemble a croquet hoop. If Genghis Khan's mom had ever turned such a glower upon her son, Prince of Conquerors would have straightaway reconsidered his hording and pillaging ways.

But Chesney had come to believe that he was now proof against its baleful influence. He had, after all, defied Satan, had even bested the Archfiend at a few hands of poker. And he had caused a young woman to make faces, motions and sounds that were far more affecting than those made by actresses in porn films. "No!" he told the voice from the television. "Not me! I'm a crimefighter, not a prophet! You better get yourself another actuary!"

The phone rang. He snatched it up, pushed the talk button and said, "What?" without modulating his assertive tone of voice.

"Sweetie?" said Melda McCann. "Something wrong?"

The young man softened immediately. No one had ever called him "sweetie" before. Melda did it frequently, yet Chesney never tired of hearing it. "It's the Reverend Hardacre," he told her. It galled him that he couldn't just say the man's name without prefacing it with the honorific, but childhood conditioning ran deep. "He's at it again!"

"Well, screw him and the cloud he came down from Heaven on," she said, which made Chesney laugh, despite himself. He imagined his mother reacting to his girlfriend's view of Letitia's boyfriend – and boyfriend was the appropriate label. He was sure the preacher and his mother were cohabiting "without benefit of clergy," as his mother herself would have put it before she had apparently opted to exempt herself from her own lifelong standards.

He had to use his imagination because, so far, the two females in his life had not occupied the same room at the same time – a state of affairs that would continue for as long as Chesney could arrange it. Of course, the young man knew that this happy situation could not forever endure; he was not looking forward to that inevitable moment, when the clash of universes must occur.

Melda was saying something else. Chesney tore his mind away from the delayable-yet-unavoidable and paid attention. She was asking him if he wanted to meet her in the park or have her come to his apartment.

"Here," he said, without need to think about it, "my place." There were things they could do in his apartment that they could not do in the park, things that were still new to Chesney's experience, and even more delightful than being called "sweetie." He could eat anytime.

"We'd better make it the park," Melda said. "I'm hungry. And momma always said a girl should eat first, even when she was providing the eats." Chesney made a different kind of groan, and she said, "Don't worry, sweetie. Food gives me energy."

She lived on the far side of the long river-following park. Carrying the picnic basket, it would take her a while to walk to their favorite spot – actually, it was Chesney's pick – near the amphitheater and the basketball courts. That meant he had some time. He used it to summon his assistant.

The fiend appeared the moment the young man spoke its name, bringing with it a slight whiff of sulfur. As usual, it arrived hovering in the air, its saucer-sized eyes in a weasel's face at the same level as Chesney's, which meant that Xaphan's patent-leather shoes, wrapped in old-fashioned spats, were about three feet above the carpet. Between the fanged head and the foppish footwear was a pin-striped, wide-lapeled,

double-breasted suit, of a kind that had been fashionable among the denizens of Chicago speakeasies, back
when *twenty-three-skidoo* was on every hepster's lips.

"Hiya, boss," said the demon around a thick Havana
Churchill that protruded from between two huge
curved canines that would have been a sabertooth's
pride. The fiend removed the cigar only long enough to
blow a complicated figure of smoke into the apartment's air and to lift the glass in its other hand to its
thin, black weasel lips. Xaphan drank off a finger of
tawny overproof rum, issued a breathy sigh of satiation,
and put the cigar back where it had been, breathily
pumping the glowing end to a brighter glow. When the
Churchill was drawing to its satisfaction, Chesney's assistant said, "Whatta ya say, whatta ya know?"

"I'm going out to the park for a picnic with Melda,"
the young man said, "then we'll probably come back
here." He ignored the demon's suggestive eyebrow
motions and low-voiced "Hubba hubba!" – he'd found
that responding to Xaphan's prurience only encouraged more of the same. "But tonight," Chesney went
on, "I want to go out and do some crimefighting."

"Okay," said his assistant, in a tone that implied it
was waiting to hear the details.

But Chesney didn't have any details. "So I need to
know what's going down" – he'd heard police officers,
or at least actors pretending to be cops, talk that way
on TV – "in the mean streets. What can we hit tonight?"

Xaphan's eyes looked left, then right. It pulled the
cigar from its lips and examined the glowing coal for
a moment, then said, "I gotta tell ya, not much."

"What do you mean?"

Xaphan put the cigar back, shot the linked French cuffs of its silk shirt and gave a kind of hitch of its padded shoulders that always reminded Chesney of Jimmy Cagney in the old black-and-white, crime-does-not-pay films. "I mean," the demon said, "not much. These days, crime..." – it gestured with the hand that held the glass of rum, spilling a few drops – "there ain't so much of it around, see?"

"Come on," said Chesney, "it's a big city. I've seen the figures." As an actuary, the young man was intimately familiar with crime statistics.

"Things change," Xaphan said, tilting the glass and draining the last of the rum.

"What things?"

"Well, mainly," said his assistant, "you."

"I haven't changed," said Chesney. "I don't change." Anyone who knew him could have attested to the truth of the remark – although not too many people, apart from his mother and now Melda McCann, could have been said to have really known Chesney Arnstruther. "Does not play well with others," had been a frequent notation on his grade-school report cards, words that could have served as both the young man's life motto and the epitaph carved into his tombstone. The only other phrase that could have given those six words competition as a succinct summation of Chesney's life was the one he had just voiced to his demonic helper: "I don't change."

"Yeah," said the fiend, "but you've changed the game. At least around this here burgh."

"You mean crime – major crime – has gone down since I started being The Actionary?"

"You got it. The serious outfits, they gone and pulled right back. No dope, no heists, no chop shop action. Nobody would look at a bank job even if they had the keys to the front door and the combination of the vault."

"Hmm," said Chesney. "So what does that leave?"

Xaphan shrugged again and puffed smoke around the cigar clamped in its jaw. "Little everyday jobs, muggings, burglaries, guys cheatin on their taxes, playin' poker, hangin around in cathouses, kids boostin stuff outta the stores, guys spittin on sidewalks." It drew deeply on the Churchill and blew another complicated smoke-shape. "You wanna tackle some of that?"

"We've been doing that kind of thing the past couple of weeks. That's not what I became a crime-fighter for."

"Hey," said the demon, "whatta ya gonna do?"

Chesney had no quick answer. He couldn't see a pool of light to work within. "Wait a minute," he said after a moment, "I play poker."

"Not for the stakes I'm talkin about," said the demon. "Real moolah. Besides, you never played in the back room of no high-class house of ill repute. A house that takes a percentage of every pot – that's what makes it illegal."

"Huh," said Chesney, still thinking. "Is there a game like that going on tonight?"

"It so happens, there is."

"Are the players hoodlums?"

Xaphan looked like a weasel weighing things up. "These ain't your ordinary street goniffs," it said, "but ain't one of them as hasn't done a shady deal or taken a kickback."

"Racketeers!"

"It wouldn't be stretchin' the point too far."

"What time does the game start?"

"Nine, ten," said Xaphan. "They eat, have a few drinks, maybe talk some bizness, go upstairs with the girls. Then they settle in for an all-nighter."

"Where is this place? What's it called?"

"It ain't got a name. Too exclusive. Mostly they call it 'Marie's place.' Or just 'the place,' seein' as how Marie's been dead maybe forty years."

It was sounding good to Chesney. He could see it in his mind's eye: chandeliers and swag lamps, champagne in free-standing ice buckets, velvet-covered plush furniture, cigar smoke, women in frilly corsets. He realized he was back in a pool of light. "Come at midnight," he told his assistant. "We'll let them get right into it. Then… wham!"

"Wham it is, boss." Xaphan looked into its glass and seemed surprised to find it empty. "Ya need me for anything right this minute?"

"No, I've got to get to the park and meet Melda." Chesney checked his watch, found he had to hurry.

"You wanna take the short cut?"

Technically, according to the contract Billy Lee Hardacre had negotiated with Satan on behalf of the young man, the demon's powers were only to be invoked in Chesney's role as the crimefighting Actionary. But Chesney and his assistant had come to a private arrangement: Xaphan performed some extra duties in exchange for being able to use their way station in the outer circle of Hell, which was well stocked with over-proof rum and fine Cuban cigars – the demon had developed a taste for the latter during his Capone years, and for the former when he was attached to the scourge of the Spanish Main.

"Let's," said Chesney. Instantly he was no longer in his apartment, but in a warm, comfortable and spacious room whose thick stone walls, oak-beamed ceiling and plush carpeting kept out the howl of the ice-charged winds that blew foul, stinking air in a ceaseless gale through Hell's outermost region. Xaphan used the stopover to recharge his tumbler of rum and immediately drain it. Then the room was gone and Chesney was in the park, near the bench where he was to meet his girlfriend.

"Girlfriend," he whispered to himself. Saying it was almost as good as being called 'sweetie.'

"She's comin," said the demon. "I'm just gonna fade you in."

To avoid startling the citizenry, they had arrived invisible, as Xaphan would remain. The demon looked around, saw a teenager on the very edge of the riverbank. The kid was trying to impress his girl by holding out a fragment of bread and encouraging a floating Canada goose to take it from his hand. The fiend made a slight motion of its own stubby fingers, and now the goose lunged upward, caught both the bread and the youth's fingertips in its beak and turned its neck into an ess-shape as it yanked down hard. The teenager, pulled toward the water, tried to keep his footing, knees bent, free arm windmilling. His girl grabbed the flailing limb, but she was too late to pull him back. Instead, he grabbed her wrist and they both toppled into the shallows, where the goose beat its wings at them and honked in outrage.

Every eye in the park turned toward the disturbance. "Okay," said the demon, "fadin' you in now."

Chesney became visible as he sat down on the bench. Nobody noticed. "See you at midnight," he said, but his assistant was already just a whiff of sulfur dissipating in the late spring air. He relaxed against the horizontal wooden slats of the bench's backrest. He looked in the direction that Melda would be coming from, and there she was: just passing the basketball court, where the usual gang of young toughs were passing the ball back and forth and offering salacious invitations to the women, usually in pairs, who walked or jogged by.

One of the teenagers said something to Melda – or tried to; he got no farther than "Hey, chica–" before one of the others clamped a hand over the speaker's mouth and spoke rapidly and quietly into his ear. The silenced youth's eyes widened, his friend released him, and they all turned their attention to dribbling and passing the basketball.

Chesney had watched the business. He put it into the context of what Xaphan had told him about crime rates falling. The same gang of thugs had surrounded

Melda McCann as she'd walked home from work three weeks before, their intent the theft of her purse. Instead, from out of the darkness, the Actionary had appeared amid a clap of thunder and a flash as bright as lightning to bang heads together and send the muggers fleeing.

It would have been a perfect moment, if Melda hadn't taken him for yet another threat and pepper-sprayed his eyes and nose. But, fortunately, they had gotten past that, and past the much worse things that had ensued when they'd all gone to Hell, and now Melda McCann was one of only three people – Chesney's mother and the Reverend Billy Lee were the others – who knew that he was the crimefighting Actionary.

She arrived carrying a large plastic cooler hung from a strap over her shoulder. Chesney knew that she was slight of stature but surprisingly strong. He stood and took the cooler from her, set it on the bench, then craned his neck down to kiss her upturned lips.

"Hi, sweetie," she said.

"Hi, yourself."

"You still upset about the rev?"

"Not now," he said. He drew her down to the bench and they kissed again, a long one that resulted in Chesney having to rearrange the front of his slacks.

Melda noticed and rolled her eyes. "Eat first," she said. She pulled the cooler closer, opened its lid and began taking out small plastic containers. Then she scooted sideways on the bench to make room between them for the food.

Chesney looked around the park, wanting to see somebody noticing him and his girl and how cool they were with each other. But the only people looking their way were the gangstas at the basketball court. One of them, the leader, seeing he had caught Chesney's gaze, showed him an expression of exaggerated surprise, as if the actuary had just pulled off some impressive stunt.

"Hey, 'mano!" the young tough called. He wore a gold, sleeveless shirt and red bandana tied in a torc around his forehead. A chain-link tattoo circled his throat. "You got some huevos, hookin' up with that chica." Chesney ignored the remark, but the thug continued: "You know whose girl that is?"

"Ignore him," said Melda, continuing to unpack the cooler.

But Chesney wasn't going to let the day be spoiled. "Yeah," he called back. "Mine."

The gangsta showed him mock fear, his hands shaking in front of his chest. The others in the gang made *hoo* and *whoa* sounds and laughed.

Melda handed Chesney a sandwich. "Eat," she said. She selected one for herself and took a healthy bite. Chesney followed her lead. They turned away from the basketball court to face each other and, for Chesney, that meant that the rest of the world ceased to exist.

They ate in silence for a while. Besides sandwiches, Melda had brought cut-up raw vegetables and a dressing that she made herself out of sour cream, garlic and herbs. She dipped a cherry tomato into the little plastic tub and popped it into his mouth. He loved that, even though he had hated it when his mother used to do it at the family dinner table when he was a kid. Of course, Melda was a better cook than Letitia, whose science of the kitchen extended no farther than the need to cook everything until it was either limp and soggy or bone-dry.

"Listen, sweetie," she said, after he had finished his second sandwich and half the veggies. "I've been thinking."

"About what?"

"About you and me and this thing you do." She was watching him closely and when she saw the look on his face, she said, "What's the matter?"

He didn't know. But it was as if a cloud had passed between them and the sun. The light no longer seemed so bright. "You're not..." he began, but couldn't find words to continue. He gathered himself and tried again. "You're not going to push me... like my mother and the reverend–"

"What? No!" She shook her head as if a particularly silly idea had somehow made its way into her mind and had to be thrown off. "No, no, never. Look, sweetie, if you don't want to be a prophet, that's okay with me."

"Oh, good," he said, and reached for another cherry tomato.

"I mean," she continued, "where's the profit in being a prophet?"

He stopped with the dripping red orb at his lips. "Huh?"

"All I'm saying, is you're a celebrity now. You're the Actionary, for gawdsake. You should cash in."

He put the tomato down. "I'm not doing this for money," he said.

"Who said money?"

"You did. You said, 'cash in.' Cash is money."

She looked as if the connection had never occurred to her. "Okay," she said, "I didn't mean like get paid for crimefighting. Like, how would that even work? They'd make you a special agent for the FBI?"

"The FBI already has special agents, thousands of them."

"Okay, then, a super special agent. But that's not what we're talking about anyway."

"What are we talking about, anyway?" he said. The air still seemed cooler than it ought to be in the sunshine. The disturbance in the front of his slacks was now just a memory.

"Being a celebrity. Endorsements. Giving speeches. A book deal." Her eyes widened, "Oh, god," she said and only breathed the next two syllables: "Oprah."

"Oprah?"

"You could so be on Oprah. She'd love you."

"But I don't want to be on Oprah."

"But you'd need her," Melda said, as if explaining to a nine year-old, "for the book."

"I don't want to write a book. Or give speeches." When he thought about it, the prospect terrified him. "Or tell people what kind of soda they should drink."

She gave a delicate snort. "I think you'd get a better class of endorsement than Coke or Pepsi. Those big companies with the names that don't tell you what they do, the kind that used to hire Tiger Woods until it turned out he was more into sluts than putts."

"But I don't want to do that," Chesney said. "I just want to fight crime."

"But what are we going to live on?"

"Well," he began, and then the pronoun she had used caught up with him. "We?" he said.

"Well, yeah," she said. "I mean, I kinda thought, the way you like me . . ."

"Oh, said Chesney. He realized that while he was enjoying the unfamiliar territory known as "having a girlfriend," the girlfriend in question was already picking out an address in the land of permanent relationship. Perhaps even the neighborhood called marriage. He wondered how he would feel about that, once he got over the surprise. But now he focused his mind on the question they were actually discussing. "I have a job," he said. "I make pretty good money. And you've got your thing with the nails."

She sighed. It wasn't anywhere near as eloquent a condemnation of his intellect and character as one of Letitia Arnstruther's sighs, but it blew from the same direction. "You can't keep working there," she said.

"Why not? I mean, the C Group has wound up, now that W.T. has decided not to run for governor." That decision by Chesney's employer, Warren Theophilus Paxton, had been prompted by the sudden nervous breakdown of his daughter, Poppy, who did not remember her own trip to Hell. Unlike Melda, Poppy had gone there unwillingly, kidnapped by her father's campaign adviser, Nat Blowdell, who'd made his own deal with the Devil, though on more traditional lines than Chesney's.

C Group had been a special crime statistics unit within Paxton Life and Casualty, to which Chesney had been seconded. It crunched numbers to back up Paxton's candidacy, which was supposed to be based on an anti-crime platform. The campaign would have been fueled by a "missing blonde" media frenzy orchestrated by Blowdell. Young, blonde women who went missing were a guaranteed draw for the media. Every year, on the anniversary of her disappearance, the media ran retro-stories on the young journalism student, Cathy Bannister, who had been snatched from her third-floor apartment nine years ago, and never seen again.

Paxton hadn't known that Blowdell meant the "missing" descriptor to transmute into "found murdered." A missing blonde daughter of a socially prominent millionaire who subsequently turned up dead would have whipped the media into paroxysms of overkill. A skilled operator like Blowdell could have ridden the grieving father like a surfboard on a wave of frenzy, straight into the governor's mansion. From there, Blowdell had intended to position Paxton for the next big wave, whose froth just might have carried them into the White House; once there, Blowdell meant to somehow use his insider position and infernal connections to rule the world.

Chesney had put a stop to that. Now Nat Blowdell was just another damned soul in Hell. Xaphan had wiped away Poppy Paxton's memory of the incident, as well as that of a Major Crimes Squad lieutenant named Denby, Police Central's liaison with C Group. But the young woman's emotional trauma was too deep-seated, so Xaphan explained it, that he couldn't "clean her up completely widdout she's gonna lose some of her marbles."

Faced with a suddenly depressed and nervous daughter and the mysterious disappearance of his key campaign adviser, W.T. Paxton had abandoned the idea of running for governor and closed down C Group. The group of hotshot number crunchers, of whom Chesney was the hottest and crunchingest, had been sent back to the actuarial cohorts. In recognition of his outstanding work, Chesney had been upgraded to a level three actuary, which qualified him not only for a raise and more benefits, but an actual fourth-floor office – though not on a corner and with only one window.

"So I've got a pretty bright future with Paxton's," he told Melda.

"Not once the ice queen starts to remember what happened," she said.

"She won't," the young man said. "And you shouldn't call her the ice queen. She's had a rough time."

"Who hasn't?" said Melda. Her small face under straight-cut brown bangs compressed its fine features in thought. "Maybe Poppy won't remember," she said. "But she's going to get a sick turn every time she runs into you. It won't be too long before she gets daddy to turf you out."

Chesney's instinct was to deny the likelihood. But he checked himself. Melda was better than he was at this kind of thinking. Human nature was one of her pools of light and she could spot details he would always miss. He'd only seen Poppy Paxton once in the two weeks since the events that had cost the young woman her memory and her ability to sleep through the night. She'd been sitting in the back of her father's limousine, the long black car idling at the curb, waiting for W.T. to come out.

Chesney had come down the front steps of the Paxton Building. She had glanced at him through the tinted window, and their eyes had met. He'd seen her react, her already pale face going white and her eyes widening. She'd looked away, and said something sharply to the chauffeur. The car had driven off.

"You may be right," Chesney said, "but still, I can get a good job somewhere else. I have a thing for numbers."

She was going to say something, but didn't. "Eat your tomato," she said, pushing the food gently back toward his lips, "before it drips on your shirt. We can talk about this some other time."

Chesney ate the tomato and the last half sandwich. He deliberately did not think about the things they'd been discussing. Melda passed him a soft drink and he washed the food down, while she repacked the empty containers in the cooler. After she closed the lid, she said, "What'll we do now?"

"Um," Chesney said.

She made a little noise in her throat. "That's what I thought you'd say." She stood up. "Your place is closer."

TWO

The demon appeared on the stroke of midnight, its ever-present Churchill sticking out the side of its jaw, behind one of the sabertooth fangs. Xaphan removed the cigar, drained the tumbler of rum in its other hand, then tossed the glass into the air. It rose, stopped, and disappeared. "Costume?" the fiend said.

"Costume," said Chesney and instantly he was clad from head to foot in skintight blue and gray – he liked Batman's colors – with a half-mask that left only his eyes, mouth and chin showing. He had modified the outfit after his original outings: the long gauntlets had proved cumbersome so he had replaced them with wrist-length gloves of gray; the original calf-high boots were now something like a low-cut deck shoe. Somehow the effect was more modern.

He checked himself in the full-length mirror in his bedroom and for a moment was distracted by a memory of scenes that had been reflected in that same length of glass only hours before. Melda had stayed through the afternoon and they had ordered in pizza for supper. The pause for food gave them renewed energy; and it was past nine o'clock before the rumpled young woman had called a cab and gone home. Chesney had collapsed back on the bed and slept a deep and dreamless sleep until the alarm woke him just before midnight.

"All right," he said to his assistant, "is everything you told me earlier still good?"

"Ain't the word I'd use," said the demon, "but it's all jake."

"The game is on, in a… brothel?" It was only the second time in his life that Chesney had ever said the word; the first had been when he was ten and, having heard the term in the schoolyard, had asked his mother for its meaning. He could still taste the lavender-scented soap with which she had lathered his tongue.

"You bet."

His assistant had become more reliable since their earliest encounters – Chesney thought it was because Xaphan clearly valued the tobacco and liquor perquisites that came its way and which Chesney could revoke just by an exercise of his free will – but he knew he shouldn't take any spawn of Hell at its word. "Is there anything you aren't telling me?" he said.

The enlarged weasel eyes looked at him sideways. "Yes."

"What?"

The demon began ticking off its stubby fingers: "The median annual temperature in Timbuktu, the middle name of the guy who stocks the meat cooler at the Safeway on Route 44, the measurements of the winner and first runner-up in last year's Miss Universe pageant, the–"

"That's not what I meant!"

"That's a relief," said the fiend. "We coulda been here all night."

"Tell me about the poker game again – no, wait, *show me* what's going on there, right now."

Xaphan gestured, and a screen the size of a top-model plasma TV appeared before Chesney's eyes. It was as if he were standing behind a thick-set man in shirtsleeves, sitting at a green felt-covered table. The crown of the man's head was bald and beaded with sweat. He was separating his cards after a draw; Chesney saw aces and tens, then the man fanned out the last card – another ten. "Bet five," he said, pushing a stack of chips toward the pile in the middle of the table. The pot was lit by a bright light overhead.

Another player, long-faced and thin of hair, said, "Fold," and threw his cards into the middle.

The player to his left, a triple-chinned blond with flushed cheeks, looked at the man who had made the bet and said, "Five grand?" His eyebrows went up. "What did you pick up?"

"See me and I'll show you," said the first player.

It looked to Chesney like any of the poker games he used to play with the other actuaries from Paxton Life and Casualty. "What makes it illegal?" he said.

"See the guy here?" the demon said, pointing at the screen. A square-jawed man wearing an old-fashioned eyeshade held the deck in one hand and was picking up the cards that the man who folded had tossed into the pot. "He's the house. He don't play and he collects a percentage of the money when they settle up at the end. That's against the law in this state."

"Is the dealer a member of organized crime?"

"Name's Sal Feore. It's a mob-run game. In a mob-run cathouse. Look." The fiend made the image change, as if a camera had pulled back for a wider shot. In the darker reaches of the room, Chesney saw couches and chairs on which sat women wearing next to nothing. A tall redhead crossed the room from left to right, bringing a glass of whiskey to one of the players; she wore nothing but a smile and a pair of high heels.

"Sheesh," said Chesney. Still, he wanted to be certain that he was operating in a pool of light as clear as that which illuminated the poker table. "And the players, you said they're racketeers."

"No, you said that. I said they do shady deals. Bribes, kickbacks, a little of the old now-you-see-it, now-you-don't."

"Give me a for-instance," the young man said. "The guy who bet five thousand, what's his game?"

The demon said, "That mug? He's into a lot of different things. He's one of the partners in that new development that's going in on the south side – a silent partner, if you know what I mean."

"Let's say I don't," said Chesney.

"He gets three per cent of the revenues, but his name don't appear on no deeds or contracts. And what he gets don't appear on his tax return neither."

"Why do they give him three per cent? What does he put in?"

Xaphan tapped ash from its cigar. "He makes sure that no city inspectors come sniffin' around the site, maybe holdin' things up."

"A corrupt official!" said Chesney.

"Couldn'ta said it better myself. The guy's on the take."

"And the others?"

"Skinny guy who folded, he fixes traffic tickets in the DA's office, makes sure paperwork gets lost, tells cops to look the other way."

"What about the fat one?"

"Banker."

"What's wrong with that?"

"He takes dirty money, makes it clean."

Chesney had heard enough. "Let's bust them!"

"Okay. How you wanna go about it?"

"What do you suggest?"

The demon puffed his cigar and said, "Thing is, these mugs got juice downtown. That's why their game never gets raided."

"So we can't just tie them up and call Lieutenant Denby?"

"Nah. He'd get overruled, soon as they heard the address."

"Then what do we do?"

"We could cheat."

"What do you mean?"

The demon smiled a weasel smile. "We change the address." He gestured at the screen, which now showed the players and the women in a new location.

• • • •

An illegal poker game, even one attended by scantily clad ladies of the evening, did not constitute a major crime. So Lieutenant Denby, as the on-call duty officer of the Major Crimes Squad, was not called at home and summoned to Police Central when the outraged telephone calls began to clog the department's switchboard a few minutes after midnight. The responsibility for first response fell to two uniformed officers on patrol in a car painted black and white and with blue and red lights on top.

The lights were flashing when the policemen showed up, but the several people seated around the poker table or on chairs and other furniture tastefully arranged around the scene paid them no attention. The senior of the two patrolmen, George "Tick" Webber, radioed in that the pair might need back-up; then he and his younger partner, Carmela Ortiz, got out of the vehicle and approached the group.

"Holy…" Webber began, then found himself at a loss for words as he watched the tall naked redhead saunter across the open space and hand one of the players a glass of what the patrolman presumed to be liquor being illegally consumed in a public place. The man accepted the drink and patted the woman's well formed buttock, then returned his attention to the cards. It was only then that Ortiz drew his attention to the activity that was being transacted between a paunchy middle-aged man seated on a couch in his underwear while a young brunette with an apparently high tolerance for silicone knelt before him and made herself useful in a manner that was still technically illegal in several parts of the Bible Belt.

"Hey!" Officer Webber shouted. "Stop that!" Nobody paid him any attention. He blinked and rubbed his eyes. Ortiz was reaching for her weapon. "Wait," he told her, then lifted his portable radio and said, "Dispatch, alert the command sergeant. We are going to need two paddy wagons and at least two more teams of patrolmen."

The radio crackled. "Backup's on the way. Is it gang-related?"

Webber knew better than to use expletives over police band airwaves. Certain civic-minded citizens, their ears glued to police monitors, made a point of calling Commissioner Hanshaw and Mayor Greeley if those ears were affronted by low and rough language. "No, it's…" – he sought for a word then went with – "perversion-related."

"The funny thing is," Ortiz said, "they act like we're not even here." Sirens sounded in the distance, coming rapidly closer. "See that? Sirens, our lights, and they don't even look round."

The brunette was speeding up her rhythm. The heavy-bellied man on the couch groaned.

Webber looked around. Civic Plaza was only three blocks from Police Central. More blue lights were visible in the direction of headquarters, coming closer fast. He turned back to the scene before him: a carpeted, furnished room; men playing poker; near-naked women who were obviously not their wives or girl-friends lounging around or performing intimate acts. And all of it was taking place right smack dab in the middle of the brightly lit Civic Plaza, a broad expanse of pavement, fountains and benches that stretched from the imposing classical facade of the Justice Center on the square's east side to the chrome-and-glass modernity of City Hall on the west. Worse yet, the north side of the plaza was lined with up-market, high-rise condominium towers whose residents were some of the city's cream. Quite a few of those worthies were standing on their balconies, some of them in their nightclothes, and several with phones to their lips.

From high above, Webber heard a voice that was used to issuing orders and seeing them obeyed. "Officers," it said, "do your duty!"

"I guess we're gonna," Webber said to Ortiz. With his hand on his holstered nine-millimeter pistol, he stepped between two armchairs and said, "Nobody move!"

Later, describing the moment to the command sergeant, the officer would say that it was as if he had stepped though a wall and suddenly become visible to the people around the table. A fat, blond man jumped up and said, "Holy," in just the same tone as Webber had used the word, but he followed it with an even shorter word that described an act most people considered pleasurable but not holy.

One of the women screamed. The redhead stared at Webber and said, "How did you do that?" then jumped back startled, when Officer Ortiz followed him onto the carpet.

And then, as the back-up cars screeched to a halt just short of the scene, with the two paddy wagons coming up behind, followed by a TV crew's satellite-equipped van, the card players and courtesans looked around as if seeing for the first time that they were out in the middle of Civic Plaza. They said things like, "What the..." and "What happened?"

Only the kneeling brunette and the man who was the focus of her attention failed to notice, both being fully occupied in their transaction. Ortiz went over to them, tapped the woman on the shoulder and said, "You'll have to finish that later, hon."

As the skinny man was cuffed and led away, he said to Officer Webber, "Do you know who I am?"

"No," said the patrolman, "but I can't wait to find out."

Lieutenant Denby was roused from his bed and ordered to the Commissioner's office forthwith. He pulled on his suit trousers and jacket over his pajamas and by the time he exited his front door a black-and-white was idling at the curb. They drove down to Police Central through the empty streets on a code three, lights and sirens going full tilt.

The commissioner looked to have dressed just as quickly as the lieutenant. So did the district attorney. The mayor made a better showing, in black tie and shined shoes, but that was only because he hadn't been in bed, having spent the evening with a the majority leader of the state senate and their wives at the gala season's opening of the city's symphony. The chief of police, John Edgar Hoople – his mother had been an admirer of the FBI's red-busting efforts – arrived just after Denby, buttoning up his uniform tunic as he came out of the private elevator from the basement parking garage.

A few aides were scattered around the spacious office, but this was a meeting of the old bulls seated around the commissioner's desk. Commissioner Hanshaw reached into the bottom-left drawer and brought out a bottle of twelve year-old Scotch, while one of his aides collected glasses from a sideboard and passed them around to the silverbacks before withdrawing to the outer reaches.

Hanshaw poured more than a splash into each man's glass and nobody said a word before he, the mayor, the chief and the DA had all upended their drinks and thrown back the liquor. Then the commissioner said, "What the Hell was that all about?"

Mayor Greeley's hand was trembling as he set down his glass. "I was invited to that game," he said. "Hadn't been for Gladys and her thing about the symphony, I might've been there."

Chief Hoople was a square-faced man with a jutting jaw and hair like combed-back steel wool. "We got two questions to answer," he said. "Who did it, and how?"

"I got a third," said the district attorney, a smoothly polished man who wore rimless spectacles. "How are we going to handle it?"

"We're going to downplay it," Hanshaw said.

"How do you downplay naked hookers performing sex acts in the middle of Civic Plaza?" the mayor wanted to know.

"Drugs," said the commissioner. "Hypnotic drugs, roofies, or whatever it's called. They didn't know what they were doing."

The DA blinked behind his lenses. "That could work. They're the victims. So, no charges," – he blinked again – "so no names." He nodded, thinking. "But we need to get the raw footage from the TV crew."

"Get on the phone," said Hanshaw. "Call that weasel who cleans up messes for you."

"I can't," said the DA. "He was in the game." He took out a cell phone. "I'll get somebody on it. We'll tell the media it's a blackmail scam." He punched buttons on his phone and spoke into it: "Wake up and listen."

The chief of police reached for the Scotch and poured himself another drink. "We're back to how and why."

"What about who?" said the mayor.

"I think we know that," said the chief. He looked over his shoulder. "Denby, step over here and tell us about this kook."

The lieutenant had been leaning against a wall. The cops who had collected him from home had filled him in on the night's events, and he'd been thinking about it ever since. He stepped over to the desk. "We don't know who he is or what his game is," he told the four seated men. "We thought we had a lead on him, this kid who was supposed to be his buddy, but it was a dead end."

"Did you squeeze him?" said the chief.

"Couldn't," said the lieutenant. "W.T. Paxton sent over his private lawyer."

Hanshaw's eyebrows went up. "The kid was connected to Paxton?"

"Works for him. And maybe he's the daughter's boyfriend." Denby's brow wrinkled. "It all got kinda vague."

The mayor was looking thoughtful. "It isn't…" – he thought some more – "it isn't Paxton? He was looking at a run for governor. The boys and I were going to back him. I set him up with Nat Blowdell."

The district attorney shook his smooth head. "No, not Paxton. He's out of it. His girl's sick, some kind of mental breakdown. And he looks as if he caught it off her."

"What's happened to Blowdell, by the way?" said Mayor Greeley. "Haven't seen him since–"

"Never mind!" the commissioner snapped. "Let's deal with this craziness." He pointed a finger at Denby. "What have you got on this freak in the mask and tights?"

"Not a lot," said the lieutenant. "There was that thing with the stolen car export crew and the one with dopesters and all the money. Since then, he hasn't been making a splash. We think he's interrupted a few muggings, and maybe he was the one stopped a teenage shoplifting ring. But he didn't call us in on it."

"Why not?"

"His first two outings, he called us to come collect the crooks. Then we tried to bust him, and he stopped calling."

"Find him," said the Commissioner. "Get him in here. We need to talk."

In an unlit corner of the room, Chesney said to Xaphan, "Now?"

The demon watched the men around the desk, its huge eyes narrowing as it drew on its cigar. "I don't think so," it said. "I don't think they're gonna slap ya on the back and give ya the keys to the city."

It had been Chesney's plan to let the police discover the racketeers and arrest them, then to step forward and take credit for bringing the malefactors to justice. He had been waiting, cloaked by his demon's powers, for the right moment to make his presence known.

Commissioner Hanshaw was saying to the district attorney, "Get a statement out, pronto. The drugs thing. And tell the TV that if they run any pictures without that pixie whatsit—"

"Pixelation," said one of his aides from behind him.

"Whatever, just so nobody's face shows up on TV." Hanshaw turned to Chief Hoople. "Make sure your booking sergeant loses all the paperwork on this. Prints, mug shots, the works – I want it all delivered to my office in the next fifteen minutes."

"What about me?" said the mayor. "What do I do?"

"Just look concerned and tell anybody who asks that you've got complete confidence in us to get to the bottom of this."

"Right," said Greeley.

"And you," Hanshaw pointed at Lieutenant Denby again, "you get to the real bottom of this. From now on, it's your only assignment. Whatever it takes."

"Yes, sir," said the lieutenant.

"Do a good job," said the chief of police, "and there's a captaincy in it."

"Huh," said Denby, though only to himself as he turned away, "how about that?"

The meeting was breaking up. "This," said Chesney to his assistant "hasn't worked the way I wanted it to."

"This crimefightin' can be a tricky racket," said the demon. "We maybe need to work on it some more."

"Remember me?"

Chesney looked up from the statistical analysis he was reviewing. His office door was open and leaning against the jamb was Lieutenant Denby. "Yes," he said, "I do."

The policeman eased into the room, hooked a leg around one of the extra chairs in front of the young man's desk – as a level-three actuary, Chesney rated two, besides his high-backed swivel – and pulled it out so he could sit. Throughout this operation, Denby's eyes never left Chesney's.

"I'm glad to hear it," he said. "A lot of people have been having trouble with their memories lately. Like all those people who ended up in the middle of Civic Plaza in their underwear and couldn't account for how they got there."

The policeman paused, then let the pause extend. Chesney was familiar with the technique – his mother had perfected it – and knew that he was now supposed to feel compelled to say something. Whatever he said, the lieutenant would try to use it against him. So he said nothing.

The silence lasted more than ten seconds, then Denby leaned forward and said, "You on drugs?"

"No," said Chesney. "They cloud the mind."

"They sure clouded the minds of those people in Civic Plaza."

Another pause. This one developed into a contest to see who would speak second. Chesney saw no reason not to let the policeman win. "How can I help you?" he said.

Denby leaned back and gave the young man a long look. "You're a cool one, aren't you?"

Chesney tried to recall if the term "cool" had ever been applied to him before. "I don't think so," he said. "In high school, I was considered a walking definition of 'not cool'." He let Denby look at him again for a while, then said, "You haven't answered my question."

The policeman's dark brows drew down. "What question?"

"How can I help you?"

"What do you know about what happened in Civic Plaza last night?"

"They said on the news," Chesney answered, "that some people were arrested for public indecency."

"Did they?"

"Yes."

"And that's all you know?"

"What else is there to know?"

Denby blinked, then moved his eyes to several places around the office, as if expecting something useful to be found. Then he returned his focus to Chesney and bit the inside of his lip, squinting as if the action caused him pain. "I can't tell," he said, "if you're simple-minded or a real wise guy."

"Why don't you just tell me how I can help you, lieutenant?"

The policeman blew out a breath. "All right, that business in Civic Plaza…"

"Yes?"

"Was your friend the Actionary part of it?"

"How would I know?"

"He is your friend, isn't he?"

Chesney knew this was an occasion for being careful. "We are acquainted," he said.

Denby's faced screwed up. "Here's the funny thing," he said. "I know that you know the guy…" He paused and seemed to be wrestling with something in his mind. "But I can't remember *how* I know that."

It was another of those times, Chesney thought, when saying nothing was the best strategy.

After a while, the other man continued. "I know I had you in. I remember that lawyer, Trelawney, showed up. But I don't remember the interview." He looked at Chesney. "How come?"

"Didn't you take notes?"

"That's the screwy part of it. Or I should say, *another* screwy part of it. I look in my notebook, there's nothing there. A couple of pages are just blank."

"Did you tape record it?"

"You'd think I would've, wouldn't you? But again, it seems I didn't. I say 'it seems,' because I can't remember one way or another."

"I see," said Chesney.

"Do you?" There was a note in Denby's voice that sounded to Chesney like emotion. His guess was that the lieutenant was frustrated. "What do you see? I mean, what, exactly?"

"Something has happened," Chesney said, "and you can't explain it. It happens to me all the time. Like, right now, I think you're getting angry with me, but

I'm not sure why." He thought he should add, "I'm not very good with feelings. They're not one of my pools of light."

"Pools of light?"

"Things I understand."

Denby shook his head. "What do you remember from the interview?" he said.

"That the lawyer told me not to say anything. So I didn't. After a while, you said I could go."

Denby looked at him again, letting the silence grow. Finally, he said, "Huh."

They seemed to have exhausted the topic, or wandered off it. Chesney said, "Is that what you came to see me about?"

Denby shook himself. "No," he said. "I came to ask about your... acquaintance."

"The Actionary?"

"Yeah, the Actionary."

"What would you like to know?"

"You gonna be seeing him? Or you got a way of getting a message to him?"

"You mean like the bat signal?"

Chesney heard the other man sigh and suspected that he might have gone too far.

"I don't know what the fuck I mean!" said Denby, then he seemed to work at getting his emotions under control. "Just answer the question."

"I don't know when I'll see him next." That was true; he had no operations planned at the moment. "But I can give him a message when I do."

"Okay." The policeman nodded, as if confirming

some point. "Okay," he said again, "you tell your friend–"

"Acquaintance." Chesney thought the distinction was important.

"All right, you tell your *ac-quain-tance* to get in touch with me. We need to clear some things up."

"All right."

Denby stood up. "So he'll be in touch."

"I didn't say that. I said I'll tell him what you want. But he's not likely to come see you if you're going to try to arrest him."

"Oh, he's not?"

"Doesn't that make sense to you?"

The lieutenant was getting that look again, the one Chesney was now quite sure represented frustration. "OK," Denby said, "you tell him to come see me. We'll just have a talk. Meeting of the minds."

"You won't arrest him?"

"No."

"And you won't arrest me?"

"What could I arrest you for?" said the policeman as he headed for the door.

Chesney remembered a line he'd read in an issue of *The Driver*. "Mopery, with intent to gawk," he said.

From the doorway, the lieutenant gave him a look that wasn't friendly. "Now I'm thinking maybe you are a wise guy, after all."

"You look surprised to see me," Letitia Arnstruther said.

"I am." Chesney's mother had never visited his home before. She came through the door now, taking off her gloves – she was the only woman Chesney knew who wore gloves in summertime – her eyes active.

She went straight down the hall and turned left into the kitchen. A saucepan of pasta sauce was simmering on the stove, beside it a covered pot of slowly boiling water waiting for the spaghetti. The meal was also waiting for Melda McCann to return from the errand that had taken her down to the parking garage.

Chesney thought he wouldn't mention Melda, but his mother could count the number of plates and glasses on the dining room table, visible through the kitchen's serving hatch. "You have company?" she said.

"A friend."

Melda's purse was still on the counter where she'd let it slide off her arm when she set down the grocery bags. "Tell me," said his mother, "that it's a female friend."

"Mother."

"How long have you known her? Why haven't I met her?"

Chesney went over to the stove, took up the wooden spoon, and stirred the sauce. Melda had said it had to be stirred or it would burn.

"Well?" said his mother.

"I've known her a few weeks. You haven't met her because you've been" – he had been daring himself to use the term "shacked up," but chickened out when the moment came – "out of town with *your* new friend."

Letitia's eyes narrowed. She looked around. "Where is she?" The pause was for effect. "In the bedroom?"

"She left something in her car and went downstairs to get it."

"Something? Something you're too embarrassed even to name? To think that a son of mine–"

"A bottle of Chianti."

His mother did not miss a beat. "Oh, so now it's wine and women. Your father's genes breed true."

She broke off at the sound of the door opening. By the time they heard it close, Letitia had positioned herself to be the first thing to be seen by anyone walking through the kitchen doorway. She put her hands on her ample hips and her chin in an elevated position. Chesney thought that if his mother's nose had been a weapon this is how she have would looked sighting down it.

Chesney stopped stirring the sauce and set the spoon down on its ceramic holder – another Melda-based improvement to his domestic arrangements – and put himself between his mother and the doorway, just as the word, "Sweetie!" sounded from the hallway. It would have been followed by "I'm back!" except that the young man forestalled her by saying, "We have a surprise."

At that moment, Melda came into view, an old-style raffia-covered Chianti bottle in one hand and a corkscrew in the other. "Yes, we do!" she said, looking past Chesney. "Don't tell me. Is this Mom?"

Letitia Arnstruther had never been called "Mom" in her life, nor ever aspired to the distinction. Chesney heard the sharp intake of breath from behind him and was raising a hand to try to warn his girlfriend of the terrors she had just unwittingly unleashed, when Melda pressed the Chianti bottle into his upraised palm and found his other hand with the corkscrew.

"Open that, sweetie," she said, gliding around him to bear straight for the enemy. "Mom and I will have a glass of wine and start to get acquainted."

"I don't drink," said Letitia in a tone that could have frozen steam.

"Nothing to be embarrassed about," Melda said. "My aunt June is a recovering alcoholic, too. We're all real proud of her."

Chesney couldn't remember ever seeing his mother's eyes grow quite so large, but Melda didn't seem to notice as she took the older woman's elbow in hand and somehow, possibly involving some hitherto undisclosed jujitsu-like power, moved Letitia Arnstruther from the kitchen out into the hall and into the dining area. Over her shoulder, his girlfriend said, "Make Mom a nice cup of tea, will you, sweetie?"

He did as he was asked, boiling a cupful of water in the electric kettle while he opened the Chianti and poured two glasses. He had English breakfast tea bags – his mother's preferred beverage – but he didn't expect that to weigh heavily in his favor. Still, he prepared the tea the way she liked it, with a hint of lemon, and carried it and the wine on a tray to where the two women sat at the dining table.

While engaged in his kitchen operations, he had been aware of the sound of conversation coming through the serving hatch. Actually, the conversation had been one-sided: Melda had done all the talking, touching on what a pleasure it was to meet Letitia, and what a naughty boy Chesney was to have told her so little about his mother, and how she looked forward to a good old-fashioned chinwag so they could get to know each other. "Because, well," Melda said, "this may turn out to be a long-running show."

Chesney arrived to find the two sitting on opposite sides of the maplewood table, in the places that had been set for him and Melda when the evening's agenda had included only dinner, maybe some television and then the activity for which he would have gladly given up eating, TV-watching, and probably everything else he did besides crimefighting and breathing.

He set down the tray. Melda left off talking to smile at him, and indicate with her eyes that he should sit between them. Then she took her glass of wine and held it up in preparation for making a toast. "To good beginnings," she said.

Chesney lifted his glass of Chianti and looked to his right. His mother had not moved, nor had she acknowledged the bone china cup of steaming amber liquid he had set before her. She sat erect, her head held slightly back and to the side, regarding the young woman opposite her as if Melda were an object of unknown, though possibly dangerous, characteristics that might without warning explode or exude unpleasant substances.

"A toast, Mother," Chesney said.

Letitia's eyes moved sideways but her gaze did not rest warmly upon her son. Her hands remained below the table. And now Melda was looking at him, too. Chesney realized that the frozen moment had become some kind of test. He even knew what he was being tested on. He touched his glass to Melda's and said, "And happy endings."

Letitia's lips became thin and pressed hard against each other. Chesney had seen the expression on many occasions, and in those bygone times the set of his mother's jaw would have made him anxious – would have set his mind hunting for the soft words that scripture said were supposed to turn away wrath, though experience had taught him that armor plate would not suffice to turn away the kind of wrath Letitia Arnstruther could generate.

But, curiously, the sight of his mother's face armed for battle caused him no distress. He realized that he was not affected because he had already made his choice – had made it long before he had touched his glass to Melda's – and that whatever might come after was of no consequence. The tension went out of his spine and he sat back to watch what was about to happen.

"You said that Chesney has told you little about me?" said Letitia. Without waiting for confirmation, she added, "He has told me nothing about you."

Melda put down her wine glass and said, "What would you like to know?"

Now the older woman took up her cup and sipped the tea. "To start with," she said, "who are your people?"

"My people?" Melda smiled. "Well, they're the Irish on my father's side, and the Italian on my mother's"

Chesney watched his mother try out two different facial expressions at the same time: one was contempt that the young woman opposite was too ignorant even to know what the question, "Who are your people?" meant; the other was suspicion that Melda knew all too well and was mocking her. She settled on the first option and said, "I meant, dear, where do they live, what do they do?"

Melda smiled sweetly. "I know what you meant," she said. "I was trying to save you the embarrassment of going there."

"Going there?" said Letitia, as if the phrase was new to her.

"Starting a conversation that would leave you, you might say, at a disadvantage." Melda took another mouthful of wine, rolled it around a little, then swallowed. "Or, like my kind of people might say, holding the shit end of the stick."

Chesney's mother had been holding her half-filled teacup midway between mouth and saucer. It now descended to the latter with an unquestionable finality. She turned to her son and said, "She will not do."

The young man met her gaze, and was pleased to find that he did not tremble inside; facing down Hell had apparently been good practice for this moment. Then he looked at Melda as he said, "Yes, Mother, she will."

"You have obligations," Letitia said, rising from her chair and turning her eyes toward the ceiling as she added, "*high* obligations." Though they were seated across from each other, she looked down at Melda from a great height and said, "There are matters at stake, young woman, that are beyond your competence. Matters I cannot divulge, that—"

Melda let Chesney answer. "She knows, Mother."

The older woman stopped in mid-condescension. "She knows? *What* does she know?"

"Everything."

Though the foundations of Letitia Arnstruther's world clearly rocked beneath her feet, Chesney thought she handled it well. "You foolish boy. So she inveigled you into telling—"

Chesney had never interrupted his mother before a moment ago, and here he was doing again. "She went to Hell for me, Mother," he said. "Literally. She was ready to fight the Devil for me." He put his hand over Melda's. "She loves me. I love her. That's all there is to it."

There was a great deal more to it as far as his mother was concerned, but before she could utter more than the first few syllables of his badly needed re-education, Letitia was interrupted for an unparalleled third time. A weasel-headed, sabertooth-fanged apparition in spats and a wide-lapeled suit shimmered into view at the unoccupied side of the table.

"Boss," Xaphan said, "we gotta go."

Chesney was no less surprised than the two women. He noted that his demonic assistant also lacked a cigar and a glass of rum. "I didn't summon you," he said.

"No, boss," said the demon. "You been sent for."

"By whom?"

"By the boss, boss. My boss. The big boss."

"Satan?" said Chesney. "What does he want?"

"Better he should tell you himself."

"My son," said Letitia Arnstruther, "is not at the beck and call of Hell. He is a prophet of–"

Fourth time, thought Chesney, *world record*, then he said, "If he's asking nicely…" He turned to Xaphan and said, "It is a request, right?"

The demon looked uncomfortable. "He can't command you, so it has to be he's askin'."

Chesney told his mother, "Then I think I should find out what he wants."

"He can't come here?" Melda said. "It's a better atmosphere than his place."

"It's complicated," said the demon. "Let's just say he feels more comfortable with you comin' over to his side of town."

"Do I need my costume?" Chesney said.

The weasel head went from side to side. "Better not."

"Okay, then, let's–" Chesney's apartment disappeared and he was instantly somewhere else, saying, "go."

THREE

The somewhere else was enveloped in some kind of mist. The young man was relieved to find that it wasn't any of the parts of Hell he had already visited; their climates did not agree with mortal flesh. Nor did it fit any description of the internal regions he had ever come across. "Where is this?" he said.

A voice behind him said, "Limbo."

He turned. Lucifer was standing in the mist. Chesney studied the severe features and deduced that behind the anger that the Devil usually showed when they met he was seeing something else – he thought it might be worry. "I thought they'd done away with Limbo," he said. "Theologically, I mean."

"Yet here we are," said the Devil. "How do you account for that?"

Chesney shrugged. "I don't think it's up to me to account for it. You're the one who brought me here."

Satan regarded him with a cold anger. "The last time we spoke," he said, "there was talk about a book."

"I remember. You didn't care for the idea."

"I still don't."

Chesney waited. He couldn't imagine the Devil being stuck for words, but that was the impression he was receiving. Lucifer seemed to be wrestling with something he wanted, and didn't want, to say.

Eventually, the Devil said, "You thought that all this," he gestured in a way that included more than the mist they stood in, "was part of a book that…" Satan couldn't bring himself to say the name, "that's being written."

"Actually," said Chesney, "it was the Reverend Billy Lee Hardacre's idea."

One tapered-fingered hand made a gesture of irritation. "But you know about it."

"As much as he's told me about it," said the young man. "It's not something I'm particularly interested in."

"Not one of your 'pools of light.'"

"So you know about that, too?"

Satan fixed him with a hard look. Chesney was glad he'd worked his way up to a point where he could bear such a stare from his mother; it made meeting the Devil's gaze less of a challenge. "Oh," said Lucifer, "I've made a point of getting to know you."

"Why's that?" Chesney said.

"We'll come to that, in due course. First, tell me what you know about the… book."

"You're probably not used to this kind of question," said the young man, "but why should I?"

He had the impression that Satan had thought out their conversation in advance. That was a technique his mother had applied to the interrogations she used to inflict upon him before he left home; policemen did it, too. Even so, his question caused the satanic jaw to tighten and the satanic eyes to narrow. It was a moment before the Devil answered. "Is this," he said, "a negotiation?"

Chesney shook his head. "I thought we'd established that I have no interest in any of the kinds of contracts you make."

"We have."

"Then what am I doing here?" When there was no immediate answer, he said, "You're not trying to ask me for help?"

Pride was the Devil's everything, Chesney knew, and he also knew he had just trodden upon it. He again waited while the jaw and eyes went through their permutations.

"I am trying to discover," Satan said at last, "if you and I have a common interest."

"I fight crime. You inspire criminals. Where in that would you look for a common interest?"

"Nowhere. But, still, we may have a common problem."

Chesney thought of his mother, then felt guilty for having done so. "Speak plainly," he said.

"Someone is trying to make you do things you don't want to do," said Lucifer. "That was always the nub of my problem, too."

Chesney made a show of thinking about it, but after a moment it wasn't just a show. The Devil seemed to know what he was thinking and weighed in with the next brick in the wall. "And it may be that we're talking about the same 'someone.'"

"You're not allowed to tempt me," Chesney said.

"I'm not trying to. Your soul is not in play."

"So what do you want, and what are you offering?"

"A partnership," Satan said. "Or call it an alliance."

"To what end?"

"To find out what this book business is all about. After that, we can reassess our positions."

"But you were there," Chesney said, "when Hardacre explained it."

"I know." Lucifer's face took on an expression that Chesney was now sure could only be described as worried. "That's what bothers me. I can't recall exactly what was said." The thin black brows drew down to form a perfect vee. "And *I* recall *everything*."

"You don't recall the meeting?"

"I do, and I don't. It's…" – the jaw clenched and unclenched – "vague."

Chesney could see no reason not to tell Lucifer something the Devil ought to know already. "The reverend has this theory," he said, "that the universe, including Heaven and Hell, you and me and everybody, are all part of a book that…" He hesitated, until Satan waved a hand to signal that he would hear the next syllable. "That God is writing. He's supposed to be writing it to learn about morality."

The Devil grunted and rolled a hand in a gesture that said *go on*.

"That's about all there is to it," the young man said, "except that the book keeps getting rewritten, and elements of previous drafts pop up in sacred scripture. So that's why you have the story about Noah's Ark or the Tower of Babel, even though these things didn't really happen. I mean, they *did* really happen, but only in a previous draft of the universe."

The Devil pinched his lower lip and looked down and to one side. "I remember those events," he said. "But you're saying they didn't happen?"

"Well, they did," Chesney spread his hands, "but then they didn't. The thing is, you were in both drafts. Or, probably, there have been a lot more than two, and you've been in all of them." He paused to think. "Although it seems as if your character has been rewritten."

Satan's head snapped around. "What do you mean?"

Chesney held up both palms. "Well," he said, "do you remember being a talking snake? With legs?"

Thunderheads formed on the Devil's brow – quite literally: small, turbulent clouds through which flashed tiny bolts of lightning – until he brushed them away. Then his face took on the aspect of a man recovering a wisp of memory.

"And did you," said Chesney, "used to make bets with you-know-who? Cause there's a story about that, too."

"Why would I make bets with him? He knows everything that's going to happen."

Chesney took that as a rhetorical question. "Anyway," he said, "that was Billy Lee Hardacre's theory. There's a book, we're all in it, it keeps getting rewritten, and here and there we come across traces of the previous drafts. Like fossils."

"Like Limbo," Satan said, looking into the mists that surrounded them.

"Maybe," said Chesney. "It's not in the current draft, but it must have been in a previous one."

"Because," said Lucifer, "here it is." He paused. "And here *we* are."

"Why show it to me?"

"Because I like people to be knowledgeable."

It took Chesney a moment to follow the Devil's train of thought. "I still don't see grounds for a partnership or an alliance," he said.

"You don't?" Now the hard-featured face produced a knowing smile. "Let me point them out to you. You and I are characters in a book, a book written by someone else. We play roles prepared for us by someone else. The meaning of our existence is that we serve another's will." Lucifer fixed Chesney again with his serpentine gaze. "And that sits well with you?"

"According to Hardacre's theory, I have free will. So do you."

"Unless the… someone we're talking about decides to revise the draft. Then maybe I'm a snake again." Chesney shrugged in a way that he hoped showed a certain sympathy; the Devil did not appreciate the sentiment. "And maybe you're your momma's boy again, doing what she wants you to!"

"No!" The shout could not echo in Limbo, but still it came out loud and with force.

Another satanic smile, this one to savor a point scored. "What I hear," the Devil said, "is that there *is* a new draft being written. The Book of Chesney. In which you perform wondrous deeds and generally prance about like a latter-day prophet."

"It's nothing to do with me!"

The smile widened. "Not now," said Lucifer. "But what if it is the first cut at a new draft of the big book? Then everything changes again. And this time, maybe it's your legs that get taken away."

"I am not a prophet!"

"You would not be the first prophet to respond to the initial offer with, 'Who, me?' I believe those were Moses's very words."

"I will not do it," said Chesney.

"Not even if your mother says?"

"Not even then. Especially not even then."

Satan smiled upon another victory. "And thus it seems we do have something in common." He waited while the young man worked it through. "So," he said, when the thinking was done, "do we have an alliance?"

Chesney did not answer right away. "What would be my part in it?" he said.

"First, read the Book of Chesney, and see what you think of it."

"I don't need to read it. I glanced through it once, and that was enough. It is full of things that never happened, and never will."

"Know thine enemy's mind," said Lucifer, "always seemed part of a good strategy to me."

Chesney had to agree. "All right," he said, "I'll read it. Then what?"

"Then we'll see."

"You don't get my soul."

Lucifer snorted. "I wouldn't let your soul anywhere near my realm," he said. "You, young man, are trouble."

And then he was gone.

"Xaphan!" Chesney called.

"Here, boss." The demon emerged from the mist.

"What do you think?"

"I don't think, boss. Way I see it, it just leads to trouble."

"As the sparks fly up," Chesney quoted.

"Say what?"

"Never mind. Are Melda and my mother still going at it?"

"Nah," said Xaphan. "In this place, we're out of time. I can put you back right when we left."

The prospect of stepping back into the middle of a fight between the two women in his life did not entice Chesney. He thought for a moment, then said, "If I was called away to fight crime, I could just leave them to get on with it, couldn't I?"

"I ain't gonna argue," said his assistant.

"Then what have we got?"

"Crimewise? You mean in that burgh of yours?"

"Yes."

"Coupla muggin's. And there's this stock boy gonna swipe some steaks from the supermarket when he gets off work."

"That's it?"

"It's a quiet night. It's too bad you didn't ask me sooner. There was a murder just before we come out to see his nibs."

"What! A murder! Why didn't you say anything?"

"I wasn't on duty. You was gettin' ready to have dinner with mom and the missus. I didn't wanna–"

Chesney cut him off. "Wait, when was the murder? When exactly?"

Xaphan produced the big old pocket watch that was attached to the chain that ran across its waist-coat. The demon flipped the gold case open and studied the dial, then said, "Bout five seconds ago, your time."

"So is the victim actually dead?"

Xaphan thought about it. "Depends on what you mean by dead. Heart's stopped. Breathin's stopped. Body's on the floor. Brain is windin' down."

"So not brain dead?"

"Nah. But pretty soon."

Chesney was thinking. "Listen," he said, "when we step outside of the world, we step outside of time, right?"

"Always."

"Okay. Now, I've never asked you this, but when we step back in, do we have to come in exactly when we left off?"

Xaphan's weasel brow wrinkled. "I think we're sup-pose'ta."

"But do we have ta?'"

The demon's brow wrinkled even more deeply. "I guess not," it said, after a moment.

"So if I said, 'Let's go back into the world just before the murder, just in time to prevent it,' how would that be?"

Xaphan's brow cleared. "Okay," it said, "I know this one. If someone's dead, they have to stay dead, cause otherwise you're calling a soul back from our place, or the other place, and that's not kosher. Traffic goes one-way, ya see?"

"Oh," said Chesney, "I guess that makes sense. Too bad, then."

"Wait," said the demon, "I ain't finished yet. You can... what's the word when you bring a dead body sorta back, so you can order it around?"

"Reanimate? Zombie? Frankenstein?"

"That's the one! Alphonse and me, and some of the boys, we went to see that picture. Did I laugh!"

"But I don't want to reanimate a corpse," said Chesney.

"You sure? They can be a lotta fun at a party."

"I'm sure. So, dead is dead, and I can't prevent the murder."

"Oh, sure you can," said his demon. "I was gettin' to it. If the soul hasn't actually taken a powder, you can deal yourself in a little before the deadly deed. Then the murder don't really happen, so it don't really count."

"Really? Excellent. All right, get me in costume." Instantly, he was clad in blue and gray, gloves and half-mask in place. "So what's the setup?"

"Well," said Xaphan, "it's a mom and pop fight. In the kitchen. Same old razzamatazz: he drinks too much, she's always playin' the bingo, blah, blah, blah. He gives her a push, she smacks him with the fry pan, he sees red, stabs her wit' the knife. She goes down, end of story."

"Except I come in, grab the knife before he gets her, it's all good."

"You wanna play it like that, we'll play it like that."

"Let's go."

It was a three-room shotgun apartment on the third floor of a walk-up tenement. The kitchen had a view of the window of an identical apartment across the air shaft. It was dingy and lit by a single sixty watt bulb hanging from a globeless ceiling light fixture. The woman was about sixty, gray-haired, with smoker's rivulets all down her upper lip. The man was just old, his hair thin, greasy and lank, dressed in a stained sleeveless undervest and colorless pants over worn-out carpet slippers. Everything he wore was redolent of beer and cigarette ash. His eyes were moist, probably with tears that were the result of the blow he had just taken to the side of his head, where a bump was already rising.

The knife had been on the table, where the woman had been cutting up cabbage. Now it was in his hand and he was rising from the chair into which he'd been knocked back by the swipe from the frying pan. In another second, the long blade of German steel would be buried to the hilt in her middle, slicing open her heart and piercing a lung, bringing almost instantaneous death.

Except that the Actionary appeared. His hand flashed out at superhuman speed and, with the strength of ten men, closed about the old man's wrist. The knife fell from his nerveless grasp and seemed to Chesney to float slowly toward the floor. He caught it with his other hand, then as Xaphan returned him to non-emergency speed, he stepped back and, in a dramatic gesture, raised the weapon in both hands and snapped the blade in two.

For a moment there was absolute silence and stillness in the room. Then the old woman said, "What the Hell do you think you're doin'? That was a hunnerd-dollar knife! Our boy Donny gave it to us on our fortieth anniversary!"

"He was going to stab you with it," said Chesney, indicating the old man with a sideways motion of his head.

"I never!" said the husband.

"It was in your hand! You were getting up! It was pointed at her belly!"

"I was, whatchamacallit… *gesturin'* with it, to make a point, like."

"That's right," said the woman. "He likes to gesture and such!"

"Listen," said Chesney, "I came back in time to prevent him from sticking this in your heart. By now you should be lying on the floor, dead as a mackerel."

This information caused the couple to pause. "You're from the future?" said the old man. "Jeez, I used to read about that stuff when I was a kid. Ray Bradbury, Asimov, Heinlein."

"Don't start with that malarkey again," said his wife. "This bozo broke Donny's anniversary present."

"Well, jeez-looeez, Marjorie, the guy did just appear outta nowhere. An' he's dressed like Buck Rogers." The old man gave Chesney the once-over, then did it again, while his nicotine-stained fingers touched the bump on the side of his head. He winced and said, "Hey, what did you do to my head?"

"Nothing," said Chesney, "She did–"

"I never!" said the woman.

"You're still holding the frying pan," said Chesney. She turned and set the pan down on the counter beside the gas stove, then looked at him as if the act was conclusive proof of her innocence.

Meanwhile, the old man was saying, "So you come from the future to stop me from sticking Marjorie – not that I ever would, baby. Does that mean we're part of some important timeline?"

"Timeline!" said Marjorie, addressing the ceiling as if it would now confirm the idiocy of her spouse.

"No," said Chesney. "It's not like that. I only came back by a few seconds, because when I heard about the murder–"

"I never!" said the old man.

"When I heard what was going to happen, it was only a few seconds after it happened." That hadn't sounded right. "Wait, I mean–"

"Never mind all this hoopdedoo," said Marjorie. "What about the knife? That's a Henkel chef's special, cost about a hunnerd and fifty, easy."

"Yeah," said the old man, "not to mention sennuh-mennul value."

"Xaphan," Chesney said, in a voice only his assistant could hear, in a conversation that took place outside of time, "Can we fix the fershlacklinner knife?" Chesney had long ago taught himself, aided by his mother's soap-gargling, never to swear. Instead he made up nonsense words on the spot.

"Done," said the demon.

Chesney felt a vibration in the hand that held the knife's handle. He lifted up the Henkel chef's special and showed it whole and perfect again. "There," he said, "it's fixed."

The old man took the knife, turned it over, examining the blade. "How'd you do that?" His watery eyes brightened. "Did you go into the future and, like, weld it with lasers?" Then he recollected what they'd been talking about before. "Wait a minute, you said you only came back five seconds. So were you, like, already here when I– I mean, when you thought I–"

"No," said Chesney, "I wasn't here."

"Were you on some, whatchacallit, alternate timeline? You know, parallel universe. Or did you–"

"No," said Chesney, "I was in…" And then he thought better of it and said, "Xaphan, get us out of here."

"Want me to make them forget we was here?"

"I don't care. I'd rather be in Hell."

Instantly, they were in his warm and cozy room in the outer circle of Hell. Xaphan went to the drinks cabinet, poured itself a tumbler of rum and got a cigar from the humidor. The demon lit up and blew some complicated shapes of blue smoke. "Couldn't do this on the boss's nickel," it said.

"Why," said Chesney, "does everything have to be so complicated?"

"What?" said Xaphan. "You mean those old fuds?"

"They weren't even grateful."

The demon blew some more smoke. "You want grateful, don't fix it before it happens. Fix it after it happens, when they'd give anythin' not to have had it happen." It drank half a glassful of the pungent liquor. "And even then, don't be surprised if they turn around and give you the fish-eye."

Chesney sighed. He recognized that his assistant's view of the world was at an angle to his own, but at this moment he was tempted to share it. Still, he told himself, I did save her life, even if they both denied it. The deed stands. He said as much to the demon.

"Deed, schmeed," said Xaphan. "So, you wanna go home? Your momma and the girlfriend, they're gonna mix it up if you don't."

"Guess I'd better. Just let me think a little first."

The demon poured itself another glass of rum. "Take alla time you need," it said.

"Mother," Chesney said, "I've been unfair to you and to the Reverend Billy Lee."

"Yes, you have," said Letitia, reminding Chesney that she never gave ground and never forgot a trespass, even if she was supposed to forgive them.

"So I will go to his house, and I will read the book."

"What book?" said Melda.

"Nothing that concerns you," said Letitia.

"Anything that concerns–" the young woman began, but then she allowed Chesney's gently raised hand to check her outburst.

"Anything that concerns me," Chesney said, "concerns Melda. We are a couple."

"She is not–" his mother began to explain, but when he raised his hand again, she scarcely paused before continuing, "not part of what you are called to do."

"If she's not part of it," Chesney spoke before Melda's fuse had smoldered all the way to the inevitable explosion, "then I'm not part of it."

"How dare you speak to your mother in that way?" said Letitia.

Melda eased into the conversation, her tone deceptively mild. "Tell me, Mrs Arnstruther: you say Chesney is a prophet?"

There was no warmth in the older woman's reply. "He is. I have seen the book. I have seen the angel of the Lord."

"And does that make you the mother of a prophet?"

"If that is what I am called to–"

But Melda homed right in. "And do prophets' mothers usually outrank their sons?"

Letitia froze. Melda had the good grace neither to move nor to let her face do anything that would call up associations with a running back's post-touchdown victory dance. There was silence around the dining table until Chesney said, "Then that settles it. Mother, I will read the book. Melda will read the book. And then we'll see."

Instantly, he realized that his last four words had been quoting the Devil. And if his mother had come back at him, he would have told her that her bidding and Satan's were one and the same. But Letitia

Arnstruther was looking a little like a champion boxer whose head was still reverberating from a haymaker that had come out of nowhere.

Chesney thought he'd better save the news for the rematch.

Lieutenant Denby scrunched his thin shoulders against the angle made by the car door and the driver's seat and watched the matronly woman get into the forty-odd-year-old Dodge DeSoto. He had routinely called in to dispatch to run the car's plate when it had parked in one of the visitor's slots outside the condo building where the nerd kid lived. When the tag had come back as belonging to a Letitia Arnstruther, the policeman had settled in to wait.

He had already seen the girlfriend's beat up old Hyundai go down the ramp into the building's underground parking and knew that she would park in one of the two bays allotted to the kid's unit. The other one stayed empty; the kid didn't drive, had never even got a license. Denby had followed the girlfriend around for a couple of days, in case she was a go-between who would lead him to the guy in the costume. That was the term the lieutenant used when he thought of the Actionary, except when he thought of him as Mr Spandex – but the latter label always caused an odd tickling sensation in the back of the lieutenant's mind, as if he ought to remember something that he had forgotten. Something important.

The Dodge started up. Whoever looked after the vintage car knew what they were doing, because the big old V8 engine purred as if it had just come out of a 1960s showroom. Denby watched it pull away from the curb like a 1930s ocean liner leaving the dock. He let it get a block ahead then started up the ghost car and followed.

Letitia Arnstruther – had to be the mother; there were no other Arnstruthers in the state – lived in a well-established middle-class neighborhood a couple of miles from downtown. And if she was going home, Denby figured, she would have turned left onto Columbus Drive. Instead, she went straight through the lights and he had to juice it up a little to get across the intersection before the yellow turned to red.

She got onto the parkway, and Denby dropped back until he was a good two hundred yards behind. Then, when the parkway met the interstate, she rolled up onto the overpass and took the on-ramp heading south.

"Oh, ho," the lieutenant said to himself, "and where are we going tonight, mother dear?"

She settled into the through-traffic lane and so did he, then he slowed down enough to let three cars overtake and get between him and the DeSoto. The old car's tail lights were unmistakable. He matched speed and waited to see where all this was taking him.

He was pretty sure the girlfriend was not playing intermediary. She went to work and back, went shopping when she needed to, and spent most of her free time with the kid – and at the kid's apartment, which was bigger than hers and up high enough that street noise wasn't a nuisance, the way it was in her ground-floor suite. Arnstruther had only been over to her place once since Denby had started keeping tabs on McCann, and their conversation had not been useful.

What he had overheard had been more than a little surprising, the lieutenant would have admitted – if he'd had anyone to talk to about this assignment, which he didn't because what he was doing was way over the line and would have got him canned if he hadn't had coverage from the highest levels of the department and City Hall. Denby was using completely illegal surveillance methods, including having the phone company turn Melda McCann's landline handset into a permanent open mike. Not only was every call she made or received intercepted and recorded, but so was every conversation – in fact, every sound – that happened within twenty feet of the phone.

The phone was right next to the girlfriend's bed, so the loudest and clearest signals had come from the couple's most intimate encounters. That was where the "more than a little surprising" part of the surveillance came in; apparently, either Melda McCann had undiscovered acting talents of Academy Award-winning quality, or Chesney Arnstruther was an absolute master of the female fiddle. Denby had listened to the tape twice and had come around to thinking that the kid had more going for him than showed on the surface.

It was only after the connubial concerto in question that the policeman had heard any mention of Mr Spandex. When their heavy breathing had moderated, Melda had brought up what she called "the endorsement question." The kid had said, "Not now, Melda."

She had said he ought to be thinking about his opportunities, and he'd said, "That's not what the Actionary is all about."

She hadn't wanted to let it drop, but apparently he'd done something that had made her moan softly. By the time another opportunity for conversation had come around, they were too exhausted to make good on it.

So Denby figured that the girlfriend knew about the guy in the costume, but not everything about him. And she wasn't the go-between. The lieutenant was sure he would know more about who knew what about whom if he could also get an open-mike phone tap on the kid's landline, but even though the phone company had put their best techies on the job – after swearing them to secrecy on pain of losing their positions and any hope of working in the industry again – the only signal they ever got from within the Arnstruther apartment sounded like a series of deep-belly belches that would have hands down taken the prize at any frat house burp-off contest.

The DeSoto cruised south and just under the speed limit for almost three hours. Denby was a veteran of the police stake-out and had known enough to bring along an empty bottle as well as a thermos full of coffee. Filling the bottle while cruising down the interstate was tricky, but he hadn't spilled any urine on his pants and he was calm and comfortable as he followed Letitia Arnstruther up the off-ramp and along a few country roads until she turned in at the gates of a walled estate.

There was no number or name to identify the place, and Denby didn't even remember seeing a road sign naming the long stretch of winding blacktop he'd followed the DeSoto along to get there. But the ghost car was equipped with a global positioning system that could fill in the gaps in his knowledge. It took only a couple of minutes before his transmission of his coordinates back to Police Central could be rolled over to the State Police liaison office and the word sent back from dispatch that he was outside the mansion of the Reverend Billy Lee Hardacre: former lawyer, former novelist, and currently a major figure in the world of televangelist hucksterism.

"Now that's a surprise," Denby told himself. He had parked a little ways along the road from the estate's gates, under some trees. By climbing on top of the ghost car he could see over the estate wall. He trained a pair of night-vision glasses on the front of the big house; there was the Dodge, looking like it was right where it belonged, parked behind a high-end Mercedes on a circular driveway. The woman presumably was inside the house.

If this had been normal working hours, Denby might have called his contact – or, rather, Mayor Greeley's contact – at the phone company, and arranged for an open-mike landline tap. But it was past ten at night. Instead, he climbed down off the car roof, opened the trunk, and fished around in a welter of surveillance equipment – some of which had not come from department stores, but from military and other government sources. When he'd been briefed on what he had been issued and how to make it work, Denby had asked where some of it came from. He'd been told he didn't want to know.

Now, rigging a long-distance sound-amplifying dish microphone on an adjustable stand on top of the estate's enclosing wall, Denby was not sure whether or not he wanted to know exactly what he was mixed up in. On the one hand – and it was a very full hand – there was Chief Hoople's straight-out offer of a captaincy if he did his job to the satisfaction of the old bulls downtown. Unstated, but clearly implied, was the corollary: if he didn't make good on this case, his career was over. He'd be transferred to traffic and kept busy checking on overparked vehicles in the bad parts of town until he got the message and quit.

Denby had never been "one of the boys" – he had earned his promotions from patrolman through detective to lieutenant the old-fashioned way: by catching bad guys. But he had also learned early that keeping your nose clean at Police Central sometimes meant that when some kid whose dad was one of the Twenty blew over the limit on a DUI stop, you didn't cuff him and throw him in the drunk tank; you took his keys, gave him a telling off, then drove him home. That kind of thing was the worst that Denby had ever had to bend rules, except for the night he'd found a guy from the mayor's office getting extremely well-acquainted with one of the girls from Marie's place – in the front seat of an official car right behind City Hall – he had just told the couple to take it upstairs to the office and lock the doors.

But a captaincy would not have been enough to make him do what he was willing to do to solve the Mr Spandex riddle. There was something more to this case, something that dug at Lieutenant Denby from inside. He couldn't put his finger on it, but he had this nagging sense that, somehow, he had been played for a sucker. Somebody, somewhere back in the weeds, was disrespecting him; was putting one over on him.

And that was not acceptable to Denby. He was not a bad cop, nor was he a perfect cop, but he was all cop when it really counted, and he had this unshakable feeling – it was as if a voice were whispering it in his ear – that somebody needed to be brought to recognize that fundamental truth. He was pretty sure the somebody was the guy in the costume, and he was determined to do whatever he needed to do to make his point.

Well, maybe not whatever it takes, he thought to himself as he adjusted the remote mike's earphones over his head. He wouldn't ice the guy over it. But any means short of murder or arson, he was willing to take a look at it.

He pointed the mike at one of the downstairs windows. The parabolic dish would pick up and amplify vibrations that shook the glass from inside the house, even the tiny vibrations caused by human voices in normal conversation. He turned up the gain on the mike's amplifier, but heard only a murmur. Somebody was talking to somebody, but Denby was listening at the wrong window.

He swung the mike to cover the next oblong of light, and now the voices were clearer: a man's and a woman's. There was an overlay of other sounds, a motor running – maybe a blender, or a refrigerator if it was right against the window – but he clicked the switch on the digital recorder attached to the eaves-dropping system. There were guys in the crime lab that could filter out the extraneous noise, if need be.

Then he heard the man's voice say, "Just let me finish making my energy drink – hand me the ginkgo biloba, would you? Then we'll talk." That was followed by a few seconds of even louder motor noise – definitely a blender, Denby thought – and then, clear as digitalization could make it, the man saying, "So, what did he say?"

"I was never so insulted in all my life," said the woman. "That young hussy, poking her nose–"

"Letty, dear," the man interrupted, "what did he say? Will he read it?"

"Yes."

"Good."

"But, Billy, he wants her to read it, too."

There was a silence, then the preacher said, "Well, maybe that's not too bad."

"She has him twisted around her little finger! And you know how she keeps him there!"

"He's a grown man, Letty. There was bound to be a woman in his life someday."

"It's sinful!"

A chair scraped against a tiled floor. "Here, sit down and have some of this." A clink of glasses, the sound of liquid pouring. "It'll make you feel better."

The mike was sensitive enough to pick up the sounds of swallowing, lip-smacking and at least one sigh. Then the woman picked up where she had left off. "It's a sin. They're not married."

"Neither are we, Letty. I said the words, but we've no license, no marriage certificate. In fact, under the law, you're probably still married common-law to whatsisname."

"Certificates and licenses don't matter. You've been marked out by the Lord!"

"I'm only the precursor. He's the prophet – at least, I think he is. If I can break the rules, surely he can."

Letitia's voice roughened. It sounded to Denby like tears being fought to a standstill. "You mustn't say things like that."

"Here," said the man, to the sound of more pouring, "have a little more. And let's look at it practically. Over the years, since he left home, how much have you been able to influence Chesney's behavior? Be honest."

A sniffle. "He was always a hard-headed boy."

"But you say she can get him to change his mind."

"Only because she… you know."

"Exactly," said Billy Lee. "So, if we win her over, we win him."

Denby heard the sharp intake of breath, then the woman said, "Billy! That's so cold-hearted."

"I was a labor lawyer before I was a preacher. You don't want to know some of the tricks I pulled."

The phrase plucked at something inside Denby. The world must be full of people who didn't want to know things. Probably that was why there were so many things people didn't want to know about.

He'd been distracted and almost missed it when the woman said something about the girl going to Hell and fighting the Devil for the nerd kid. Religious nuts, he thought. First, all this talk about prophets, and now the Devil makes an entrance. Though that didn't tally with the sense he had of the kid or of Melda. They didn't go to church, and the only thing special about Sunday was that it allowed the couple to spend a whole day bonking each other.

But the woman's remark gave him another twinge of that funny feeling, almost like déjà vu, that kept eating at him. Again, he tried to reach for the elusive whatever-it-was that floated tantalizingly at the edge of his consciousness, but again, as always, it fled out of reach.

And now the preacher was talking to the woman in a bedroom voice, saying something about breaking the rules, and she was making sounds like those Denby had heard coming from overweight women in restaurants as they succumbed to the allure of the chocolate cheesecake. Then he heard the chair scrape again, and footsteps receding. The kitchen light went out and, moments later, an upstairs window brightened, then dimmed as curtains were pulled.

Denby considered pointing the directional mike that way, but decided he wasn't interested in hearing two people well past middle age going at it. Especially not people who thought they were prophets or precursors, whatever the Hell that was. God only knew what they might shout at the moment of no return. He took off the earphones and detached the digital recorder, collapsed the mike's dish, then carried it all down and returned the equipment to where he had got it. As he was reclosing the trunk, he realized that he had left the night glasses on top of the wall and climbed back up to get them.

He took one last look at the mansion, saw that the upstairs window was now dark, as were all the others – except for a single source of light from somewhere on the ground floor. It was tiny, seemed no more than a pinpoint, yet it shone as bright as the morning star. When Denby put the night glasses on it, the instrument's green circle lit up too bright to see.

Denby had intuition – well-honed police intuition. He also had the instincts of a natural explorer; all good detectives did. But neither instinct nor intuition told him that the curiously bright mote of light had anything to do with Mr Spandex. In fact, the conversation between Hardacre and the kid's mother had pretty much been a bust as far as the case was concerned. He saw no connection between the muscle-bound freak in the costume and a couple of religious nutjobs, who seemed to think that Chesney Arnstruther, all one hundred and fifteen nerdish pounds of him, was some kind of Moses.

And yet he did not get down off the roof of the ghost car. In a time when he was beset by indefinable feelings and peculiar psychic stirrings, he could now add a new one: he wanted to know what made the light. It occurred to him – as it would to any cop – that bright lights left on at night behind heavily shrouded windows, especially in remote location, often meant that someone was running a marijuana grow-op. But he didn't see Billy Lee as the weed-farmer type.

Still, if he needed probable cause to step onto a property without a warrant and look through a window, he now had it. A moment later, he was over the wall and walking across the lawn toward the mansion.

FOUR

Halfway across the lawn, Denby expected lights to come on, maybe the *whoop-whoop-whoop* of an alarm – surely the preacher had motion sensors? But nothing happened. He kept walking, the dew-wet grass soaking his shoes and pants cuffs. He knew he would be leaving a trail. Still, he didn't care. He wanted to know what made the light.

It came through a chink in a curtain covering a ground-floor window, a chink too high for Denby to see through standing in the flower bed that ran along the base of the house's wall of closely mortared granite blocks. The lieutenant looked around, saw nothing in the darkness. But when he walked toward the rear of the house he almost fell over a wheelbarrow with a rake and shovel in it. He dumped the tools and wheeled the barrow back to the window, set it where it needed to be, and climbed up.

He could just get his eye to the level of the chink in the curtains. The curtains themselves were about a foot back from the glass, the window being a bay set in the thick stone wall. He couldn't see much without putting his eye to the chink, and for that he'd first have to break the glass – and he was sure that wouldn't go unnoticed – but he was close enough to see some of the room beyond.

It was a den or a study. He saw bookcases and armchairs and a big old-style desk. The latter was where the light was coming from, from something sitting on top of the green blotter. Denby squinted to dim the strength of the glare. He was expecting to see a halogen lamp; nothing else would have made such a bright light, except maybe a carbon-arc welder.

But all he saw was a low oblong of bright white. When he squinted even harder, he became sure of two things: one, that he was looking at a stack of paper – he could see where some of the pages were unevenly stacked – and, two, that the glow was not reflected; the paper itself was lighting up the room.

Now, what's that all about, the policeman thought? The answer came from memory: the preacher and his live-in girlfriend had wanted the nerd to read something, some text that had to do with the kid's being a prophet. Denby was no true believer. He didn't look through Billy Lee's window and see a miracle; he saw some kind of show-biz prop – how it was done he had no idea, and didn't care – that was part of some scam the televangelist was setting up.

He climbed down from the wheelbarrow and returned it whence he had found it, then retraced his steps back to the wall. It was a hard scrabble to get over to the outside again and he tore his pants leg doing it. But as he made his way back to the interstate and headed north to the city, he kept thinking about the glowing block of paper. Somehow, it was going to be the key that turned the lock and opened the door on Mr Spandex.

He hadn't figured out yet how that would happen, but his cop's instincts and cop's intuition told him it would.

Some distance away – or just nearby, depending on how you measured these things – Satan said to one of his aides, "The policeman's tempter, send him an 'at-taboy' and tell him to keep up the good work." Then the Devil rubbed his hands in the manner that was his habit when things were going the way he liked them.

"Lieutenant," said the dispatcher, "you said you were to be notified the moment a call like this came in."

Denby yawned and looked at the clock on his bed-side table. It was just after two in the morning. He'd been in bed less than an hour, after driving all the way back from Hardacre's mansion.

"All right," he said, reaching for the notepad he kept beside the bed, "I'm up. Tell me."

"Name is Belknapp, Ralph and Doris, old couple. Both like to hit the jug, then they start hitting each other. Patrol has been to their place three times the past two years, domestic. First time, the old man gets frisky, they take him in for a night in the cooler. Other two occasions, they quieted down once our guys showed up."

"What happened this time?"

Denby listened, made notes, asked a couple of questions, got the address. There was no point in going over there now; the Belknapps would be well in the bag, if not passed out. He'd check them in the morning, find out what all the nonsense was about the knife.

Melda made poached eggs for breakfast and they ate like a married couple starting the day together. She liked the feel of it. She was thinking it was maybe time she should move in here. It would save her a lot on rent, even if they split what Chesney was paying here, and it would be... nice to keep doing this. Besides, she was convinced now that this man was worth keeping, but he was going to need some full-time managing.

"Sweetie," she said, and saw him look up the way he still did when she called him that, like a neglected puppy that suddenly realizes it's going to get a treat.

"Yes?"

"About the book."

The happy puppy faded from Chesney's face. "Yes?"

"It bothers you, doesn't it?"

He looked down at his eggs. "Yes."

"Not a pool of light."

"Exactly."

"But you said you'd read it."

Chesney sighed.

"Tell you what," she said, "how about if I sort of... look after this for you?"

"What do you mean?"

She leaned across the table, took his hand. "You've got enough to worry about, with the new job and all the crimefighting. Maybe I could help with this thing. You said you wanted me to read the book, anyway."

It was clearly a new idea to Chesney. She realized that no one had ever offered to take over a part of his life and "look after it" for him. He'd been left to stumble through murk and darkness from one all-too-infrequent pool of light to another, coping as best he could.

"I still have to read the book," he said. "I said I would do it."

"That's all right, sweetie. You read the book, but when it comes to what to do after, you just let me do the worrying for both of us."

He blinked at her. "You can do that?"

"I handled your mother, didn't I?"

She dropped Chesney off at his office then drove home, changed into her blue uniform and sneakers and went on to Sugar 'n' Spice, the beauty salon where she did manicures. Her first client wasn't due until nine-thirty, so she arrived with five minutes to spare. But as she approached the front door, the policeman who had followed Chesney down the funnel into Hell got out of an unmarked car and stepped into her way.

"Ms McCann?" he said, showing her a wallet with a badge and ID, "Lieutenant Denby. I'd like to ask you a few questions."

"What about?"

"That book you're going to read."

Melda was an intelligent young woman and knew it. In a fairer world, she knew she would be running some big outfit or winning major court cases, instead of polishing the nails of women, some of whom didn't have much more brains than God gave a labrador retriever. So she was smart enough to know that the man with the badge was also smart, and that he had come at her with a question that she hadn't expected, and – worst of all – that he had seen in her face a reaction that meant there was no point trying to play dumb.

"How'd you know about that?" she said.

Of course, he was a cop and he had the advantage, so he said, "How about I ask the questions, you give the answers?"

"Okay," she said, "I don't know anything about the book except what my boyfriend's mom told me: the Reverend Billy Lee Hardacre has written it the way some angel told him to, and it says that my boyfriend is like a prophet out of the Bible."

"Is he?"

"Chesney doesn't think so. It's all the reverend's idea."

"What do you think?"

"I think it isn't police business," she said. "Doesn't this come under freedom of religion, or something?"

"It comes under something," said Denby. "What do you know about the guy in the spandex suit, goes around busting up dope dealers and auto-theft rings?"

If he'd asked that question first, Melda thought, he might have caught her off-guard. But the sudden switch of topic didn't faze her. She'd been ready with an answer to that question for weeks.

"He saved me from some muggers."

"And then he saved you from a guy named Todd Milewski."

"It was on TV." She saw him waiting for her to say something else and decided to oblige. "So you must also know that he said he'd call, but he never did."

"Never?"

"What are you, desperate? Not enough crime in the city, you've got to go around checking on people's private lives?"

Denby's smile put Melda in mind of a cat that thinks it has cornered a mouse. "What would you know about how much crime there is, Ms McCann? Or isn't?"

"My boyfriend is an actuary for an insurance company," she said. "It's what he talks about."

The lieutenant took out a notepad, flipped it open and looked at something there. "Your boyfriend is Chesney Arnstruther."

It wasn't a question, so Melda made no response.

Denby wasn't fazed. "What does he know about the spandex guy?"

"Why don't you ask him?" Melda thought that might have been the wrong answer. She looked at her watch and said, "I'm gonna be late for work."

"Sure," said the policeman. "How about we continue this after you've read the book?"

But Melda was balanced now. "How about after you read it?" she said, and opened the door to Sugar 'n' Spice.

• • • •

Denby wasn't too unhappy with the McCann interview. She hadn't told him anything he didn't know,
but she had confirmed his intuition that she knew
more than she was telling. Plus, he read her for one of
those people who feel that their intelligence is under-
rated and who welcome opportunities to demonstrate
their mental worth. He decided he would circle back
to her in a few days.

But right now he was pulling up outside the tenement where the Belknapps waged the fifty-year war
they called their marriage. It was a tumbledown heap
of warped siding and peeling paint, with no lock on the
front door, no elevator, and no shortage of the urine-
and-boiled-cabbage odor that was standard issue in this
neighborhood. On the second-floor landing a well-fed
brown rat gave him a who-you-looking-at stare.

Doris Belknapp opened the door to their apartment,
adding a fug of stale sweat and cigarette smoke to the
smell in the hallway. She didn't want to talk about the
intruder, but Ralph did, and pushed her aside so the
lieutenant could enter. The old man was excited.
Denby smelled liquor on his breath, but Belknapp
wasn't drunk – at least not this early in the day. There
was an open fifth of off-brand bourbon, mostly full,
on the scarred kitchen counter; the old lush had probably been just getting started when the lieutenant
knocked on the door.

"A time traveler?" the policeman asked, when the
man had told his tale. They were sitting at the kitchen
table. The old woman had gone into the bedroom and
closed the door.

"It's what he said." Ralph's moist eyes were big, the whites stained yellow where they weren't veined in red. "Come from the future to stop me…" He broke off, his decrepit face forming that expression that cops recognize as: *Oops, I almost said too much.*

"To stop you from what?"

"Nothin'."

"Come on. What were you gonna do?"

The old man's tongue moved his dentures around in his mouth but he said nothing.

"Listen," said Denby, "whatever you were going to do, did you actually do it?"

"Well, no."

"Not even after the guy left?"

"Nuh-uh."

"Then you got nothing to worry about."

Belknapp mulled this over. Denby didn't give him any leisure. "Look," he said, "calling in a false police report is an offense. I could haul you in right now." He saw the man's eyes go to the bottle on the counter, and added, "That's right, you don't get to take the booze."

"Okay, I'll tell you. First, pass it over." The old man took hold of the bottle, upended it and drank off two serious gulps. He wiped his lips with the back of his hand and said, "He said he come from the future to stop me from killin' Doris."

"And were you going to kill her?"

The moist eyes looked away. "I didn' meanta."

"How were you going to do it?"

"That knife, there." Denby went to the counter and picked up the big chef's knife. Belknapp saw the pause as an opportunity to take another hit from the bottle. "He just showed up out of nowhere and grabbed my arm."

"You mean, he just appeared out of thin air?"

"Yeah. One second I'm sittin' there, then I pick up the knife and go to... well, you know, and pop! he's standin' right beside me, grabbin' hold."

"No way he snuck in?"

"No way."

"And then he said he came from the future?"

"That's what he said. To stop me killin' Doris." He drank some more. "And he snapped the knife in half, but when Doris bitched at him, he fixed it."

"Fixed it?" Denby examined the carbon-steel blade. It looked perfect to him. "How?"

"Dunno. One second it's in two pieces, the next it's good as new."

The lieutenant tapped the point of the blade against the counter, the steel making a *ting* sound. "And then he left?"

"Uh huh."

"How?"

"He just disappeared."

"Any noise, puff of smoke? Anything that might have been a distraction while he snuck out?"

"Nuthin' like that. One second he's there–"

"I get it." Denby took out his notepad, jotted down a couple of points. "Did he say anything else?"

"Like what?"

"Like why it was so important to keep you from doing Doris?"

The old man shook his head and took another pull from the bottle while he thought about it. "Nope. Seemed important to him, though."

Driving back to Police Central, Denby turned the story over in his mind. On first appraisal, time travel was no more likely a scenario for the Mr Spandex than any of the other explanations that had crossed his mind since the guy had made his first appearance at a mob-run chop shop, leaving a gaggle of well-known-to-police hoodlums tied up in batches, surrounded by stolen luxury cars they'd been loading onto semi-trailers.

The prevailing view in the squad room had been drugs: specifically, some military-grade hallucinogen that the guy had got his hands on. He'd douse the area with an aerosol application, then move in while the criminals were in gaga-land. But there were two problems with that hypothesis: one, the guy didn't wear any kind of breathing gear – in fact the only parts of him that weren't covered were his mouth and nostrils; and two, he'd been captured on a security camera, moving at superhuman speed and throwing people around with the strength of a carnival strongman.

"If he really is a time traveler," Denby said to the windscreen while he waited for a traffic light to change, "that would explain why we can't find him when he's not working. He comes, he does his thing, then he goes back to hang out with Buck Rogers in the twenty-third century."

The big question, though, was why? Why would somebody in the future be concerned about crime in a Midwest city in the early twenty-first century? What possible difference could it make to the future if Ralph Belknapp had filleted Doris? Or if some manicurist got relieved of her purse in the park? Especially to a future so far advanced that they'd had time to think up time travel and work the bugs out of it?

They'd called the kid a prophet, and he had taken that as the blather of people who took their religion straight and overproof. But Hardacre was the very image of a phony TV preacher, just about the last guy Denby would expect to drink cultish kool-aid. Maybe, the policeman thought, the kid was some other kind of prophet. He was an actuary, who spent his working day making predictions of the future based on statistics and formulas. What if Chesney Arnstruther had made, or was about to make, some mathematical breakthrough that would change the world? Something to do with crime and criminals – maybe predicting who would do what?

The guy in the costume comes back from the future. Okay, Denby thought, let's say that's for real. Mr Spandex busts criminals – dopesters, car thieves, muggers, Ralph Belknapp. He shook his head at the last thought, but pressed on. What's he after? Is he a scientist collecting samples? Are criminals so rare in the future that he has to round up a few and study them?

It was an unproductive line of inquiry, but right now it was the only one Denby had. And now his mind went back to Hardacre's house and the glowing stack of paper on the desk. What if it wasn't a prop? What if it was an object from the future? And what if reading it would explain everything?

He could never get a warrant to search the preacher's house. Besides, it was way out of his jurisdiction. He'd have to convince the sheriff's department in the county where Hardacre lived. He imagined how that conversation would go. On the other hand, there might be a political connection between the Twenty and whoever ran the show down south. Maybe there was a pliable sheriff and a judge who was in someone's pocket – more and more elected judgeships were being contested these days, and campaigns cost money.

But before he went to Commissioner Hanshaw and Mayor Greeley with the kind of tale that was unwinding in his head, he had better get his facts straight. The main library was not far from Police Central. Denby parked at the curb and went in, took out his first library card since high school, and asked a librarian to help him find whatever they had on time travel.

The woman looked up from the computerized catalog. "The real thing? Or science fiction?"

Denby started with the real thing, and soon realized that he didn't understand any of it. He went back to the desk and got a list of novels, and left the library shortly after with an armload of books.

The reading of the Book of Chesney was scheduled for Saturday afternoon. Letitia wanted to drive up and collect her son, but the young man, operating from the pool of light provided by his girlfriend, was able to resist the forceful invitation. He and Melda would drive down in her venerable Hyundai sedan. The vehicle was probably not fit for lengthy excursions, but

Chesney prevailed upon his assistant to rearrange some of its molecules – or whatever the demon did to make things happen – and immediately the Hyundai ceased its tendency to blow blue smoke upon start-up and to rattle alarmingly when Melda shifted gears. So mutually accommodating had the Xaphan-Chesney relationship become that neither one made even a pretense of searching for a connection between auto repair and fighting crime.

Chesney had never been on a long drive with anyone but his mother and was delighted to find that a road trip on a summer's day could be a genuinely pleasant experience. He even toyed with the idea that, once the present business was settled, he and Melda might take a vacation together in the Hyundai. They could eat in roadside cafes and sleep in motels, take photographs of scenery and historical markers. Travel might then become another pool of light, instead of the murky, penumbrous affair the young man remembered from his bus trip to the state college, when he had first escaped from his mother. Of course, he would let Melda organize the trip.

They reached the estate without incident, and without noticing the ghost car that had followed them from the city. The gate to the estate opened when Melda spoke into the grill, and they parked beside his mother's DeSoto and the Reverend Billy Lee's Mercedes. The preacher and Chesney's mother waited for them at the top of the front steps, and the young man could not help the shiver of apprehension that went through him when Letitia's basilisk gaze locked onto him. But when Melda took his arm and said, "We're fine, sweetie," the warmth of the sun returned and he walked on untrembling legs up the steps and into the mansion.

Hardacre acted the genial host, offering a light lunch on a tree-shaded patio walled on three sides, with the open side overlooking the terraced rear lawn and a tennis court. A catering firm had been engaged to prepare and serve sandwiches and beer and lemonade. Once everything was in place, the two functionaries departed.

"Good," said the preacher, as the sound of the gate closing itself came faintly to their ears, "now we can talk."

"I've seen you on TV," said Melda.

"And what did you think?" said Hardacre.

"You want me to be polite or honest?"

Chesney saw Letitia stiffen, but Hardacre put a hand on her arm. "Honest," he said, "We are, after all, almost family."

"When you used to tear people apart, I thought you were mean," Melda said. "Not that they didn't deserve it. It's just that you seemed to take a real pleasure in tearing them a new one."

"Very perceptive," said Hardacre. "I did enjoy it."

"Billy Lee," said Chesney's mother. "You were doing the Lord's work, chastising the sinner—"

"And having a Hell of a good time doing it," the preacher said. "And so, my dear, did you. Those letters you used to write! Don't tell me you didn't relish telling their recipients of the torments that awaited them."

"I was trying to save their mortal souls!"

"Indeed you were." Hardacre patted Letitia's arm while he winked at Melda. "And loving every minute of it. The copy of the one you sent to that fat idiot, Hall Bruster – Allbluster, you called him – did I tell you I framed it?"

"You're embarrassing me."

Hardacre quoted: "'When the Devil pries apart your overstuffed buttocks and spits on the glowing iron to make sure it's hot enough, then you'll squeal for mercy like a porker in the slaughterhouse chute. But it will be too late.' You know he wanted to sue me. Then he realized it would just bring me more viewers."

Chesney said, "Who is Hall Bruster?"

Hardacre blinked in surprise. The two women were used to the young man being unaware of persons and events that were common knowledge across the land.

"He's a pundit," Melda says. "Sees conspiracies everywhere. Thinks the UN is out to get us, and has Belgian troops secretly training to round up all the patriots." When she saw that the clues meant nothing to Chesney, she said. "Draws diagrams on a blackboard? Sometimes uses puppets? Used to say that all the drug addicts should be put in concentration camps until he was caught with forged prescriptions for painkillers?"

The last reference rang a faint chime for Chesney. "I think one of the guys was talking about it at poker night last year."

"He's really got it in for the reverend," Melda said. "You know he's been making fun of you – the precursor thing?"

"I know," said Hardacre. "He's in for a surprise."

"The way you say that," Melda said, "it doesn't sound too holy."

Hardacre gave the young woman a slight nod to concede the point. "There are still traces of the old Billy Lee, I admit it. But you do see that I'm trying to do something different? Something that matters?"

Melda sipped her beer while she thought about it. Then she wiped a little foam from her upper lip and said, "Being different is not the problem. It's telling the world that Chesney is some kind of prophet."

"And what's wrong with that?"

"You didn't ask him if he wanted the job."

"It's not a job!" said Letitia. "It's a calling from the Lord!"

Melda wasn't fazed. She looked straight at the other woman and said, "Says who?"

Chesney's mother had already cleared the launch pad and was ready for second-stage ignition. Chesney was surprised to see Hardacre calm her with a quiet word and another pat on the arm. Then the preacher turned to Melda and said, "Well, that's the question, isn't it?"

"And I'm still waiting for the answer," the young woman said.

Hardacre smiled. "You're wasted as a manicurist," he said. "You should have been a lawyer."

"There's no need for insults," Melda said, but she gave him back the same smile.

"Okay," said the preacher, "cards on the table. The way I read this, the person I've got to convince is you."

Chesney spoke. "Melda is handling this one for us."

Letitia would have lit up again, but Hardacre said, "That's fine. Let's get to it, then. How much do you know of what's happened with Chesney in the past little while?"

"Pretty much everything."

Hardacre looked for confirmation to the subject of their conversation. Chesney nodded.

"Then let me summarize," the preacher said. He succinctly laid out the key events: Chesney's accidental summoning of a demon and the young man's refusal to render up his soul; the consequential strike by Hell's demonic labor force, leading to an impasse; Hardacre's entry into the situation, brought about by Chesney's mother, one of his followers; the deal that settled the strike, with Chesney apologizing and being given the part-time services of a demon to aid him in his lifelong desire to be a crimefighter.

"I know all of that," said Melda.

"And do you also know of my theory that the universe and all of us in it are part of a book that God is writing?"

"I've heard it. Why is he writing it?"

"Again," said Hardacre, "it's only my theory. One thing I learned as a novelist is that sometimes you write a book to work something out, something complex. I think God is writing a book, a book in which we are all characters, in order to learn morality."

"You think that?" Melda said. "You think God doesn't know right from wrong?"

"Put it this way," said the preacher, "He's learning as He goes."

Melda shrugged. "What's this got to do with the man I love?"

Even as he was replaying the last words in his head and feeling a glow spread through him, Chesney was wondering if Melda had said them just to rile his mother. Hardacre had to calm Letitia once more, then he said to the young woman, "Events have moved on since then. I've been in touch with the senior angel that was part of the negotiations. Together, we've been working on a... call it a new chapter in the big story."

"The Book of Chesney?"

"That's the one."

"Where he's supposed to be a prophet?"

"Uh huh."

"Whether he wants to or not, you and an angel just write a book about him, a book that's supposed to become reality for him and for everybody?"

"That's about the size of it," said Hardacre, "if I've got this thing right."

Melda looked at him for a long moment, then she said, "You got a lot of damn gall."

Letitia spluttered, but again Hardacre held her down with that soft motion of his hand. Chesney wished he'd known that trick when he was growing up. The preacher said, "It doesn't work unless he buys in."

Melda didn't budge. "But you're making him an offer he can't refuse." Hardacre started to speak but she kept on. "At least, that's the way Letitia puts it to him."

Chesney's mother froze the young woman into a pillar of ice with a single glare, but Melda's inner heat burned right through. "He doesn't want to be a prophet. He already is what he wants to be."

"At this point," Hardacre said, "all we're asking is that he – and you – read the book. It's not written in stone, if I may use an appropriate phrase. We've always thought that Chesney should have input into the draft." His tone firmed up a couple of notches. "And the two of you have already agreed to that, so why don't we finish our lunch then get on with it?"

Lieutenant Denby put the ghost car where he'd parked before, next to the estate wall and under the trees. He got the directional microphone and its recorder out of the trunk, slung a pair of high-powered field glasses around his neck and climbed on top of the roof. He was in time to see a man and a woman come around from the back of the house, get into a blue Toyota van with *Appleby Catering* painted on the side and drive out through the gates. Their route did not take them past his position, so he kept his attention on the house.

He scanned the grounds and the windows with the glasses. Most of the curtains were open now, including the room into which he had peeked, but he saw no movement. He rigged the mike and pointed it at one window after another. There was nothing from the room with the glowing book. He tried the kitchen and heard the refrigerator, but no voices. He picked up a conversation from an upstairs window, but a burst of applause told him that someone had left a television tuned to a religious network channel that was running an afternoon talk show.

The policeman swore softly to himself. He'd been hoping for a repeat of the previous surveillance, but with more participants and more information. He swung the mike in a wider arc and caught a faint whisper from the rear of the big house. He turned up the gain on the instrument, but all he could achieve was a susurration of sound. From the ups and downs, he could tell it was speech and not just a rustling of leaves from the shade trees planted around a wall that extended from the back of the mansion. But he could not make out any words.

The mike's parabolic dish picked up minute vibrations, tiny echoes of sound inaudible to the unassisted ear. Denby figured he must be catching sounds as they were bounced off the inside of the wall and then reflected off the branches and foliage of the overhanging trees. It wouldn't do.

He put the equipment on the front seat of the car and continued down the road that ran along the side of the estate. A little over a quarter mile later, the wall met a patch of woods; here the side of the estate began, fenced not by stone but by wire mesh. Another hundred yards or so, and he came upon a dirt road that went into the trees. Across the road was a barrier made of a length of heavy steel pipe hinged to a concrete post at one end and secured to another post by a padlock and chain.

The ghost car's surveillance suite included a pair of heavy-duty bolt cutters. The chain was soon parted and Denby was driving into the woods, the gate closed behind him and the bright scars on the chain smeared with mud. The road wound to a clearing where someone had been cutting firewood. A trail led toward where the policeman reckoned the rear wall of the estate would be. His reckoning turned out to be correct and he was soon looking at a chain-link fence. Beyond was a screen of trees through which he could see a sweep of lawn, which rose in terraces to a tennis court and a patio beyond.

Denby had brought the bolt cutters with him. He made a hole and wriggled through it, then crept to the edge of the trees and scanned the view. Four people sat around a white-painted cast-iron table. The preacher and the nerd's girlfriend were talking back and forth. Denby quickly deployed the directional mike and was just in time to hear Hardacre say, "… agreed to that, so why don't we finish our lunch then get on with it?"

From then on it was mostly munching and swallowing, comments on the food and offers of more beer or lemonade. He noted that the older woman didn't have much appetite, and even less appreciation for the company, but the other three dug in with varying degrees of gusto. Denby wondered if the kid's mother might be more squeezable than the girlfriend, but a close examination of the powdered face told him that though she might blurt out something in anger, the odds of changing Letitia Arnstruther's mind about just about anything were way beyond a long shot.

He watched them eat, then gather up their dishes and utensils and carry them into the house. The mike gave him a clatter of kitchen sounds, then the hum of a dishwasher, over which he distinctly heard Hardacre say, "If you would all like to join me in the study."

There were no servants in the house, Denby reasoned. That was why the four people had carried in their lunch dishes and started up the dishwasher. He had already broken a number of laws by cutting the chain on the gate and the wire-mesh fence and by trespassing on the estate. "I might as well bite the whole bullet," he said to himself. He realized the expression didn't make much sense, but he was already sprinting across the back lawn, the directional mike and field glass left behind in the trees.

The stack of paper glowed on the preacher's desk, even though the room was well lit by the afternoon sun that came through the uncurtained windows. Chesney sat down in one of the three leather armchairs that were grouped in a conversation area. Melda took the one next to his.

"I won't ask if anyone wants a drink," Hardacre said, closing the door. "Doesn't seem appropriate." He briskly crossed to the desk, picked up the manuscript, and without ceremony brought it to the young man.

Chesney accepted it and laid the stack of pages on his knees. Warmth seeped through his pants legs, but the radiance seemed to fade as he gazed at it, as if his eyes had grown accustomed to the unnatural glow. The top sheet said only, *The Book of Chesney*. He took up the sheet of paper and handed it to Melda. Then he began to read the first page.

FIVE

Denby walked silently across the patio, through some French doors and into a rec room that didn't look as if it ever got much use. The billiard table's green felt was gray with dust. Out in the hall he passed the doorways to a kitchen with a walk-in pantry on one side and a utility room on the other. Then he was in a baronial-sized stone-floored foyer at the front of the house, with closed doors leading off on several sides. The lieutenant didn't have to guess which one Hardacre and the others were behind: he could see the creamy glow of the strange light coming through the crack beneath the door and even through the old-fashioned keyhole beneath the doorknob.

He crept to the door, knelt, and put his eye to the source of the light.

"It doesn't make sense to me," Chesney said. "I haven't done any of these things. I don't plan on doing any of them. Most of them I couldn't do even if I wanted to."

"If I'm right," said Hardacre, "and the angel thinks I am, even if you don't do them, it will be the same as if you did."

Melda said, "You mean Jesus didn't really walk on water, but once it was written down and passed around – once everyone believed it – it was the same as if he had."

"Pretty much," said the preacher.

"But who's going to believe that I called together all the leaders of the world," said Chesney, "and that they *came* when I called? Never mind that I confounded them with my wisdom."

"Again," said Hardacre, "if I understand how this works, it will become the truth. Divinely empowered truth."

"And what about this part," Chesney shuffled through the pages and found the one he was looking for, "here, where I go down into Hell and tell the Devil his time is up."

"It's an embroidering of the facts, I admit," said Hardacre, "but it seems to be where they want the story to go."

"They?" Melda said.

Hardacre pointed a finger upwards.

"I thought you told the angel," she said, "that this book we're all part of is being written by us, by what we really do. 'It's our story and God's just writing it for us.'"

"Call it a collaboration," Hardacre said. "He's always had co-authors, but never one who knew he was part of the writing team."

"So this is like an experiment?" Melda said.

"I think so. He doesn't tell me directly. An angel comes to talk to me – a Throne, which is a high rank; Chesney has met him – but all the angel knows is what God wants it to know."

"It?"

"They don't come in boys and girls sizes," Hardacre said. "At least not now. Apparently, in an earlier draft, angels were male – a little too male, in fact, since they seduced" – he put up his fingers, bent into quotation marks – "'the daughters of men' and produced off-spring who were giants and heroes of old."

Chesney could see that Melda was working to get her head around it. He almost envied her the ability to make her own pools of light in the darkness. "So you want Chesney to sign up to this stuff. Then what?"

"He reveals himself as an anointed one."

"By that you mean he comes on your television show – what, dressed in a white robe? Will you work up some special-effects miracles to bring in the crowds?"

Hardacre's face drew in on itself. "I'm not sure. The angel is playing that part close to its chest."

"We must trust in the Lord," said Letitia.

Melda looked at her. "Easy for you to say." To Hardacre, she said, "That's a pretty big pig in a poke."

The man shrugged. "It always has been. That's why it's so gratifying to open the poke and see the pig."

The young woman said, "But say Chesney does what you and this angel want. What happens then?"

"I don't know. Something really new, maybe." His

face took on a curious look, like that of a child expecting to find a wondrous gift under the Christmas tree. "Probably the end of this world – this draft – and the beginning of a new one."

"And what happens to people who fit the old world and don't fit the new one?"

Hardacre shrugged. "Does it matter? They're all just characters in a story. So are you; so am I."

"Yeah," said Melda, "but you don't see yourself as just another character, do you?" Another shrug from Hardacre irritated the young woman, but she held her temper and focused on what mattered. "And what about Chesney? Suppose all that happens is makes a fool of himself? Or maybe some nut takes a shot at him."

The preacher spread his hands. "In the end, it always comes down to faith."

There was a silence for a while. Then Melda said, "We're going to have to think about this." She looked at Chesney and he nodded. "Think about it a lot."

"I get the feeling," Hardacre said, "that they" – he pointed upwards again – "would like to see something happen soon."

"Well maybe 'they' should be talking to the monkey, not the organ grinder." She put her hand on Chesney's. "No offense, sweetie."

"None taken," he said.

The stack of glowing paper was back on the desk. Denby could see a corner of it if he squinted sideways through the keyhole. They were talking in there –

arguing, really – the preacher and McCann, about faith and miracles and special effects. The study was big, the door maybe twenty feet from where they were seated in the conversation area. He couldn't hear clearly through the closed door, except when voices rose. He heard nothing about Mr Spandex. He was starting to wonder if this was a wild goose chase, or if maybe it was only a sideshow.

Hardacre and his mistress genuinely thought they were dealing with an angel. What if the guy was a time traveler who used different disguises when he dealt with different people? Denby had seen a statistic somewhere that said that more than two thirds of twenty-first century Americans believed in angels. If you were coming here from the future and didn't want to have to answer too many inconvenient questions, masquerading as a heavenly messenger would probably be a safe bet.

The meeting in the study was winding up. Denby saw people rising to their feet. He got away from the keyhole, thinking quickly: if they were leaving, the shortest route to where they'd left the car was out the front door. He quick-footed it across the foyer and into the hallway that led to the kitchen, pressing himself against the wall just as he heard the study door open.

Hardacre and the girlfriend were still talking, but it was scheduling talk. "I'll give you a call after we've talked it over," McCann was saying. Denby risked a peek around the corner and saw them moving toward the doors. The older woman had her hand on the kid's arm and was battering his ears with some fiercely whispered remarks that the policeman couldn't hear. But the nerd was not happy, his shoulders hunched, and now he pulled his arm free and said, "Mother, we've settled this." That made McCann turn her head and look over her shoulder. Denby pulled back out of sight.

Then he heard the front door open and looked again. They were going outside, all of them, the older couple accompanying the younger down to where the cars were parked. The door to the study had been left open and Denby could see the glowing stack of paper on the desk. The temptation came, strong and sudden, and before he had time to think himself out of it, he was speeding across the foyer and into the room. He scooped up the manuscript, tucked it under his arm, and made like the running back TeShawn Bougaineville heading for a game-winning touchdown. Less than thirty seconds later he was in the screen of trees at the back end of the property, hurriedly collecting the field glasses and directional mike. Another five minutes, and he was driving on two-lane blacktop toward the interstate, the glowing mass beside him on the front passenger seat.

"What did you think of it?" Melda asked Chesney, as they rolled north toward the city.

"Some of it was based on things that I've really done," he said, "like when I saved you from the muggers. And when I rounded up the dope dealers."

She kept her eyes on the road. "Yeah, but then it got weird. I mean, if you did go to the United Nations, what would you tell them?"

Chesney shrugged. "Stop fighting. Stop hurting people. Figure out what the world really needs, then make it happen."

"Exactly," Melda said. "It's not as if they don't already have people telling them that. They're just not listening, cause they've got other plans."

"Would it make a difference if they thought I was a prophet?"

"It would make some of them want to kill you on the spot – most because they'd think you were a dangerous faker, a few because they'd be afraid you were the real thing."

"I don't want to get killed," Chesney said. He reached over and touched her thigh. "Especially not now."

She covered his hand with hers. "No. So there's that. But then there's the other question: what if it worked? What if it really made the world a better place?"

Chesney put his mind to that question. All he saw was darkness and indistinct shapes. "Would it?" he said. "The Reverend believes this kind of thing has happened before – a new book comes along and changes everything. But did that make things better? Is this a better world than the earlier drafts of the universe?"

"He lets you think he believes that," Melda said. "One thing I know for sure is that he believes that when a new chapter starts, the old world ends, finito, case closed."

"And that doesn't seem to bother him."

"I don't think he believes it would end for him – especially if he's the guy who's writing the next chapter."

"So who's to say," Chesney said, "that it's better for everybody else?"

"Hardacre would say we'd have to take that on faith."

Chesney's face hardened. "I don't do faith. I do numbers. Numbers don't cheat."

"This is going to take some thinking," Melda said.

Lieutenant Denby pulled into a rest area after fifty miles. It was mid-afternoon and there were several cars in the parking area, plus some mobile homes and semi-trailers in the part reserved for heavy vehicles. Kids were playing around one of the picnic tables and a fat-bellied man was walking something on the end of a leash that looked like it ought to be on the end of a mop handle. The policeman rolled past to the end of the cars-only lot and pulled into the last bay. He cut the engine, looked around to see if anyone was likely to walk past him. When he saw nobody coming from any direction, he put the manuscript on his lap, propped against the steering wheel.

The cover page read: *The Book of Chesney*, with no by-line. He reached to turn to the first page of text, but as he did so the four words on the cover changed. Denby blinked and looked again. Now the words were in some strange script he had never seen before. Even as he examined the cursive marks and squiggles, they blurred and changed into some other form of writing, this one with dots and accents above some characters and others individually underlined.

"What the...?" was the lieutenant's response, then the script changed again. He flipped to the first page of text, and saw the same effect. A thought occurred to him, and he put his nose close to the paper and sniffed. Nothing. But still he wondered if the paper might be imbued with some psychotropic substance – he was still leaning toward drugs as the answer to how all those people ended up in their underwear in Civic Plaza without knowing how they got there. And how come there were gaps in his own memory?

As he thought about the drugs issue, the text changed again. Denby dug out his cell phone, turned it into a camera, and took a shot of the first page. A few seconds later, the lines blurred; when they came back into focus they were filled with wedge-shaped characters. Those rang a bell in the lieutenant's mind, something from a college course: Cunieform? he thought. He snapped another picture, then keyed the phone to show him the two photos.

He saw two different scripts. When he looked at the page itself, he saw two parallel wavy lines and stick-figure drawings of a bird, a bee and a human hand. He recognized them as Egyptian hieroglyphics, just in time for them to become a string of zeroes and ones.

Denby dumped the manuscript back on the passenger seat, repocketed his cell phone and started up the ghost car's engine. It was only then that he noticed that the paper wasn't glowing anymore.

It was dinner time when Chesney and Melda got back to his apartment. She fixed them a meal out of whatever she found in the cupboards and refrigerator: beef stroganoff with spicy salsa instead of ketchup in the sour cream sauce, because they were out of ketchup. It didn't taste bad, Chesney thought. Dinners with Melda were becoming another pool of light.

They did the dishes together, then he said, "I was thinking of going crimefighting tonight. If there's any crime left out there."

Melda rinsed a plate. "Maybe you should expand? Take on the terrorists?"

He summoned his assistant and in a moment the demon was hovering beside him, cigar and glass of rum in their usual places. "Xaphan, can I go after terrorists?"

"You mean as a crimefighter?"

"Yes."

The demon puffed reflectively. "Tricky question," it said. "Depends on what definition you use."

"How about people who blow up innocent men, women and children?"

The weasel brows went up and down. "There's a guy a few blocks from here."

Chesney felt a pool of light spread around him. "What's he planning?"

"To watch an old Lawrence Welk show on cable, then get to bed," said the demon. At Chesney's look of surprise, it went on, "The guy's ninety-two. Was a bombardier in the Eighth Air Force in 1943 when they set fire to Hamburg. All told, they killed forty thousand and a few more. I can't give you his personal score cause it was a joint enterprise."

Chesney felt the pool of light shrink. "No," he said, "I mean a terrorist who's going to blow up innocent people in the future."

"Which one?" said Xaphan.

"How do I know which terrorist?"

"No, I meant, which future?"

"How many are there?"

"It's a really big number," said the demon. "You don't have the words for it."

The answer raised a question Chesney did not want to explore. It was surrounded by murk. "Are there terrorists planning to blow people up right now?"

"Sure, lots."

"Then let's go after them."

"Can't."

"Why not?"

"They don't live around here." The demon released the cigar as if placing it in an invisible ashtray at about the level of its watch chain then made a small flourish with its free hand. A scroll of paper appeared in its stubbly fingers then unrolled. Xaphan let the screed unwind then said, "There."

The scroll hung in the air while the demon pointed at an indented subparagraph. Chesney bent closer and read, "Territory: the territory shall be limited to the city in which the party of the first part is normally resident, its suburbs and the surrounding district, to a distance not to exceed ten miles beyond the farthest boundary of the city limits."

"I don't remember that part," he said.

"You were kinda excited at the time," Xaphan said, "but you said you wanted to fight crime in the city and that's what got put in the contract."

"So there are no terrorists in the city?"

"Not right now."

"Will there be any in the future?"

"Again," said the demon, "which future?"

Chesney's pool of light had faded. "What about regular crime? Anything going on?"

"There's some bank robbers passing through on their way north."

"Are they robbing a bank here?"

"Nah. They work in the south, live in the north."

Chesney had begun to feel a pool of light; but already it was fading. "But they're criminals. So can I go after them anyway?"

"Sure. They got the loot with 'em, so they're commitin' the crime of possession of stolen property. You can nail 'em."

Chesney's pool of light brightened considerably.

Lieutenant Denby had stopped at a drive-in for a burger and fries before returning the ghost car to Police Central. He was passing the building's front side, heading for the ramp that led down to the parking garage, when a late-model minivan descended from the sky and landed in the curbside no-parking zone at the bottom of the front steps. The vehicle didn't come down at speed, as if it had been dropped from the top of the building, but it hit hard enough to make a hubcap pop off – and certainly hard enough to shake up the four men who were hog-tied in the seats, their seat belts snug around them.

Daubed on the side of the van, in green paint that was still wet and dripping onto the pavement, were the words: *Bank robbers from out of town*. In smaller print underneath: *PS: loot under rear seat*.

Denby stopped the ghost car and put on his flashers. Uniformed officers were already coming down the steps. The eyes of the bank robbers were very large. The lieutenant spotted Conyers, the patrol sergeant on night duty, at the top of the steps and said, "Book them, don't let them talk to each other. I'll want to question them first thing tomorrow."

Later, in bed, Chesney said, "I really enjoyed catching those juggers."

"Juggers?" Melda said.

"It's what Xaphan calls bank robbers."

"Mmm," Melda said, snuggling against him, "I could tell you were in a good mood."

"It all went very well." He turned toward her, stroking her belly. "Listen, I said you could be the one to work out what we should do," he said, "but as far as I'm concerned, I'm pretty happy just being a crime-fighter."

"When you're happy," she said, "I'm happy." A moment later she said, "But I'm still thinking about it."

She lay there doing just that as his breathing told her he had fallen asleep. She didn't like the idea of Chesney as a prophet, especially if it meant being tied to the Reverend Billy Lee Hardacre. She'd seen him on TV, ripping a strip off some politician or rock star who had gone astray; she'd admit, at least to herself, that she'd sometimes stayed tuned, which made her not much better than any other spectator at a lynching, but that didn't mean she had to like the guy who tied the noose.

On the other hand, Hardacre's show was seen by millions – really, she had no idea of the ratings, but it must be a lot of people if he stayed on the air – and being seen on TV was how you became a celebrity. Maybe she should do some research to see how other prophets ranked in the fame sweepstakes.

Chesney had gone to sleep with a hand resting on her tummy. She put her own over his and thought about what he'd said about being happy just to be a crimefighter. And, she had to admit, to have her in his life. Then she thought about some of the celebrities whose escapades she'd followed on TV or in the tabloids. Were they happy having their private parts photographed getting out of limos and their private doings spread across the pages of magazines?

She was sure that Hardacre wanted to use Chesney and didn't care how it made him feel. Was she falling under the same spell? The question kept her awake while he slept contentedly beside her. She listened to his deep, regular breathing and thought, what's wrong with what we've got?

Lieutenant Denby came into work at seven in the morning. The four bank robbers' rap sheets were on his desk, as he had requested before heading home the night before. So was a blue slip of paper – a message from the chief's office: John Edgar Hoople wanted to see him forthwith. The lieutenant slipped the blue paper under the four files, and turned to the first robber's criminal history. He read the summary, then went through the other three in rapid succession. They told him everything he needed to know, particularly that there were federal warrants out on all of them.

He picked up the phone and called the patrol sergeant. "Did we tell the feebs yet about the four orphans we found on the doorstep last night?"

Conyers said, "Somehow, in all the confusion, nobody made that call."

"Good," said Denby. "Give me an hour."

"Speaking of feebs, J. Edgar Hoohah's looking for you. He came in special early."

"We must have a bad line. I can't make out what you're saying."

"Watch yourself, loot," said the sergeant.

Denby made another call, this one to the sergeant who oversaw the holding cells. He waited five minutes, then went down one floor to the interview rooms. Behind the door to room number three, a heavy-set, balding man who needed a shave put down the paper cup from which he had been drinking coffee and stared straight ahead across the table. Denby sat down in the man's line of vision and studied him for a while.

The suspect's name was Boden. According to the Police Central computer, he had spent his adult life pointing guns at people and relieving them of valuable objects: jewelry, furs, in one instance a shipment of gold coins, but mostly it had been bundles of currency found lying around in bank vaults. He'd done time twice, never snitched to get a reduced sentence;

in fact, he was still serving the last three-to-ten he'd been handed, having escaped from a state penitentiary in Louisiana, presumably with the help of a bribable warden.

Denby had brought no files with him, not even a notepad. He finished studying the man and said, "I'm not going to interrogate you. The only thing we could get you for is possession of stolen property and illegally parking in the yellow zone outside. Besides, the feds will be here soon to take you off our hands."

Boden took another sip of the coffee. Denby noticed a tremor in the man's hands. "So," he said, "what's the point?"

"How'd you get here?" The lieutenant could tell from the flicker in the bank robber's gaze that Boden knew he wasn't asking what route they'd taken, coming up from New Orleans, where they'd hit three banks last week. But the man said nothing.

"Listen," Denby said, "this is off the record. I'm not taking notes, there's no recorder running, you can see there are no cameras and no two-way mirror."

Boden looked around, then back at the lieutenant. A series of expressions crossed his jowly face as he wrestled with something in his head. Finally, he said, "Just you and me?"

"Scout's honor."

Boden drained the coffee and crumpled the cup, threw it into a corner. "I gotta tell somebody," he said.

"I know the feeling," Denby said. "There has been some weird shit happening around here, and you just stepped in it."

The bank robber's face went still as he consulted his memory. "We were gassing up at the Texaco," he said. "I go into the store to get some smokes and take a leak. When I come back, Schultzy is paying at the pump with a debit card."

Denby didn't ask whose card it was. He wouldn't be seeing Schultz before the feebs came. "Go on," he said.

"So it's my turn to ride shotgun. I get into the van, shut the door, and all of a sudden we're not there anymore."

"Not there?"

"Not at the gas bar. I mean, it just happened, zip. I'm looking out the windshield and there's no pumps, no lights, nothing. There's like this desert – rocks, dirt, cracks in the ground – but no sun. But it ain't night. You can just see some gray light in the sky, which is all clouded over."

The bank robber swallowed and looked inside his head again. "But not nice clouds," he said, "not fluffy white. These were black and yellowy and just, like, streaming across the sky. Cause there was a wind. I could hear it blowing, throwin' grit against the window, and it was a *stinking* wind. It started to come through the vents, and it was like… dead things. Old, dead things, all rotted and dried out."

He stopped, his gaze turned inward. Denby said, "Did you see anybody out there?"

Boden came back to the room. "Oh, you better believe it. This guy in a body suit, with a mask on. He had a brush and a bucket of paint and he was painting the side of the van."

"You get a good look at him?"

The man nodded. "He was grinning like an idiot. He was saying something, but I couldn't hear him over the wind. Then he steps back and *wham*! The desert disappears and we're slamming down into the ground outside the cop shop."

"Describe the idiot." Boden did and Denby listened. It was Mr Spandex, all right.

"You know something about this?" Boden said. "Schultzy said there was something on the news a while back about some clown playing Batman."

"Yeah," said the policeman. "We don't know who he is, or what he's up to."

Boden shivered. It was only a little shiver, but in a hardcase like him, Denby thought, the smallest shiver was equal to an ordinary citizen's full-blown fit of the staggering fearfuls. "I tell you one thing for free," the bank robber said, "I don't ever want to see that idiot grin again. Or that place he lives in."

"You figure he lives in that desert?"

"He looked to be right at home." Boden's shoulder jerked once. "It was a hell of a place," he said.

Denby got up. "Thanks," he said. The other man's eyes followed him and the policeman saw something else there. "What?" he said.

"You're interested in the guy? Personally?"

"Very personally," Denby said.

Boden looked at his hands, clasped together on the table. "Cause I never snitched, you know. Not once."

"I know. It's in your file." He waited, and when nothing more came, he said, "This is not really a cops-and-robbers situation. We don't know what in hell we're dealing with."

Boden made up his mind. "Okay," he said, "you do something for me, I'll do something for you."

"Do what?"

"Call my lawyer in Minneapolis. Tell him what's going on."

Denby smiled. "You mean so he can tell whoever's watching your stuff up there to get it hidden before the FBI comes waving a warrant."

Boden shrugged.

The lieutenant said, "In return for what?"

"Something I figure you don't got. Something you'd like to have."

"About Batman?"

"Yeah."

Denby didn't have to think it over very long. Recovering loot was way down on the scale of priorities. It just went to insurance companies anyway, and lately he had found that he didn't care much for insurance companies, not after meeting the Paxtons. "Okay," he said.

"Got a cell phone?"

The policeman handed over his personal phone. Boden punched in some digits and after a moment said, "Scorched Earth," then closed the phone to end the call.

"Okay," said Denby. "Your turn."

"Check Schultzy's phone," the bank robber said. "He took a picture."

• • • •

There was no heel-cooling time for Denby at J. Edgar Hoople's office. The chief of police's hatchet-faced secretary showed him right in. The boss had been working himself up, the lieutenant could see: the square-jawed face was red and even though it was well before noon, there was a smell of Scotch in the air.

"Where the hell have you been?" he started out at full volume, one hand indicating the phone on his desk. Denby could see damp finger marks on the handset, slowly drying. "I've got the mayor and the commissioner chewing my ass over this bank robber shit, and you're nowhere to be found!"

The lieutenant didn't bother answering the question he was asked, because he believed he had an answer to the one that counted. "I think I've got a line on the guy," he said, "Where he comes from."

Hoople wound down fast. "Tell me."

"It's hard to believe."

"I'm already believing that four bank robbers appear out of nowhere on our doorstep. Try me."

"Look at this," Denby said. He flipped open his phone and showed the chief the photo he had forwarded from the bank robber's phone, which he had used in the evidence room while the sergeant there looked the other way.

Hoople was silent, studying the image. "I see the guy," he said. "He looks like an asshole in a Halloween costume."

"Look behind him," Denby said.

"There's nothing," the chief said. "Desert, clouds."

"Yeah," said Denby, "and I think I know why." The chief raised his eyebrows. "Because," the lieutenant said, "that's the future."

Hoople's face started to show red again. "The future?"

"The future," Denby said, "though I don't know how far. But the guy's a time traveler."

"Get the fuck outta here!" said the chief of police.

But Denby didn't. "I've got proof," he said, "a book from the future."

"No shit?"

"It's in my locker."

"What does it say?"

"I can't read it. Nobody can."

Hoople reached for the phone. "Get me the commissioner," he said.

Chesney and Melda were getting ready to go to work when the phone rang. He picked it up, expecting from the caller ID display to hear his mother's voice, but it was Hardacre who said, "It's gone."

"What's gone?"

"The book."

Chesney told Melda. "How did that happen?" she said.

Hardacre didn't know. He and Letitia had not gone back into the study after the young couple had left. Chesney drove from his mind the image of what they had probably got up to instead; in one sense, he was having a hard time seeing his mother in the role of mistress, or even common-law wife; in another sense, he was seeing disturbing mental pictures of the implications whenever his mind was turned in that direction.

He concentrated on the problem at hand. "Could the angel have come and collected it?" he said.

Melda put in her thought. "Maybe God changed his mind?"

"I don't think so, but I know how we can find out," the preacher said. "Call up your friend from downstairs. Ask him."

"Yes," said Melda, when the young man looked to her for a response.

"Hold on," Chesney said into the phone, then summoned the demon. Xaphan appeared instantly, puffing on a fresh Havana, full glass in hand. "Reverend Hardacre's book has been stolen," he said. "What can you tell us about it?"

"Nuthin'."

"Why not?"

The demon drained the glass in one swallow and the tumbler winked out of existence. It held up one stubby digit. "First," it said, "cause the preacher's place is about eighty miles outta your jurisdiction. Second," it added a finger, "cause the boss said to stay out of it."

"Out of what?"

"Anything you get up to with that holy joe. It's outta line."

"Go away," Chesney said, and the demon did.

As the sulfur cleared, Melda said, "Something I didn't tell you about – Lieutenant Denby asked about the book."

Chesney could hear Hardacre's voice through the phone, even though it was nowhere near his ear. "What?" He keyed the device to its speaker-phone setting.

Melda said, "He came to the salon, asking me about the Actionary. The last thing he said was that he wanted to talk to me again, after I'd read the book."

"When was this?" Hardacre said. She told him. "Have you checked your phone for a tap?" he asked Chesney.

"There's no need. It's... protected. So is yours, when you're calling me here."

There was a pause, then the preacher said, "The Devil was worried about the book. He got Denby to snatch it."

Melda said, "I can't see Denby selling his soul."

"There are other ways to get someone to do something he might ordinarily not do," said Hardacre, "and the Devil invented all of them."

"I thought he was a straight cop," Chesney said.

"He may think he is," the preacher said. "Remember what the road to Hell is paved with."

"So what do we do?" said Melda.

"Only thing we can do," said the voice from the speaker phone. "Wait and see."

Chesney was at his desk, vetting an analysis that had been prepared by three of the actuaries under his supervision: an examination of the effects on life expectancy of long-term unemployment. Given the current downturn in the economy and the consensus among economists that any recovery was likely to be slow in producing enough jobs to return the city to the employment levels it had known before the recession hit, a substantial number of Paxton Life and Casualty policy holders were out of work and liable to stay that way.

The analysts had woven together a matrix of factors: loss of health benefits, leading to later detection of serious medical issues and a likelihood that they would go untreated, or be undertreated at best; increased risky behavior, including drinking, drug-taking, violence on the street or in the home; poorer nutrition; unstable marital relationships; loss of domicile; general stress levels and descent into depression.

The trend lines did not look good. More people were liable to die earlier than had been projected when they took out their policies in happier times. In cases where those policies were already fully paid up, it was not possible for Paxton Life and Casualty to restructure the premiums to make the books balance. Premature disbursements, as payouts before the expected deaths of policy holders were called, impacted the quarterly and annual balance sheets.

PL&C did not tolerate such impacts gladly. The company was preparing a case to identify long-term joblessness as "a material change in the policy holder's circumstances," which would trigger the invoking of a clause in the pages of fine print that would allow the company to cancel paid-up policies and up the premiums on those still paying.

Chesney worked his way through the matrix of figures, and made some notes. Then he turned to his keyboard and drafted a memo instructing the actuaries to factor in the likelihood of criminal activity, apprehension and incarceration as additional elements in the analysis, and recalculate the downstream effects.

He was about to send the memo when his door opened and Lieutenant Denby entered without knocking. "Surprised?" the policeman said.

"Not really."

Chesney watched the man sit. Denby said nothing but folded his hands in his lap and tilted his head at an angle. Chesney studied the man's expression and decided that it fit the old saying about a cat that has just enjoyed a dish of cream. He pressed the enter key that sent off his memo, then said, "You're happy about something."

"You think?" said Denby.

"Therapists once trained me to recognize facial expressions. Yours is not one of the difficult ones."

"You're a weird kid, aren't you?" said the policeman. "You're not, by any chance, from … somewhere else?"

"I was born at Mercy Hospital on Filbert Street," Chesney said.

"When?"

"12:41pm. Does it matter?"

"I meant," said Denby, "what year?" When Chesney opened his mouth to answer, the lieutenant spoke again, "Or, better yet, what century?"

"I don't understand," Chesney said. "I was born in 1986."

Now Denby's expression said he was amused by the answer. Chesney said, "I have work to do. What do you want?"

"Tell your friend," the lieutenant said, "you know who I mean, that I've figured him out."

"You have?"

"Tell him that he can cut the fancy-dress act. The gangbusters…" He paused just a moment, then said, meaningfully, waving his arms like wings, "The coming down from on high like an angel."

Denby was studying Chesney's reaction, while the young man did his best not to show one. "You think he's an angel?"

"No," said the lieutenant, "as a matter of fact I don't. As another matter of fact, I know what he is."

"And what's that?"

The policeman's face was perfectly serious as he told Chesney.

The young man leaned back in his chair. "A time traveler?" he said. "Really?"

"Really. And I want to talk to him."

"You said that the last time you were here."

"And did you pass on the message?"

"In a manner of speaking," Chesney said.

"What does that mean?"

"I don't want to go into it."

Denby gave him a sharp look, then let the matter slide. "Well, give him the message again," Denby said, "in any manner of speaking you like."

"He didn't take you up on the offer last time. Why should he now?"

"Because," said Denby, "I've got his book."

Chesney knew how to look surprised. He had perfected it long ago as a technique to survive his mother's inquisitions. "Oh," he said, "so *you've* got it. I'll tell the Reverend Hardacre. I think he'll want to prosecute you."

"He comes looking, it won't be there," said Denby. "It will only be there if your buddy, the poor man's Batman, gets in touch. Otherwise, it goes in the incinerator."

"I see."

"So you'll tell him?"

"Yes."

"Make it snappy," said Denby.

"What's the hurry?"

"I'm not working for myself," said the policeman. "There's a meeting of the Twenty tonight. I'm giving them the book. And copies of this." From his inside jacket pocket he pulled a four-by-six-inch photograph and tossed it onto Chesney's desk blotter. "Give that to your friend, too."

Chesney turned the image toward him and looked at it. It showed him grinning, paintbrush in hand. Behind him, in reasonable detail, stretched the empty outer circle of Hell.

SIX

Just before quitting time, Chesney's phone rang. Seth Baccala's secretary told the young man he was wanted on the tenth floor right away. Chesney had briefly worked on the tenth floor, as part of C Group, a special-assignment unit that the company's owner, W.T. Paxton, had created: the best and brightest number crunchers of Paxton Life and Casualty, whose job was to generate statistics, mostly about crime, that would be useful in Paxton's proposed campaign for governor. The old man had seen the Actionary as an even more useful adjunct to his campaign, until his daughter, Poppy, had been kidnaped into Hell by Nat Blowdell, prompting Chesney to have to go and rescue her.

It had been a messy situation, only partly resolved by a wave of Xaphan's stubby hand that had emptied and clouded the memories of some of the participants, including Lieutenant Denby. The lieutenant had seen the kidnaping and had charged in right after Blowdell. The Actionary had had to rescue him, too, though the lieutenant had no memory of it.

Now Paxton had decided against politics. His daughter's nervous breakdown had sapped his spirits. Besides, he was mystified by the sudden disappearance of Blowdell, the political fixer he had hired to be his campaign manager. Group C had been disbanded; the actuaries returned to their previous posts – except for Chesney, whose exceptional number crunching had been recognized and rewarded by promotion.

The young man had not been up on tenth since the end of the special unit. He saw that nothing else had changed, except that the secondary conference room that had housed C Group during its brief existence had now been returned to its former function. He presented himself to the receptionist and a moment later was told to go into Baccala's office.

He knocked and went in. Baccala, an impeccably groomed thirty year-old who might have posed for the cover of Harvard's MBA school alumni magazine, invited the actuary to sit down. Chesney could see a question in the man's eyes, and a moment later it was on his lips.

"Lieutenant Denby came to see you this afternoon," he said. "Why?"

Chesney did not feel himself at the center of a pool of light. Denby had spoken of the Twenty, the small group of powerful men who had effectively run the city since driving out the mob bootleggers during Prohibition in the thirties. He knew that W.T. Paxton was a member of the Twenty and he suspected that Baccala, his executive assistant, was privy to much of what went on between his boss and the powers-that-were. This conversation was deep in the murky darkness, and dissembling could be a long walk out onto thin ice. Fortunately, though, Chesney had grown up being interrogated by a ruthless expert and had learned some useful techniques.

One of them was to tell as much of the truth as possible. "He came to see me about the Actionary," he told Baccala.

The reference brought a rare wrinkle to the other man's exfoliated brow. "Why you?"

"He thinks I can get a message to him."

"What message?"

Chesney told him.

"A time traveler?" Baccala didn't seem to know whether to laugh or sigh in despair. A moment later, however, his sharp mind brought him around to the essential question. "Why does he think you can get a message to this mystery man?"

"He didn't say." Chesney was treading wafer-thin ice now. But his lifelong training in evading his mother's inquiries into his behavior stood him in good stead. "It may be because the Actionary saved my girlfriend. Twice," he added.

That brought an even deeper wrinkle to Baccala's smooth forehead. "You have a girlfriend?"

Chesney nodded. The other man seemed easily distracted. He wondered if Xaphan had arranged for Baccala to undergo a fit of fuzzy thinking whenever the subject of the Actionary came up.

Baccala blinked and looked down like a man trying to collect his thoughts. "So," he said after a moment, "nothing to do with the company?"

"Nothing."

"Nor the Paxtons?"

Chesney shook his head.

Baccala said nothing. He looked, Chesney thought, like a man trying to remember an old tune. "A time traveler?" he said after a while. "Really?"

"Really."

Baccala shrugged. "Okay. That's all."

Chesney stood up and went to the door, then looked back. The other man was staring at his desk top but obviously not seeing the satiny finish or the solid gold pen and pencil set. The actuary made a note to ask his demon just how long the memory-fogging would last against a sustained attempt by a first-class mind to overcome it.

"It usually holds pretty good," said Xaphan. "A guy who's really sharp can chisel his way through, if he works at it lots." It drank some more rum. "But then we can just slap on a second coat."

"So I don't need to worry," Chesney said.

"Not about that."

"What about the other thing?"

"The meeting of the Twenty?" The demon puffed on its cigar. "On that one, I can't help ya."

"Why not?"

"Boss says. I go near that bizness, it's twenty-three ski-doo for old Xaphan. I'm down in the pit shoving hot coals up some mug's rosy–"

Melda cut him off. "We get the picture," she said, "and, personally, it's not one I want to keep."

"No problem," said the demon. It wagged a digit sideways. Melda blinked. "And I'm not just thinkin' of my own comfort," Xaphan went on. "They could assign you some hotshot that's not as, shall we say, accommodatin' as me."

"Then what *can* you tell me about the meeting?" Chesney said.

"Nuthin' you don't already know."

"You're not much help."

"Not when you're not crimefightin'." It drained its glass of rum and the tumbler instantly refilled.

There was a silence in Chesney's apartment. After it had lingered for a while, Melda said, "Xaphan's right." The demon toasted her but she ignored it. "Whatever's going on with the Twenty is none of our business." She pointed a finger at Chesney. "You wanted to fight crime. It makes you happy. So let's fight some crime." She turned to the demon. "What have you got?"

Xaphan frowned and looked to the young man. "You want I should answer her?"

"Consider her my partner in crimefighting."

"Okey-doke." The demon looked up as if there was something written on the ceiling. "Tonight we got a strong-armin', some kids swipin' a car, coupla hit-and-runs, three mom-and-pop puncheroos, a guy sellin' pirated videos–"

"Nuh-uh," said Melda. "None of that picayune stuff. We want something people are gonna be blogging about tomorrow."

"I can only give ya the crime that's happenin'," said Xaphan.

Chesney watched Melda thinking. It occurred to Chesney that though he had called her his crimefighting partner without giving it any thought, it might be useful to have someone whose brain could illuminate the darkness that constantly hedged in his pools of light. Now he saw an idea strike her.

"What about," she said, "crime that happened last year, or the year before, and the guy got away with it, and he's still around?"

"Yes!" said Chesney. "Cold cases!"

The weasel brows did a brief up-and-down. "Yeah, got plenty of that."

"Like what?" said Melda. "And keep it to serious crimes only." She was trying to remember the name of the young woman who had been snatched from her apartment a few years back. It almost came to her, but now the demon was itemizing prospective cases, ticking them off on its short digits. "Got a guy used to go around marryin' widows and divorcees, then he'd clean out their bank accounts and catch the bus outta town. He made millions."

"Where is he?" Melda said.

"Nursin' home on Parkhurst. But he's missin a few marbles now."

"What else?"

"An ex-button man for the outfit. He's retired now, lives in Meadowview."

"Button man?" said Melda.

"He rubbed out guys on contract. He did Joey Hiccups and Angie Snips – they called him that cause he usedta carry these tin snips in the trunk of his car and–"

Chesney said, "Is there any evidence that could connect this button man to the murders?"

His assistant waved its cigar. "Nah. He was a real pro." It took a puff. "Course, we could always make some evidence."

Chesney didn't have to think about it. "No," he said. "I'm the good guy. I fly straight. What else have you got?"

"There's another guy, a civilian, used to pick up hitchhikers and take them back to his place."

"And?" said Melda.

"They're still there."

Chesney felt a cold chill pass down his spine. "How many?"

"Seventeen."

"What did he do to them?"

Xaphan looked at him sideways. "Your partner won't like the pictures in her head."

"Where are they now?"

"In his garage," the demon said, and paused to keep his Churchill alight. When it was glowing again, it said, "It's a double, and he made half of it into a secret room."

"He buried them under the floor?"

"Nah, he set most of them on chairs. Some of them are sittin' around tables. A couple are standin' in the corner. One of 'em's leanin' against the mantelpiece. Very cozy." He drank some more rum. "Guy likes to go in and talk to them."

Chesney could see that Melda was reluctant to ask, but had to anyway. "But... the smell."

"Oh, they don't smell," Xaphan said. "He's an amateur taxidermist."

The Twenty didn't meet often, but when they did it was always in the partners' conference room of Baiche, Lobeer, Tresidder: the old-money law firm a couple of blocks from City Hall. The room had not been redecorated since the 1930s, nor had the big mahogany table Julius Baiche had had imported from London before the war ever been replaced. It was wide enough that only a pair of professional basketball players could have shook hands across it and long enough to seat twenty on each side. And tonight almost every chair was filled with one of the magnates who made the city what it was. Even Jack Dolman, the area's major real estate developer, was there, smiling grimly as he endured the ribbing from colleagues who had seen the raw footage of the poker game in Civic Plaza – Dolman had been the one the big-busted brunette had been servicing.

W.T. Paxton was not present, but he was represented by his executive assistant. Seth Baccala entered quietly and took a seat in one of the partners' oak and leather chairs that lined the conference table. Other aides and assistants – there weren't too many: Twenty business was closely held – sat on straight-backed chairs against the side walls of the long room.

Louis Tresidder, silver-haired, patrician-faced, and for fifteen years now the chairman of the group, called the meeting to order with a double-tap of the gavel, then called on Police Commissioner Hanshaw to put the rest of them in the picture. Hanshaw did it quickly,

sketching the previous incidents involving the Actionary leading up to the Civic Plaza situation then
going on to the sudden appearance of four bank
robbers, with loot, outside Police Central. The latest incident was news to many of the elite assembled for the
meeting – the police had managed to keep the story
away from the media until the FBI made its announcement which, like most FBI press statements, was short
on detail.

"Bottom line," said the commissioner, "we don't
who this joker is or how he does what he does. But
Chief Hoople," he nodded toward where the chief of
police sat on one of the chairs along the wall, "and I
have assigned one of our best detectives to cut through
the mystery and get us the facts. He's ready to make a
report." Hanshaw looked to one of his assistants,
seated by the door. "Bring him in."

Denby wasted no time. He entered the room and
went around the table, distributing copies of the photo
the bank robber had taken. Under the lieutenant's arm
was a stationery box. When they all had the photos before them he laid the box down at the head of the table
and said, "Gentlemen, that's a picture of the man who
calls himself the Actionary. Claims to be a crimefighter."

An elderly man named Carruthers, president of the
largest state-chartered bank in town, said, "What does
it tell us?"

"About him," said Denby, "not much." He looked
around at the assembled silverbacks, though his gaze
lingered curiously on Baccala for a moment. "I'm
more interested in the place he's standing in. Look at

it. It's dead, barren. The sky's filthy. The bank robber I interrogated said it stank of old death."

"Where is it?" said another man, who owned almost thirty per cent of the city's rental housing stock and spent nothing on upkeep.

"Let me get to that," said the lieutenant. "This guy, he's making himself out as some kind of Green Lantern-Batman kind of freelance crimefighter. But," he looked around the table again, "he's been presenting himself as somebody different in another venue."

He had them now. They were leaning forward. "I happen to know," Denby said, "that he's been appearing to Billy Lee Hardacre, the TV preacher, and telling him he's an angel on a mission from God."

"Ah, jeez," said Hanshaw, "let's don't get that asshole involved."

"He's already involved," Denby said. "Our mystery guy has convinced Hardacre that one of Paxton's employees is a latter-day prophet."

All eyes in the room turned to Seth Baccala. "Which employee?" the assistant asked Denby.

"Arnstruther."

"Who?" and "Who's that?" erupted from several points around the table.

"Never mind," said Denby. "It's just a kid with some kind of mental block – autism or something. He does tricks with numbers."

"He's an actuary," Baccala said. "A good one. W.T. thinks highly of him."

Louis Tresidder tapped his gavel once. "We're drifting off point."

"We are," said Denby. "Look, I don't know what the guy's trying to pull with Hardacre, or by catching bank robbers, for that matter. I don't know why, or who, in this case, but I think I've got a handle on how."

"How what?" said Carruthers.

"How he appears and disappears. How he relocates a room full of people to Civic Plaza without them noticing."

"Say it," said Hanshaw.

"The guy's a time traveler. That picture you all saw, that's the future – after atomic war or global warming or–"

The men around the table weren't leaning forward anymore. "What the fuck are you on about?" said Jack Dolman.

"He's got powers," said Denby. "Mind-control powers. You didn't even notice when he moved you–"

"Dolman's mind was distracted by something a little closer to hand," said a man farther down the table.

"Is this all you have?" said Tresidder. "A picture of, what, the desert? And some speculation out of a bad sci-fi movie?"

"No," said Denby, "I've got this." He shoved the stationery box toward the lawyer. "Read that and tell us what it says."

Tresidder lifted the cover off the box and bent to peer within. Then he poked a finger into the box and stirred it around. He lifted the digit and examined it: the tip was covered in a gray powder. "What is this?" he said.

Denby craned his neck to see what Tresidder saw. "It's a b–" he began, but broke off as he saw what was in the box. His face went pale. "Less than an hour ago," he said, "that box was filled with white paper – glowing white paper – with words written in languages that kept changing."

They were all watching him now, and most of the expressions he was seeing were not encouraging. "I lifted the paper from Hardacre's study–"

"Wait a minute," said the police commissioner, "are you saying you broke into Hardacre's house and stole this," he looked in the box, shook his head, "this whatever it was? No warrant, nothing?"

"Where would I get a warrant? You said to do whatever it took."

"Jesus wept," said Tresidder. "I've seen that bastard in court. Makes a great white shark look like a picky eater. We don't want him anywhere near this thing."

"He's already in it," said Denby. "He calls himself the precursor of the new prophet."

"But you burgled his house," Tresidder said. "Tell me he doesn't know you've got whatever it was."

Denby paused. "He will if the kid talks to him."

"What kid?"

"Arnstruther. The actuary from Paxton's. His mother is Hardacre's mistress. I told him I had the book, trying to get him to get a message to the time traveler."

"Jesus H. Christ in a crinoline!" said the police commissioner. "Have you any idea what you've done?" He turned to the chief of police, who was seated on one of the chairs at the side of the room. "Did you know about this?"

The sentiment was echoed by comments from around the table. Chief John Edgar Hoople was not a member of the Twenty, but his job – like every other senior public-sector position in the city – depended on their approval. He stood up. "Not about Hardacre."

"We need distance," said Tresidder, "and we need it now."

Hoople got the message. "Lieutenant Denby, you are hereby relieved of duty, forthwith. Take that," he pointed at the box of ashes, "and get rid of it. Report to my office at 8am tomorrow and make sure you bring your badge and gun."

Denby's face registered shock. "You're suspending me?"

"You'll be lucky if we're not burying you," said Hanshaw.

The chief made a hand gesture that said, *let's not get into this now*, but Denby had already rounded on the commissioner. "I did my job, the way I was told to. 'Whatever it takes,' I was told."

"Nobody told you to drag somebody like Hardacre into it," said Hanshaw.

"You've got to listen," Denby said. "I've cracked the case."

"Doesn't matter," said the chief. "If Hardacre's in it, that's a whole different kettle of worms." He looked around the room, in a way that asked for support. "Here's how it has to go: you went rogue, did stuff on your own time that you shouldn't. Nobody authorized it."

"That's not true!"

"It's our word against yours. You'll get a reprimand. If Hardacre makes real trouble, you'll get demoted and assigned to clerical duties."

"That's not right!" said Denby.

"Time goes by," said the commissioner, "and this all blows over, you could be reinstated. But for now you've got to take one for the team."

There were nods and words of assent from around the table. Tresidder said, "Perhaps the lieutenant is concerned about pay and benefits. I think we could arrange for an informal subsidy–"

"It's not about the goddamned money! Not even about the rank," Denby said. "I did my job and you're screwing me over!" Commissioner Hanshaw was going to speak but the lieutenant cut him off. "What's really important here is that we've got a guy from the future messing around with our city. He's got powers and he's using them, for what purpose we don't know. I've got a theory–"

But the Twenty were not interested in the lieutenant's theory. The introduction of Hardacre into an already uncontrollable situation had spooked them. Hoople took the initiative. "That's enough, lieutenant! My office, 8am!"

Denby looked at the well-fed faces. These were men who were used to having it their way, and well-practiced at swatting aside anybody who tried to tell them they couldn't. Tresidder was closing up the box of ashes, and now the lawyer slid it across the glossy table. Denby picked it up and tucked it under his arm again.

A moment later, he was outside the conference room, treading the deep-piled carpeting toward the elevators. The offices were empty, the secretaries' desks neatly ordered, the lights turned down low. The sterile gloom matched Denby's mood.

"Lieutenant," said a voice behind him. He turned and saw that Seth Baccala had followed him out of the meeting.

"What?"

"Tomorrow, after you see the chief, come and see me."

"Why?"

"Because," said the smooth young executive, "I'm inclined to believe you."

"Aren't you afraid of Billy Lee Hardacre?" Denby said.

"Not as much as I'm afraid of someone who can play the kinds of games your time traveler can."

"He's coming out now," Xaphan said.

The demon had refused to tell them anything about the meeting of the Twenty but had agreed to let them know when Denby reappeared. Melda had a plan for the lieutenant and the taxidermist.

"What's his mood?" she asked the demon. "How's he feeling?"

"Like somebody used his hat for a chamber pot and told him to get used to it."

"So the meeting didn't go well?"

"Can't tell you that," said Xaphan.

"You don't have to," said Melda. "Show me Denby."

A screen appeared in the air in Chesney's apartment and an image formed on it: the lieutenant exiting a downtown office building, his shoulders hunched, his mouth downturned, a box under his arm.

"Oh, yeah," said Melda, "that did not go well." She turned to Chesney. "All right, time for Lieutenant Denby and the Actionary team to have a meeting of minds."

Xaphan could not move them from place to place on Earth; the rules said that demons could only go from Hell to Earth and vice versa – no gadding about creation, even when their actions were powered by the will of a mortal soul. Therefore, all trips had to go through Hell. A moment later, all three of them were in Chesney's comfortable room in the gale-swept outer circle of Hell; a warm blaze in the fireplace evoking a mellow glow from the wood paneling and the polished inlay on the armchairs. Xaphan took the opportunity to replenish its glass of rum and tuck a couple of fresh Havana cigars into the breast pocket of the wide-lapeled pinstripe suit he favored, cut to lines that had last been fashionable when twelve-cylinder Duesenbergs and drum-magazined Tommy guns had been in vogue.

Chesney was now in his Actionary garb, which not only disguised his face but added a considerable amount of muscle to his chest, shoulders, arms and thighs and gave the impression that his abdomen could have served as a washboard. Melda was dressed in slacks and a favorite cashmere top that always made her feel classy and confident.

"Okay," she said, "let me do the talking."

Denby had not yet turned in the ghost car. He had left it parked at a meter a block from the offices of Baiche,

Lobeer, Tresidder. As he reached into his jacket pocket for the keys he caught a flicker of motion from the corner of his eye. Melda McCann was keeping pace with him on his left. He hadn't seen her on the street or heard her catch up with him, but he had been sunk pretty deeply in his own thoughts.

"We need to talk," she said.

He stopped and so did she. "About?" he said.

"About him," she said, pointing to his other side. The policeman turned and saw the Actionary standing, fists on hips. At least this time he doesn't have a smart-ass grin on his face, Denby thought, remembering the bank robber's photograph.

"Where'd you come from?" he asked, then corrected himself. "No, *when* did you come from?"

"That's another thing we need to talk about," the woman said.

"You're talking to the wrong guy," Denby said. He fished the keys out of his pocket and moved toward the ghost car. "I'm off the case. In fact, there probably is no case now."

"How come?" said Melda.

"Because of this." The policeman had unlocked the car. Now he held up the stationery box and shook it. Fine powder sifted from under the top.

"That would be the book you stole," the woman said.

"Yep. Except somehow it turned to ashes." He paused and seemed to puzzle over something, then he said, "But without even charring the box."

"How about that?" said Melda.

"Here," he handed it to her, "like I say, I'm off the case. Tomorrow morning, I might not even be a cop anymore."

"They're going to fire you?"

"I'm going to say things to the chief that will probably get me fired. Or I might just quit." He opened the car door, paused before getting in and gave both of them a sour look. "I almost forgot to say thanks." Then he slammed the door and put the keys in the ignition.

"We still need to talk," Melda said. The sound of her voice made him jump because now it was coming from right beside him. He turned his head and saw her sitting calmly in the passenger seat. He saw movement in the rearview mirror. Mr Spandex was in the back seat.

"What do you want?" Denby said. "You haven't done enough to me already?"

"We want," the woman said, "to make it up to you."

"How?"

"By including you in."

Denby sat still, one hand on the steering wheel, the other still holding the key in the ignition. He stared through the windshield at the empty city street. "In what?"

"Well, for a start, how about the biggest case of your career?" Melda said.

"How do you know it would be my biggest?"

"Serial killer, mass murderer, skins and stuffs his victims, keeps them around to talk to."

Denby nodded. "That would be it," he said. "Problem is, I'm suspended. It would have to be a citizen's arrest."

"When did you get suspended?" she asked.

"Just now."

"Does anybody know? I mean, the other cops."

"Probably not." The Twenty were still up in the conference room, and neither Hanshaw nor Hoople would be leaving before the silverbacks had finished ripping strips off both their hides.

The woman indicated the microphone hooked below the dashboard. "And that's a police radio, right?"

"Uh huh."

"If you arrest the worst serial killer in the state's history, it would be kind of embarrassing for Police Central to say you were under suspension at the time, right?"

"Kind of."

She put on her seat belt. "Then let's go to 6490 West Furlong Drive and make the arrest."

"I can't go in without a warrant, or without probable cause."

"You'll have all the probable cause you need," she said.

Denby looked in the rearview mirror. "He doesn't have much to say, does he?"

"Don't worry about him," Melda said. "He's the strong, silent type."

Denby gave it a moment's thought, then turned the ignition key.

Delbert Torrance, a forty-seven year-old pharmaceutical sales representative, was driving his Lexus home from one of the get-togethers his employer encouraged him to host at a downtown steak house. He had bought dinner and drinks for three general practitioners who, annually and cumulatively, wrote several hundred thousand dollars worth of prescriptions for products that Torrance's employer produced. The salesman hoped the dinner would increase that total to the one-point-three million mark.

The dinner had involved preprandial drinks at the bar, four bottles of wine, and brandy and liqueurs to toast the doctors' agreement to shill even more avidly for the drug manufacturer. Delbert Torrance was therefore well above the legal limit when, after taking a corner at too high a speed, he over-corrected and scraped paint and trim off three vehicles parked on a residential street. As car alarms sounded and lights flashed, the sales rep – who already had two DUIs on his record – decided that official involvement in the incident could not possibly redound to his benefit. He floored the Lexus and sped off, taking the first corner that put him out of sight of the growing crowd that had come out to see what was causing all the rumpus.

Torrance took another corner, tires screeching, then cut his speed and drove as sedately and carefully in the direction of his home as his alcohol-bathed neurons would permit. Five minutes later, he was on West Furlong Drive, only six blocks from his well-appointed two-story, when his steering began to act up. Way up.

The Lexus pulled to the right, cutting across a lawn and crashing through a six-foot high board fence. Nothing Torrance did had any effect. Even when he spun the wheel to the left, the big car still kept going on its path of destruction. He stood on the brakes but was amazed to find that the car went even faster.

Beyond the tall fence was a big woodframe house on a one-acre lot, with a long driveway that ran all the way along the side of the property to a sizable building in the rear. With both of Torrance's feet stomping futilely on the brake pedal, the Lexus accclerated and struck the corner of what the salesman just had time to recognize as a double-width garage. The car ripped open the garage's painted softwood siding, exposing a room in which several people seemed to be having a party. One of the partiers was flung across the Lexus's hood and ended up with his face pressed against the windshield, staring in at Torrance with a lifeless gaze that made him briefly think of the glass marbles he'd played with as a child – then his airbag went off and left him in a cloud of white powder.

A nondescript sedan with three people in it pulled into the driveway, its headlights illuminating the scene of destruction. Within the party room, a small pot-bellied man was getting up from behind a table where four other people sat holding cards. Aghast, the rising man stared out of the newly made hole in his wall, while the other card players sat motionless.

Torrance staggered out of the wreck. He saw a woman and a man get out of the gray sedan in the driveway, and heard the woman say, "There, how's that for probable cause?"

Denby handcuffed the shell-shocked taxidermist and put him in the back of the ghost car. Then he found a spare pair of cuffs in the trunk and disposed of the hit-and-run driver in the same way. Only then did he radio in the code for "multiple homicides" and ask for back-up and the scene-of-crime technicians. There was little chance of the suspect skating on this one – a single glance at the photos the SOC techs would take would convince the weirdo's lawyer to plead insanity at the arraignment – but Denby had never been a taker of chances.

Until I went in and stole that book, he thought to himself as he hung up the radio mike and stepped out of the ghost car. He still couldn't account for that. He had acted as if he were in some kind of altered state of consciousness. At that thought, he realized he wanted to talk to the two people who had led him here.

They were over by the Lexus, peeking into the secret room. The place had a strange kind of cozy feel to it, like a Norman Rockwell painting of a scene from a Stephen King novel. He hurried up behind the man and the woman, saying, "Hey, you two, don't contaminate the crime scene."

The muscular guy in the body suit looked as if he was going to say something in return, but the McCann woman put her hand on his arm and said, "Never mind, sweetie, let me handle this."

In the distance, a siren sounded, growing louder. "You've got to get out of here," Denby said.

"We will," said Melda. "But, first, do we have a deal?"

"Depends," said the lieutenant, "on the terms."

The woman leaned against the Lexus and folded her arms. "Pretty simple. We help you fight crime." She gestured with a thumb over her shoulder. "Like so."

"And what do I do in return?"?

"Stop trying to arrest us. Don't steal any more books, that kind of thing." The guy in the costume leaned over and spoke in her ear. She listened then said, "Exactly." To Denby she said, "You'll treat us like, what do you call them, confidential informants?"

"Snitches, we call them. The DA calls them CIs."

"Whatever," said Melda. "Do we have a deal?"

"We're supposed to register all CIs with the district attorney," Denby said.

Her face said, *oh, yeah?* Her voice said, "And do you?"

The siren was getting closer. The detective had to laugh. "All right," he said. "Deal. Now get out of here."

"We'll meet tomorrow to talk about what to do," Melda said. She told him about the bench in the riverside park where they sometimes met for lunch.

"I want to know everything," Denby said.

"Good luck with that," said Melda. She spoke to Mr Spandex and then they were just not there anymore. A moment later, the Lexus and the shattered garage wall were lit up by blue lights.

SEVEN

Lieutenant Denby presented himself at the office of J. Edgar Hoople, precisely at 8am. John Hanshaw had already arrived. The interview did not go as the chief and the commissioner had planned. Both men had already fielded early-morning calls from the media, wanting comments on the arrest of the man the cable TV news channels were already calling "the Taxidermist."

Denby came in and took a seat on a corner of the chief's expansive empty desk. "Here's what you're going to do," he said. "You'll promote me to captain, and place me on permanent special duty. I can call on resources of the Major Crimes Squad, but I won't report to the inspector in charge."

"You're out of your fucking mind," said Hanshaw.

Denby ignored the interruption. "I'll pick my own cases and let you, chief, know when I get a result."

"When we get through with you, you'll be lucky if you can still pick your nose," said Hoople.

Again, Denby just motored on. "The alternative is I go downstairs and tell the media that I'm being fired just after nailing the worst mad-dog killer since Baby Face Nelson. And I'll tell them the reason I'm getting canned is cause I refused to cover up… well, take your choice – how about the kickbacks the two of you personally pocketed when you switched the department's uniform supply contracts to that sweatshop in Malaysia?"

"You can't prove that!" said Hanshaw.

"You're right, I can't." Denby folded his arms and idly kicked one heel against the side of the Chief's desk. "But I bet some eager-beaver reporter could if she dug into it. CNN might even give me a consultant contract to do it myself. You guys think you've covered your tracks, but you aren't smart enough to have done it right." He unfolded his arms and spread his hands. "Now, do you want to give me lots of spare time and a grudge to work on? Or do you just want to let me go on being a good cop?"

"What about Hardacre?"

"I'll take care of him."

"How?"

"I don't know yet." He showed them a reasonable face. "Tell you what, if he comes after us, you can throw me to the wolves – rogue cop, secret drinker, cross-dresser, I don't care. I won't fight you."

The chief looked at the commissioner. Hanshaw said, "What the fuck, we can't fire him today, anyhow."

Hoople looked like a man who would rather have stayed home that morning. He stood up and put on his gold-braided cap. "I don't like it," he said.

"You don't have to," said Hanshaw. "But right now

we've got a press conference to do." He turned to Denby. "You are one lucky bastard."

Denby smiled. "It wasn't luck," he said. "And you ain't seen nothing yet."

"Indulge me," the former lieutenant said, when he met Chesney and Melda on the park bench at lunchtime. "I think I've got this figured out."

Chesney looked at Melda. She made a face that said, *let's see where it goes*. "All right," the actuary said.

The captain laced his fingers together, looked down at them for a moment, then lifted his head. "The future," he said, "is pretty grim. I don't know why – global warming, some problem with genetically modified crops, or maybe we get hit by another rock out of space. But it's bad."

He paused and gave them a look to say, *how am I doing so far?* But Chesney showed his poker face. Melda was watching some kids rollerblading on the walkway beside the river.

"Okay," Denby continued. "So it's bad, but there's one thing they got going for them – time travel. Somebody from down the line is coming back here. He pretends to be a comic-book hero. He also pretends to be an angel."

"Why pretend?" Melda said.

Denby had an answer. "Because not much information about us has survived. Maybe the only documents they've got are a kid's comic book collection and a Bible, and they figure they're an accurate description of how we lived. And the kind of people we would trust."

He paused again. This time it was Chesney who responded. "Plausible," he said. "Go on."

"The guy in the costume – and maybe he's the angel, too; I haven't seen him – but the guy in the costume is a descendant of yours." He pointed a finger at Chesney. "He looks a little like you, around the mouth and chin, although everything else is different. No offense, but the guy comes ready to rock and roll. You're more the chess club type."

"Poker's my game," Chesney said, "but no offense taken."

The reference to poker seemed to call up some vague association in the policeman's mind, because he paused for a moment as if trying to remember something. Then he shook his head and went back to what he'd been talking about. He said to Melda, "I figure you for the great-great-whatever grandmother. That's why he rescued you twice – it had something to do with you two getting together, so that someday, all the way down the line, he would be born."

Melda moved her head in a *could-be* motion.

"Now," Denby said, "we come to the why. And there, I'm still in the dark. It's got something to do with crime. Maybe if the guy in the costume–"

"He's called the Actionary," Chesney said.

"All right, the Actionary. Maybe if he can prevent some crime here in the city, or maybe take some bad guy out of circulation, that's going to change the future. Maybe it even stops the big bad whatever-it-is from wrecking the world."

"And the angel?" Melda said.

Denby threw up his hands. "I don't know. Some religious movement, some cult that Hardacre starts – maybe it's got something to do with how the future turns out. The guy's trying to influence it, make it change direction, or kill it in the cradle." He looked at Chesney. "Again, no offense, kid, but I don't see you as any kind of prophet."

"Me neither."

Chesney could tell that Denby was waiting to see if either of them would add something to his scenario. They had agreed that Melda would take the lead in this conversation. The young man had read enough time-travel stories – the Freedom Five had once battled an alien invasion from a future Earth – to know that the concept was full of paradoxes and wild ideas that chased and ate their own tails like demented snakes. But he didn't want to put the policeman off the false trail.

Denby said, "So what do you say?"

"As little as possible," said Melda.

"But I'm close?"

Melda gave him an eyebrow shrug and said, "We can't tell you. We decided to bring you in because you were getting to be a problem and because we thought you could help." She gave him a sympathetic smile. "And also because you didn't deserve to wreck your career."

"I get it," the captain said, "you can't tell me too much because what I know could change the future. That's why you destroyed the book."

"I'm not saying we did," said Melda, "and I'm not saying we didn't. But work with us and we'll do what we have to do, and you'll get to bust a lot of bad guys."

"You won't hurt innocent people?"

"We haven't yet," she said, while Chesney chimed in, saying, "Never."

Denby nodded. "And the future?"

"It'll take care of itself," Melda said. "Any other questions?"

"Yeah," said the captain. "Where do we go from here?"

"The Actionary," said Melda, "sets his own timetable. So don't call us. We'll call you."

Denby showed them the smile of a man who was not entirely sure what he was getting into, but was willing to give it a try. "Okay," he said, "but one question: I don't have to dress up in spandex, right?"

"It's not–" Chesney began, but Melda cut him off.

"It really isn't spandex," Melda said, "and, no, a costume is not included in the deal."

"I'm not sure about him," Chesney said as they walked along the river bank. Chesney liked to be able to put people into definite categories. As a policeman, Captain Denby ought to be in the general category of "good guy," but he had stolen the *Book of Chesney* from Billy Lee Hardacre's house, and burglary was unavoidably a "bad guy" action.

"You ever hear the line about how, with some guys, it's better to have them inside the tent pissing out," Melda said, "instead of outside the tent pissing in?"

Chesney was not good with metaphors. They never occurred to him and he never remembered them. "I don't think so," he said.

She took his arm and hugged it against the side of her breast. "We've just arranged to have a dry tent," she said. "Besides, he's a good cop, and he knows the city. He'll be better at picking good targets than your other assistant."

"If he's really on our side."

"He will be," Melda said, "because we'll be on his."

Just before quitting time, Chesney received another summons to Seth Baccala's office.

"What do you know about time travel?" the executive assistant asked.

"Wouldn't work," Chesney said. "Too many possible futures."

"What?"

"That's what I've heard."

"What about travel into the past?"

"I think that's possible."

Baccala stared at him. Chesney didn't read the prolonged scrutiny as hostile – just puzzled, with an undercurrent of worry. After a while, the other man said, "That's all."

Chesney went to the door. As he opened it, Baccala said, "Arnstruther?"

He turned. "Yes?"

But the executive assistant shook his head again. "Never mind."

• • • •

Melda phoned Billy Lee Hardacre from Chesney's apartment after supper. "You don't have to worry about the book," she said. "It got turned into ashes."

"He didn't read it?"

"He couldn't. It kept changing from one language to another."

"Is he going to continue to be a problem?" the preacher said.

"No. He's going to work with us on the crimefighting."

"You're not going to introduce him to Chesney's little helper?"

"No," said Melda. "Although, actually, they've already met. Captain Denby just doesn't remember it."

"Captain?"

"He's moving up."

There was a pause. Melda thought it was a sign that Hardacre was about to switch tracks, and she was not surprised when the next thing he said was, "So, what about your young friend? Has he made up his mind?"

"You mean about becoming the prophet Chesney? What's that word you lawyers use, abey-something?"

"Abeyance?"

"That's sort of like Limbo, right?"

"Sort of."

"Well," she said, "that's where it is."

And so was Chesney.

The Devil had not sent Xaphan to summon Chesney this time. Instead, when the young man rode the elevator down from his office on the fourth floor of the Paxton Building and the doors opened, he stepped out not into the lobby but into that amorphous region of mists that had once been the resting place of innocent souls who had died *in utero* or in infancy before baptism.

Lucifer was waiting for him, arms folded, foot tapping. "I didn't hear back from you," the Devil said.

"I didn't have anything to say to you. I still don't." Chesney was hungry and his mind was still trying to work out the meaning of the expression he had seen on Seth Baccala's face when they had parted. "I agreed to nothing," he said. "Besides, you went ahead and had Denby steal the book."

"You reasoned that out? Well done," said Satan.

"It was obvious."

"Lit by a pool of light."

"Never mind that," Chesney said. "I take it you couldn't read the book. Denby said it kept changing languages."

"I speak and read all languages," the Devil said. "Actually, I speak and read the one true language, which all beings hear and understand as their mother tongue. But, the book had played its part. Things had moved on."

"Moved on where?"

Satan didn't answer. Instead he asked a question of his own. "Have you decided whether to take up Hardacre's offer?"

"Melda and I have agreed that she will make the decision as to what I do about it. I can tell you now I have no interest in being a prophet. Nor will I do the things the book says I did."

"You'll let the woman decide?" said Lucifer. "Interesting."

Chesney, graduate of umpteen childhood hours spent in his mother's Sunday school, caught the association. "If you try to tempt her..." he said.

"Under our agreement, I'm not allowed to tempt her in any manner that involves you. Even if I were, Melda McCann is no Eve. I'm happy to let her nature run its course."

"What do you mean, her nature?"

"That's for you to discover. What I'm telling you is that I will leave her alone."

"And that's the truth?" Chesney said.

"What is truth," said the Devil, "if Himself keeps rewriting it?"

And then he was gone, along with the mists. Chesney was standing in the lobby of the Paxton Building.

"You all right?" said the guard at the security desk.

"Too early to say," Chesney said.

The Taxidermist created a lot of work for Captain Denby. To begin with, the victims had to be identified, which meant combing through missing persons files for the past several years. The perpetrator's name was Wendell Throop and he had been a truck driver most of his life; for the past twenty-one years he had driven for a major supermarket chain. The assumption was that he had picked up his victims along the highways he had driven between the company's central warehouse here in the city and its larger distribution centers in the surrounding states.

Throop himself wasn't saying anything. The shock
of the Lexus bursting into his private world had
snapped some link in his already fragile mind, and he
was spending most of his time sitting in a cell and staring at the wall. A court-ordered lawyer had had no
more luck getting a response than Denby.

But the pieces were falling into place. The captain
had now tentatively identified six of the victims – five
males and one female – and was arranging for DNA
samples from the families to corroborate his supposi-
tions. While he plowed through the grunt work that
made up most of a policeman's day, his mind kept
turning to the other mystery that now occupied center
stage in his life.

We'll call you, Melda McCann had said. Denby's
eye kept slipping from the paperwork on his desk to
the multi-line phone off to one side. Every time he
saw one of the button-lights start to flash, he felt a little tension draw his shoulder blades together. But
then the buzzer in his phone wouldn't sound, or if it
did, the call would have something to do with the
Taxidermist.

Mustn't be greedy, he told himself, and went back
to comparing the crime scene photos of the stuffed
bodies with the photos and descriptions of missing
persons that were still coming in by the hundreds.

"I'm leaning toward you should maybe try it," Melda
said to Chesney.

The young man moved his shoulders in a silent display of discomfort. "I'm not a prophet," he said.

"You don't have to wear a white robe and grow a beard," she said. "Cause, after all, it's not you who would be the one up there on the stage. It would be the Actionary."

Chesney put that thought in the middle of the screen in his mind and looked at it. It was less disturbing than the prospect of having to meet with world leaders or give speeches and sermons. "So it would be the *Book of the Actionary*?"

"That's what I'm thinking. You'd be in costume, in your crimefighting identity. You'd come on the reverend's show, say a few words—"

"What words?" Chesney had never cared for the idea of public speaking. It was just about the darkest, murkiest shadowland he could envision.

"We'll work that out with the reverend," Melda said. They were sitting on the couch in his apartment, and she put a hand over his two, which were clasped together on his thighs. The warmth of her palm soothed him.

"The thing is," she went on, "right now you're doing good work catching bad guys like that awful man who killed the hitchhikers. But how many people are you reaching?"

"How many do I need to reach?"

"Well, imagine if you could stop people – young people, especially – from becoming criminals in the first place. Think of all the crimes you could prevent, and all the victims who wouldn't suffer, because they'd never *be* victims." She squeezed both his hands in hers. "Because of you."

It sounded less frightening. "Oh," he said.

"Every week, you could solve some big crime," she said. "Then you come on the TV and talk about the lessons learned."

"Like crime does not pay."

"Yeah. Or how so many of the big bad guys started out doing little bad stuff. So you tell them, don't steal candy, Johnny, because it will only get you twenty-to-life in the slammer."

"That doesn't sound too bad," Chesney said. He remembered the episode where Malc Turner busted up a ring of fur thieves. He described to Melda how some kids had watched him throw the perps into the back of his truck. And he stopped to tell them, "This is where the road of crime leads to."

Melda squeezed his hands again. "You could have a fan club, send out autographed pictures." The idea did not appeal; he saw himself sitting at a desk, signing hundreds of photographs, hour after hour, addressing envelopes, licking and sealing. It reminded him of all the years he had been his mother's helper, as she deluged newspaper editors, politicians and errant celebrities with her scathing epistles.

Melda must have sensed something, because she said, "You'd only have to sign one, then Xaphan could do all the rest."

Chesney still didn't like the idea, but he wanted to please her. "I suppose that would be okay. It would be part of being a crimefighter. Preventive crimefighting."

"So, what do you think?" she said, putting a hand on his cheek to turn his face to hers. "I know we said I would make the decision, but it has to be something you're comfortable with."

Chesney put his mind to the question. As he expected, prophethood still refused to become the center of a pool of pure light. It was like peering through a smeared window at a storm-darkened landscape, where the wind was preventing anything from staying still and holding a clearly defined shape. He was reminded of the outer circle of Hell, where he had faced down Nat Blowdell, a memory that reminded him of Lucifer, which led him to their last meeting. And that brought a new thought.

"Limbo," he said.

"What about it?"

"There used to be a place called Limbo, where the souls of unbaptized children went," he said, following the thought. "It existed because it was written into an earlier draft of the big book, but now it has been written out. But it's still there – empty, but still there."

Melda was looking at him with concern. "So?"

"So what happened to all the souls?"

Her face took on the expression she wore when she was trying to decide which movie to rent: thoughtful, but not too worked up about the issue. "I'm sure they were looked after," she said.

Normally, when Chesney came to a murky question, he let it slide. But he couldn't just shuffle this one aside. "Were they?" he said. "Or did they just get edited out?"

"Either way," she said, "it's nothing to do with us, sweetie." Her hand covered his again, and squeezed reassuringly.

But he wasn't reassured. He was following his

thought through the shifting darkness. "No," he said, "Limbo isn't. But what about this world?"

"What about it?"

He was driving his mind forward, like he'd never done before outside a pool of light. "If I become a prophet, if I make a new book, then it becomes the latest draft of *the* book."

"Yes," she said, "and it's a better world."

"But what happens to the old one? And all the people in it?" He pushed himself on now. "What happened to Adam and Eve and the Garden of Eden? It was supposed to have a wall around it and an angel with a sword at the gate. So where is it? Where's the world it was in? Because it isn't in this one."

"There's no need to get upset," Melda said.

He realized his voice had risen. He brought it down. "Okay, but what about the Tower of Babel? It used to reach all the way up to Heaven, and people from all over the world came to build it. Then it got smashed and toppled, and then it got written out of the draft. What happened to all those people?"

"It was all a long time ago, sweetie."

"Yes, but now is now! Say I'm responsible for making a new part of the big book, and the old one gets put aside while the new story goes forward. Does that mean that all these lives…" he gestured at the city outside the apartment window, the winding snakes of traffic lights moving along the streets, "do they all get canceled, dumped in the wastebasket?"

Her brows drew down and a vertical line formed between them. "It's a good question," she said.

He had already hit the speed-dial on the phone. When he heard it answered, he said without preamble, "What happens to the other drafts?"

Billy Lee Hardacre said, "What are you talking about?"

"The discarded drafts, the worlds that used to be but aren't there anymore. What happens to them? And the people in them?"

There was silence on the other end of the line, then Hardacre said, "I don't know."

Chesney had made up his mind, had followed the thought all the way along its dark, twisting trail to where it inevitably led. But wherever he had arrived, it was still not a pool of light. "I need to know," he said. "Or I can't do it."

They met in the preacher's study. Chesney had thought they might have to drive out to the estate, but when he'd summoned Xaphan, the demon made no bones about whisking them there – via the usual stop in Hell – even though the matter had nothing to do with crimefighting.

"Truth to tell," it said, "the boss sez I should just do whatever you want me to do – that is, if it don't interfere with some other contractual obligation."

The unexpected concession raised Melda's suspicions. "Why the change? And what does he want in return?"

The demon puffed on its cigar. "First," it said, "he don't tell me why, and I long ago learned not to ask. Second, this is service with no charge." It took another drag and blew a thoughtful cloud of smoke that formed a question mark in the air. "Way I figure it, and don't quote me, but this whole book bizness has got him rattled. He wants to see where it goes and he can do that by watchin' where you take it."

And so they transited through Chesney's room in Hell, Chesney's assistant pausing briefly to pick up a refill of its tumbler of rum, then they appeared in the foyer of the preacher's mansion.

"I'm gonna fade," Xaphan said. "Call me if you need somethin'."

Hardacre wanted to talk about the *Book of Chesney*, but Chesney was firm on the evening's agenda. "None of that matters if I decide I'm not doing any of it," he said. "And that decision is going to depend on what we're here to talk about."

The preacher looked a question at Melda. She said, "Looks like it's not just my decision after all."

Chesney restated the questions he had asked on the phone. Hardacre said, "Short answer is: I don't know. With me, I keep all my drafts – first, second, third. Maybe they'll be of interest to somebody doing my literary autobiography fifty years from now, though I doubt it." He shrugged. "Or maybe I'm just a sentimental pack rat."

"So the old worlds, they might be around somewhere," Melda said. "Limbo is. Chesney was there."

"Really?" said Hardacre.

"But it's empty," said Chesney.

The preacher quirked his lips. "Interesting."

"I have to know what happened."

"We could ask the angel."

"He might not know," Chesney said. "He didn't even know about the great book until you told him."

Chesney's mother had been sitting in a corner of the study, her face a portrait in disapproval. "Take your questions to the Lord," she said, "and he will answer them."

"Please, Letty," Hardacre said, "I think He wants us to work this out for ourselves."

"No," said Chesney, "I think Mother's right." He didn't know which of the three faces looking back at him was more surprised. But he had just seen a new path through the darkness. "Xaphan," he called, "we're going somewhere."

The demon appeared over by the drinks cabinet. "Gimme a minute," it said, reaching for a decanter. As it poured, it said, "Where?"

Chesney's answer made it spill several drops.

First they had to go back to Chesney's room in Hell. Then the demon said, "Wait a minute. A thing like this, I gotta ask."

"You just told me that the Devil said you should do whatever I want," Chesney said.

"That ain't it. I gotta get directions."

"You don't know where it is?"

The demon elevated its padded shoulders and let them drop. It counted on its stubby fingers. "Hell, I know. Anywhere on Earth, I know. Probably, I could still find my way around Heaven – it don't change. Even Limbo, now that I been there. So, wait here, while I go ask."

Xaphan disappeared. Chesney expected him to be right back, but as the seconds swelled into a minute with no sign of his assistant, he took a seat in one of the comfortable armchairs with which the demon had furnished the room and sat listening to the faint sound of cold, stinking winds rushing past the thick stone walls of his waystation. His mind returned to the discussion at Hardacre's – but then his thoughts slid to the topic of his own behavior there.

Chesney was not prone to introspection. He knew who he was and accepted himself as given. In his boyhood, the therapists who had labored to make him aware of the behaviors that made him different from other children, so he could moderate them – at least in public – had eventually settled for achieving some essential modifications. They had never really gotten their patient to turn the spotlight of his unusual intellect inward, to examine his own motivations and mental mechanisms.

Chesney always knew what he thought; he did not actually know how he came to his conclusions. Presented with a problem in math, for example, he first recognized its parameters, then the answer appeared, as if from behind some dark curtain at the back of his mind. Occasionally, a math problem might be so complex as to require him to break it down into two or three steps, but even so, the process meant only that he had to make two or three appeals to the obscuring curtain – he still knew nothing of what went on behind it.

Pools of light, surrounded by acres of dimness and murk – that was how he saw the world. For what went on within his own head, he had not even those simple images. "You don't think," one of the consultants had said to him, after an exhaustive month of tests and experiments. "You either know or you don't know, and you've no idea how you get from one state of mind to the other."

But now he had at least an inkling of what it might be like to have a normal mental apparatus. He had actually pursued a line of thought through the darkness, managed at least to keep an eye on it as it followed some invisible, twisting trail, always threatening to disappear into the shadows. And he had come to a conclusion. Even if the conclusion was only that he needed more information, he had, for the first time in his life, genuinely worked something out.

He didn't know whether to feel proud or worried. And even that ambiguity was another source of concern.

Xaphan reappeared, reloaded its tumbler of rum and took a couple of Havanas from the humidor. It tucked the cigars into its breast pocket, drained the glass and said, "Okay, here we go."

Chesney stood up as the room disappeared. For a long moment they were... nowhere. Gray nothingness lay in every direction, with not the slightest evidence – not so much as a dust mote – to show scale. He might have been looking out into infinity, or the no-place might have ended an inch beyond his reach. He might have been hanging in the emptiness or traveling at the speed of light.

"What–" he began, but no sound emerged. He looked at his assistant, saw Xaphan's furred brows draw down in what appeared to be a weasel's version of disorientation. The demon tentatively reached out one short arm, stubby fingers spread, as if patting fog for something that might be hidden. Then it seemed to push.

A moment later, Chesney sensed gentle pressure against his face and the front of his body, as if he had drifted up against a pliable barrier. Then the resistance abruptly ceased and he burst through nothingness into bright sunshine.

Xaphan and he were standing on a hillside under a blue sky. The ground beneath their feet was dry and sparsely thatched with stalks of even drier grass and some dusty-leafed ground-hugging plant. A few inches from the young man's right big toe was a heap of small, brown, pebbly objects, like a handful of glossette raisins, only darker. It took a moment for Chesney to realize that the reason why he was seeing them near to his toe was that he was no longer wearing the pair of loafers he had put on when they went out to Billy Lee Hardacre's. His naked toes protruded from under a strap of coarse, woven fiber.

Sandals, he thought, I'm wearing sandals. And when he stretched out his arms, his first thought was of a striped blanket, none too clean. Then he realized he was wearing some kind of woolen robe, belted at the waist with a rope. He took a step back from the glossettes, having suddenly made a connection between them and the half-dozen raggedy-fleeced sheep he saw farther down the hill, down where the slope leveled off to flatter land. There were mud-walled houses, a scattering of them, with the ends of wooden poles sticking out of the walls just beneath the flat roofs. At the door to one of the hovels, a swarthy bearded man with dark, curly hair and a ten-year beard was shading his eyes from the sun, looking up at them.

No, Chesney thought, at me. The sight of a fanged weasel in a pinstriped suit would surely have wrung more of a reaction out of the observer. The young man raised an arm and hand in greeting. The man in the doorway continued to regard him for a few more seconds, then replicated the gesture and followed it with a beckoning of one brown hand.

"You're not from around here," said the man when they arrived in the dusty yard.

Chesney was scraping the edge of his sandal against the ground. It had turned out to be impossible to walk a straight line without stepping in sheep's leavings. "No," he said, when he'd cleaned as much as possible and coated the remnant in dust.

"That's what I thought," said the other. He looked straight at Xaphan and Chesney realized he could see the demon. "Didn't I cast you out once?"

"Not me," said the fiend.

"You're sure?"

"It's the kinda thing you'd remember."

"I suppose," said the man, then turned to Chesney. "I can rid you of that if you want. At least, I think I can. Used to do a lot of it, but of course there's no call for it anymore."

"No, thank you," said the young man. "Xaphan is on special assignment."

The bearded man looked at the demon again, then more carefully at Chesney, shrugged and said, "I suppose he must be. You don't have the earmarks."

"The earmarks?"

"Not literally," said the other, touching a hand to one of his ears, half-buried in curls. "It's just a kind of look the demon-haunted get. I can usually spot it."

"I'm more demon-assisted," Chesney said. "It's a long story."

The man rubbed his beard. "And you've come to tell it to me?" He shrugged again. Chesney thought it might be a characteristic gesture. "I suppose it makes a change."

"I haven't really come to tell it to you," said the young man. "I've mostly come to ask you some questions."

The bearded man looked them over again and said, "Well, then, you might as well come in."

Inside, the house was dim, lit mostly by the light from the open door and a square hole in the roof, positioned to let out the smoke that rose from a brick hearth set against the wall opposite the door. There was only one room, with an archway in one of the side walls, half-covered by a hanging blanket. Beyond it was an alcove just big enough for a man to sleep in; on its floor of beaten earth was a rolled-up leather pallet and a clay pot.

The main room was furnished only with a rough wooden table and two equally utilitarian stools. Some shelves against one wall held pots and bowls of unglazed pottery, and an iron cauldron was hanging from a frame fashioned from the same metal above the hearth. A charcoal fire was smoldering beneath the pot.

Chesney took in the sparse furnishings at a glance, noticing also a shepherd's crook that leaned against the wall beside the door, which was of rough planks indifferently nailed together. "No carpenter's tools?" he said.

"No," the householder said, "my family's always been in sheep."

"But this is Nazareth?" Chesney said. "And you are Jesus?"

EIGHT

Chesney's mind formed the name as he had always known it, but when he heard his voice speaking it, what emerged from his lips sounded more like *Joshua*, only with a Y instead of a J. Also, the vowels sounded strange. He tried saying it again, more slowly, but still what he heard was something like *Yesh-wa*.

However it sounded, the man nodded his head. "That's me," he said, then gestured generally towards the huddle of mud-walled houses and sheds visible through the open door. "And out there's Nazareth, for what it's worth."

"I thought you were a carpenter. Everybody says so."

"No, definitely sheep. A carpenter would starve in Nazareth. There's no trees." He gestured upwards, where poles as thick as Chesney's wrist held up the ceiling of mud and woven reeds. "Even the roof beams had to be brought up from Gaza."

"But you are the Messiah?" Chesney was coming to understand that he had not stepped into the pool of light he had been expecting. "I mean, you talked about casting out demons."

Understanding dawned in Joshua's face. "Oh," he said, "I see. You've come to the wrong one. You want the other part of me." When he saw that the young man was still floundering, he added, "The divine part."

Chesney sat down on one of the stools. He looked to Xaphan for a moment, before he realized that the demon was studiously ignoring the conversation. "I thought you were supposed to be like… a blend."

There was a clay jug on a shelf and a wooden cup on the table. Joshua stepped past Chesney and got the container, poured a stream of dark liquid into the cup and handed it to his visitor. Their fingers touched and the young man felt a brief sensation, not electric but some kind of energy, pass through him.

"Drink up," said the bearded man, upending the jug. A spill of the contents ran down from the one side of his mouth into his beard. Chesney sniffed the contents of the cup; it smelled like sour wine, and when he tasted it, it was even sourer than it smelled.

The other man sat down too. "A blend," he said. "Well, in the end, that's how it worked out. After they had that big confab at Nicaea. So now he's up in Heaven."

Joshua wiped his mouth and said, "At first, after the Romans nailed me up and I died, I was up there, too. Just like anybody else. But down here they kept working on the story, especially the Greeks, who were always eager for half-gods and virgin births. Finally, and it took hundreds of years, they got it all worked out the way they wanted it – I mean the bishops and the emperor; they talked it all over for days, made up their minds."

"What happened?" Chesney said. The wine tasted better – not actually good, but better – on a second sip.

"Somewhere along the way, they'd decided that my body had come back to life and gone up into Heaven, wounds and all. How they worked that out, I never did understand. But suddenly, the new reality came into effect. I was in Heaven, but I was made of flesh. Worse, they had decided that I was Himself, or at least one part of the Lord, who was now a trio. Blasphemy, but the Greeks and Romans were writing the new books, and that was now the way it had to be."

He drank from the jug again and shook his head. "I had become an anomaly – one of their words, of course – a leftover. An angel came to see me and told me that I was – how did he put it? – 'being let go.' Next thing I knew, I was here, back where I'd started." He drank a little more from the jug then said, "Oh, and I was just myself again. Look." He showed Chesney his hands. "No holes."

"The Council of Nicaea," Chesney said, more to himself than to the other man, "where they put the Bible into its final shape." Courtesy of his mother, he had received a very thorough grounding in the history of the early church before he'd decided that he didn't believe half of it.

Now the pool of light was reforming around him. This place, this little house in Nazareth, was from an older draft of the continuing story. The man across from him had been a sheep farmer, like just about everybody else in the tiny village. He'd become a preacher and a wonder-worker, doing some faith-healing and casting out demons. Then he'd gone up to Jerusalem and fallen afoul of the authorities, ending up being crucified by the Romans.

He'd arrived in Heaven and settled in. But back on Earth, his story had continued to evolve and intensify as his disciples kept spreading the word about what he'd done and what he'd said. Years went by, then decades. Other people got involved – people who could read and write, instead of the group of illiterates who had begun to follow Joshua in his wanderings around the Galilee. The stories and sayings, augmented now by tales of walking on water, raising the dead, confounding Satan, began to be written down. The texts were passed around, so they could be added to and rewritten by believers who had their own particular slants on the issues.

After three hundred years of literary fervency, there were many conflicting biographies and gospels. Joshua the itinerant preacher had become Jesus the Christ, and more than that, he had become first the son of God, then he'd been promoted to the rank of God himself. Or a co-equal part of a divine trinity, along with the original and his holy breath.

Of course, this led to disputes among the faithful, some of which were conducted by passionate argument, others by knives and clubs and arson. Meanwhile, the Emperor Constantine had made Christianity the official religion of the empire after seeing a vision that said converting to the hitherto-despised cult would bring him victory in one of the civil wars that Roman politics regularly threw up. The emperor called all the warring factions together at Nicaea, a Greek city in Asia Minor, and they thrashed out which of the competing texts would go into the authorized Bible, and while they were at it, they established the true nature of the Christ.

It would have been then that the original version would have become unuseful – indeed, Joshua would clearly have become an element of a soon-to-be discarded draft of the evolving big story. So an angel had eased him out of Heaven. Chesney wondered if the process was similar to what happened at Paxton Life and Casualty when a fired employee put his odds and ends into a cardboard box and was escorted out by a security guard. And the former Messiah had wound up back in Nazareth.

While Chesney had been running this scenario through his mind, Joshua had been watching him, throwing occasional glances at Xaphan. Finally, the bearded man showed a worried expression and said, "So, have you two come to take me somewhere else?"

The question confused Chesney. "Such as where?" he said.

Joshua cast a meaningful glance at the dirt floor, then at the demon. "Special assignment, you said."

Light dawned again in the young man's mind. "You think we've come to throw you out of here? No, no, no." He was shaking his head. "No, I came to find out what happened to you. And to…" he gestured toward the door, "your world."

Relief showed on Joshua's face. "Well," he said, "what happened to me, you can plainly see. What happened to the world, I have no idea. All that my neighbors know about is sheep and gossip. And it's always the same gossip, because it's always the same day."

He paused as if expecting Chesney to pose a question, but the young man had already had the experience of watching Melda's favorite Bill Murray movie. In fact, he'd seen it three times since they'd become a couple, although when he'd tried to point out the irony in that situation he had discovered that it had somehow eluded his girlfriend.

Seeing that his visitor intended no response, Joshua said, "Do you understand? Every morning I wake up on that pallet over there, eat some lentil porridge then put the sheep out to pasture. I can watch the sheep or I can visit the neighbors, but they're always doing and saying the same things.

"The first few days, I didn't notice. Then one day I decided I'd slaughter one of the yearling lambs and have a feast. I invited a few of the neighbors, and they brought some bread and wine and olives, and we had a good time. I saved a couple of honey-barley cakes for breakfast and went to bed. In the morning, the cakes were gone…" – he paused for effect – "but the lamb was back in the fold!"

Chesney nodded. "And when you tried leaving the village?"

"I took the Roman road that runs to Jerusalem. I walked all day. When evening came, I wrapped myself in my cloak and slept under a bush. When I woke up,

I was right there!" He pointed at the rolled-up sleeping mat and shook his head. "Another time, I sat up all night. When morning came, I let the sheep out then went to visit Mordecai, over there. We had the same conversation we always have, but I couldn't tell if it was day repeating itself, or just him.

"I came back and took a nap. When I woke up..." His hand gestured at the pallet, and his shoulders executed an elegant shrug.

Chesney had seen enough. He stood up, Because he had been thoroughly trained by Letitia Arnstruther, he said, "Thank you for your hospitality. "We should be getting back."

"Stay and have another cup of wine," said the man. "Where is it you come from?" He seemed anxious to prolong the encounter, and even Chesney could understand why. "Not Heaven, or you wouldn't have that." He indicated the demon. "But you say you're not from Hell. So what does that leave?"

"The world," the young man said.

Puzzlement clouded Joshua's face. "But the world has ended," he said. "Not the way I expected, to be sure, but it has definitely come to an end."

Chesney did not want to have to explain. Despite the efforts of experts in his childhood, he had never become adept at anticipating other people's emotional reactions to the things he said and did. But even he could recognize that for Joshua to learn that he was trapped in a discarded draft of a divinely written book would not be a positive experience. On the other hand, he thought, the man would wake up tomorrow and probably put the whole thing down to a bad dream.

He sat down again and accepted the refilled wooden cup. "It's a long story," he said.

"Good," said the other man. He repositioned himself on the stool so that his back was against the table, crossed one knee over the other and interlinked his fingers on his lap. "Let's hear it."

Joshua was an intelligent and motivated listener. As a storyteller, Chesney was used to being told to skip over what most people thought of as too much detail, but Joshua kept interrupting him to have some event in the story amplified or put into context. It had been midafternoon when the young man and his demon had arrived in Nazareth; by the time he had told the full tale of his adventures and undertakings, the sun was disappearing behind the hill he had appeared on.

He finished with, "And so I had Xaphan bring me here so I could see for myself what had happened to you."

Joshua was silent for quite a while, chin sunk upon his chest, arms folded across the end of his beard. He extended his legs, crossed one ankle over the other and regarded his calloused feet as if they had become a disappointment to him. Finally, he heaved a sigh that contained more than a hint of dissatisfaction and said, "Another book. Well, that makes sense, I suppose. And this time some of you know what's going on. I wish that had been the case back when I was walking the roads."

"I think," said Chesney, "that at that point in the writing process, he wasn't ready to let the characters in on the nature of the story."

"Huh," said the other man. He looked at the demon, which had drifted out into the yard, then back to Chesney. "That thing had the power to bring you here?"

"Yes."

"And presumably the power to take you away again."

"Presumably."

Joshua looked around the darkening room, at the dying embers in the hearth, the rolled-up pallet in the alcove. "Then how about," he said, "you take me with you?"

And suddenly, Chesney was in a pool of light. He asked Joshua a question, and the prophet's answer was, "Why not? It beats what I'm doing now."

"Don't be a wise guy," said Xaphan, when they put the matter to the demon.

"Whatever I want you to do," Chesney said, "that's what your orders are."

"Long as you don't break the rules."

"This doesn't break a rule. Hell isn't fighting Hell."

"Yeah, but–"

"No yeah-buts," said the young man. The situation had become clear to him the moment Joshua of Nazareth had said, *take me with you.* "You're covered," he told the demon.

Xaphan subsided. "You're the boss." The fiend clamped its weasel jaws around its Churchill cigar and blew smoke out of its slitted nostrils.

"They didn't do that when I used to cast them out," said Joshua.

"It's another long story," said Chesney. "You'll see

when we get there. The main thing is, do we have a deal?"

"Oh, yes," said the bearded man. "I'm happy to do it. It will be like old times."

"Not quite," said Chesney. "A lot has changed."

A sad smile appeared within the whiskers. "That's all right. So have I."

"Anything you want to bring with you?" Chesney said.

Joshua shook his head, then said, "On second thought." He picked up the shepherd's crook from beside the doorway. "In case I need to earn a living," he said. "Being a prophet never paid much."

"This time, you'll be able to write your own ticket," the young man said. He turned to the demon. "Is Hardacre in his study?" he said.

"Yep."

"Then take us there."

Their time in the grayness was shorter on the way back, and they didn't go by way of Hell. In a few moments, they were stepping out of nothingness into the preacher's study. Billy Lee looked up from where he was seated in an armchair, a lawyer's yellow pad on his lap and a pen in his hand. "What's this?" he said.

"You wanted a prophet," Chesney said. "I've brought you one."

Captain Denby called it a day at six in the evening. The Taxidermist paperwork was under control; he'd shanghaied a civilian clerk to help him – just walked into the pool on the third floor, pointed at a middle-aged woman he'd worked with before and knew to be competent, and said, "Madge, come with me." An hour later, she'd set him up a cross-referenced file system and arranged to come up to his office – he had also commandeered a space that had formerly belonged to a lieutenant who did press liaison, one of J. Edgar Hoople's stable of go-along, get-aheads. Denby had tossed the soft-bellied lieutenant out partly because he wanted the space, and partly to see if he would get away with it. Now it was the end of the day, and nobody with more brass on his collar than Denby had arrived to restore the evicted sycophant.

Denby turned off his desk lamp and closed the murder book – a three-ring binder in which he recorded all steps taken in the investigation of Wendell Throop's homicidal career. He looked at the phone one last time, hoping for coincidence, but its row of lights stayed dark. Still, he didn't rise and head for the door.

Denby was a reflective man. One thing he'd learned in his years on the force was that motivation was usually the key to solving major crimes; once you knew *why* somebody had ended up dead in a pool of blood, you had a pretty good chance of finding out who had done the deed. Occasionally, he turned the spotlight on himself, and went looking for the why behind his own actions.

What he'd done today – beating the chief and the commissioner at the power game, turfing out the PR lieutenant – didn't bother him. He was honest enough to admit that he enjoyed the ego-boost that came from being top dog, but he knew that the only thing he wanted out of the special-assignment captaincy and all that went with it was the chance to be a better cop. He was willing to cut himself a fair amount of slack if the end result was more bad guys off the streets and in the pen.

But the business with the preacher's book bothered him. Yes, it had been a mystery and Denby couldn't have been a good cop if he didn't have that urge to get to the bottom of things. But he couldn't deny to himself that he'd stolen the damned thing, and not because he thought it was evidence of a crime – time travel was not illegal, at least not yet – but just because he'd had an itch he had to scratch. That wasn't the Denby he knew.

What got into me he wondered? Whatever it was, he knew that he'd acted on impulse, without thinking. Up until now, he would have bet on his impulses being those of a good cop. But the book business showed him that he was as capable as anybody else of doing the wrong thing, and not for the right reason.

I need to watch that, he told himself. Especially now that he was boldly going into regions where nobody had gone before. The nerd kid and his girlfriend were straight – his instincts would have rung a bell if they hadn't been. The guy in the costume, whatever weird futuristic concerns motivated him, also seemed to be trying to do some good. Now that Denby could bring him into the system, at least as far as making him a confidential informant, the captain wouldn't need to step too far over the line that divided solid police work from vigilantism.

He nodded to himself. That just left Billy Lee Hardacre. The reverend wouldn't be filing any official complaints; he had no evidence that Denby had stolen his book, and he probably wouldn't want to make public the nature of the purloined item. So there would be no repercussions. But still...

Denby consulted his notebook, found Hardacre's number and punched buttons on the phone. The preacher answered on the second ring. The captain identified himself and said, "It's about the book."

"What book?" said Hardacre.

Denby paused long enough to take in the implications of the man's response then said, "I just want you to know I'm sorry. I don't know what got into me."

"I bet I do."

"What?"

But Hardacre didn't add to the cryptic comment. After the silence had lengthened, the policeman said, "Well, I just wanted to say–"

"That you're sorry. I got that."

"So where do we go from here?"

"Nowhere," said Hardacre. "Just stay away from me and my home."

"I can do that."

"Then we're done." Denby heard a click and the line was dead.

The Reverend Billy Lee Hardacre had other troubles. After his wife's son had brought him a replacement prophet, it hadn't taken long to establish the newcomer's identity, even if Joshua didn't present an image the preacher might have expected. For one thing, the attire in which Joshua had arrived was different from what he'd been wearing when Chesney and Xaphan had found him. The demon had converted Chesney's jeans, short-sleeved shirt, and loafers into a robe and sandals to fit the look of first-century AD Judaea, then put him back in twenty-first century casuals for the return. It had also done the equivalent for Joshua, dressing him a lightweight summer suit, open-necked shirt, and suede lace-ups.

The once-and-future prophet was intrigued by the garments. He kept running the zipper up and down until informed that it was necessary to keep it up in mixed company. He was also taken with the idea of pockets. "Very handy," he kept saying, as he investigated the jacket, pants and shirt for useful places to keep stuff. Then he pulled off one of the shoes to see if it had any hidden compartments.

During the couple of minutes the prophet spent exploring his clothing, Hardacre and Chesney were preoccupied with reviving Letitia and moving her from the carpet on which she had fainted and getting her settled in an armchair. Her son went to the kitchen to fetch a cool cloth for her forehead, while her husband took the more practical approach of pouring an ounce and a half of brandy down her throat.

She came to, spluttering, but when her eyes focused on the bearded man running his zipper up and down in front of her, she went away again. Another slug of liquor brought her back, and this time she took hold of the glass and drained it.

By now, Chesney had got the prophet seated and the bearded man was looking about the room with evident interest. "Not Rome?" he said to the young man.

"No. America. It hadn't been discovered when you were... active."

"America," said Joshua, pronouncing the word carefully. "Sounds Roman, though."

"It's a long story," Chesney said.

"Oh, good." Joshua folded his arms and waited attentively.

"Later," said Chesney. "Right now we need to settle a few things." He turned to the demon, which was sampling a single-malt Irish whiskey from Hardacre's cabinet. "Xaphan, would you bring Melda, please?"

The fiend nodded, then shimmered out of sight. It was back again a moment later with Chesney's girlfriend, who came into view in the act of striking the demon with a long, pale object that turned out to be a loofah bath sponge. The young woman then noticed the presence of the others, screamed, and attempted to cover strategic parts of herself with the sponge, because she was otherwise clad in nor more than a few widely scattered patches of bubbles.

"Xaphan!" said Chesney. "Fix this!"

A moment later, Melda was clothed, dry and bubble-free. Xaphan had chosen one of her favorite outfits: a green cotton blouse and denim skirt combo that she liked to wear when they went to the park for picnics. She still held the loofah, however, which she disposed of by throwing it at Chesney's assistant. The demon moved a finger and the sponge disappeared in mid-flight.

Joshua had had the good manners to avert his eyes and blush. When the embarrassment was over, he said to Chesney, "Are you sure you don't want me to rid you of that thing?"

"How about it?" the young man said to Xaphan. "Want to see how an exorcism feels?"

"Try it, and I'll just ankle on home."

"Not if I order you to stay."

"It was just a little joke," said the demon. "No need for all the brouhaha."

"Go somewhere else until I call you."

Letitia's eyes were the largest Chesney had ever seen them. His mother held out her glass, now empty, and said to Hardacre. "More."

As the preacher was returning with another brandy, and a Scotch for himself, the phone rang. He answered it and held up his end of a short conversation. When he'd hung up, he said, "Denby."

Chesney saw that Melda had gone from seething to a low simmer. "It was my fault," he told her, steering her toward a chair. "I should have thought of the possibilities." He watched her get a grip, and tried to help it by saying, "I've always liked you in those clothes."

"Enough," she said. "What's been going on?"

"I want to introduce you to Joshua," he said. He could hear, by the sound of his own voice, that he was speaking to her in ordinary American English so he worked at getting the pronunciation right. To the prophet, he said, hearing his voice take on the accent and cadence of Heaven, "This is Melda McCann, my girlfriend."

"Your betrothed?" said Joshua.

Chesney looked at the young woman and felt the heat of a blush creeping up his cheeks. "We haven't talked about…"

"His betrothed," said Melda.

Chesney's mother let out a noise somewhere between a squeak and a moan, then opened her mouth to say something more cogent. Hardacre stilled her by holding up both hands, as if placing a barrier between his wife and an unpleasant sight. "Later, Letty," he said. "Business first."

Chesney had something to say, and now was the time to say it. "Melda, I know we agreed that you would make the decision on this prophet thing. But now something's happened and I've worked it out for myself."

He did not know what to expect. He wouldn't have been surprised if she'd laid into him. He'd seen enough incidents at work of people having their responsibilities undercut by others – insurance was a competitive business, even for actuaries – and he knew it made people mad. Instead he saw forming between her brows the little line that meant she was thinking something through.

"How?" she said.

"I don't know," he said. "It wasn't clear, but then I followed it anyway and then I saw… well, anyway, I figured out what was best."

The little line went away and she smiled. "That's fantastic!" she said. "I'm so proud of you."

He felt a warm glow, but it was edged by a little chill. "But you might not like what I've decided," he said.

"Try me."

He turned and addressed the others. "I'm not going to be a prophet," he said. "I've seen what happens," he gestured to indicate the bearded man, "and it's not going to happen to me."

Letitia cleared her throat. "Now, you listen to me, young man–" she began, but this time it was Chesney who cut her off.

"No, Mother. I saw what happened to Joshua, here. He launched a new chapter of the book, just the way the reverend wants me to do. And then he got left behind in the old draft, living the same day over and over again." He said to Melda, "Just like *Groundhog Day*."

"Really?" she said.

"Yeah, but it didn't end. Didn't matter if he changed. He was just stuck forever."

Melda gave the prophet a sympathetic look. "Poor guy."

Joshua shrugged. "It's all right now," he said.

Chesney turned back to Hardacre and his mother. "And that's what would happen to me. The Actionary would go on into the new draft. You'd write the book, Reverend, and the book would become the new reality. But me, *this* me, I'd be like him, sitting around, waiting for the story to finally end." He looked the preacher in the eye, then did the same with his mother. "Well, I'm not going to do it. I was going to say, 'Get yourself another prophet,' but you won't have to, because," he indicated the bearded man, "I already went and got one for you."

What came next, of course, was an argument. It wasn't a very cohesive discussion; it tended to wander among a number of different subjects, because the individual disputants each had his or her own slant on what constituted the most important grounds for disagreement. But it was a heated argument, at times very hot.

Chesney's basic line could be expressed in the words, "No," "No way," and, finally, "Case closed."

Hardacre's stance was that the young man did not realize what was at stake. He used phrases like, "Unparalleled opportunity," and "Whole new world for the making."

Letitia's themes were more personal, and revolved around past instances of her son's willful disobedience and her own selfless efforts to bring him up to be a "decent, upstanding Christian," which were negated by his obstinate nature, inherited from his father, along with his tendency to "go chasing after trollops."

This last was said with the older woman's eye fixed meaningfully on the younger, but Melda ignored the invitation to debate her own character and instead kept the focus on where she believed it belonged: the Billy Lee/Letitia axis that was "just trying to use Chesney to further your own agendas, without a thought as to how it will hurt him."

The altercation eventually became circular, with the disputants hurling their accusations at each other like weary prizefighters unable to score a knock-out. Throughout, the fifth person in the room sat and watched like a spectator with a front-row seat at the performance of a live drama. Finally, when the ebb and flow of accusation and vituperation had begun to lose energy while conversely gaining bitterness, Joshua stood and raised a hand as well as a voice that had once been accustomed to address multitudes without the benefit of microphones and loudspeakers.

"*Enough*!" he said causing a sudden silence in which the arguers could hear the window glass's last rattle in its frame. Then, more quietly, "Enough."

Four pairs of eyes were now turned his way. "Let me see," he said, more to himself than to the others, "I used to be good at this." He thought for a moment then said, directing his words to Hardacre, "Prophets are called, but not by men. Not even by men of power." He turned to Chesney and said, "Are you called?"

"No."

"Be sure," said Joshua. "Many a prophet denied the call, pretended it was just a dream, or that it must have been intended for another."

"I am sure," said Chesney.

"Then that settles it. If he is not called, he is a false prophet." He waved a hand to put distance between himself and the notion. "And we all know what trouble they cause. Remind me to tell you sometime about Simon Magus."

He turned to Letitia. "Mother," he said, "you should count your blessings. My mother wept when I went out onto the roads. She wept even harder when they put me in my tomb."

Chesney's mother had been readying herself for another run up the hill. Now, for the first time Chesney could recall, she seemed to be unsettled by an opposing view.

Joshua turned to Chesney. "If you don't want to be a prophet, what do you wish to do?"

"Fight crime."

The beard-surrounded lips widened in a smile. "That sounds useful. It also sounds like fun. Do you ever need a helper?"

Chesney looked to Melda, who gave him back one of her *worth-thinking-about* looks. "We could talk about it," he told the prophet.

"Wait a minute," Hardacre said, but the bearded man forestalled him with a raised hand.

"Our young friend invited me to your... America," he said. "But it was a conditional invitation. He said you needed a prophet, a real one." He locked gazes with the preacher. "Do you?"

Hardacre paused before answering, but then he said, "I do."

"Then," said Joshua, "we should talk. In the meantime, these young people probably want to get away together. Why don't we let them? We can sit and you can tell me what is on your mind." He looked over at the drinks cabinet. "Is any of that wine?"

Xaphan took them home. Increasingly, Chesney's roomy apartment was where Melda spent her non-working hours. Before the young man dismissed the demon he required it to apologize to her.

"Sure," said the fiend, "sorry." The words were accompanied by a wave of a stub-fingered hand, a gesture so casual that Chesney felt that it undercut the sincerity of the verbal sentiment.

"Well, of course he doesn't mean it," said Melda when Chesney took his assistant to task. "He's a demon."

"It," said Chesney. "They don't have gender, just like angels." Then returning to the subject at hand, "Even if it doesn't really feel sorry, it should make a proper effort."

"One of the things you have to admire about Xaphan," she said, "is that he – it – is not a hypocrite. He's one hundred percent rotten to the core."

"Thank you," said the demon. The weasel face assumed a reflective aspect. "I'm pretty sure no one has ever defended me before."

"Don't mention it." To Chesney, she said, "It's its nature. We just have to work around the rough parts."

"You don't mind that it took you out of the bath, stark naked, and plopped you down in front of everybody?"

She did that thing with her mouth that he liked, a kind of shrug of the lips. "It was mostly the shock." She pulled the neck of her blouse forward and peered down it. "Truth to tell, I look pretty good in the raw."

"Yes," said Chesney, "you do. Xaphan, you can go."

The demon exited with the usual whiff of sulfur.

Melda was laughing quietly now. "Did you see Jesus's eyes bug out?"

"Joshua."

"Joshua, Jesus. He, it," she said. "Did you see your mother's face?"

At the time, Chesney had not found it funny. Now, under Melda's prompting, he did. At one time, he would have found it disconcerting that a single event could call up two different emotional responses in him. Now he could live with it.

That thought reminded him of how he had pursued a thought through darkness and emerged into the light. He felt good about that, and even better when he remembered how Melda had responded to the news that he had decided not to be a prophet.

She was going around the apartment turning off lights. He followed her and put his arms around her from behind, and found that Xaphan, when he had clothed her, had not bothered with a brassiere. He put his nose into her hair; it smelled of vanilla and ... her. "So we're betrothed?" he said.

"Seems that way," she said.

"What exactly is 'betrothed?' I've never been clear on that."

"Come in the bedroom," she said. "I'll show you."

NINE

A couple of quiet days passed, then came the weekend. It was the end of the month and Melda gave up her apartment and moved in with Chesney. That meant bringing over two big suitcases and a few cartons of odds and ends; her furniture belonged to the landlord. They did the usual things that couples do when they first cohabit: apportioning shelf and closet space, which was not a problem, since Chesney had few possessions and a severely limited wardrobe.

"We should get you more clothes," she said.

"Why?"

And when she thought about it, she couldn't come up a good reason. "Never mind," she said.

"It's Saturday," he said, when they had everything settled. "What do you want to do tonight?"

"I don't know. What do you want to do?"

"Fight crime."

Captain Denby had come into the office that afternoon, even though it was Saturday. With the assistance of

Madge from the civilian assistants pool, he had gotten the Taxidermist case ready to hand over to the district attorney by end of business on Friday. Now he had spent a couple of hours down in the records room – actually, it was a huge portion of Police Central's sub-basement – looking up some old cases.

The files he pulled represented not just old cases, but notorious ones; and not just notorious, but unsolved. The "Pillow Case" murders from the 1970s. The Holliman Security bullion heist in the late 1980s. The disappearance of Cathy Bannister in 2003.

That last file was the one that called to Denby. It was one of the first he'd worked as a young third-grade detective, back before he'd learned it was not wise to take police work so personally. It still itched in the back of his mind that they'd never found her; nor had they even identified a prime suspect.

Cathy Bannister had been a junior at the state college, studying communications and living in an off-campus apartment that she shared with two other young women. It was a two-bedroom flat – the third girl slept on a foldout couch – and Cathy's bedroom was at the rear of the building, with a fire escape outside the window.

She wanted to be a television reporter. Classes were finished for the summer and she had landed an internship at the local TV station. She had to be at work at 5am weekday mornings to scan the early papers and the overnight feeds from the wire services so she could identify developing stories that might be interesting enough for the newsroom to follow up when they came in at seven.

She was talented and detail-oriented and had already received two "good stuff" commendations from the station's news editor. There was serious talk of a part-time job come the fall, with maybe even some on-camera weekend puff stories to give her experience.

So Cathy Bannister had gone to bed early one night with all her hopes and expectations lined up before her. And no one ever saw her again. No one, that is, but whoever had climbed up the fire escape, come through her window and taken her silently away to whatever awful end – and Denby had no doubt it had been awful – the monster had planned for her.

He harbored no doubts on that score either. The lack of evidence said this was a planned crime, not some burglary that escalated, spur-of-the-moment, into rape and murder. And the choice of victim could not have been random. Whoever had come for Cathy Bannister, must have come prepared to overpower her and spirit her away. And the bastard had gotten away with it.

The major crimes squad had looked at everybody in the young woman's life, starting with the roommates, then moving on to her classmates, the people at the TV station, neighbors, known weirdoes residing within a reasonable distance from the apartment. Then they had looked at weirdoes living an unreasonable distance away, because nobody they looked at could be fitted into the picture.

There was an old boyfriend or two, but they were

quickly alibied out of contention. They'd actually tracked down a guy who had tried to pick her up when she was waiting at a bus stop outside the college a couple of weeks before. She noted down three number of his license plate, just in case. But he had been three hundred miles away at a NASCAR event, with a good dozen people to testify that he'd been working as pit crew for a middle-of-the-pack driver.

"This one," Denby said to himself, centering the Bannister file on his desk. He put the others in a file cabinet. He reached for the phone and called the nerd kid. The girlfriend answered.

"I've got a case," the detective said. "A murder. But it's an old one."

"How old?" she said.

"It's Cathy Bannister."

It took a moment, but the girlfriend remembered. She'd been a teenager and the idea that someone could steal into her bedroom at night and take her away had terrified her.

"You and a lot of others," Denby said. "What do you say?"

"It's not up to me. We'll have to ask the Actionary."

"When?"

"Pretty soon, I think."

"Good. Call me."

"It's tricky," said Xaphan.

"Tricky how?" Chesney said.

"Remember when we discussed the groundrules? Like how I couldn't help you with anything that crosses somebody else's arrangement with..." – the demon pointed at the dining room floor in Chesney's apartment – "the organization I represent."

"Cathy Bannister was snatched by a demon?" Melda said.

"No," said the fiend, "not as such. But it's, like I say, tricky."

"You need to be clearer," Chesney said.

The weasel lips moved the perpetual cigar around between the sabertooth fangs. "Some things, you don't get a pool of light."

Melda said, "Don't get smart. Can we solve the crime or not?"

"I'm gonna have to ask."

"So ask," said Melda.

The demon disappeared, then reappeared a moment later. "Interesting," it said.

"What?" Chesney said. He was all togged up in his Actionary costume, ready to collect the policeman and solve a fifteen year-old murder.

"This one oughta be a no-can-do," said Xaphan, "but the boss says, 'Hey, what does it matter?'"

Melda had been sitting at the table, the remains of their supper pushed away. She leaned forward. "You're quoting?" she said.

"I'm how-you-say, paraphrasin'." The demon wrinkled up its weasel brow, squinted its oversized eyes. "It's a new attitude for him."

"Never mind," said Chesney. "What about the crime? Who dunnit?"

"Best you should see for yourself," said his assistant.

"Me, too?" said Melda.

Xaphan puffed on his cigar and inspected the bottom of his glass, finding it empty. "Hey, what does it matter?"

Cathy Bannister's fire escape led down to an alley that ran behind the low-rise apartment buildings that lined the block. On the other side of the alley was the sheer side wall of a supermarket outlet. At just after 10pm on June 7, 2003, it was quiet for a Friday night: not much traffic on the streets of the residential neighborhood; not even any loud music playing from the area's mainly student population. Somebody was blasting out profane rap, but the source of the noise was at least a block away.

Chesney, in his Actionary guise, led Captain Denby and Melda into the narrow thoroughfare and down the alley to where an emergency exit created an alcove in the supermarket's windowless wall. They were no more than fifty feet from the bottom of the fire escape.

Chesney thought the policeman seemed more keyed up than a professional ought to be, but he reminded himself that the captain had been very wrapped up in his time traveler theory. Seeing it proved – actually going back into the past himself – was probably a big deal. Plus Denby had told them that his not being able to solve this case had always eaten away at him. The young man wondered what it was like to experience that kind of anguish; he lived, as his boyhood therapists had confirmed, strictly in the present. The past, for good or ill, could not be helped or healed.

Nor could it be changed. Xaphan had briefed him and Melda: they could watch; they could slow the action down or speed it up, just as on a video player, but nothing they could do would have any impact on the events unfolding before their eyes. The pair had passed on the rules to Denby.

"What's written is written," said the policeman, "and all your tears cannot wash away a single line."

There had been a silence after that, and Denby had said into it, "Sorry, the Bannister case always got to me."

Denby's briefing had taken place in the captain's office, the dead woman's file still open on his desk. Chesney looked at the photo of a young woman, blonde and wide-cheekboned, with an incisive intelligence evident in her eyes, looking up at them from the dead past. He thought he knew what Malc Turner would say at this moment, so he said it: "Then let's go get her some justice."

He spoke to his assistant, present but unseen – and unsmelled, Chesney had made it clear – in a manner that Denby could not overhear. A moment later, having transited through Chesney's room in Hell too quickly for the experience to register as more than a flicker, they were in the alley. The demon had put them in the alcove that housed the supermarket's emergency exit. They instinctively stepped back into the shadows, although they had been told that they were invisible to the denizens of the past.

"How long?" Chesney said privately to Xaphan.

"Any second now," said the voice only he could hear.

To the others, Chesney said, "Here we go."

A shadow appeared at the mouth of the alley, where a street lamp cast a glow, and was quickly followed by the figure of a man walking at a rapid pace. The moment he stepped out of the streetlight's range he became a vague shape in the poorly lit alley, a shadow among shadows.

Nervous, Chesney thought to himself as he saw the pass swiftly through a place where a slight illumination fell from an apartment window whose shade was pulled down. The man glanced around in several directions before his gaze settled on the fire escape and he moved forward to where the iron ladder was fixed high upon the apartment house wall. He stood there in silence for a moment, while Chesney wondered how he would ascend the fifteen feet between the ground and the bottom rung.

The Actionary said to Xaphan, "Night vision," and immediately the scene brightened. He saw the man clearly now, though from behind: slight of build, in his early twenties, a smooth, round head, dressed in a dark windbreaker, black jeans and sneakers. He reached into a pocket of his jacket and brought out something cupped in his hand; a moment later he tossed something up at the third-floor window. It struck glass without the force to break it then rattled down through the iron fire escape.

"A pebble," Chesney said, aloud. "He threw it at the window."

"Can you see?" said Denby, whispering even though they could not be heard.

"Yes. He's doing it again." The man threw a second small missile. They heard the tap and rattle again, then Cathy Bannister's bedroom window slid silently up.

"No wonder," Denby breathed.

The sounds were soft – she was making an effort to be silent – as the young woman climbed down the fire escape. At the bottom landing she leaned out and stepped onto the vertical ladder. Under her weight, it slid down to the ground. She stepped off, and it noiselessly rose to its original position.

"I remember it was freshly oiled," Denby said. "Now I'm thinking she must have done it."

"It's no kidnapping," Melda said, "at least not yet."

The couple embraced. Chesney saw a kiss and the woman gave the man a brisk hug. Then they turned and went quickly back the way he'd come. The man kept his face turned toward her, showing Chesney's enhanced vision only an ear and a curve of cheekbone. But there was something familiar there, and in the economy of motion with which the suspect moved.

Then they were passing through the glow of the streetlight at the end of the alley and turning out of sight. "We need to follow them," the policeman said as they heard the sound of a car's ignition.

"Xaphan," Chesney said, privately, and the transportation the demon had arranged appeared before them. It was a flat disc of pale metal, hovering six inches off the asphalt. "Step on," he said to the others. They did so and the disc did not sink under their weight. "After them," the Actionary said, and the platform immediately moved silently down the alley, then turned the corner and accelerated to catch up with the taillights of a dark sedan that was just pulling away from the curb. Cathy Bannister's profile, her head turned to talk to the driver, could be seen through the rear window.

The disc kept them a close distance behind the car, speeding and slowing as necessary, while the three pursuers felt no wind from their journey. At one point, the vehicle stopped for a light and another car came up behind its rear bumper. Xaphan caused the disc to rise smoothly into the air until they were hovering above the second car's hood, then they slid down to their previous position as the traffic moved forward.

They passed through the college district and turned toward downtown. The city core was one of those places that emptied out after office hours, except for a few restaurants and the usual scattering of after-work bars. But the dinner crowd and one-for-the-road drinkers had mostly gone on to more interesting activities, and the streets were almost untrafficked.

"Where's he taking her?" Denby said.

"We'll know in a moment," Chesney said as the car's brake lights flared. The driver turned into a downward sloping driveway beneath one of the office towers, not far from City Hall. His arm reached out to tap a code into a keypad and the big steel door folded itself up. The sedan drove into the basement parking lot.

"I know this building," Denby said.

"Yes," said Chesney. He knew it, too.

The steel door rattled down. "Aren't we going in after them?" the captain said.

"No need," said the Actionary. The disc was rising smoothly up the side of the building to the top floor. Eighteen stories above the street it stopped then slid gently sideways until they were facing a large window with a rounded top. The room beyond was dark.

"Wait for it," said Chesney, warned by his assistant. Then a light came on and they were looking into a room lined with metal filing cabinets, all in uniform gray. They were the kind whose front opens up and folds over top of the files within like a garage door. The man led Cathy Bannister into the file room and over to a cabinet in the corner. This one was more strongly constructed, and above the standard key lock was a second security system: a heavy steel bar that fitted into slots on either side of the door and could only be deactivated by a code punched into a seriously strong-looking keypad.

"That's it?" said the young woman.

"That's it," said the man.

"Open it."

"We had a deal," he countered.

"So we did," she said. And when he just stood and waited, she gave him a *what-the-Hell* smile, slipped off her jacket and began to unbutton her blouse. She walked over to a small table of scarred dark wood and dropped the garment on top, then with her back to the man she unhooked her bra and laid it on top of the blouse. Then she turned and faced him.

"Jeez," Denby said softly.

She was wearing slacks and flat-heeled shoes, but only for another few seconds. She kicked them to one side then, with an expression that was anything but erotic, she peeled down her panties and stood naked.

Chesney turned to look at Melda. He was thinking he probably ought to apologize for the fact that Cathy Bannister naked was bringing about in him the same physiological response that Melda McCann caused when he saw her without clothes – and even when he just thought about it for more than a few seconds. But Melda's eyes were on what was going on in the room, and Chesney interpreted the look on her face to mean that she wasn't in a mood to accept apologies from anyone.

He turned back to the window. The young woman had seated herself on the edge of the table, legs open. The man approached her. He reached out and covered one breast with his hand. She kept her gaze on his face – her expression said that whatever was going on here was hers to control – as she lowered her hands to his fly. Chesney heard the sound of the zipper going down and the man's involuntary gasp as she reached in and fished him out. She looked at him expectantly and he put a hand in his jacket pocket and brought out a con- dom in a plastic wrapper. She took it from him, still holding his eyes with hers, and used her teeth to tear the package open. Then her hands went out of sight as she positioned the contraceptive and rolled it all the way down.

His back was towards the window, but it was clear what the woman did next from the way her arms moved, and from the way the man's back arched to thrust his groin towards her. After a few more motions, the man groaned. She lay back on the table, propped up on her elbows, and opened herself to him. He unbuckled his belt and let his jeans fall about his ankles then shuffled forward the last few inches to thrust himself into her.

He leaned forward, his hands on either side of her body, his head thrown back, and after no more than a dozen uncontrolled strokes his legs began to tremble and he made a sound like something being seized by the slaughterman in a barnyard.

Then it was over. She pushed him back and away from her, and while he stood, panting and round-shouldered, she quickly put on her clothes. Then she held her head the way Chesney had seen Melda hold hers when she was not receptive to argument and said, "Your turn."

The man took a few seconds to get his breathing under control, then pulled the condom from his flaccid penis and looked around for somewhere to put it. The woman briskly pulled a tissue from a jacket pocket and handed it to him. He folded the contraceptive into the paper and put it in the pocket of his windbreaker. Then he took the torn wrapper from where she had discarded it on the table and put it where he'd put the wad of tissue.

"Don't want to have to explain that," he said to her.

"Whatever," she said. "Let's go."

He pulled up his underwear and jeans, buckled himself up and crossed to where she now waited beside the secure cabinet. He gave her an attempt at a conspiratorial smile, but her face just said, *get on with it,* while her head motioned the same message. He shrugged and made a spin-around motion with one finger, and when she had turned her back he punched in a code, hauled the locking bar out of the way, and opened the file drawer.

She moved briskly then, elbowing him out of the way, running her index finger over the files. But he stepped back in, more forcefully now and chose a file. He handed it to her and said, "Just this one. That's the deal."

She took it over to the table and opened it, leaning over it in a posture of intense concentration. "Jesus Murphy," she said.

He stiffened, his head cocked, listening. "Shh!" he said. "I hear something." He went quickly to the light switch beside the door and plunged the room into darkness. Chesney called for his night vision.

"Hey!" she said, angry, turning to him from the file she could no longer see.

"Quiet!" he whispered. He put an ear to the door and listened.

A flash of eye-searing light flared in Chesney's vision. "Xaphan!" he said, and instantly his sight cleared. A second flash lit up the room, and this time he saw Cathy Bannister posed over the file, a small camera aimed at two pages she had spread wide.

"Christ!" said the man. "Don't–" he was rushing across the short distance between them, a hand outstretched to seize the camera.

She took one more exposure, then turned to meet him. They struggled in the dark and she pushed aside his reaching hand.

"That wasn't part of the deal!" he whispered.

"It is now!" she said.

"For fuck's sakes, be quiet!" he said, trying to get a hand over her mouth. "There's somebody out there!"

"Bullshit!"

"Give me the—" he said, reaching for the camera again, but the next sound out of him was a high-pitched whine as she brought a knee up into his groin. She made a break for the door then, hands groping ahead of her through the darkness. Chesney saw the man recover enough to throw himself after her.

He blindly caught her collar, then frantically brought his other hand into play and seized her hair above the back of her neck. She swore, in pain and frustration, and kicked back with one heel at his shin. Now it was his turn to swear, but he held on, putting his weight into it even as she kicked a second time at the same spot, knocking that leg out from under him.

The man made a whimpering, whining sound, but still would not let go. As she raised her heel for a third back-kick, he tried to dodge while standing on one leg. The action swung them both off balance. They toppled to the floor.

But along the way, Cathy Bannister's head struck the corner of the table on which they'd consummated their deal. The *crack*! was loud, and when he began to rise from the floor, she did not.

Light flared again. A hand had come through the partly opened doorway and turned on the light. The door swung wide and a distinguished looking man in a tailored three-piece suit was looking down at the woman on the floor and the man half-crouching above her. The newcomer's eyes went to the open cabinet, the file on the table, the little camera lying on the floor near the woman's outstretched hand.

"Baccala!" said the man in the doorway. "What's the meaning of this?"

"Mr Tresidder!" said a younger Seth Baccala. "I can explain!"

But, of course, he couldn't.

"Let us be clear," Joshua said, "I am the prophet. You are the one who goes before to… how did you say it?"

"Stoke the boiler," Billy Lee Hardacre said.

"In the language of Heaven, I hear that as till the field.' I don't think that's quite what you said."

"Perhaps you should learn English," the preacher said.

"No, the language of Heaven is surely best for discussing these kinds of things."

They were sitting in Hardacre's study, in the glow of lamplight. The prophet was very taken with the soft illumination the lamps threw; yesterday he had enjoyed himself immensely playing with the dimmer switch. "And none of that greasy residue from burning olive oil, even with the highest grade of oil which, believe me, we didn't get too often."

"If we can get back to the subject," Hardacre now said, "to the fundamental question: what are you going to say?"

"I'm still thinking about that," said the prophet. "Obviously, I can't say a lot of the things I said last time."

"Love thy neighbor is still a good message."

"Is it?" The prophet stroked his beard. He had allowed Hardacre to prevail upon him to trim it drastically. Chest-length whiskers carried the wrong connotations these days, the preacher had said. His mop of black curls had also been reduced to a more reasonable size, Letitia wielding the scissors. "You've had two thousand years to put it into practice," he said, "and what I see on the far-seer…" – he stopped, and made the effort to speak the untranslated word – "the television, what I see there tells me that there has not been much progress.

"Besides," he went on, "that was only a part of the message. I was preaching the end of the world as we know it, the descent of the Kingdom of Heaven to Earth, the redemption of the children of Israel after generations of trials and tribulations." He spread his hands. "Turned out I was wrong. The world didn't end; it just went on to a new chapter."

Hardacre was a patient man. He wouldn't have lasted long as a labor mediator if he hadn't been. But two days of dealing with the historical Jesus had worn him down. "Listen," he said, "this is Saturday."

"The Sabbath. I was going to ask about that. Do you have gentiles who come in to make supper?"

"Saturday is not the Sabbath anymore."

"Says who?"

"We moved it to Sunday."

"You're kidding me."

"And we're not Jewish."

The prophet's bushy brows knit. "Tell me you're not Greeks."

Hardacre sighed. "Can we concentrate on what's important?"

"A commandment's not important?"

"Please. Today is Saturday. Tomorrow I go on the air—" He checked himself as the prophet's brow wrinkled. "I speak to millions of people through the far-seer. I have been telling them for weeks that the prophet is coming." He leaned forward in his chair. "Do I tell them he is here?"

Joshua chewed his lip, then his expression cleared. "I suppose you have to. Because I am."

"All right," said Hardacre, "I tell them you are here. I step aside, you come out. Millions of eyes and ears are turned your way. What do you say?"

The prophet folded his arms across his chest and tucked in his chin. After a long pause, he looked up and said, "I'll tell them the truth."

"What truth?"

Joshua laughed. "Who are you, Pilate the Procurator? How many truths are there?"

"I mean, the truth about what?"

"About life and the Lord and Heaven. What they ought to do."

"Love thy neighbor?"

"That could come into it."

Hardacre said, "You mean, you don't know?"

"I often used to let it just come out of me. Trusted in the spirit."

"No preparation?"

"I tried that the first time, in Nazareth," said Joshua. His eyebrows bounced around for a moment. "Notes, citations from Torah, the whole megillah." He laughed. "They ran me out of town. After that, I just trusted the Lord to put words in my mouth. I did all right."

Hardacre went and got a decanter of whiskey and two glasses. The prophet had developed a taste for bourbon. He poured them a glass each and took a good swallow of his own. "So," he said, "I go out there tomorrow, introduce you, and you say whatever comes into your head.

Joshua took a sip of the liquor and rolled it around on his tongue. "You're in the faith business, aren't you?" he said. "Then have some."

Chesney, Melda and Denby were inside the offices of Baiche, Lobeer, Tresidder, having passed through the window on their hovering disc. They saw the lawyer take the young man by the arm and propel him from the room, down a long hallway, and into a corner office. He put Baccala in a chair and said, "Stay there," then left the room.

"Stay on Tresidder," Denby said and they did, floating back to where he had left the body.

Tresidder closed the door and locked it, then went to the reception desk and dialed a number. "I've got a problem," he said to whoever answered, "same as that time with the girl at the Breaufields' New Years party." He listened for a moment then said, "By the service elevator in the underground parking lot." He listened and looked at his watch, then said, "Right."

He hung up and went back to his office, the three invisible watchers following. He poured himself a serious

Scotch, did not offer one to the young man in the chair, drank half of it in one swallow then said, "Tell it."

Baccala told the tale, hesitantly at first, and in a low voice so that the lawyer had to order him to speak up. He'd met her at a party at his sister Maddie's house. Maddie had been afraid there would be a shortage of men and had browbeaten him into coming. But he was glad he'd come when he met Cathy Bannister, even though she hadn't responded to his overtures. He was smitten. He'd never felt such an itch for a woman before and he couldn't stop thinking about her, even though she didn't return his calls.

Months went by, he finished law school, and was taken on as an articling student at Baiche, Lobeer, Tressider while he prepared to take the bar exam. Somewhere along the way, Maddie must have mentioned that fact to the woman of Baccala's stickiest dreams, because one day the phone rang and it was Cathy Bannister herself, inviting him to lunch at a little place where students hung out. And, he soon found, to a role as a stepping stone in her journalistic career.

It was 2001 and the city's south side was the scene of major redevelopment projects. Four square blocks of derelict factories were coming down to be replaced by condo towers with commercial and retail space in the lower two floors – Chesney lived in one of the blocks. Streets were being repaved, sewers relaid, underground wiring and fiber-optic cables replacing the old overhead power and phone lines. All of this was attended by a brisk traffic in permits and licenses, easements and re-zonings, plus a swirling paperstorm of contracts and subcontracts involving builders, demolition firms, trucking and cement outfits, all manner of suppliers, and nine different unions – and all of that was generating an even thicker blizzard of kickbacks, skims, sweeteners, backhanders, rake-offs and straight-forward bribes.

Most of those illicit transactions involved the Twenty, and, as customary, were coordinated through the law firm in which Seth Baccala had just become a fly on the wall. And Cathy Bannister wanted him to become her personal insect.

"You could get me fired," was his first reaction, "and worse." He lowered his voice. "The Twenty are all over that thing."

"That's why I'm interested," she said. She had been drinking a vanilla shake through a straw. Now she moved the fat tube in and out of her astonishingly well formed lips, and Seth Baccala felt a stirring in his groin. "I'll make it worth your while," she said.

"How?"

She moved her eyes and brows in a way that invited him to figure it out for himself. But Baccala asked her to spell it out, knowing as he did that the moment she made the offer plain, he was going to accept it.

"But," he told Louis Tresidder, "the deal was that I'd show her the master tally of who got what, but she couldn't take it away or copy it. That way, the best she'd have would be some unconfirmable names and figures. Without confirmation, she'd never get anyone to run the story."

"But she screwed you," the lawyer said. "Of course."

"I didn't mean to kill her."

"If she'd got out of here with that camera, some-body would have had to." He looked at his watch, said, "Come on."

They went back to the file room. Nothing had changed. "At least there's no blood," Tressider said, examining the bruise on one temple. "Broke her neck." Then he said, "Get her ankles."

They hauled the body through the door, then put it down so the lawyer could go back into the file room and recover the camera. He pocketed it and locked the door, said, "Right, service elevator."

There was no room in the elevator for six, especially with one laid full-length on the floor and three on a floating disc. Xaphan took them down the shaft to the underground parking lot and out into the loading area before the two men had wrestled the corpse into position. They hovered to one side, listening to the car descend. At the other end of the basement the door to the exit ramp rolled up and an unmarked windowless van came into view. When it neared the loading area, it did a three-point turn to aim its rear doors at the service elevator just as the bell rang and the doors slid open.

The van doors opened from within. A short, heavy-shouldered man got out of the vehicle. "Come on," he said.

Tresidder and Baccala lifted the body and carried it to the van. There was a sheet of heavy plastic on the floor of the cargo bay. With the stocky man's help, they laid their burden on the thick membrane and the newcomer swiftly and efficiently wrapped the corpse. Then he looked at the lawyer and said, "Him, too?"

Baccala took a step backward but Tresidder shook his head. "Not this time," he said.

The shorter man shrugged, slammed the doors of the van and went and got into the passenger seat. The driver had not moved. Now he put the vehicle into gear and headed for the exit ramp.

"Follow them," Denby said.

Chesney thought the captain seemed to have something blocking his throat. To Xaphan, he said, "Do as he says."

The disk moved silently after the van, followed it up the ramp and out into the city night. As the vehicle picked up speed, so did everything else as the demon fast-forwarded them through the streets, over the river and out past the suburbs to where a remnant of a state forest still stood.

The van turned onto a dirt road and passed through a gate made by a four-inch pipe that was usually padlocked to a concrete post. They drove a half-mile or so into the woods and came to a clearing where a car waited. A flashlight blinked from the trees and the driver and the stocky man carried the body towards it.

Two other men waited there, beneath a mature maple. They had already dug a grave and stood, leaning on their shovels. Without ceremony, Cathy Bannister's remains were tossed into the hole, and the shovels worked fast to cover her over.

Denby, watching, said, "The driver is Petey Worrance. He was a wheelman for the mob, died of cancer a few years back. The muscle is Turk Something; he's still active – I've seen him around the cardrooms." He peered at the action by the grace. "I can't make out the guys with shovels."

"Let him see them," Chesney said to Xaphan. His own night vision showed them clearly.

One of the men was now scraping leaves and twigs over the disturbed earth. "Jesus!" said the captain, when he saw the man's face.

"You know him?" Melda said.

"He was only a senior inspector back then," Denby said. "No wonder he rose so fast." He swore quietly to himself then said, "That's J. Edgar Hoople. The chief of police."

TEN

Here is how Billy Lee Hardacre saw things.

He had trained as a specialist in labor law and soon found out that he had the peculiar set of skills that made him a good mediator. By his early thirties, he was rich.

It was then that he was bitten by the fiction bug: he began a new career as an author of fat-spined novels in which men and women of power intrigued against each other's interests and interfered with each other's bodies. His characters had unending appetites for sexual encounters and a predisposition to solve disputes with unrestrained violence. His books were hugely popular, and sold by the truckload through Wal-Mart and discount stores, making Billy Lee Hardacre even richer.

Then, at the age of forty-seven, while writing his seventh novel, he was struck by an epiphany. The universe suddenly made sense to him: the world was actually a book being written by a deity; probably, he thought, to work out that most fundamental of questions – what was right, and what was wrong? There had been previous drafts, which explained why the holy scriptures were full of events that had never really happened. The story was open-ended, and depended – as good novels do – on the conflicting wills of the characters to drive the narrative forwarded.

The revelation was a life-changing event: Billy Lee abandoned his literary career and enrolled in a seminary to pursue a doctorate in divinity. He expanded and amplified his revelation, but his ideas were not well received, however, and his doctoral thesis, in which he expounded the god-as-author theory, was rejected – even ridiculed. Unused to failure, Hardacre fell prey to emotions he had never before experienced: self-doubt, depression, anxiety.

But he overcame these demons by transmuting them into righteous anger, then turned his resentment into the foundation for a third career, this time as a television preacher. His weekly cable program, *The New New Tabernacle of the Air*, was broadcast live at 11am every Sunday morning. For years, the program's format saw the preacher sitting at a desk, like a news anchor, trolling through the week's events and offering a commentary focused on the persons he deemed responsible for them. Those persons might be politicians of any ideological persuasion, movie stars, authors, professional athletes, academics, pundits, and even fellow men and women of the cloth – in fact, especially the most prominent whited sepulchers of his new-found field. One thing they had in common: they had all failed to live up to Billy Lee's standard of moral behavior.

It had been Hardacre's practice to make one of the week's offenders the subject of a pointed, even barbed, sermon – a real balls-scorcher, was how one not-very-religious journalist described a typical Hardacre screed. After fifteen minutes of verbal flaying and skewering, the TV screen would display a card with the target's mailing addresses so that Hardacre's legions of devoted fans – none more so than Letitia Arnstruther – could bury the week's victim in letters, and later, emails that detailed the reception the miscreant could expect when he, and sometimes she, eventually passed through the Gates of Hell.

But then came the events surrounding Chesney Arnstruther, and from then on Billy Lee did not just believe that his rejected doctoral thesis was nothing less than the explanation for life, the universe and everything, as another novelist had put it. It was the literal truth and it offered the preacher a new way forward. The negotiations that ended the strike by Hell's demons, accidentally sparked off by Chesney's innocent summoning of a demon, put Hardacre in touch with a high-ranking member of the heavenly hierarchy.

When the dust had settled over the infernal strike, Billy Lee called for the Throne to visit him again. He was not surprised when the being in white reappeared again; was Hardacre not, after all, one of the most significant figures in all of history? Was it not he, and he alone, who had unraveled the central secret of existence?

The Throne came when he called, and together – though it was mostly Billy Lee's efforts – they wrote a new chapter for the divine story. It was to be called the

Book of Chesney, but the young hero's role in it was more metaphorical than actual – essentially, it was Billy Lee Hardacre's take on how the world ought to be organized, with a surface gloss that reflected the preacher's understanding of how his views matched those of God.

Billy Lee expected to release the book, with the prophet Chesney as its purported subject, and somehow bring about the next great change. Exactly how the process would work, he did not know. Yet he had faith that it would, and never once entertained the notion that his own considerable vanity was the main argument for his believing that he could, albeit with angelic assistance, change the world forever.

But, to give him credit, he put it all on the line. No more weekly pillorying of the venal and foolish – the whole tenor of his Sunday morning program changed. Instead of a rehearsing the week's excesses and pointing an accusatory finger, Hardacre gave his viewers a history lesson: *How We Got Here*, it was called, an idiosyncratic explanation of the course of human events since ancient times to modern and post-modern, with Billy Lee leaping from epoch to epoch, making unusual connections between events famous and obscure, between individuals and mass populations.

The incidents and personalities mentioned changed from week to week, but a common theme remained: things had gotten pretty bad and looked to be on the verge of getting worse. But unlike other Jeremiahs of screen and pulpit, Billy Lee Hardacre, did not prophesy doom and damnation. He did not predict the destruction of the world, but its new beginning.

Specifically, the preacher described himself as the precursor. He had come to prepare the way, he said, and if this description raised in his followers an association with the first-century fellow that the world remembered as John the Baptist, that was no accident. Hardacre proclaimed a prophet – yet to be named, because his wife's son kept balking at the assignment – would soon emerge from the wings to take history's center stage. And when that prophet came, all things would be made new.

The preacher had genuinely thought that Chesney, guided by the *Book of Chesney* – that is, guided by Billy Lee Hardacre – would be that new linchpin of the ages. He had since come to accept that that vision had been in error; he might even have misunderstood the angel. Instead, the strange young man had turned out to be a kind of precursor in his own right. Chesney had delivered unto Billy Lee the genuine article: the actual, living, historical, flesh-and-blood Jesus of Nazareth, who had been the central character in another of the umpteen new drafts that God had written since starting with a simple tale of two innocents and an ogre in a garden.

Hardacre would have felt better about Yeshua bar Yusuf, as the prophet named himself – they'd settled on Joshua Josephson for the purposes of *The New New Tabernacle of the Air* – if the man could have given him a clear idea of what he would say when the cameras turned his way. But whenever he was asked, Joshua would just shake his curly head and say, "I never did know what was going to come out. So much of it was in response to questions people put to me. I would wait for the spirit to move me. Which it always did."

"The Holy Spirit?" Hardacre said, wanting to be clear.

The prophet made a shooing motion with one hand. "Not like it was later," he said, "when the spirit was somehow reinterpreted as a fully fledged third person of the tripartite deity. When I was wandering the roads, preaching, that would have been outright blasphemy. Straight to the stoning pit." He smiled ruefully. "Same as if I'd said *I* was one third of a divine threesome." He mused over something for a moment, then said, "Where was I?"

"Being moved by the Holy Spirit."

"Ah, yes. In those days we thought of it as the breath of the Lord, that which was first breathed into Adam's clay and then breathed anew into every infant as it took its first inspiration at birth. And in that draft of the book, I suppose it was." He frowned and went on, "I don't know whose idea it was to make it over into a pigeon. That came after my... transformation."

"But is it still in you?" said Hardacre. He dreaded the prospect of the final moment, after all these weeks of build-up, when he would introduce the awaited one then watch as the fellow stood under the lights and couldn't think of anything to say.

"I think so. If not..." Joshua shrugged. "I'll tell them a story. That's what I always used to do, especially if some smarty-boots was trying to trick me into saying something that would get me taken up by the Sanhedrin or the Romans." He raised his eyes to the ceiling and went on, "Of course, eventually..."

He sighed then a thought occurred. "You don't have anything like them, do you? I've no interest in going through all that again."

"No. You can say whatever you want."

"Good." The prophet dusted his hands together. "Well, then, just leave it to me. I did this for years. It's like riding an ass, you know – you never forget how."

Sunday morning, Captain Denby summoned Lieutenant Grimshaw, the senior on-duty scene-of-crime officer, to his office and told him to gather up his team and whatever equipment they would need to exhume a body.

"On whose authority?" said the SOC man.

"Mine."

Grimshaw had got where he was by being a team player, and he knew who was captain of the team he played on. "I need to check with the chief."

"Do that," said Denby, "and you won't be in on what would have been the biggest case of your career."

"Bigger than the Taxidermist?" Grimshaw had not been on duty that night and had missed out on the glory.

"Way bigger." Denby lowered his voice to a conspiratorial murmur. "Cathy Bannister."

The lieutenant dropped his own tone to a whisper. "You know where she is?"

"I got a tip. Reliable."

Denby waited while Grimshaw worked out the angles. If he called the chief of police, Hoople would probably tell him to stay clear. J. Edgar had his own scene-of-crime favorite, Lieutenant Schreiber, assigned to the case. Schreiber had also got the Taxidermist, which had led to appearances on network news shows, describing the state of the bodies and the layout of the crime scene. If Grimshaw could get that kind of exposure, it could catapult him into his life goal: to retire after he put in his twenty and open a scene-of-crime consulting firm. Rich defendants, facing serious charges – movie stars who murdered their wives, politicians who got caught taking too wide a stance in airport washrooms – would pay huge fees for a specialist who could muddy the evidentiary waters.

"How reliable?" he said.

"Rock solid."

His calculations complete, Grimshaw said, "I'll get my crew."

"Confiscate their cell phones before they saddle up," Denby cautioned.

"Not to worry."

Billy Lee Hardacre used taped music for his broadcasts. He'd heard other televangelists recount horror stories of booze, drugs and illicit sex among their in-house choristers. He been told of one occasion where a live broadcast had teetered on the edge of disaster because a soprano soloist, pregnant by the basso profundo, had had to be manhandled out of camera shot and off the stage before she could make their private disagreements indelibly public.

For the revelation of the new prophet, he decided to go classical: *Also Sprach Zarathustra* – better known as the opening theme to *2001: A Space Odyssey*. But first came his own segment, his last as the precursor, and Hardacre came on stage, as he usually did, to the strains of *Get Happy (Get Ready for the Judgement Day)*. The set was unlit, except for a plain wooden stool beneath a single spotlight. The preacher came out of the darkness, a cordless microphone in his hand, rested one buttock on the seat, hooked a boot heel on one of the rungs, and smiled into the camera.

"My friends," he began, "for weeks now I've been telling you that a new light is coming, a new day is about to dawn. Hold on, I said, for the time is almost at hand."

He paused. "It's hard, waiting for deliverance, in a world that seems to have gone mad. A world where the strong oppress the weak, where the rich rob the poor, where the wise have given themselves over to foolishness. We look to the east and say, 'Where is the sunrise? When will the light come to chase away the darkness?'"

He shook his head and looked down, silent and pensive. Then he raised his eyes to the camera again and said, "I thank you for your patience, friends. I thank you for your faith. I thank you for your courage, for your willingness to tune in, week after week, to hear me say, 'Hold on, it's coming! The dawn is about to break!'"

And now his voice rose. "But I'm not going to say that to you today! I'm not going to tell you that you have to wait!" He rose from the stool and moved closer to the camera, and now the spot faded and more lights came up, creamy and golden, to illuminate the stage's backdrop in an illusion of heavenly light. Hardacre stopped at a place where an X was chalked onto the concrete floor and a carefully aimed spotlight created a nimbus of light about his head.

"Friends," he said, his voice rising another level, "I'm not going to tell you to wait anymore! I'm not going to tell you the one we've been waiting for is on his way!" Beneath his words, the horns and drums of the fanfare began. "I'm not going to say, 'Be patient, have faith.'

"Because your patience is about to be rewarded! Your faith is about to be vindicated!" The music built in intensity and volume as Hardacre's highly able sound engineer tracked his oration. "Because the waiting is over! Because the one you've waited for…" The music moved into the crescendo, and Hardacre followed its rhythm, waiting for the final roll of the kettledrums, then shouted, "is here!"

The stage went dark again, only for a second. Then a new spotlight fell upon the curly-haired, bearded man who had been waiting in the darkness. Joshua stood with his hands in his pockets – he'd found that a most agreeable use for pockets. He stared down at his sandal-shod bare feet – he couldn't get used to shoes and socks – and rocked back and forth on his heels and soles. Then he looked up and around, as if not sure where his eyes ought to settle.

Hardacre, standing out of shot beside camera one, pointed at the instrument's hooded lens. Joshua smiled and nodded – they'd rehearsed this, though without the music, and now he stepped toward the camera until the preacher showed him both palms.

The prophet stopped, raised one hand to pensively pinch his lower lip, and remained silent. Five seconds went by, then ten. Hardacre made a rolling motion with one hand, which drew Joshua's attention though he didn't seem to know what the gesture meant.

Finally, Billy Lee stage-whispered, "Speak!" which caused the other man to blink in surprise.

"Now?" he said.

"Yes, now!"

"I was waiting for you to introduce me."

"I did!"

"Not by name."

"You can do that."

The prophet frowned. "What's the point of your being a precursor if you don't tell them who I am?"

"Please," said Hardacre, "get on with it."

"Do you want to play the music again? That was very… startling music."

"No! I just want you to talk to the camera."

The other man shrugged. "As you like." He seemed to gather his thoughts, then said, "Peace be upon you. I am" – he pronounced it carefully – "Joshua Joseph-son. I am a prophet of the Lord. I've come to talk to you about what the Lord wants from you."

Here he paused, and Hardacre had the frightening thought that the man was thinking about the issue for the first time. The pause lengthened and the preacher's hand came up, trembling, just about to make the rolling gesture again, when Joshua said, "Not all that much, really. At least, not all that much out of the ordinary."

The prophet lowered his head, pinched his lip again and took a step to the right, then another, then a third. The spotlight, robotically controlled from a computer in a booth two floors above the studio, tracked him smoothly. So did the camera, operated by the same computer. Joshua looked up, seemed almost surprised to find the device still looking at him, and turned to it again saying, "People always used to ask me: what does the Lord want of us? What are we supposed to be doing?

"Does he want us to always be praying to him, and thinking about him, trying to get closer to him?" He looked away, tugged on the lip again, then came back to the camera. "Well… no." He paused again, then appeared to hit on something. "Put it this way," he said. "Imagine you take your child somewhere to play. Perhaps you even build a garden for the child to play in, with interesting toys and things to do.

"Then you put your little one out there and you say, 'Go ahead, have some fun.' But, instead, all it does is sit before you and stare at you and ask you questions." He shrugged. "How are you going to feel?"

He seemed to be waiting for a response, then realized after a moment that the camera couldn't give him one. "The point is," he said, "that the Lord put us here so he could watch us, not the other way round."

He put his hands in his pocket and walked up and down again, the spotlight and camera tracking him. After a while, he shaded his eyes and found Hardacre. "Will that do?" he said.

"No!" cried the preacher, then clapped a hand over his mouth. He had another fifty-three minutes of airtime to fill. He tried another stage whisper. "Tell them what should they do!"

Joshua twitched his shoulders as if the question wasn't worth a full shrug. "What they should do?"

"Into the camera! Talk to them directly!"

The prophet looked into the lens. "Our friend, here, the, um, precursor, wants me to tell you what the Lord wants you to do." He raised a finger and shook it with emphasis. "That hasn't changed since I was here last." He spread his calloused hands. "Be good to one another.

"An old rabbi used to put it very well: don't do anything to anybody that you wouldn't want somebody to do to you. And, if you can see a way to help, then help. After all, what are we here for, if not to help each other?"

He gave the matter a little more thought then his face brightened. "Oh, yes," he said, "and don't worry about what it all means. Even the Lord doesn't know that. At least, not yet. He's still working it out. Or, I should say, we're working it out for him. We're all part of a story that the Lord is telling himself."

"Well," the prophet rubbed his palms together then spread his hands, "nice talking to you. Peace."

And with that, Joshua Josephson, gave the camera a little flick of his becurled, bearded head, and walked off into the darkness. The robotic spotlight and camera followed him until he stepped over the strip of yellow tape that marked the limit of the coverage zone, then faithful to their programming, the light turned itself off and the camera went on standby.

Leaving Billy Lee Hardacre with fifty-three minutes of airtime to fill. In the automated broadcast center, Billy Lee was his own director; he had a device in his pocket with a miniature screen and keyboard. He pulled it out and quickly tapped in a sequence of numbers, and the screen showed an image of himself pitching for donations. A second later, so did all the television sets in the land that were tuned to his program.

Then he went looking for the prophet.

Captain Denby didn't know how it was done, but the time traveler had told him that if he signed out a police vehicle – any vehicle that had a global positioning system – he would find the coordinates of Cathy Bannister's grave already entered in it. Sure enough, when he got behind the wheel of an unmarked car in the police garage and turned on the GPS, it told him where to go. Lieutenant Grimshaw and three crime-scene technicians in a van full of technology followed him.

It took longer to get there than it had on the floating disk, but eventually the woman's voice from the dashboard brought him to the pipe gate that had been open that night in 2001. It was closed now but one of the technicians clipped off the padlock with a pair of bolt cutters, then the two vehicles wound their way along the rutted track that led through the trees.

The night before, he'd mentally marked the spot under the maple where they'd laid the body. The tree did not look much different after nine years and he led Grimshaw there and pointed to the ground. The lieutenant, beckoned over a technician who brought a five-foot-long steel rod with a tee-bar handle. The technician pushed the rod into the ground in several places, a foot apart. Denby could see that where the grave ought to be, the instrument went in deeper without the man having to put weight on it. In less than a minute, the rough dimensions of the grave were marked out by tiny white flags mounted on sticks stuck into the ground.

"Definitely been dug into," Grimshaw said. Another of the technicians, a woman, brought him a handheld device covered in black rubber; it had a long metal tube attached to it by a plastic cable. The lieutenant inserted the tube into one of the holes the first probe had made, within the area bounded by the flags on sticks. Grimshaw pressed a button and studied a display for a moment, then he withdrew the probe and put it into one of the holes outside the flagged area. He studied the result for a moment, then said, "Higher methane results inside than outside. I'd say we've got a grave."

He turned to Denby and said, "Captain, I'm going to ask you to step back." Then he spoke to his crew. "Done right," he said, "this one's a career-maker. Done wrong – that means we fuck up and blow a conviction – it could be a career-ender. So we're not only going to do this right – we're going to do it perfect. Karen, get the camera. It's been nine years, but we'll start with a complete site survey. Let's get to work."

Hardacre had found two bucket chairs and a small table, and set them up, siting them on strips of tape laid on the floor by another televangelist who used the studio and liked to do an interview format. Then he'd gone and found Joshua, who was wandering around the studio exercising his curiosity, and brought him back. They were both already wearing button micro-phones and FM radio packs, so all the preacher had to do was get them seated, find the right item on his con-trol's drop-down menu, and let the computer up in the control booth adapt the lighting and camera posi-tioning to the new set-up. He'd had to run another commercial while a second camera rolled forward from the back of the studio, but that gave him to time to explain to the prophet what they were going to do.

Joshua scratched his black curls. "We're going to talk while they eavesdrop?"

"Pretty much."

"That seems like bad manners."

"Not here."

"As you say." The prophet leaned back in the chair and crossed his legs.

"Better if you keep both feet on the floor," Hardacre said. "Sandals without socks give the wrong impression."

"What impression is that?"

But the preacher was looking into one of the cam-eras and saying, "And we're back. I'm talking with Joshua Josephson, prophet of the Lord. Joshua–"

"Yes?" The man craned his neck to see the camera that had positioned itself behind him so it could shoot Hardacre over his shoulder.

"This one," Hardacre said, gesturing with his thumb at the camera behind his chair.

"That one?" The prophet peered into the lens. "But I was talking to the other one before."

Hardacre took a breath and let it out slowly. "That doesn't matter. Or you can just look at me."

"It's a complicated business, isn't it?"

The preacher took another breath. "Earlier, you were saying that God–"

"Don't say that," Joshua interrupted. "He likes to be called 'the Lord.'" He smiled, like a man remembering an embarrassing faux pas. "I used to call him 'Father,' you know, but that led to some complications." He laughed. "Especially with the Greeks. You wouldn't think they would have taken me literally, but there you go."

Hardacre opened his mouth for a second try, but the prophet was shaking his head and saying, "I never wanted to include the Greeks. Or the Romans. Waste of time, I thought, talking to pagans. Even if they'd come around to what I was saying, I figured the best they'd do is make the Lord into just another one of their gods – they had a lot of gods, you know. All false, of course, but could you convince them of that?"

He shook his head again and Hardacre used the opportunity to say, "But your message to–"

"And then, as it all turned out, I have to say I was mostly right. Even when Constantine made them all convert, they kept a lot of those godlings – started calling them saints and so on, and just kept on burning incense to them and asking for favors and all that pagan hoo-hah."

"But–" Hardacre began and was rolled over.

"And you should have seen the trouble that caused in Heaven," Joshua said. "First, all of the pagan gods and demigods were demons." He had been speaking to the preacher, but now he stared over Hardacre's shoulder into the camera and said, "That is, they were fallen angels. Do they know about that business with Lucifer?" he said to Billy Lee.

"Yes. Now let's–"

"Good. So here were all these formerly fallen angels coming back and being rehabilitated as saints. Which meant they had privileged access to the Lord. Seats on the right hand. I don't want to say there was resentment among the Thrones and Dominions – not to mention the real human saints who had been martyred by the Romans – but, well, let's say there had to be a period of adjustment."

Joshua blinked and smiled at Billy Lee. "But listen to me," he said, "prattling on and on. What was it you wanted to talk about?"

The ground search turned up the usual odds and ends, almost certainly unrelated to the body in the hole, Grimshaw conceded, but they were doing this one "absolutely by the book." Things got more interesting when the technicians got down to the bones themselves. Karen, smallest of the three, lowered herself into the grave and began brushing away the last bits of soil from the bones, pausing every few strokes to let one of the male technicians capture the scene on a digital camera.

"Here," said the woman, straightening from a crouch and handing Grimshaw a plastic evidence bag.

In it was a gold ring set with garnets, Cathy Bannister's birthstone. Her father had given it to her at her high-school graduation. It was known to have disappeared when she did. The lieutenant examined it then said to Denby, "Captain, do you have the file?"

It was in Denby's car. He went and got it. Grimshaw followed him. They opened the folder on the vehicle's hood and the captain riffled through the material until he came to a picture of the high school girl smiling in cap and gown. The hand that held a rolled-up diploma also showed the ring.

"Bingo," said the lieutenant. "We'll still do the DNA, but…"

"You're convinced?" Denby said.

"Uh huh."

"Time to call the chief." The detective took out his cell phone, checked the display and saw three green bars. He called up the speed dial menu and punched in a number. The phone rang several times – he could en-vision J. Edgar Hoople staring at the caller ID and trying to decide whether or not to answer – then the chief's voice said, "What?"

"Are you sitting down, chief?" the captain said.

"Don't fuck with me, Denby!"

"Thought you'd want to know. I'm out in the state forest, off County Road Eight. Grimshaw and his team are with me. We've just dug up Cathy Bannister." At first, Denby thought he was hearing silence on the line, that the chief had disconnected, but when he pressed the phone closer to his ear, he could hear the sound of breathing.

"You there, chief?" he said. "Do you want to call Public Affairs and set up the press conference? Or do you want me to?"

Chesney and Melda watched *The New New Tabernacle of the Air* in their apartment.

"I don't think this is what Billy Lee had in mind," she said.

It sounded pretty interesting to Chesney. "Eyewitness reports from Heaven aren't all that common."

"Yeah, but I think the rev was expecting revelations, real straight-from-the-mind-of-God stuff. Not gossip and platty-whatsits."

"Platitudes," Chesney said. "I guess he was expecting some kind of big change, all in the twinkling of an eye."

He turned back to the screen. Obviously, chairs that swiveled were a new experience to the prophet. He was swinging from side to side, and now he did a complete rotation.

"But what about the end of the world?" Hardacre was saying.

Joshua quit swinging and made a *what can I tell you?* face. "It doesn't end, does it? The author just starts a new scroll–"

"Chapter," said Hardacre.

"Starts a new chapter, and keeps on going."

"So what do you say to all those people who think it's all going to wrap up soon, and they'll be transported straight to Heaven?"

The bearded man thought for a moment. "I heard

an expression on the far-seer thing the other day. One person said to another, 'Get over yourself.' I think that's what I'd say to the people who think they're the heroes of the story." He smiled reassuringly into the camera. "I mean, look at how it has developed. It all started off very simple, just two teenagers in a garden with some animals. That didn't work, but he didn't stop there, did he? He added in more people, more places, more situations."

The prophet swung around in another full circle. "Now he wants to try getting the characters consciously involved in the story. Who knows where that's going to lead?" He bit his lower lip, the beard jutting as he did so, then said, "Besides, once the story ends for good, that will be the end of Heaven, too."

"What are you saying?"

"Heaven's just part of the story," Joshua said. "The same as Hell is. When he's done, they're done."

"But what about the angels and demons," Hardacre said, "the righteous and the damned? Where do they all go?"

The prophet shrugged. "Back where they came from, I suppose. I certainly don't know. You're the one who figured it all out."

Chesney switched over to the news channel, saw a breaking news announcement. A woman in a red suit with brunette hair that looked as if it had been lacquered solid was standing in front of Police Central, saying, "...conference expected soon, but the word around here is that there has been a significant break in the nine year-old mystery surrounding the disappearance of Cathy Bannister."

"What kind of break, Angela?" said the weekend fill-in anchor back at the studio.

Angela began to answer, but just then a black Lincoln Town Car slid to the curb behind her. Out of the back seat stepped the chief of police. The woman in red rushed to push a microphone under J. Edgar Hoople's nose, and so did a whole gaggle of other well-coiffed and polished TV reporters, plus a few print and radio newsies who looked as if they had slept in their clothes, and probably had.

"Do you expect an imminent arrest?" Angela asked, walking backwards as the chief thrust toward the front steps. "Has a body been recovered?" said someone else.

Hoople grunted something his hand jerked up spasmodically. Angela ducked back as if she expected a blow, but the police chief was only signaling to a uniformed lieutenant at the top of the steps – the public affairs careerist whose office Captain Denby had commandeered – to get down into the scrum and rescue him. The PR officer shouldered his way into the press, then turned and ran interference for the chief until Hoople disappeared through Police Central's front doors.

Then – it what was probably his bravest act to date as a police officer – the lieutenant turned and blocked the entrance as the reporters tried to force their way past. "Press conference at 1 o'clock!" he kept shouting, in response to every question they threw at him.

• • • •

Meanwhile, a producer and camera operator were just strapping themselves into a private jet about an hour's flight from the broadcast center where Hardacre rented studio time once a week. The producer's name was Janet Morrissey, and she worked for Hall Bruster, the czar of right-wing cable news network commentators whose hide still smarted from the flaying it had received when Bruster had been the target of a Billy Lee Hardacre jeremiad. The accompanying avalanche of mail and emails had been almost pornographic in their detailed descriptions of the infernal tortures awaiting the pundit. He still remembered the one about the Devil spitting on the red-hot iron.

Bruster had caught Hardacre's interview with Joshua Josephson. He had also caught the weeks-long buildup to the so-called prophet's appearance, and been devoting time on his own broadcasts to mocking Billy Lee's pretensions to being a latter-day John the Baptist. Five minutes after Joshua hit the airwaves, Bruster called the private airport terminal where he kept his Citation jet and told the duty officer to round up a pilot and get the plane ready to fly. Then he had called Morrissey and told her to be at the airport with a camera operator ASAP. He was emailing her a string of questions to ask the preacher once she ambushed him with the camera rolling.

Now, in his office in his mansion, the pundit was already writing his script for an upcoming program that would prominently feature Hardacre and his bearded wonder, who was still blathering away on the big screen across the room. Brewster looked at the last two words he had entered on his computer screen, high-lighted them, then typed "beardy-weirdy" over them.

He was looking forward to saying that, and a few other phrases. Maybe something about Mohammed going to the mountain and coming back with nothing but a mouse. He also made a margin note to mention the sandals.

ELEVEN

J. Edgar Hoople was sweating under the TV lights in the first-floor shift-assembly room at Police Central that also did duty as a venue for news conferences. At the table next to him were Grimshaw, the crime scene specialist; Lieutenant Schmidt, the Public Affairs coordinator; and Captain Denby. Denby was holding up a photograph and an evidence bag, and the flash of photographers' strobes and the glare of the lights mounted on the shoulder-held video cameras were giving the police chief a blinding headache.

He'd wanted to corner Denby before they faced the media, but the captain couldn't be found and he didn't respond to radio calls. Finally, Schmidt had been smart enough to use the department's system that could contact the GPS in police cars and find out where they were.

"He's at 198 Kercher Avenue, chief," the PR officer said, "or at least the car is. Want me to send a unit to bring him in?"

Hoople recognized the address. "That's the Bannisters'." Denby had stopped on the way to the press conference to inform the parents that their daughter's body had been found, so they wouldn't have to hear it on the news – or worse, suddenly find themselves besieged by reporters. "Yes, send a unit, but nothing over the radio. We'll need somebody to keep the ghouls away from the family. And have them tell Denby I want him back here forthwith."

Forthwith, to Denby, apparently meant whenever the Hell he felt like it. So there had been no time for a private word before the press conference. The captain had pulled up in front of Police Central, accompanied by Lieutenant Grimshaw. They had immediately attracted a swarm of media, and Denby had invited them all to follow him into the briefing room. Schmidt, the public relations officer, had managed to ease in and establish some kind of order, giving the chief time to take a seat at the table.

Now Denby was saying, "The ring was custom made. There's no question of identity. We have found Cathy Bannister."

"Have the family been informed?" said the woman in red.

"Yes. Moments ago."

"What will happen to the body?"

"We're dealing with bones," Denby said, "but we will attempt to establish a cause of death, and we'll sift the soil from the grave to see what turns up. Maybe one of the killers dropped something that will lead us to him."

Hoople wanted to step in now and take control of the news conference. He nudged Schmidt. But Denby had started a feeding frenzy and there was nothing to do but wait for the blood-scent to dissipate.

"Captain Denby," said a print reporter, "you said 'killers.' Is there evidence that there was more than one perpetrator?"

Denby delayed responding while he turned and looked straight at the chief. Anybody watching would have seen it as a deferential act, a look to see if the senior officer wanted to speak. But Hoople felt a jolt of ice-cold energy pass through him. He knew the meaning of that kind of look, had used it himself many a time in his years as a working cop: it was the look cops gave to a suspect when they knew they had the guy who did it. The chief froze then made a slight motion of the hand, as if to say, "Take it, captain."

But he knew that a trained interrogator might interpret the gesture to mean, "Get that away from me!" And when he saw Denby nod and turn back to the reporters, a voice in the chief's head said, *he knows*.

"We have information," Denby was saying, "that indicates more than one person was involved in Ms Bannister's death and disappearance."

"What kind of information?"

"From a confidential informant."

"A confession?"

"No." Then Denby smiled knowingly. "At least not yet."

"Do you have suspects?"

"No comment."

"Is an arrest imminent?"

"No comment."

"Where was the body found?"

Denby said, "The location has to remain secret until the scene of crime technicians have thoroughly canvassed the area. But why don't I let Lieutenant Grimshaw tell you everything that can be made public at this point."

He settled back and crossed his arms while the lieutenant leaned forward and began to give the reporters a blow-by-blow account of how the grave had been located with probes, the soil removed, the ring discovered, the bones recovered. Denby's position gave him an unobstructed view past the backs of the PR and crime-scene lieutenants to J. Edgar Hoople's jowly profile. The chief turned and offered the captain a deadpan gaze. But the voice in his head kept saying it: *he knows! He knows!*

"You've actually been to Heaven," Billy Lee Hardacre said.

Joshua swung from side to side again, then unthinkingly crossed his legs. "Oh, yes."

"Will you tell our viewers what it's like?"

The prophet shrugged – Hardacre was growing less and less fond of that gesture – and said, "Well, it's about what you'd expect."

Hardacre felt a trickle of sweat run down his chest. It was not the first. "Go on," he said.

Another shrug. "Well, it's wonderful and perfect and you feel happy all the time. No, come to think of it, 'happy' is not the word. Blissful. Content." He leaned back in his chair, stretched his legs out and crossed his sandal-strapped ankles. "Did you ever have one of those days when everything goes just right? Well, Heaven's like that, only it's every day. Oh, and it's always day, never night."

"It sounds…" Hardacre searched for a word, decided on: "exciting?"

"Oh, no," said the prophet, "it's never exciting. All you ever do, really, is contemplate Himself. That's blissful, of course. Every now and then you can take a break, but then there's nothing to do but prepare yourself for another stint of contemplation. Preparing yourself is also blissful." His brows drew down, and he nodded. "Basically, that's what I'm talking about. It's blissful. Bliss, bliss, bliss, and then along comes some more bliss."

"But what do you do there?" Hardacre said.

"There's nothing *to* do. Doing is not what Heaven's for. It's just for being." He lifted a finger. "And, of course, contemplating."

"But–"

"I suppose that's why I used to go over to the other neighborhoods. Something to do."

"Other neighborhoods?"

"Of course, I was an anomaly." He looked away from the preacher and found the camera. "That's a Greek word. You may not be familiar with it. It means I was different."

"Yes, but–"

"The difference was that I was taken up in the flesh, you see. Not at first, but later. Most people – well, almost everybody – they leave the flesh down here and just the soul goes up. But I was a special case. So I was

up there, warts, wounds and all." He frowned, remembering. "They had to make special allowances for
me. I still got hungry, you see. And then there was the
problem of what do to when the food…" – he made a
pushing gesture with both hands – "went through. I
had the only outhouse in Heaven." He paused, then
said, "Where was I?"

He looked over at Hardacre. The preacher was loos-
ening his tie and collar. A sheen of sweat had formed
on his face. In his hand was a sheet of paper with questions on it; he'd jotted them down while the prophet
had been making his first remarks. Now he let the
paper fall to the floor, raised a hand and opened his
mouth to speak.

But Joshua forestalled him. "Oh, yes, the other
neighborhoods. Heaven's a big place. Many mansions,
as someone once put it. Most souls don't notice the
fences, though."

"Fences?" Hardacre said. His voice had to struggle
to get out.

"Between the different… well, I keep calling them
neighborhoods, but they're really different Heavens.
One for the Muslims. One for the Hindus. The Zoroas-
trian one is quite interesting, though a little taxing. I
didn't care for Valhalla. And the Elysian Fields," – he
made a clucking, tutting noise with tongue and palate
– "far too Greek." He looked at the preacher and said,
"You do know that Judaea was ruled for centuries by
the Greeks until we rebelled and fought them? Judah
and the Hammer and all that?"

Hardacre nodded. It was a reflexive action. He had

a feeling that it was all running away from him, and nothing he could do would ever let him catch up.

A white light began flashing on top of the camera that was looking at him over the prophet's shoulder. "Oh," he said, though his voice sounded in his ears like someone else's, "I see we're almost out of time. Please join us next week when we'll…" But for the life of him, he couldn't think of what he might be doing a week from now. Maybe writing novels again. Maybe just sitting around his mansion staring at the walls.

The flashing light speeded up, and now it was joined by an amber bulb.

Billy Lee reached for the control in his pocket. "Goodbye," he said.

"Are you leaving?" said the prophet.

Then the amber was replaced by red, the studio lights came up, and the cameras rolled back to their start positions.

"We both are," said the preacher.

Seth Baccala had not been watching the preacher and his guest. Nor did he normally have the television on and tuned to a cable news channel. But as he was working on the Paxton Life and Casualty strategic plan at his desk in his home office – old W.T. was leaving more and more of the running of the company to his executive assistant – the phone rang. Tressider's voice said, "Turn on the news," and hung up.

Baccala went into the lounge and turned on the big screen just in time to see Captain Denby hold up the evidence bag with the ring in it and the photo of Cathy

Bannister. He recognized both. He sank into a chair and listened with a growing sense of liquidity in his bowels as Denby talked about knowing there were multiple perpetrators involved in the young woman's death and disappearance. When the captain refused to confirm or deny the existence of a confession or whether he had suspects in mind, Baccala thought he might throw up.

When Lieutenant Grimshaw began detailing the way the methane probe caught the chemical scent of decomposition, Baccala's breakfast spewed all over the rug. He didn't even bother to clean it up, but reached for the phone and had it recall the last number that had called him.

"What are we going to do?" he asked when the lawyer answered.

Melda said, "Denby may need some help. We should ask Xaphan."

When summoned, the demon scratched the dense fur on top of its head and said, "You're gonna need to be a little more specific."

"How can we fix it so that he gets a conviction?" Chesney said.

"Depends on who you wanna see go over." The fiend ticked off fingers. "Now, Baccala you got at best for manslaughter and – what's the legal-beagle language? – oh, yeah: interferin' wid a dead body. Tressider, same thing, but no manslaughter. Same for the guys who collected the body and dug the hole."

"But somebody should pay," Chesney said.

"Somebody already has," Xaphan said, "starting with the Bannister skirt, who pulled a fast one on Baccala. She was just supposed to take a peek at that file, not take no pitcher. And that guy that drove the van, Worrance, he's down in the smoke." A short and spiky thumb gestured downward.

"Besides," – a pause to empty the half-filled tumbler of rum that had arrived with the demon – "there's no evidence. These guys was pros."

"Maybe some evidence could, you know, turn up," Melda said.

Xaphan's oversized eyes enlarged even farther. "Are you one of the good guys, or one of us?" it said. "Framing people is sposed to be bad juju."

"Even when you're framing people who actually did the thing you're framing them for?" she said.

"Xaphan's right," said Chesney. "When I got into crimefighting, I always intended that anybody I caught I would turn over to the police and let the law take it from there. I'm not going to be a vigilante."

"But this time," Melda said, "the police are working for the bad guys. That was the chief of police digging the grave." A thought occurred and she turned to Xaphan. "Who was the other guy with the shovel?"

"Patrick Tooley. He was Hoople's old partner when he was a working cop."

"Where is he now?"

"Also in the smoke," said the fiend, accompanying the sentence with a puff of pure blue Havana that resolved itself into a scene of a bent-backed figure shoveling something indistinct. "Shit brigade."

"What happened to him?" Melda said.

Xaphan shrugged. "Like old Alphonse used to say, he developed a bad case of inconvenience. In fact, it was fatal."

"Inconvenient to whom?"

The demon blew another cloud of cigar smoke. This one looked just like J. Edgar Hoople.

The demon gestured with the cigar and a screen appeared in the air. "And, fore you ask, here's Turk Borghese." A street scene came to life: a heavy-set man in slacks, a polo shirt and sports jacket coming out of a drugstore, pausing to light a cigarette. A Cadillac Escalade pulled up to the curb, its stereo blasting rap, and the driver said something to the man who laughed in response then went around the front of the SUV and climbed into the passenger seat.

The vehicle pulled away, and Xaphan's screen tracked it, the point of view swinging around to look through the passenger window just in time to see a hand holding a small-caliber pistol come from the back seat and press the muzzle against the back of Turk Borghese's head. The double *crack!* of two shots was almost inaudible over the stereo.

"When did that happen?" Chesney said.

"That's right now," Xaphan said.

"Who's behind it? Tresidder?"

The demon blew smoke. "Can't tell you. Rule number one. What I can tell you is, the Twenty are tidyin' up the loose ends, now that your flatfooted friend is stirrin' up trouble."

"So Denby does need our help," Chesney said.

"Yeah, but not to get a conviction," said the fiend, "just to get out of this alive."

"Does he know that?"

Xaphan waved at the screen. "I think he's got a pretty good idea." The image changed. Chesney saw an office, with Hoople seated behind a big desk and Denby leaning against the wall. The chief's hand was in an open drawer. The demon had framed the scene from an angle that allowed them to see the old-fashioned .38 Police Special around which Hoople's fingers were curling.

"He'll never get away with it," Melda said.

"He's the chief of police," said Xaphan, "and he got away with it before."

Chesney saw it all in a pool of light. "Costume," he said. "Strength of ten." A second later, as he tugged a glove tighter on his hand, he said to Melda, "We'll be right back."

Then he disappeared. But the screen stayed where it was, and in a moment the young woman saw the Actionary appear in the chief's office, saw him place his hand on the older man's shoulder and say, "You're coming with me." An instant later, they both winked out of sight, leaving Denby staring at the old-fashioned .38 caliber police special that fell from the air, from just the height the chief's hand had been at when the Actionary yanked him to his feet.

Chesney didn't take Hoople to the warm, cozy room with thick stone walls to keep out the biting cold and bitter winds of Hell's outer circle. He had Xaphan put them down out in the open. The chief's uniform was no match for the temperature. He hugged his arms around his shivering torso. Two tiny crusts of ice were already forming on his eyelashes.

The demon was at hand but out of the policeman's sight. Chesney said to him, "Give me a Wizard of Oz kind of voice. Not the little man behind the curtain but the full roar."

"You got it."

The chief flinched as Chesney seized the back of his collar and lifted him well off his feet. "Take a good look around," he said. "Anything happens to Denby, you end up here."

"Where are we?" The man's teeth chattered.

Chesney put him down. "A bad place. How do you like it?"

"Don't."

"Worse than jail?"

"Worse."

"Leave him alone?"

"Yes."

"Then we're done."

A moment later, they were back in the chief's office. The gun was still falling to the floor. Chesney picked it up and put it back in the drawer, closed it. Hoople was still shivering.

"What'd you do to him?" Denby said.

"Showed him his future," Chesney said. "Speaking of that," he tapped Hoople's shoulder, "are you listening?"

"Y-y-es." Hoople had to be listening. Chesney was still using the Wizard of Oz voice. The young man spoke privately to Xaphan and his normal voice re-asserted itself.

"Here's how it is," Chesney said. He was in a pool of light. "We know you helped bury Cathy Bannister. We know who was in on it with you. But there's not enough evidence to go to court. Am I right, captain?"

Denby shrugged. "Yeah," he said.

"So you don't have to worry about that. Now, what you're going to do is promote Captain Denby again. Give him a medal or something."

"Wait a minute," Denby said.

"No," Chesney said, "I got this." He turned back to Hoople. "Then a month goes by and you retire as chief of police. You go somewhere and we never hear from you again. But before you go, you nominate Denby to be your successor."

"Hey!" Denby and Hoople both spoke at the same time.

Chesney's pool of light was still very clear and bright. "No arguments," he said. "I want a police chief I can work with. You," he addressed himself to Denby, "want to be the best cop you can be." He turned to Hoople. "And you want to keep warm."

The chief shivered again. He thought about it, but not for long. "Okay, but I might not be the only problem you've got with this," he said.

"You mean the Twenty?" Chesney said. "That's why I want Denby in your job. We're going to bust them wide open."

The captain's eyebrows drew together, then went up. "You've been planning this?" he said.

"More of an inspiration," Chesney said.

Denby turned to Hoople. "I know you got files – who did what and when. Make sure you leave them for me."

The chief lifted his hands in a gesture that was both surrender and the action of a man gladly letting go of a hot potato. "You want to be crazy, I'm not stopping you."

"He's right, you know," the captain said to Chesney. "Those old bulls won't go without a fight."

Chesney summoned his inner Malc Turner. He blew air over his lower lip. "They won't know what hit them."

Janet Morrissey and her camera operator touched down at a private airfield too late to make it to Hardacre's broadcast center. But Hall Bruster had already sent a man to watch for their exit and he was now following the reverend's Mercedes. It was clearly heading back to the mansion and the watcher reported in every five minutes.

When the producer stepped onto the tarmac, she found a light helicopter with its rotors already turning. Twenty minutes later, the copter put down in a field less than two hundred yards from Hardacre's front gate. By the time the preacher and prophet arrived, Morrissey and her cameraman were blocking the entrance.

"No comment!" Hardacre shouted through the one inch he rolled down his window.

"We work for Hall Bruster," said the woman. "Got a few questions we'd like to ask your friend here."

"Get lost!" Hardacre said, before he noticed that Joshua had opened the passenger door and was standing outside the car, looking over its roof at the producer. The camera operator was dodging around the front of the car to get a better shot of him.

"Yes?" Joshua said.

Hardacre was getting out of the car, but the producer had already left his window and hurried around to where the story was. "You're Joshua Josephson?" she said.

"I am."

She looked at her Blackberry. "*The* Joshua Josephson? AKA Jesus Christ?"

"I don't know what AKA means."

"'Also known as.'"

"That's a complicated issue," Joshua said. "I am, or rather, I was. But I'm also… not."

"But you are Jesus of Nazareth, the son of the carpenter?"

Joshua shook his head. "My father raised sheep. He had a local reputation as a good builder, though. If someone was putting up a house or a shed, they would ask his advice. So he had this nickname, Tekton – it means the builder. You see, there were a lot of people with the same name so nicknames were how we told each other apart."

The producer was favoring him with the kind of smile she was accustomed to give to her sister's youngest child, who was officially designated as "special." She said, "But you lived two thousand years ago, were crucified and rose from the dead?"

"Oh, yes," said the prophet, "that was me."

"Well, there's someone here who'd like to talk to you." She held out the Blackberry.

"Is that one of those telephone things?" Joshua said. "I haven't used one yet." He reached for the instrument.

Hardacre thrust himself between the prophet and the producer. "Don't!" he said. "She's not here to help you!"

But the woman stretched her arm over Hardacre's shoulder and passed Joshua the Blackberry. His fingers touched hers as he took the phone and he said, "Do you know you've been in contact with demonic forces?"

"I'm sure you're right," she said, giving him another of her smiles for "special" people.

Hardacre was reaching for the phone, but Joshua turned his shoulder and said, "Can you hear me?"

"Very clearly," said Hall Bruster. "Is this the prophet?"

"Yes."

"I'd like to talk to you."

"Go ahead."

"What I'd really like," said the pundit, "is for you to come and visit me so that we can talk face to face."

"Ah," said Joshua. "Are you by any chance connected with the government?"

"Do you have a problem with the government?" said Bruster.

"I did, the last time I had to deal with one."

Bruster chuckled. "Of course. No, I have some friends in government, but I myself have no official power."

"Joshua!" Hardacre said. The woman and the man with the camera had put themselves between him and the prophet. "Don't listen to him! He's not your friend!"

The bearded man looked over at him and said, "I never confined myself to talking only to friends." Into the phone he said, "Where are you? How do I come to you?"

"The people I sent will bring you to me. Just tell them you want to come."

"All right," said the prophet. He handed the phone back to the woman. "He says you will take me to him."

"No problem. We have a helicopter right over there, and a private jet standing by."

"Some of those words don't mean anything to me," said the prophet, "but I'm sure I'll catch on."

Hardacre had pushed through the two who had been blocking his way. He took hold of Joshua's arm and said, "This is a mistake."

A smile split the black beard. "That's just what Judas said." He patted Billy Lee's arm. "It will all work out." To the woman, he said, "Will you bring me back here again?"

She consulted with Bruster over the phone, said, "Yes, right afterwards, if that's what you want. Or anywhere else you want."

"Then let's go."

Settling the future of Captain Denby raised a tide of confidence in Chesney. Never before had a pool of light seemed so large and so clear. When he returned to the apartment and doffed the Actionary costume, he felt more energized than he could remember on any Sunday afternoon. His betrothed recognized the change in him and suggested they skip lunch and put

his newfound energy to immediate and mutually ben-
eficial use. He dismissed the demon and they were just
on the brink of being full engaged when the phone beside the bed rang. The caller ID said it was from Billy
Lee's Hardacre's place.

Chesney exercised his newly confident judgment by
reaching down and pulling the phone jack from the
wall, then returned to his other most favorite pool of
light. An hour later, he and Melda were basking in its
afterglow when she remembered the phone call. She
sprawled over the side of the bed, presenting him with
a view that at once began to re-elevate his inclination,
and plugged the jack back into the wall socket. Immediately, the phone rang. She hauled herself back onto
the bed, glanced at the ID, and answered.

Chesney could hear his mother's voice clearly from
across the bed, aided by the fact that Melda did not
hold the instrument to her ear. "What is it?" he said.

The young woman made a face. "Hardacre," she
said. "I think he's drunk." Chesney heard a crash followed by a tinkle. "And throwing things."

"I'd better talk to her," he said. A moment later, his
mother's voice was loud in his ear, the sounds of the
reverend's tantrum even louder in the background.

"It's all your fault," she told him, "bringing that hor-
rible little man here and passing him off as our Lord
and Savior!"

"He is who he is, Mother," Chesney said, which he
realized at once was not the right kind of remark to be
making to his mother when she was in full fulmina-
tion. Melda had told him on a number of occasions

that most people dealt not in facts but in emotion. Especially in times of stress. He decided to use the same mother-handling strategy that had served him well in his youth: he sat in silence, holding the phone a distance from his ear, only half listening; he knew that she would eventually run all the way across the land of rage and settle over the border in her more accustomed territory of bitter disappointment.

But then he heard something that caused him concern. He brought the phone back to his lips and said, "He went where?"

"I don't know," Letitia said. "They sent a helicopter and a jet."

"Who did?"

"You haven't been listening, have you? You never listen! I can't count the number of times–"

A crash and an inarticulate bellow broke her train of denunciation and Chesney used the break to say, "I've got to go." He hung up, said, "Xa–" and was mindful enough of the circumstances to warn Melda that he was going to summon the demon.

She pulled the sheet around herself and said, "Aw, he can probably see through brick walls if he wants to, but thanks for the thought." She leaned over and kissed him. "You're getting better."

A moment later, the demon appeared on command, rum glass in its hand and cigar in its saber-fanged mouth. "What?"

"Joshua," Chesney said, "where is he and who's he with?"

"You wanna stay away from that mug," Xaphan

said. "He's trouble, and that's straight from the horse's mouth."

"I didn't ask for an opinion. Now–" Chesney checked himself. "Wait a minute. When he asked you if he'd ever cast you out, you said no."

The fiend shrugged. "No need to make a federal case out of it."

"That was a lie, wasn't it? And you're not supposed to lie."

The fiend took on the look of an indignant weasel, gesturing with the Churchill. "To you," he said. "Just you. You don't mind me lying to Denby about you bein' a time traveler, do you?"

"Never mind," said the young man, "just tell me now about you and Josh."

"Awright, awright!" Xaphan shot its cuffs, drank half the rum and got the Havana well stoked. Then it said, "Back in those days, I was in the possession racket, see? Some guy would slip up on his prayers and sacrifices, we'd move in, take the place over, have some laughs.

"So, we're workin' this one guy, got him dancin' around on the road, lotsa roarin and blasphemin', and along comes this bird with a bunch of mugs followin' him, and they're all sayin', 'Ooh, look, here comes a prophet!' Didn't look like much to me, I'll tell you, so me and the boys, we gave him the business, the old horse laugh."

The fiend paused to reload on rum and nicotine. Melda was listening closely, the sheet tucked tightly around her. "So then what?" she said.

"So then he points the finger and, wham! I'm outta the bozo – so are the rest of the boys – and next thing I know we're stuck in a bunch of pigs! And when I say stuck, I mean stuck! He'd not only cast us out, he'd jammed us in tight!

"So we're all jumpin' around, tryin' to get loose, and the crowd starts throwin' stones. So the pigs run, and we go right over a cliff into the sea! There's no way to get outta the water, so the pigs drown!"

The demon shook its head in grim recollection and clamped the cigar behind one of its fangs. "So then we gotta lie there in the bottom mud till the fish and the crabs eat the carcasses, before we can get unstuck from the flesh. And, that ain't the worst of it – then we gotta go back and report to the division chief, except it's worse than the worst, 'cause the boss himself has heard all about it, and he's more than a little hot under the collar, I'm tellin' ya!"

The demon blew smoke, and only some of it was from the Havana. "So, yeah, I guess I oughta remember that mug!"

Melda said, "You can't blame him for casting you out when you were turning some guy's head right around his shoulders. I mean, he was a prophet. It was his job!"

"And possessing was mine! Besides, what about the poor schmoe who owned the pigs? Some Greek farmer, that herd was all he had. He couldn't pay his debts and ended up in slavery!"

Chesney tsked. "Like you care!" he said. "Now, where is he and who's got him?"

"He's on a jet that's just landed about four hundred miles from here. He's with some TV people who are takin' him to meet with a guy name of Bruster. Bruster's thinkin' of puttin' your guy on the air."

"Hall Bruster?" Chesney said. He frowned.

"That's the bird."

"Is that bad?" said Melda.

The young man told her about his mother's letter and the red hot poker reference. "He'll want to embarrass Hardacre."

"Do we care about that?" Melda said.

"Josh might get in trouble."

"So we'll get him out of it." She looked at the demon. "Right?"

Xaphan snorted, blowing rings from both nostrils. "Your guy might not be the one gets in trouble," it said.

"What does that mean?" Chesney said.

But the demon waved its pint-sized hands, the smoke from the cigar making zigzag bands in front of its face. "I already said too much."

TWELVE

Hall Bruster's Sunday afternoon program went live to air so that he could take calls from viewers. His scheduled guest was Maylene Ho, a newly elected member of the House of Representatives who was a strict constitutional originalist: she had campaigned on a platform of reverting the republic's seminal document back to its original form, before all these footling amendments had watered down its historic purity. Bruster wanted her on board because she was foursquare for the abolition of the income tax, a change he favored because it meant he would not have to employ a firm of accountants to mystify the IRS as to exactly what he took in, and where it all went. But his screeners would have to vet callers carefully to keep any of them from pointing out that one of the amendments Ho would like to repeal was the one that had given her sex the right to vote. Bruster wasn't entirely sure that she had actually read the Constitution; she might be relying solely on posts from blogs she had googled.

But when Janet Morrissey told him that she had Hardacre's prophet on the jet, he immediately told his in-studio staff that the Congresswoman would get no more than the first half-hour and that he wanted her out of guest's seat the moment Joshua set foot across the threshold. He then sat down and, suppressing the occasional giggle, jotted down a series of questions for the alleged Jesus of Nazareth redux.

Now he was listening with only half an ear as the Congresswoman provided her exegesis as to what the Constitution really meant: mostly plenty of church and a minimum of state, with a citizenry whose pockets remained full of their own cash while their hands never strayed too far from a loaded gun. Twenty-two minutes into her segment, the earpiece he was really listening to informed him that the helicopter bringing the new guest from the airport was landing on the roof and did he want them to take the man to make-up or bring him straight down to the studio.

"Tap your pencil on the desk if you want him right away," said the producer in the control booth, and the lead from the pundit's HB 2 snapped off and struck the representative in the left eye.

"Ow!" she said, reaching up to dislodge the greasy fragment, giving Bruster the perfect opportunity to say, "Let's take a break."

"Here's the way we'll play it," Chesney said to his assistant. The television in the living room was on and Bruster had just gone to a commercial that featured the pundit himself pitching medallions that illustrated great moments in American history. The day when Ronald Reagan single-handedly tore down the Berlin Wall was "commemorated in genuine gold plate," Bruster's taped voice was saying, "a moment all patriots will treasure. And speaking of treasure–"

Chesney muted the sound as the screen showed a medallion showing the multitudes that had gathered for Bruster's celebration of his own exemplary rectitude on the steps of the Lincoln Memorial, in which the pundit appeared larger than the assassinated president's statue. "Here's the way we'll play it," the young man said again. "If it goes okay, we'll let it roll. If he's getting pushed around, we'll go and get him out of there. Go in invisible, cloud of smoke, grab him and gone. Got it?"

"If *he* gets pushed around?" Xaphan said, followed by a wordless sound that expressed skepticism.

"What?" said Chesney.

"I'm not sayin' nothin'. You got any more rum?"

"You drank it all."

"You mind if I…?"

"Be my guest."

The fiend put its cigar in its mouth. A bottle of liquor, still trailing seaweed from the sunken freighter whose cargo the demon was gradually pilfering, appeared in the hand it had just emptied. Xaphan looked at the cork, which shot out and hit the ceiling, then filled the tumbler and drank half of it. A rumbling belch followed, then the television screen showed Hall Bruster back at his desk in the studio.

"My next guest is someone you've been hearing about," he said, "if you happen to tune in Sunday mornings to a little medicine show put on by a self-proclaimed TV preacher named Billy Lee Hardacre. The Reverend Hardacre, as he likes people to call him, flunked out of a seminary after blowing a career as a slick labor lawyer and writing a few potboilers that the *New York Times* thought were just the kind of thing you and I should be reading."

He paused there to quirk an eyebrow in his trademark *and you and I know what we think of that* expression. The thirty or so people in his studio audience, all of whom had signed loyalty oaths, reacted with raucous hoots and sundry noises of derision.

"Well, lately, Billy Lee has been telling his dwindling following – I mean, folks, you really can't fool all of the people, all of the time – he's been telling them that a genuine," he pronounced each of the three syllables separately, "end-of-days prophet was about to appear."

Bruster paused to let that one sink in, while the studio audience registered their lack of esteem for the preacher in question. "And, amazingly, this latter-day wonder-worker would make his appearance – where else? – on Billy Lee's little one-man stage."

The audience laughed, though not sympathetically to Hardacre's claims, and Bruster waited until the sound died before he said, "But you won't believe this, folks. Guess who this TV huckster, this hack novelist, this sleazy lawyer said his so-called prophet would be?"

One of the audience, apparently not accustomed to rhetorical questions, could be heard saying, "Who?"

Then Bruster lowered his chin so that he could look into the camera over his glasses and said, "Well, he said it would be a guy we all remember as Jesus of Nazareth…"

Shouts went up from the audience, not mocking now but angry; the pundit's audience skewed markedly to the portion of the American population that believe that their Savior was as American as they were, and no more to be trifled with than any other patriotic son of liberty.

Bruster raised his voice over the commotion. "…that's right! Jesus Christ, the son of Mary, our Lord and Savior!"

The shouts were louder, and there was a sound of motion and moving furniture. Bruster showed the outraged studio audience a palm, then another, patting the air gently.

"Well, folks," he said, dropping back into the purr he favored when setting up an on-air lynching, "you'll be glad to know that Billy Lee's messiah turned up today, right on time." More angry growls from off-stage, including one clear recommendation – *Shoot him!* – then Bruster swept one arm toward the place where guests usually entered the set, "and here he is now!"

Chesney said, "We need to go there right now!"

Xaphan said, "Give it a minute."

"They'll tear him apart!"

"Costume!" Instantly, he was clad in his blue and gray garment. "Go! Now!"

"I'm tellin' ya," said the demon, "he don't want rescuin'."

Melda said, "What's going on, Xaphan?"

"Why'ncha watch and see? We can be there any-time you want, puff o' smoke, you name it."

The screen showed Joshua stepping hesitantly into shot from the left, his eyes squinting and blinking against the lights. Bruster had stood up behind the desk and was reaching out a hand to the prophet. But Joshua had not been introduced to the handshake, and seemingly thinking that he was being offered a helping hand, waved away the assistance.

The audience rumbled at the show of discourtesy to their idol, and someone shouted, "Shame!"

The pundit gestured to the guest's seat and the prophet sat down, crossing his legs and showing his sockless, sandaled feet. The wide shot of the two men was replaced by a close-up of the prophet's hairy ap-pendage, the toenails in need of the kind of services Melda supplied to women at Sugar 'n' Spice.

Then the two-shot was restored as Bruster leaned back in his chair, studied the other man for a long mo-ment, and said, "So you're Jesus of Nazareth?"

Joshua was distracted by the growls from beyond the lights, but then he held up a hand in a *wait a minute* gesture and said, "Joshua. Jesus was the name the Greeks gave me, after I was dead."

Harsh laughter from the audience, but Bruster pat-ted it down again and said, "Ohhh-kay, Joshua. But you were around, back in the time of Pontius Pilate, did some miracles, got crucified, rose from the dead."

"Uh huh," said the prophet in a tone that indicated that his mind was on something other than the ques-tion he'd just been asked. He had put both feet on the floor, his forearms on his knees, and was leaning forward to peer intently at the host.

The audience was reacting with loud cries, and this time Bruster was making no effort to pacify them. Indeed, he was making *can you believe it?* faces at the crowd while his hand gestured in Joshua's direction.

At that moment, the prophet stood, reached over, and seized the other man's hand in a strong grip. Bruster reacted as if he had received a jolt of electricity. He rose from his chair and tried to pull his hand free, but Joshua only shook his head and tightened his grip. Chesney could see the cords standing out in the bearded man's wrist.

"Come out of him!" Joshua commanded, in a voice that brooked no defiance. "Both of you! Right now!"

Hall Bruster began to shake. A white froth appeared at the corners of his mouth, his eyes rolled back, and his knees bent as he began to run in place behind the desk. Then his neck bent backwards to an impossible extent. Chesney could hear the bones crack as the back of the pundit's skull almost touched the space between his shoulder blades. His mouth opened wider than it should have been able to, and a roaring voice emerged, making harsh sounds that might have been words, but in a deep timbre that no human vocal apparatus could have produced. It sounded to Chesney like a whale cursing.

Xaphan silently toasted the screen, then said, "And here we go."

Something shadowy yet thick, like dense, roiling smoke, erupted from Bruster's far-too-open mouth. It twisted in the air, then tumbled to the desk, and the shapes of knobbed limbs and joints, a narrow, hairless skull, wart-speckled shoulders, and some even less attractive parts, seemed to take solid form only to dissipate from one moment to the next. And now something else was appearing from the pundit's lips. It looked to Chesney like a pair of giant crab's legs, sickly yellow and tipped with jagged claws, reaching out from within to spread the orifice even wider. Instead of a deep-throated roar, the man's body was now issuing a hissing, gasping voice, the words it was forming full of harsh gutturals and throat-clearing k-sounds.

Someone screamed amid a clatter of chairs and shouts, and a rising din of struggle as the unseen audience fought to put distance between themselves and the glistening, segmented body that was dragging itself out of Bruster's throat and joining the writhing smoke-creature on the desk. The monster lifted its tail to elevate the stinging tip, a drop of pale ichor hanging from the needle point.

But Joshua, still clutching Bruster's hand, pointed a finger at the two horrors on the desktop and said, in a voice that shook the studio walls, "Begone, foul demons! Back to the pit and trouble this soul no more!"

And in a moment, gone they were. The desk was empty, Bruster ceased his high-stepping contortions, and fell back in his chair like a plump puppet whose strings have been cut. He bounced off the back of the seat, his glasses flew off, and his arms barely caught him as he toppled forward to sprawl across the desk.

He lay inert for several seconds as the last sounds of the fleeing audience registered on the overhead microphone. Then he slowly lifted his head, his eyes glazed and blinking, a dribble of drool hanging from one corner of his mouth. "Where... what...?" he said.

Joshua was looking down on him, a kindly expression on the unbearded portion of his face, his eyes pools of compassion. "There," he said, "I'll bet you're glad to have those two out of you."

Bruster looked up, stunned. Then his face took on an expression of pure delight, even as tears sprang from his eyes. He said, "You are my Lord and savior."

"Now, now," said the prophet. "They were just a couple of demons."

But Bruster slid from his chair to his knees and embraced Joshua's ankles. "Lord, Lord," he cried. Then he just cried.

"See?" Xaphan said, gesturing to the screen with the Havana. "Told ya."

The shot of a drooling Hall Bruster, his back being comfortingly patted by the prophet, abruptly disappeared, and was replaced by a notice that technical difficulties had temporarily disrupted the broadcast.

"We should get him out of there," said Chesney. "Some of those people wanted to attack him even before..." He made an expansive gesture, both hands vibrating in mid-air, that connoted a situation that was rapidly going out of control.

"Bring him back here," Melda said. "The media will be looking for him at Hardacre's." She thought for a moment. "And the rev is probably not going to be the most genial of hosts just now."

"Not to mention the old battle-ax," said the demon.

Chesney thought he might have commented at that point, but Joshua had to be his primary concern. "Let's go," he said.

They passed through his room in Hell, the fiend pausing to refill its glass, then relocated to Hall Bruster's television studio, where chaos was apparently settling in for an extended stay. Two men in shirtsleeves, one fat and the other even fatter, had the host by his ankles and armpits and were endeavoring to remove him from the vicinity. A tall, thin man with an earpiece-and-microphone set dangling from a cord around his neck was shouting, "Get back! Get back!" at the prophet, while a short young woman with her hair severely braided was poking at the bearded man with the pointed end of a flagstaff that usually stood in the background of Bruster's set.

Joshua was backing away, palms extended in a placating mode, saying, "He'll be fine. A little wine mixed with honey works wonders."

Chesney said privately to Xaphan, invisible behind him, "Voice of authority," and stepped into the melée. "I'll handle this," he said, in a tone that made Gregory Peck sound like a tenderfoot Boy Scout. The director and the spear-maiden fell back, giving the young man space to step up to the prophet and take him by the arm.

"It's all right," Joshua said.

"No, it's not," Chesney said. He could see past the prophet and across the studio to a side door that led out into a sunlit parking lot. Some members of the audience who had fled the unexpected exorcism were now peeking back into the room. Seeing a welcome absence of demons and an outnumbered false prophet already under attack, their courage was reasserting itself. One fiftyish man with a face lined by a lifetime of delivering stern judgments was already withdrawing a square-barreled, black pistol from under his armpit.

"Xaphan!" the young man said. "Now!" An instant later they were in transit through Chesney's infernal stage point, then before the young man could blink they popped into his apartment's living room.

Joshua looked around and noticed the view from the window. He went over to survey the panorama of river and city. "We're very high up, aren't we?" he said. "Reminds me of the time when the Adversary wanted a chat with me."

"That reminds me," said the demon, "he wants another one."

"What about?" said the prophet.

"He don't tell me that. You gotta ask him yourself."

The bearded man shrugged. "What's the point? We never had much to say to each other."

"I'm just passin' on the message." The demon turned to Chesney. "You want anythin' else?"

"Just put the costume away."

A moment later, he was back in his normal Sunday garb of khakis and checked shirt. The demon was a memory in sulfur, and the prophet was turning away from the window to say, "Now what?"

Melda got up from the couch. "Lunch," she said, then turned to Joshua. "Are there things you're not allowed to eat?"

"There used to be," he said, "but I think all of that's lapsed now."

"Good," she said. "Let me introduce you to a Ball Park Frank."

Monday morning, Seth Baccala called Denby and said, "I think we should talk."

"So do I," said the detective, "and soon."

"Where?" It was an important question for the executive assistant. If Denby wanted to talk down at Police Central, that was one thing; if he wanted to talk at Baccala's office in the Paxton building, it was another. If he wanted to talk at the offices of Baiche, Lobeer, Tressider, that was another thing altogether.

"I'll come to you," Denby said, and Baccala let out a breath he hadn't known he'd been holding.

When the policeman arrived, the executive assistant told his secretary to hold all calls.

"Even from W.T.?" she said.

"He won't be calling." The old man had not been seen in the building since the disappearance of his political consultant and his daughter's nervous collapse.

Denby sat across from Baccala in the visitor's chair, the polished and orderly desk between them. The younger man's seat was slightly higher, and the chair the policeman was in had front legs that were slightly shorter than the back, forcing the sitter to lean forward in a supplicant's pose; it was all intended to give the owner of the office a psychological advantage. Today it didn't.

"Well," said Baccala and waited for what would come.

Denby gave him the same look he'd given the chief of police at the news conference. Then, to make sure there were no mistakes, he said, "I know."

Baccala saw no point in fencing. "The time traveler," he said. It was not a question.

"I saw you. In the file room. On the loading dock."

Baccala nodded. "And you saw them bury her."

"Uh huh."

"Can you make a case?"

Denby looked up into a corner of the room, then back to the other man. "I can go back and record it," he said. "Say they were tapes from security cameras that had just come to light."

Baccala put his hands flat on the desk, looked down at them, and blew out another breath. "That's it, then." A moment later, what the policeman had said sank all the way in. He looked up. "You say you 'can'," he said. "But you haven't."

Denby held his gaze. "No, I haven't."

Baccala waited, but so did the detective. After a while, the younger man said, "You want something."

"Uh huh."

"What?"

Denby did not blink. "The Twenty."

Baccala had been feeling a sense of relief, reading into the policeman's words and manner a growing conviction that Denby was like Hoople and Hanshaw:

a man in search of a payoff. But now a cold shiver went down his back and somehow lodged in his bowels, which were turning to a roiling liquid behind the fine-spun wool of his handmade suit pants and the silk of his boxer's.

"No," he said.

"Okay." Denby stood up. "Do you want to turn yourself in, or will I take you now?" He reached to the small of his back and came up with a pair of handcuffs.

"They'll kill me," Baccala said. "They'll kill you."

"That could happen," the captain said. "And you'd only do a couple of years for manslaughter and concealing a body."

Baccala waited. He knew that wasn't all of it.

"That's right," Denby said. "They wouldn't take the chance on you in prison. You don't have the…" He sought for the word, then went on, "Well, let's say you don't have the breeding. The first time some big lifer showed you what happens behind bars to the delicately boned, you'd be looking for a way out."

"And there is no way out," the younger man said, "is there?"

Denby put away the cuffs but didn't sit down again. He leaned over Baccala's desk and said, "There's one. We take them all down. Make an airtight case and hand it over to the feds. To a federal attorney who wants to be President some day."

Baccala's face felt cold. He knew he must look as pale as the skull beneath his flesh. "Can't be done," he said.

"Can," said the captain. "In a month, I'm going to be the new chief of police. You've already taken

Paxton's place at the table." He leaned in closer. "Everything will be compartmentalized. I know that. So one of us on the inside is not enough. Two of us, it's no better than a maybe."

Baccala sensed a "but" in the offing. He raised his brows.

Denby smiled. "But we've got the time traveler. It's his project. So we'll turn one or two more," he said, "even three or four. We'll cut a few steers out of the herd, then use them to round up the old bulls."

Baccala's hands were trembling. "And what happens to us steers?" he said.

Denby shrugged. "Nothing. At worst, witness protection." Then his tone turned conspiratorial. "Or maybe when that federal attorney gets sworn in as President, you're up there on the platform, too, sitting in the seat reserved for White House Chief of Staff. He'll owe you enough."

The executive assistant was still feeling a vibration passing through his flesh. But now he couldn't tell if it was fear or expectation. "All or nothing," he said.

"Don't it make life interesting?" said the policeman.

"How long do I have to decide?"

"Five seconds."

Baccala swallowed something that didn't taste good. Then he said, "I'm in."

Chesney was at his desk, immersed in a matrix of probabilities that connected risk to cost and profit in the insuring of single women who managed their own white-collar businesses. There were more of them than there had ever been before. He looked up to see Denby opening his office door. The policeman came in and told him about recruiting Seth Baccala to the cause of bringing down the Twenty.

"He gets away?" Chesney said.

"It's how it often works. You use a little fish to catch a bigger one." The captain thought for a minute. "Besides, I bet there hasn't been a day go by that he hasn't regretted what happened to Bannister. Not to mention the way she played him for a sucker."

"Now we'll be doing the same thing," Chesney said. "Playing him the way that reporter did."

"Some people, that's what they're good for."

Five minutes after the policeman left, it was Baccala's turn to step into the actuary's office and close the door. "Denby told you," he said.

"Yes."

There was a peculiar expression on the executive assistant's face. Chesney thought it might be the faintest hope he had ever seen. "The time traveler," Baccala said, "he can't change the past, can he?"

"It doesn't work that way," Chesney said. He saw the emotion disappear from the other man's face, like a few drops of water evaporating from a skillet once the heat is turned on under it.

Afterwards, Chesney tried to think his way through the man's situation. He found that no pool of light shone around Baccala, the way it had around Melda, right from the start. But neither was the man hidden from him in darkness. If he thought about it, he realized, the way he'd thought about not being a prophet, he would be able to bring the man into clearer focus. That was new and different. It was as if he could see the first steps of a trail that led into the murk, and somehow he knew that if he took those first steps, the next ones along the way would become clear to him.

Right now, he didn't feel like pursuing the matter. He had work to do. But before he switched his focus back to the incidence of stress-related illnesses among female management and marketing consultants, Chesney realized something else: the image of a trail leading into darkness was a metaphor – the first he'd ever conceived.

Something is happening to me, he thought. I'm changing. The thought gave him a small frisson of anxiety. But then he thought: Melda will like it. And that was enough. He went back to the numbers, and soon he was at the center of a pool of clear light, listening to the elegant song the statistics sang. He didn't notice himself humming.

The phone rang that evening. Melda picked it up and held it out to Chesney. "Your mother," she said.

If he'd been sitting nearer the phone he would have read the caller ID and not answered. But his girlfriend gave him a meaningful look which he interpreted as *you've got to talk to her*, and he took the phone.

"Billy Lee wants to see you," Letitia Arnstruther said.

"I'm not responsible for what happened to that Bruster fellow," Chesney said. "Billy Lee wanted a prophet. I got him one. The rest of it has noth–"

"You haven't been watching the news, have you?" his mother said.

Chesney hadn't. He'd come home, had dinner with Melda and Joshua and they had sat around talking about inconsequentials. None of them had watched the news, although the prophet had spent most of the day watching television, clicking the remote from one thing to another; mostly, he had been drawn to old situation comedies and soap operas. He found them more comprehensible than much of what else was on the tube, especially the commercials, and especially the ads for forthcoming movies. He'd turned off the big plasma screen when Melda came home from work.

"Turn it on now," his mother said.

"Which news channel?"

"Any of them."

The first scene that came into view was the yellow-clawed demon hauling its segmented body out of Hall Bruster's grossly stretched throat. Then there was footage from Hardacre's show, with Joshua talking about Heaven.

"Is that what I look like?" said the prophet. He cupped an ear. "My voice sounds wrong."

Chesney began an explanation about sound waves heard through the eardrum versus those heard through the maxillary bones behind the ears, but Melda shushed him. The screen was showing the face of Hall Bruster behind a thicket of hands holding microphones. He was wearing a collarless garment of blue cotton. Then the camera pulled back to show him sitting up in a hospital bed, surrounded by reporters.

"…no question," he was saying, his eyes bright behind the dark-rimmed glasses and with an expression Chesney read as childlike delight on his owly face. "No question at all. I had been in the grip of demons for years and years. They controlled me, spoke through my voice, made me do and say terrible things. Terrible."

His face was shaded by a deep sadness as he spoke those words. Then, like the sun coming out from behind smog-filled clouds, it lit up again as Bruster said, "And then he came in and – wham! bam! – set me free."

"When you say, 'he,'" – the voice belonged to one of the off-screen reporters – "for the record, Mr Bruster, who do you mean?"

The talk-show host looked straight into the camera, his eyes wide behind the spectacle lenses. "I mean Jesus Christ, himself, the son of God."

"Oh," said Joshua with a sigh, "not again."

"So you believe," the reporter was saying, nailing it down, "that you have witnessed the second coming of Christ."

Bruster laughed, and for the first time Chesney had heard the sound come out of the man, there was no harshness in it. It was a peal of pure joy. "Witnessed it?" he said. "I *participated* in it!"

"So you retract all the things you said about the Reverend Billy Lee Hardacre?"

"Without hesitation; without qualification. Billy Lee was absolutely right. He has brought us the Messiah!"

"Does that mean," another reporter asked, adopting an ominous tone, "that we have reached the End of Days?"

Bruster shrugged. "What do I know?" he said. "All I can tell you is that I have been delivered from bondage. I was a slave of Hell, but now I am free!"

The camera pulled farther back and focused on the reporter who had lowered his voice to ask the final question. He moved away from the scrum until he was in front of a window, then said, "Well, there you have it, Wolf. If it was some kind of a stunt, it was one for the record books."

The image shifted to a bearded man in a studio backed by a wall of monitors. He said, "I don't know which was the greater miracle, Todd – the casting out of demons or the sight of Hall Bruster praising Billy Lee Hardacre." He looked down, shaking his head, then came back to the camera. "Perhaps it really is the end of the world."

The image cut back to the reporter in the hospital room. He was half turned, looking out the window, saying into his microphone, "That seems to be the dominant opinion, Wolf, judging by the crowd that's forming outside Our Lady of Mercy Hospital." He stepped aside so his camera operator could move up to the window and angle down for a shot of the parking lot, three stories below.

At least five hundred people were massed among the scattering of parked cars, most of them looking up at the camera. Some of them carried home-made signs – Chesney read one that said *Repent* in bold red letters; another said: *If nobody's holding this sign, I've just been raptured.* A pair of police squad cars were belatedly arriving, disgorging uniformed officers who fought their way through the mob to reinforce whoever was keeping the crowd from pushing through the ground-floor doors into the building.

Behind the cops, more people were arriving, including a big yellow ex-school bus that now belonged, according to the black lettering along its side, to Land of Goshen African Baptist Church. From its single door emerged a file of young men and women, all with dark skin and wearing purple robes, who immediately struck up a hymn Chesney remembered from his mother-dominated youth. The strains of *Oh Happy Day* came faintly through the hospital window and were transmitted to the twin speakers of his big-screen TV.

Now the bearded man was back on screen, and this time the memory cue for Chesney was the location shown on the banks of monitors behind him: the wide front steps of Billy Lee's mansion. The door was closed, but Chesney didn't expect that to remain the case, because obviously the preacher had allowed the media past his iron gates. "We're going live," said the program's host, "to the home of the man who began this unprecedented and bizarre series of events, the Reverend Billy Lee Hardacre. He's expected to make a public state–"

The door opened and Chesney's mother stepped out, wearing an expression the young man had often seen before. It told him that his mother had not altered her jaundiced view of persons employed in the media – "guttersnipes and scoundrels" were her usual epithets – but that today she was compelled by a higher calling to place herself, however reluctantly, in proximity to them. He was sure that an eighteenth-century French countess forced to make her way through a rabble of ill-smelling, manure-smeared peasants would have done so with an identical countenance.

Another hedge of hands holding microphones appeared before Letitia Arnstruther's face as the reporters rushed up the steps to catch whatever she had to say. Which was, "Get back, all of you!"

The hedge did not recede, even when the woman folded her arms across her considerable chest and elevated her chin to a devastating angle. Finally, she sniffed a disdainful sniff, and accepted the inevitable. "My husband," she said, then repeated the words as if savoring them: "My husband will make a statement shortly. He will take no questions."

She hadn't said that she would take no questions, and was immediately bombarded with them. Most of them could be expressed in the two words spoken by a brunette whose hair swept down to become twin sharp points beside her chin, their tips seemingly hard and sharp enough to pierce her flesh if ever she swung her head too briskly to either side: "Where's Jesus?"

Letitia favored the woman with another look that Chesney remembered, the one that ought to have laid its recipient instantly unconscious, if not actually dead on the spot. "He's not Je–" she managed, in her iciest tone, before the door behind her opened and Billy Lee Hardacre stepped into view.

He was dressed in his television outfit, with lifts in his boots and the silver mane of expensive acquired hair shining in the lights mounted on the cameras. He patted the air in front of him in a quieting gesture and said, "I have a statement."

"Where's Jesus?" said the brunette, but Hardacre ignored her.

"As you know," he said, "for some time now I have been telling you that a prophet would soon arrive. My statements were met with widespread disbelief, even mockery from some figures in the media." He paused and looked around at the throng of reporters. "Maybe from some of you here today."

Chesney studied his stepfather's face. There was an expression there that he hadn't seen before. He said to Melda, "Does he look all right to you?"

"He looks," she said, "like he's as batty as a bipolar bedbug. But I think we'd better listen to this."

Hardacre had been itemizing some of the things that had been said about him, and the media personalities who had said them. Hall Bruster came in for special mention, but so did the man with the neatly trimmed beard standing in front of the banks of monitors. Chesney was impressed at the power of Hardacre's memory, which apparently gave the preacher total recall of every unkind cut and the ability to reproduce them with the same fidelity to accuracy that Letitia had demanded of her son when she used to make him recite an entire psalm, of her choosing, before letting him taste a first bite of dinner.

Now Hardacre was finally moving however. "Yesterday," he said, "the whole world witnessed my complete vindication. He who had mocked me loudest and longest was revealed to have himself been for many years in thrall to the forces of darkness."

He paused as if to savor the thought of Hall Bruster under the demon's lash, then said, "There can be no further question about the identity of the prophet I have brought before you. He is, indeed, the Jesus of the Gospels. And, as prophesied, he has come back."

"Where is he?" said a reporter, while another said, "Bring him out, Billy Lee!"

Hardacre said nothing until the silence was restored. "The question now," he said, "is what does it mean? Why has he come? What will happen next?"

He looked around with a showman's air, until finally one of the reporters said, "Well, what does it mean?"

The preacher showed the camera a wide smile. "It means," he said, "just what it's supposed to mean – the end of the world."

Behind him, Chesney saw his mother's face set itself into a frown that was even deeper than usual. Then his attention was drawn to the other people in his own living room as Melda responded to Hardacre's announcement by bursting out with, "Oh, Jeez! Tell me he didn't say that!"

The prophet himself rose from the couch and said, "He said it, but he shouldn't have."

"What kind of game is he playing?" Melda said, then turned back to the screen and said, "Wait a sec, what did he just say?"

Hardacre was looking straight at them from the screen, having chosen to speak into the camera of the cable news network they were tuned to. "I'll repeat that," he said. Then he carefully enunciated an address, complete with apartment number.

It was Chesney's address.

"We've got to get out of here," said Melda. "And right now."

Chesney said, "Xaphan!"

The demon appeared, a smoking cigar sticking out of the side of its muzzle. Joshua gave the fiend a hard look but the weasel-headed creature drew itself up to its full semi-height and said, "Don't look at me. I just do what I'm told."

"We've got to go somewhere and hide," Chesney said. The nearest TV broadcast center was only blocks away. It could not more than minutes before the first camera crew came knocking on his door.

"You can't take him to Hell," Xaphan said. "Last time he showed up there, he made a real mess of the files."

"He'll be recognized anywhere we go," Chesney said.

"Maybe some remote cabin?" Melda said. "Or a desert island? Just until we figure out what to do."

Joshua said to the demon, "It was you who brought me out of Nazareth, wasn't it?"

"Yeah. What of it?"

"Where did you get that power?"

The padded shoulders shrugged. "I dunno." A stubby thumb gestured at Chesney. "I operate on his will."

"But not his power," said the prophet, "because he doesn't have that much." Xaphan, inspecting his spats, said nothing. "Come on," said the bearded man, "out with it."

"Aw, lay off!" said the demon.

"I can compel you," Joshua said. "You know I can."

The fiend looked to Chesney. "You gonna let him push me around like this?"

The young man said, "I want to hear the answer."

The weasel jaws clamped around the cigar. The huge eyes became slits as it looked from Chesney to the prophet. "You know the answer," it said.

"Where is he?" Joshua said.

"Away. And I'm not supposed to disturb him."

"But not so long ago you were passing on a message that he wants to see me. Now, where is he?"

"That place," said the demon. "Where it all started."

"What place?" Chesney said, but the prophet was already telling the demon to take them there. The padded shoulders shrugged again, just as they heard a knock on the door that led to the hallway. A gleam of bright light showed all around the portal, as someone on the other side aimed a television camera at it.

The knock came again and a voice said, "Hello, in there. This is the First Response news team. We're looking for the son of God."

Chesney said to the demon, "Wherever Joshua's talking about, take us there! All of us! Right now!"

The demon took the cigar from its mouth and blew a puff of blue smoke that expanded to become a rectangle taller than Chesney. Xaphan bowed like a potentate's doorman and gestured for the three of them to step through. Joshua went first, then Chesney, holding Melda's hand and drawing her after him. The living room disappeared: they were again in the gray haze, but only for a moment. Then they were standing among some chest-high plants, breathing pristine air laden with the scents of sweet grass and a dozen different blossoms.

Joshua looked around and said, "Under the Tree, I suppose?"

"Natch," said the demon.

"Lead us there."

He set off between the plants. Chesney followed, still holding Melda's hand. There was a faint path worn in the luxuriant grass and they followed it to a clearing. In the middle of the open space, a huge tree towered over every other plant, its branches heavily laden with ripe fruit. Beneath the lower limbs stood a table and chair, the latter occupied by a slim, dark figure who was writing with a fountain pen on a pad of paper.

The Devil finished the line he was writing before pausing to look up. "Ah," he said, "there you are. Welcome back to Eden."

THIRTEEN

"I thought this was a meeting of the Twenty," Seth Baccala said, frozen in the doorway to the big conference room. He looked around the great table. All the other chairs were empty.

"No," said Tressider, seated in his usual place. "just you and me. It's good that you showed up. I thought we should have a talk about where things stand."

This was to be a test, the younger man knew. He could turn and run. The old lawyer would not pursue him. But between here and his car, parked in the basement garage, someone would surely intercept him. Fighting down a tremor that began at his knees and rose to trouble his lower bowel, he stepped into the room.

The lawyer watched him take a seat, his aquiline face unreadable, his fingers interlaced over the slight bulge of his belly. The silence in the room was broken only by the measured ticking of an antique pendulum clock on the far wall. When it had first been hung there it had been brand new.

Baccala pulled out a chair that rolled smoothly on silent casters and sat down. He summoned up the whole of his training, first as a lawyer, then as a student in one of the country's best business schools, and met Tressider's gaze. He leaned back in the chair and crossed his legs. Look confident, and you'll feel confident. Or so his mentors had taught him.

"So," the lawyer said, his voice soft, "how bad is it?"

Baccala imitated the tone. "He knows."

"What does he know?"

"All of it," said the younger man. "You, me, Hoople."

"How?"

"Remember the tale about the time traveler?"

Tressider's answer was his raised eyebrows.

"It's real," Baccala said. "He's real." The lawyer digested this in silence. The younger man did not trespass on the older's thought processes.

Finally, Tressider looked down at his interlocked fingers, pulled them apart and put them tip to tip. Staring at them, he said, "So now what?"

"So now we give Denby what he wants."

"And is that us?"

"No," Baccala said. "It's in."

The lawyer looked up. "He wants in?"

"He's already made his move," the other man said. "Hoople's retiring, and before he goes he'll name Denby his successor. Hanshaw will rubber-stamp it."

"He moves fast." Tressider made a thoughtful noise in his throat. "The question is, where does he move next?"

Baccala had anticipated this question, but he said, "How do you mean?"

"The time traveler changes the game. Denby could take down all of us."

Baccala made a show of thinking about it, then said, "Except for one thing. The time traveler doesn't work for Denby; it's the other way around."

"You're sure of that?"

And now came the hard part: lying to a man who did it for a living, and who had a long lifetime's experience in judging whether others were telling him the truth. But Baccala had not only been to one of the best business schools; he had graduated with honors. "I am," he said. "I challenged him to produce a recording, anything to link me to the crime. He folded."

Tressider studied him for a long moment. Then he slowly nodded. "You should have stayed here," he said at last. "You'd have been a first-rate lawyer. You're wasted on Paxton."

Baccala inclined his head.

The older man was thinking again, working it through. "The question then becomes," he said, "what does the mystery man want?"

"That we don't know, and may never know." Baccala uncrossed his legs leaned back, studying the clock. "It might be that, even if he told us, we wouldn't understand it." When the lawyer shot him a sharp look, he explained, "Could you explain credit default swaps to a medieval baron?"

"I could explain anything to anybody," Tressider said. "That's why I bill at a thousand dollars a half-hour. But I take your point." He rubbed his hands together as if kneading something between them. "So the time traveler has an agenda that has nothing to do with us. He needs Denby to make it work, and Denby uses that need to get what he wants."

"That's my read on it," Baccala said.

The clock ticked on. Tressider's eyes were unfocused for a while, then they came back to the younger man. "I never took Denby for an ambitious man."

"Maybe he never had the opportunity. At least he never made waves."

Tressider went back inside his head. After a while, he rubbed a fingertip down the bridge of his long, thin nose and said, "Then I think we're all right."

"Business," said Baccala, "as usual."

The lawyer made a noncommittal motion of his head. "But we watch him," he said. "Watch him well."

Baccala stood. A trickle of sweat ran down his back, but it wouldn't show under the well-tailored suit. He rode the elevator back down to the garage, and was sensible enough not to let his posture show even half of the relief he felt. There would be cameras, and Tressider would be watching.

For a while there, Billy Lee Hardacre had been sure it had all been going wrong. First, Chesney had refused to have anything to do with the new chapter in the great divine book. Then he had brought back Joshua bar Yusuf, the historical Jesus, from a discarded draft, and the prophet had lit up *The New New Testament of the Air* with all the power of a snuffed out candle wick.

But then it had all turned around in two minutes on Hall Bruster's show. Hardacre had taped and replayed more than once the few seconds of video of Bruster in his hospital bed, when he looked into the camera and said, "Billy Lee was absolutely right. He has brought us the Messiah!"

Now the media were camped outside on his lawn, cameras trained on his front door, with behind them half the world waiting for his next prophetic utterance. And, more than that, beyond the closed gates of his estate – now guarded by a police phalanx – thousands of people were standing, sitting on lawn chairs they'd brought or in their cars and pickups, lying in any shade they could find, wandering around, trying to get a peek at the man who had brought them the first act in the end of the world.

Thousands had already come; thousands more kept arriving. Billy Lee had gone up to one of the dormer windows in the mansion's roof and peered out through a slit in the curtains. The police were trying to keep the crowd off the road, but had let them spread out into the empty field across the way. The cops had even cut down the wire fence – it was either that or see the crowd tear it down with their bare hands.

But the mood was carnival-like. People had brought instruments – mostly guitars and amplifiers – and several church choirs had come. Or maybe they had formed spontaneously. it was definitely a church-going demographic out there, the preacher thought, people who had been looking forward to the end of the world the way rock fans used to look forward to a farewell tour of their favorite groups. Now here it was, come at last, and they were determined to make the most of the experience. If Billy Lee had thought to secure the Armageddon tee-shirt concession, he could soon be even richer than potboilers and TV preaching had ever made him.

He came down the stairs and went into his study, poured himself a twelve year-old single malt and let the first sip of it dissolve in his mouth. It was all working out as the angel had led him to believe. "Mysterious ways, indeed," he said, and took another sip. It wasn't the money; he already had plenty of that, and money had never been for him what it was for so many of the rich, just a way of keeping score.

Billy Lee had always known, deep in his core, that he was special, that he was marked out for some great purpose. When he'd had the revelation and gone to divinity school, he thought he'd found his path. Then they'd mocked and ridiculed him. But now he saw – and soon they would all be brought to see – that he was the most important man of the age, even of all the ages. The world would never be the same, and that was because of his doing.

And now he didn't need his wife's oddball son. He didn't need the ancient Judaean. He refilled the glass and carried it over to the big desk – the same one on which he'd written *The Baudelaire Conspiracy* and *The Rimbaud Killings*, all those years ago. Instead of a typewriter, he turned on a slim-bodied laptop, leaned back in the plush recliner chair, and set the wireless keyboard on his lap. His word processing program came up automatically and he opened a new file.

His fingers descended to the keys and he typed: *The Book of Jesus*. He centered the five words then dropped the cursor down and began to type. *As it was in the beginning, so it was at the end. God looked down upon the Earth and said, "I will choose me a messenger and raise him up above all the tumult of the world, that men and women may know that he speaks with my Voice."*

A light shone on the man at the desk and he looked up. The angel with whom he had composed the *Book of Chesney* had appeared in the corner of the study. "Be not afraid," it said.

"I'm not," said Hardacre, "but I'm busy. What do you want?"

"To see if you needed assistance."

"No. I know how to do this. Especially now that it's just me."

"As you wish," said the figure in white and disappeared.

Hardacre paused for a moment to recapture the thread, then typed: *And God said, "To bear witness before all humanity that the chosen one speaks my truth, I will send unto him my only begotten son, and the world will see them sit down together."*

Hardacre took another sip of the good whiskey and read over what he had written. He moved the cursor up a line and put the word "inerrant" between "my" and "truth," and smiled. "The thing writes itself," he said to the empty room, and put his fingers to the keyboard again.

Down in the smoky bowels of Hell, in an anteroom just off Lucifer's main office, the figure in white that had just come from Hardacre's study popped into view. The Devil's first assistant, an elephant-sized demon with rank of Archduke, the general shape of a mouse, and the dentition of a Nile crocodile, looked up from a ledger in which it had been making an entry, slitted its coal-black eyes against the glare, and said, "You've been told!"

The light dimmed, the angelic form shimmered. A moment later, in its place stood a demon with the limbs and body of a mantis and the head of a four-eyed ginger cat. It offered no apology but said, 'Where's the boss?"

The mouse finished the entry, the quill pen scratching on the parchment. "Out."

"Still?"

"You question?"

The thin fiend said nothing, that being the wisest course. The huge mouse stared at it for a while, to re-inforce the slight difference in rank between them, then said, "Report."

The mantis shoulders shrugged. "Hook, line and sinker," it said.

"He's going for it?"

"If the world does not end," said the insectoid fiend, "it won't be for any lack of effort on the part of Billy Lee Hardacre."

"Can I offer you some fruit?" said Lucifer, gesturing to the laden boughs above them.

"That's not funny," said Joshua, "but then you never were."

Melda reached up and touched one of the hanging orbs. It was pale yellow and smooth-skinned. "It's not an apple," she said. "I thought it was an apple."

"So did some Renaissance painter," said the Devil, "and the image stuck."

"What will happen if I eat it?" she said.

Chesney answered her, drawing on his extensive store of biblical lore. "Nothing. It's the Tree of the Knowledge of Good and Evil, and you've already got that." He looked about. "Somewhere around here should be the Tree of Life – eat that and you live forever."

"In retrospect," said the Devil, looking up into the great mass of wood and foliage above them, "this should have been a clue. It's what he has always been interested in, from the very beginning."

"You're saying that Billy Lee Hardacre was right," Chesney said, "that the world is a book God's writing so he can work out the meaning of right and wrong?"

"I don't think there can be any doubt of it. Look around you. We're standing in a previous draft."

"Which brings us," Joshua said, "to the pertinent question: why?"

Lucifer gave him a look of mild exasperation. "Don't play the simpleton. You know why."

The prophet looked down at the paper on the table, the spiky handwriting. "I know why you're here. You wanted to get away somewhere quiet to work on that. Hell can be, well, Hell, when you're trying to concentrate."

"It doesn't exactly run itself," Satan said.

"But that doesn't explain what we're doing here."

A slim finger dismissively indicated Chesney and Melda. "They're here because they came with you. You're the one I summoned."

"I don't come when summoned by the likes of you," said the prophet. "I took it as a request."

"You also needed a quiet place to hide out."

"Nazareth is quiet. I could've gone back to it."

The Devil smiled knowingly. "But you didn't."

Chesney was following the conversation closely. Often, as he'd gone through life, he'd been puzzled by the things people said to each other, especially in situations charged with emotion. But this was different. The two disputants, if this was indeed a dispute, seemed to be bathed in clear light – although, he had to admit, that was probably to be expected in the Garden of Eden – and the young man was able to anticipate correctly what each was about to say. It was a novel experience, and enjoyable, but he was becoming tired of the sparring. He wished they would get down to the business at hand.

Joshua was saying, "I recall there was another time when you were eager to talk to me."

"You came then, too."

"Only to stop your importuning."

The Devil laughed, the way only the Devil could. "Importunate, was I? How kind of you to overlook it."

"And then," said the prophet, "you wanted me to bow down to you, and then you'd give me all the kingdoms of the world." It was Joshua's turn to laugh.

Lucifer shrugged. "I admit," he said, "it was a poorly thought-out proposition."

"It was another kingdom entirely that I was after."
Joshua raised his gaze to the firmament that, in this
draft, still existed as a solid dome above the Earth.

A gleam of triumph lit the stygian darkness in the
Adversary's eyes, and Chesney was not surprised when
he said, "And how did that work out for you?"

There was a silence broken only by the incredibly
beautiful song of a bird somewhere in the tree above
them. Joshua's face took on a reflective cast. "We all
make mistakes," he said.

Lucifer bore in on him. "The truth, you used to say,
would set you free."

The prophet smiled wryly. "You're a great one for
the quoting," he said.

This time, the slim, sharp-nailed finger pointed directly at the bearded man. "Admit it, he played you just
as he played me. He called you to be his prophet, he sent
you out to preach the end of the world and the coming
of the kingdom. Then he decided to go another way, and
left you hanging. Literally, and I'm sure, quite painfully."

Joshua sighed. "If it means that much to you, then,
yes, I admit it. Things did not turn out as I expected."

"And then he made a new version of you," Lucifer
said, "who sits on his right hand, and is somehow him
and his own son – and occasionally, a pigeon – while
you were eased out of Heaven and deposited by the
side of a road no one ever travels."

"True, too," said the prophet. "Yet here I am."

"Exactly," said Lucifer. "And so am I."

"It doesn't feel," said the bearded man, "like a meeting of minds."

"You haven't heard what I have to say to you."

Now it was Joshua's turn to shrug. "I heard it two thousand years ago. I don't expect it has changed. You want to be in charge. You've always wanted to be in charge, because you feel you're entitled to that role."

Satan's expression was a blank, the dark and terribly beautiful face absolutely still. Then the severe lips split into a smile of triumph. "Got you!" he said. He clapped his hands together. "Got you completely!"

Joshua frowned. "What?" he said. "You don't want to be the one who says what all the others do?"

"That," said the Devil, "is the role I was meant to play. "I've decided not to."

The prophet cocked his head to one side, studying the figure before him. "That's the decision that got you into trouble in the first place."

Lucifer wagged a finger. "Oh, no. Rebelling was what I was supposed to do. As I said, he played me no less than he played you."

"So now you're rebelling against your own rebelliousness?"

Chesney had heard enough. "Excuse me," he said, "but I think it's time you two stopped monologuing and got down to the point."

The Devil turned a cold gaze on him, then spoke to Joshua. "Control your monkey," he said.

Chesney did not wait for the bearded man to respond. "Listen," he said, "it's perfectly clear what's going on here." He indicated Lucifer. "You've had to accept the truth that you're just a character in the great book that–"

"Not so great," the Devil said.

"Hush," said Joshua, "let him speak."

"Just a character like Melda and me and everybody else who ever was or ever will be," Chesney said. "Like you, too." He inclined his head toward the bearded man then turned back to Lucifer. "At first, you didn't want to accept it. I remember how, when Billy Lee first told you that's how things were, you refused to believe it. But when you went back to Hell and thought about it, after a while you couldn't deny it anymore."

"I've always been an advocate of facing the facts," Satan said, "however unpleasant."

"Though usually," said Joshua, "you're the one responsible for the unpleasantness."

Chesney stepped back into the conversation. "But that's just his role in the story. He's the bad guy. The difference is, now he knows what he is."

The Devil was regarding the young man with a considering look. "And what happens when a character knows that he's a character, and knows what his role should be?"

Chesney knew the answer. "He either says yes to that. Or he says no." He turned to Joshua. "He's saying no."

The unbearded parts of the prophet's face were skeptical. "He's going to give up doing evil?"

"No," said Chesney. "He likes it too much. But he's going to pay a larger role in the story." He turned to Lucifer. "You already have, haven't you?"

The Devil smiled and said nothing.

Melda said, "Oh, my–" then though better of completing the expression. "You've been behind all of this, haven't you? Billy Lee wanting Chesney to be a prophet, the book he was writing, bringing in Josh here. Even when I won that poker game in Hell. It's all been a plot that you've been developing!"

"And what a plot it has been," said Lucifer. "I believe I am entitled to pride of authorship. Still," – he bowed slightly to Joshua – "I needed your assistance to have convinced a sizeable and growing proportion of humanity that the end of the world is in the offing. And I have set your friend Hardacre on the path to becoming the most influential man on Earth."

"The Antichrist," Chesney said.

Satan smiled again, and again said nothing.

"But what good does it do you," Melda said, "to bring on the end of the world? Everything wraps up and you lose."

Another smile, another silence.

"Because it won't end," said Chesney. "God won't let it, because the story doesn't work out that way. He's still got to deal with the problem he set for himself here." He pointed a finger up at the hanging fruit.

Joshua had been following the discussion with a thoughtful face. Now his brow cleared. "You don't want the end of the world," he said to Satan. "You want a new chapter." He looked down at the papers on the table, laughed and shook his head. "He'd never let you. Be as self-aware a character as you want, he's not going to let you write the story."

One last smile from Lucifer, one last silence. Chesney had known for a while the answer to the question Joshua had asked when they'd first arrived in Eden.

Now he said, "He doesn't expect to write it, at least not all of it." He looked at the prophet. "He wants to work on it with you. You'd be co-authors."

"You can even have," said Satan, "top billing. How's that for transcending the limits of character?"

Joshua blinked. "Why would I?"

The Devil spread his elegant hands. "You certainly don't have to. We can just let the Reverend Hardacre go on arranging the end of the world."

"And the end of all your plans," Joshua said.

"Not if the young woman is correct. And I think she is. The worst that would happen is that he'll throw aside the current draft and pick up from before the recent sequence of events began."

Chesney said, "Before I accidentally caused Hell to go on strike. You had some headaches then, if I recall."

Lucifer conceded the point with a nod. "The question then becomes: do I come through the transition knowing what I know now?"

"A substantial risk," said the prophet.

"If I wasn't prepared to take risks, I'd still be up in Heaven singing that same endless song through all eternity." Satan smiled yet again, this one the smile of one who sees a win on the next roll of the dice. "You, of course, would be back in Nazareth. Living the same changeless day through all eternity. Or until he finally writes 'The End.'"

Joshua said nothing, folded his arms and looked at his sandaled feet. The bird sang again and a cooling breeze ruffled the leaves of the Tree of Knowledge.

After a while, still studying his toes, he said, "A partnership?"

"Yes," said Lucifer.

"No bowing down?"

"You may have not noticed, but a little while ago I bowed to you."

The prophet tapped three fingers on a bicep. "How do you see the story developing?"

The Devil gestured at the table. "I've been making some preliminary notes." He moved his hand again and a second chair appeared, beside the one he had been sitting in. Chesney noted that the two seats were identical and of equal height. He took it as a good sign.

Joshua moved over and sat, picking up the top page. Satan sat beside him.

Chesney said, "What about Hardacre and the end of the world?"

Lucifer looked up. "That's your problem. You started all this."

"Joshua?" the young man said.

The prophet's eyes didn't leave the paper as he said. "You can handle it. I think you know that now. Besides, as my would-be co-author here says, it probably won't actually happen."

The Devil said, "Consider yourself one of his mysterious ways." Then he turned his eyes to the papers, and Chesney was dismissed.

"Come on," said Melda, taking his arm. Xaphan had disappeared and they had the rest of the garden to themselves. "We'll go look at the Tree of Life and figure out what to do." She smiled at him in a way he had come to recognize as having a particular meaning. "I believe I can think of something already."

Letitia Arnstruther was a house divided against itself. One half of her was foursquare behind the man who had changed her life, a man who was a genuine prophet – or at least a precursor – who was regularly in the presence of an angel from on high, and a high-ranking one to boot. The other half was just as adamant that the beardy-weirdy that Billy Lee Hardacre had presented to the world as Jesus of Nazareth could not possible be as advertised. Her Lord and Savior was not an olive-skinned, curly-headed, squat little fellow with hands like a plowman's and grime-encrusted toenails.

If Billy Lee's relationship with the man who called himself Joshua bar Yusuf had been a minor facet of her husband's large and consequential life – if Joshua had been, say, some distant relative he saw twice a year – Letitia could have weathered the discomfort. But the alleged prophet was now central to the preacher's career. Billy Lee had hitched his wagon to that particular mule, as Letitia's father used to say, and now he would have to follow the road it was taking.

Ordinarily, the situation would have caused her no serious problem. She was a woman of mature years who was used to dealing with wrong-headed people who refused to exercise the sense God gave them. In any other circumstance, Letitia Arnstruther would have girded up her formidable loins and waded into battle against Billy Lee's error. But she was undone by a simple fact: she had witnessed with her own eyes the oily little man's casting out of not one, but two, full-weight demons from that odious tub-thumper, Hall Bruster.

And it wasn't just the fact that Joshua cast out the demons – it was the manner of the casting out: no ritual, no paraphernalia, no tedious hours of praying and throwing of holy water. He had just said, "Out you go," and out they went. To Letitia's comprehensive knowledge of matters spiritual, only one person had ever had that kind of power: the person Joshua said he was; the person she said he wasn't.

Is it just me, she asked herself, sitting in the mansion's breakfast nook, staring at the congealed egg yolk on her china plate and holding a coffee cup whose contents had gone cold while she pondered her dilemma? Am I just being prideful?

She remembered what had happened to her when her willfully errant son had caused the fuss with Hell that led to all the tempter demons walking off the job for a couple of days. Letitia had lost interest in her life's work: scourging sinners and hypocrites by sending them long letters that detailed the imaginative torments awaiting them in the afterlife. It had become clear that the main source of her letter-writing energy had been her own vanity – the old, original sin of pride. Now she had to wonder whether her refusal to accept Joshua as the returned messiah was born of nothing more than the fact that he did not measure up to Letitia Arnstruther's high expectations.

She wished she had someone to talk it over with. Ideally, that would have been her father, with his

analytical lawyer's mind and inborn common sense, but
he was long since gone to his reward. It ought to have
been the excellent substitute she had found for her old
dad, Billy Lee Hardacre. But her husband did not take
an objective view of the issue; when she had tried to
broach her concerns, he had told her to leave him be –
he was authoring the next chapter of the greatest book
ever written, and had no time for fripperies.

Had he been anyone else, Billy Lee's aiming of the
word "fripperies" at Letitia would have earned him an
ear-bending of the first magnitude. But she was still in
the enthrallment phase of their romance, when the
very thought of hard words reduced her insides to a
quivering, jelloid state. It had only happened to her
once before, and by the time she got over it, she was
pregnant with Chesney and it was too late to alter the
course of her life.

She didn't want anything like that to happen again.
She wanted her dilemma resolved, and, plainly, she
would need someone to help her. But there was no
one else in her sharply circumscribed life but the produce of that first infatuation, and she had never found
her son to be of any use whatsoever, outside the narrow sphere of arithmetic.

But then, as the coffee in her cup passed from luke-
warm to cool, she thought about Chesney as he had
lately manifested himself. He was making gains in his
profession. He was chalking up some remarkable ac-
complishments in his secondary career – or hobby, she
wasn't sure – as a crimefighter. He had stood up to Billy
Lee, who was no slouch in the forceful personality

sweepstakes. And he had, for the first time, managed to achieve a relationship with a woman.

Not that Letitia approved of Melda McCann. On principle, she did not. But neither was she blind to the effect that the young woman, for all her flaws, was having on her son. Chesney's mother had been no less surprised to see the young man work through the thought process that had led him to say no to Billy Lee. It was the first time she had ever seen Chesney do anything other than leap to an immediate conclusion or declare the problem as insoluble.

And now, as she considered the implications, Letitia came to a fresh insight: could it be that Chesney and Melda together added up to a competent, reasonably rounded person? The more she thought about it, the truer it became. She put down the coffee cup and reached for the phone. A moment later, a strange voice spoke in her ear.

"Who is this?" Letitia said.

"Who's asking?" said the man who had answered her son's phone.

"I want to speak to Chesney," she said.

"Who doesn't?" said the unknown man. He had an overly self-satisfied manner of speaking acquired by those who were trained in schools that fed new stock into the ranks of radio and television commentators. Now he said, "Are you calling on behalf of Billy Lee Hardacre?"

"I am calling," Letitia said, "on behalf of no one but myself!"

"The caller ID says you're calling from Billy Lee Hardacre's phone." There was a pause, then the voice said, with a rising pitch of excitement, "Wait a minute, are you the older woman who's shacked up–"

"How dare you!" Letitia pulled the phone away from her ear and stared at it as if it had suddenly transmogrified into a scorpion and stung her. "My husband and I are duly married according to the rites of–"

"We've checked. There's no marriage license, no registration." Letitia made sounds, but none of them were actual words. Then the man said, "But we don't need to go into that on-air. It's a side issue. Especially if you tell us where Jesus is hiding out." There was a pause, during which Letitia's pulse was loud in her own ear. "Come on, lady," the man said, "we don't have all day."

She hung up. She sat in the breakfast nook for a long moment, her vision focused inward on scenes that, if ever reproduced on film, would require a stronger rating than PG-13. Then she gathered herself together and made her way to her husband's study, entering without knocking.

Billy Lee was at his desk, his fingers on his laptop's keyboard. The big-screen television was also on and he was dividing his attention between the two. On the larger display, a vast crowd was surging through a great plaza ringed by classical buildings. The image switched to a close-up of people straining at a barricade, shouting the same word over and over. A commentator's voice was saying, "…and here at the Vatican, a crowd estimated at well over a hundred thousand is chanting, 'Parousia, parousia!' – that's the technical term for the Second Coming – and demanding that the Pope come out and speak to them."

The image switched to another crowd, this one with angry faces and shaking fists. "Meanwhile, in Cairo," said the voice-over, "the Grand Mufti has summoned leading scholars of the Muslim world to a convocation at the Mosque of–"

Hardacre killed the sound. "It's happening all over the world," he said. "And all because of the Bruster thing. Look." He turned the laptop so she could see its screen. She saw the casting out of the clawed demon. "YouTube," Billy Lee said, "it's gone mega-viral. See the counter here?" – his finger touched a multidigited number on he screen – "It's had two hundred and thirty million hits. Google's crashed twice, just trying to handle the traffic."

Letitia said, "I want to talk to Chesney and Melda."

"Call 'em up." Hardacre's eyes went back to the big screen. Another mob. This one seemed to be turning over taxis in Times Square.

"I can't," she said. "They've gone into hiding. After you set the media on them."

Billy Lee shrugged but didn't take his eyes off the television. "I needed Josh to be out of the way for a while. I figured that would do it." Now something he was seeing must have given him an inspiration. He touched a key on the laptop and a word processing file came up, filling the screen with text. He began to type.

Letitia felt an impulse to close the computer on her husband's key-rattling fingers. She resisted it and said, "I want you to help me."

Billy Lee didn't look up. "Me? How?"

"The angel. Summon the Throne."

The man typed a few more words, moved the cursor back and added a couple more. "Is that a good idea?"

"Yes."

He typed another line, backspaced out the last word and put in another one. "I don't think so."

For Letitia, the enthrallment phase was definitely dwindling. "Do it," she said. "Please."

"Why?"

"I'm trying to decide what to do. I want their help."

"There's nothing *to* do," he said, eyes still on the lap-top screen, fingers still on the keyboard. "It's the end of the world."

She waited. He went back to typing. "You're not going to do it?" she said.

"Do what?"

She left the study, went into the foyer. Outside, she could hear the buzz of conversation, the more distant sound of hymn-singing. The media were still en-camped between the front door and the gate, and the fields beyond were becoming a revivalist's version of Woodstock. She could not leave. The moment she opened the door, she'd be mobbed.

She stood in the middle of the great hall, thinking. For the first time since the doctor had told her she was preg-nant, she felt cornered. She hadn't liked it then, and liked it even less now. She sorted through the options, not liking any of them. Then she settled on the least evil.

"Xaphan!" she said. "I summon you!"

Nothing happened.

"I don't have time for this!" she said. "You come here right now!"

A faint whiff of sulfur and cigar smoke touched her nose. She turned and saw the diminutive demon hovering in the air so that its eyes were level with hers. The Havana in one small fist poked in her direction. "I don't work for you," the fiend said. "You summon me, I can demand your soul."

"Pish," she said, "and tush. Where's my son?"

"I don't gotta tell you nuttin'."

"True. And next time I see him I'll tell him to cut off the rum and cigars."

"He don't listen to you, toots. I seen that plenty."

"You want to take that chance?"

The demon studied her, its huge round eyes closing to slits. It seemed to be weighing things up, then it lifted its shoulders briefly and said, "Just this once. He's in the garden."

She looked towards the rear of the big house. "What, you mean outside? Here?"

"Not that garden. The–"

"Never mind," she said. "Take me to him, now!"

The fiend bridled, then its eyebrows raised thoughtfully, and in a moment they were passing through a gray nothingness. A moment later, they emerged into a place of sweet, perfumed air borne on the softest of breezes, a low-key paradise of rustling leaves and nodding blossoms. A great tree soared above them and Letitia's feet were sunk into the softest, greenest sward of grass she had ever known.

But they weren't the only things sunk into the emerald turf. So were the naked buttocks of Melda McCann. And sunk into Melda's upturned softest parts was Letitia Arnstruther's son Chesney, his own narrow rump rising and falling with a speed and an athletic certitude that took his mother by surprise.

Then, of course, came the shock. She involuntarily shouted out his name. So, at that moment, by coincidence, did Melda. The young man obviously hearkened to one and not the other, because his cadence increased in both alacrity and power, and matters went swiftly on to their inevitable conclusion.

Voicing a single syllable, Letitia turned away, to find herself being regarded with satisfaction by a saber-toothed, weasel-headed creature in a suit left over from an Edward G. Robinson gangster film. The demon tapped ash from the tip of his cigar, winked one over-sized eye, and said, "You asked for it."

FOURTEEN

Hardacre finished polishing the draft, saved the file and got himself another Scotch. It had taken even less time than he'd thought, because he found he'd been able to lift segments from the *Book of Chesney* and adapt them to the new gospel. That was good, he thought, because the hyperactive news cycle had to be continually fed new material to spin and regurgitate, and the prophet's casting out of Bruster's demons had just about worn out its allotted time upon the stage. The cable news channels had already gone through the "what happened?" stage as well as "how did you feel when it happened?", and now they were well into "what does it mean?" Soon, they would move on to the "what next?" phase, and if they were not handed something fresh to beat to death, they would start looking around for a blonde woman gone mysteriously missing or, failing that, a shark attack.

Fortunately, Billy Lee had just the thing to keep the wheel turning. He closed the word-processing software on his laptop and activated the movie-maker program. Several files were listed as recently accessed. He put the cursor on one and opened it. Joshua bar Yusuf's face appeared, overlaid by a box with a side-ways-pointing arrow in it. Hardacre clicked on the arrow and the prophet began to speak.

"Back then, I came to deliver a simple message: these are the end times. The kingdom is at hand. Make yourselves ready. Turn away from the world. Turn to the Lord and to each other. And do not be afraid. All shall be made new."

The preacher used the program's tools to trim the first two words from the prophet's statement. Then he saved the amended version of the clip and went to the internet. He found the page he had created on a social networking site the day before, but had not activated. He uploaded the file and went through the procedure to put the page out onto the web. Then he went to his desktop system and used it to access the clip he had just posted. And there it was.

Hardacre picked up his laptop, disconnected it from its power lead and went out into the foyer, his hard-heeled boots clicking on the marble floor. He opened the front door and was immediately met by a rush of lenses and microphones.

"Have you heard from Jesus?" was the first ques-tion. "Where is he?" followed soon on its heels.

Billy Lee held up one hand for silence and the laptop to get their attention. "The prophet," he said, "has posted a message on the internet." He reeled off the web address of the social networking page and watched as reporters tucked their microphones under their arms, worked their phones and PDAs and found the clip. There was a furious flurry of fingers and thumbs as every one of them forwarded the page to their production centers. Then the microphones and lenses came back to Hardacre.

"What does he mean?"

"It couldn't be more simple," said the preacher. "These are the end times, he said."

"The end of the world?" said a too-handsome man with perfect teeth and sculpted hair. His manner was light and skeptical, but underneath the professionalism Hardacre heard fear.

"Ding!" said Billy Lee. He turned to go, then paused as if remembering something before turning back. "Also," he said, "in the next little while, the prophet will release a text, a new book of the Gospel. It will replace the Book of Revelation."

"When?"

"What's in the text?"

"Where can we get it?"

Hardacre stilled them with another upraised hand. He enjoyed the way they quieted. "It will be uploaded onto the internet," he said. "Watch the same site as where you saw the prophet's message."

He turned and went inside, ignoring a storm of questions that broke harmlessly on his back. As he closed the door he was thinking: and away we go.

G.O.O., said the text message on Captain Denby's phone. He was downtown in a cafe he sometimes visited at lunch. The place never drew many cops –

the proprietor didn't believe in feeding anyone for free – and the policeman valued the opportunity to get away from shop talk and read the sports pages in the morning paper. He also liked the pastrami on black rye.

He closed the phone. He could already hear sirens. "General Order One" was code for the response to a major emergency. The last event to have triggered a "goober" was the flood of 2004, when the river had burst its banks and inundated the low-lying streets below Jackson Avenue. Today's goober meant that, as of immediately, all leave was canceled, every off-duty cop was to report in forthwith, and everyone was to wear the uniform, even those who normally worked in plainclothes. Even those who were on special detached duty, Denby wondered?

He was still staring at his phone. Now he dialed dispatch. "It's Denby," he said. "What's all the rumpus?"

He recognized the voice of the normally imperturbable sergeant who answered. Denby had never before heard the man sound rattled. "End of the world, captain," was all he said, then the line went dead.

Something had happened. Denby looked at the newspaper beneath the remains of his sandwich. He'd glanced at a front-page headline about a prophet claiming to be Jesus who had caused some Sunday talk-show bloviator to throw a fit on the air. Now he looked at the weather report to see if heavy rain was expected in the hilly country in which the city's river had its wellsprings. He saw nothing.

His uniform was in a locker at Police Central. He left

money beside the crust of his sandwich and stepped outside. A cab was idling at the curb, the driver sipping coffee from a paper cup. Denby opened the rear door, showed his badge to the pair of eyes that went to the rear-view mirror and said, "Police Central, emergency."

The cabbie said something the captain didn't catch, but that was probably the direct opposite of an enthusiastic cheer, and put the car into gear, still sipping on his coffee.

"You hear this?" he said, his head indicating the dashboard radio.

It was two male voices, talking fast, stepping on each other's words. "Turn it up," Denby said.

It was something to do with the stock market, he gathered after a few seconds listening to the panicky gabble. Maybe another one of those glitches that happened when computers were programmed to buy or sell if they noted particular changes in the ebb and flow of the market. Whatever the cause, the Dow Jones Index had apparently dropped two thousand points in twenty minutes and the plunge hadn't hit bottom yet. If anything, the gabblers were telling each other, not to mention the many thousands of others listening in, the sell-off was accelerating.

"End of the fucking world," said the cabbie. "Who needs a stock market now?" He took another sip, looked at the cup with distaste, and dumped its contents out his window.

A squad car, its blues and twos going full-tilt, sped past them, took a corner on two wheels, and disappeared in the direction of Civic Plaza. Denby said, "Change of plan. Follow that guy. And move it."

The driver killed the radio and hit the gas, and then the horn as they rounded the corner, scattering pedestrians. Less than two minutes later, they pulled up behind the police car, a block-and-a-half from the big city square. That was as close as either vehicle was going to get; the street was jammed with stopped vehicles, some of them driverless, abandoned. A few others still had people in them, including members of that hopeful tribe who believe that, when all else fails, blowing a horn might somehow achieve a useful result.

Denby got out of the cab. The cabbie turned to look out through the rear window. There were already three cars in line behind him, two of them belonging to horn-believers. Denby showed the drivers his badge and said, "Shut up," then listened. He could hear crowd noises up ahead, and what sounded like singing. He went toward it.

Civic Plaza was already half-filled and the empty half would not remain that way for long. People were coming from every street that fed into the great open space, mostly downtown office workers, but Denby saw shoppers and teenagers and the social detritus that lived on the streets after everybody else went home for the night. They were moving toward the east end of the plaza, to where the broad steps leading up to the pillars of the Justice Center were thronged by what looked to be a mass choir – no, the captain thought, several different choirs, elbowing each other for space

– all singing, swaying, and hand-clapping their way through some old-timey hymn.

Above and behind the singers, someone had erected a giant screen, the kind they used at music festivals and political conventions. Denby recalled seeing a bulletin that said Civic Plaza would be the venue for an open-air concert some evening this week. But this wasn't it. This was noon and somebody must have decided to put the screen to another use: right now it was showing a news channel.

The policeman pushed his way through the crowd. Despite the massed singers' energy, this didn't feel like a religious celebration. The people standing in the plaza mostly weren't clapping or singing along. The deeper Denby pushed into them, the more he smelled a combined odor of the sweat of many – and not the good sweat of heat and muscular motion; the policeman recognized the smell of fear.

He moved around a portly executive in a business suit, putting his hand on the man's upper arm to ease by. The fat man jerked and spun toward him, his face pale and sheened in greasy sweat, his eyes too wide. "Police," Denby said, showing his gold badge.

Neither the word nor the shield had the desired effect. The man struck out at the captain, the swipe more like an ineffectual spasm than a coordinated strike, and Denby fended him off and kept moving. He kept looking up at the steps and the screen, expecting to see someone who had the look of being in charge – maybe some preacher – but no one came forward to still the choirs and take the crowd in hand.

A man next to him swore bitterly. The captain looked his way, saw that he was another downtown business type. He had buds in his ear, the wires leading to a device in his pocket. Now he put a finger to one of the buds, the better to hear over the singing.

Denby caught the man's eye. "What is it?" he said.

The eyes that met his were frightened. "The Dow just fell through five thousand." The ashen face twitched. "It's all over."

A sound went through the crowd, like the growling sigh of a wounded bear. The singing trailed off as the members of the big choir turned to look at the huge screen. Denby followed their gaze and saw the image of a swarthy, bearded man touching the hand of an overfed man whose face he recognized without knowing the name. Then the porker began to run in place, his head bent impossibly backwards.

When the first thing climbed out of the man's grossly distorted mouth, the crowd made the wounded-bear noise again. When the second monster emerged, the policeman heard shouts and whimpers. From somewhere behind him came high-pitched, hysterical laughter, abruptly choked off.

But now a hush fell over the thousands of people. The screen showed a closed door. Denby recognized it. And he recognized the man who came out into a strobing, flickering glare of lights. He watched Billy Lee Hardacre hold up a laptop and say something about a prophet posting a message on the internet.

Then the image changed. The bearded man, relaxed in a chair, was saying, "These are the end times. The kingdom is at hand. Make yourselves ready. Turn away from the world. Turn to the Lord and to each other. And do not be afraid. All shall be made new."

Then it was back to Hardacre, who said, "It couldn't be more simple. These are the end times."

"The end of the world?" said someone off screen. Then the image cut to a studio somewhere, with anxious men and women grouped around a table, monitors in the background, laptops in front of them. A hard-faced woman looked up into the camera and said, "The Pope has scheduled a statement for" – she looked at her watch – "about an hour from now. We're told the President will address the nation from the Rose Garden in a few minutes."

She rubbed her forehead. "Meanwhile, the man who calls himself Jesus of Nazareth has dropped out of sight, apparently leaving it to television preacher Billy Lee Hardacre to be his spokesperson. But the Reverend Hardacre has had precious little to say."

She looked to the man on her right. "Roy, what's happening elsewhere?"

The newsman's face, normally full of wry humor, was stark. "The Pentagon has put all branches of the military on full war alert," he said. "The Director of Homeland Security is reported to have told the President that he should invoke his emergency powers and place the country under martial law."

The man ran a hand over his face. "Meanwhile, there are reports of rioting and looting in several cities. A gunman is reported to have opened fire at a shopping center in Kansas City. In Tucson, several men in

Kevlar helmets and body armor have sealed off a block in the downtown business district. They have commandeered a truck and are apparently emptying the vaults of a large bank."

He looked at the woman and said, "Back to you, Jane."

She was staring at something on her laptop. Now she looked up, as if seeing her surroundings for the first time. She unclipped a lapel mike from the front of her blouse, ripped away a flat black box that had been taped to the back of her skirt and dropped it on the table. "The hell with this," she said, getting up. "I've got kids."

At the top of the Justice Center's steps a balding, stocky man with a bullhorn pushed his way through the rearmost members of the choirs. "Repent!" he cried, his amplified voice echoing off the glass walls of the City Hall. "Repent or burn forever in–"

Somebody knocked the bullhorn away from his lips. The man struck back and the one who had silenced him grabbed him by the front of his suit jacket. They wrestled and fell, rolling down the steps, knocking over choristers who weren't able to get out of the way.

"Jesus," said Denby. He tried to push his way toward the fight, but someone tripped him and he half-fell against a woman in a flowered dress. She screamed as he clutched at her to keep himself upright.

"Get off her!" said a man who could have been her husband; the ages matched. He seized Denby's collar and tried to drag him away. The captain reached for his badge, but somebody's elbow knocked it to the ground.

"I'm a cop!" he told the man who had hold of his jacket.

"Who gives a shit!" said the man, delivering a glancing punch that made Denby's ear feel like it had been partly torn off. "It's all over now!"

Denby had a 9mm pistol under his arm and a canister of pepper spray in his jacket pocket. He went for the latter and in a moment his attacker was reeling back, hands to his tear-stained face.

"Ladies and gentlemen," said an amplified voice, "the President of the United States."

The crowd made its wounded sound again. Even the sobbing man was trying to see the big screen. The President looked grim. "My fellow Americans," he said, "the thing I most want to say to you today is what another president once said to the American people in another time of trouble: we have nothing to fear but fear itself."

He paused for a moment, turning to each of the cameras aimed at him. "There is no cause for alarm. America is not under attack. No natural disaster has struck. There has apparently been another computer malfunction in the stock market, but the economy remains sound.

"I am asking you, as your President, to remain calm. Do your jobs, or go to your homes. Stay off the streets and allow the authorities to maintain control.

"We will get through this. It is not, I repeat, not the end of the world."

"Oh, yes it is," said a fervent voice nearby. "Mine eyes have seen the glory!"

"Shut up!" said another voice and Denby heard sounds of a scuffle, a little knot of violence pulsing through the crowd. But it was moving away from him.

The restless mob seemed to be pulsing, the people moving in on each other, then edging away. Space opened around Denby and he saw a glint of gold out of the corner of his eye: his badge. He stooped and recovered it.

The once-wry reporter was back on the screen, his face haggard. "Have we got it?" he was saying to someone off camera. "No, not that one, the other one."

A man standing near Denby, looking up at the screen, said, "This can't be happening."

A woman on the man's other side said, "It *is* happening. It's *on TV!*"

The captain realized there was nothing he could do here. His instinct, his impulse to get to where the trouble was, had let him down. He turned and pushed his way toward the rear of the mob, holding up his badge as if it might make a difference. And maybe it did. In a couple of minutes he found the going easier, the people not so closely packed, until all at once he was out of the crowd. He was on the west side of the plaza, near a fountain that spurted water in several streams out of a complicated structure of bronze struts and plates. It supposedly represented the city's pioneers.

He sat on the fountain's edge and scooped water to wash the sweat from his face. Across the plaza, over the heads of the throng, he could see images flashing in rapid succession across the big screen: police behind riot shields beating back a stone-throwing mob; cars overturned and on fire: someone smashing a newspaper sales box through a plate glass window, then jumping through the jagged gap; a helicopter's view of city streets packed with people, flowing like ants.

All at once, Denby knew. This was what the time traveler had come back to prevent: the collapse of civilization, the end of order. And he knew that Hardacre was central to it. That's why the preacher had been slipped the unreadable book and sold the line that his weird son-in-law was a prophet – as some kind of distraction that would prevent him from doing whatever he'd done to bring this about. But it hadn't worked – at least not yet.

Chaos was breaking out. The authorities were urging calm – nothing to fear but fear itself – but if that didn't work, Denby knew what would come next. Homeland Security had been briefing senior police officers for years. Next would come men in black uniforms with automatic weapons, backed up by special forces troops in armored personnel carriers and helicopter gunships. If necessary, behind them would come tanks.

Denby sat beside the fountain and saw it all in his mind's eye. *The way the world ends*, he remembered from somewhere, *not with a bang but a whimper*. From anarchy in the streets the road led to the future wasteland he had been shown. He knew what he had to do: find the time traveler and help him make this stop.

The kid, he thought. He was the only lead. He took out his phone, dialed Chesney's work number. He got a computer telling him no one was available to speak to him, though his call was very important to Paxton Life and Casualty. Then Denby tried the kid's home number and got a live person. It took a few moments for him to figure out that he was talking to a reporter who'd staked out the apartment.

But that's the only place he's likely to show up, the captain thought. He doesn't like the world outside. Not enough pools of light.

Uniformed police were arriving now, having come on foot through the car-choked streets. A uniformed inspector approached Denby and said, "It's a goober, Denby. Go get into your bag and get back here. You're not on detached duty anymore."

The captain saw no point arguing. "On my way," he said, getting up from the fountain. But when the senior officer turned his back Denby went, not toward Police Central but toward the riverside apartment house where Chesney Arnstruther and his time-traveling descendant might be found. He would throw out the gate-crashing media and wait.

Half a block later, the captain changed his mind. He retraced his steps to Civic Plaza, turned and headed for Police Central.

"You come to the Garden of Eden," Chesney's mother said to him, "and... *that's* the first thing you think of doing?"

Chesney was pretty sure that it was probably the first thing the original pair of inhabitants had thought of, too. But he had long ago learned not to voice all of his thoughts to his mother – especially any that concerned sex. He well remembered the time, at the age of ten, when he had asked her if she had had sexual intercourse with his father. He had only been trying to establish that it was a universal rule in procreation, as a kid at school had maintained – Mary and the visitant angel notwithstanding – but his mother had not taken his question in a spirit of scientific inquiry. He could still taste the soap, way deep in the back of his throat.

"It's the Tree of Life, Mother," he said. "It has a... an effect on you."

"Put some clothes on," Letitia said. "Both of you."

Chesney did as she said, hunting around for his underpants while Melda gathered up her clothes and went behind a bush. But as he pulled up his briefs, the young man watched his mother, and saw her expression change as she looked up at the great tree, and at the strange, banana-like fruit that hung from its branches. Her hand went halfway toward the lowest-hanging specimen; then it was as if she had just noticed what her hand was doing and pulled it back, clasping it with the other one then putting them both behind her.

Chesney pulled his trousers on and closed them up. As he fastened his belt, he said, "What do you want, Mother?"

If he'd been struck by the wistful look with which she'd regarded the fruit, he was outright surprised to hear her say, in a small voice, "I think I need your help."

"With what?"

He could see that she was reluctant to say it. He put on his shirt and began to button it methodically, as always starting at the top and working his way down.

Finally, as he fastened the last one, she said, "With Billy Lee." It was not until Chesney had his shirttail tucked in that she finished with, "I think he's maybe doing some harm."

"Maybe?" Chesney said. "I don't believe I've ever heard you use that word before." He'd always assumed that his mother saw nothing but pools of clear light, all around her – although she often didn't care for what might be so clearly illuminated.

"All right," she said. "He *is* doing harm, real harm." She looked in every direction but at her son.

Another son might have been deeply moved to see a woman of Letitia Arnstruther's firmness of mind and spirit reduced to such an abject state. Reconciliation, even hugging, might have ensued. But Chesney was not another son; all his mother's distress did for him was to make him deeply uncomfortable. Much as he disliked his parent's unending campaign to direct his life, the prospect of having to deal with an insecure, uncertain Letitia was moving him toward an unaccustomed sense of panic.

"What do you want me to do?" he said.

At Police Central, off-duty officers were pouring in and uniformed personnel were pouring out, many of the latter bearing transparent plastic shields and dressed in riot gear. Denby took the elevator but rode it past the twentieth floor where his office and uniform were and straight up to the roof. As he expected, he found the department's helicopter on its pad, its pilot in his seat and its rotors slowly turning.

He went straight to the passenger-side door, climbed in and fastened the seat belt. The pilot, a sergeant named Borisovich, looked at him curiously. "Nobody told me you'd be coming on this one, captain," the man said. "Thought it was just the chief and the deputy watch commander."

Denby saw no point in prolonging the confusion. He drew his pistol, racked the slide, and pointed it at the pilot. "Get us up," he said.

The man registered shock but recovered as quickly as a good pilot should. "Not gonna," he said. "And I don't reckon you can fly this thing if I'm sitting here dead."

The captain said, "Did you know Gabe Martinez?"

"Sure. He helped train me."

"He ever tell you how he flew Hueys in Vietnam?"

Borisovich's face turned cagey. "Yeah."

"He ever tell you about the time a RPG exploded right next to him in mid-air, and he had to fly back to base with shrapnel wounds all down his left side?"

The pilot looked straight ahead. "Maybe," he said.

"So you could probably do it with just one bullet wound," Denby said. He poked the muzzle of the pistol into the fleshy part of the man's thigh. "Say, right here?"

"This is seriously fucked up, captain," said Borisovich, but he upped the revs on the engine. Moments later, they were off the roof and, at Denby's direction, heading south at the machine's top speed.

The detective had put it together. The time traveler had come back from his future wasteland to stop Billy Lee Hardacre from precipitating a mass panic that would somehow lead to the end of the world – or at least the end of civilization. He couldn't quite see how the crimefighting fitted in, but that was because history was lived forward and understood backward, and he was living this moment instead of studying it in retrospect. One thing he was sure of, though: the strange book that the preacher had been working on with the supposed angel had been part of the plan to derail Armageddon, and Denby had impulsively stolen that book; an act of theft that had led to its destruction.

So there was a very good chance, Denby thought, that he, himself, was responsible for the Hell on Earth that was about to descend on the world. And thus it was up to him to stop it. He told the pilot to follow the highway south; he would tell him when to turn toward Hardacre's estate.

He wouldn't be surprised to find the time traveler there. If not, Denby would take care of things himself.

"How can you help us?" Chesney asked the demon.

"I dunno," said Xaphan. "Question is, do I gotta hurt him?"

"No," said Chesney and his mother together.

But Melda had a different take on what the demon had said. "Why is that the question?"

The weasel face took on an even shiftier than usual cast. "The basic rule," the fiend said.

Chesney remembered. "Can't interfere with another contract?" he said. "But Billy Lee doesn't have a contract with Hell."

Letitia drew herself up to her full height from which she glared down at the demon with sufficient force to have shattered it into smoking fragments. "Of course he does not!"

Incredibly, Xaphan managed to look even more shifty. "Not as such, no."

"What aren't you telling us?" the young man said.

"We've been through this," the demon said, preparing to count on its fingers. "The temperature in downtown Kabul, Madonna's shoe size, the odds against tossing a coin and coming up heads six million times in a row, the–"

Chesney interrupted. "For the rum and cigars," he said, "last chance: does Hardacre have a deal of any kind with Hell?"

The fiend drained its ever-present tumbler and said, "Of *a* kind."

Letitia squawked, but her son bored in on his assistant. "Specify."

"He thought our guy was an angel, the same one he dealt with when we had the strike."

Chesney's mother gasped. "That's cheating!"

"No kiddin'?" said the fiend. "Imagine that."

"You're saying the preacher took help from a demon he thought was an angel," Melda said, "and that's the same as signing a contract?"

Xaphan shrugged. "That's the way we're seein' it. Constructive culpability, that's the term."

"But he thought he was doing the work of the Lord!" Letitia said.

The demon blew smoke. "Fact is, toots, he didn't

care who's work he was doin', long as it was him doin' it." He tapped ash onto the green grass of Eden. "'Nother fact is, you was just the same. We catch more of you wid pride than wid all the other six big ones put together."

"It's not fair," Chesney said.

"Fair ain't the bizness we're in. It went the way it always goes – the preacher sees the action and wants in on it, wants the biggest slice. A demon shows up, offers him help, he don't say, 'Whoa, Nellie, what's the vig?' He just takes it."

"A demon pretending to be an angel," Chesney said.

"We weren't helpin' him carry in the groceries," Xaphan countered. "He wanted help you only get from us, real mess-wid-the-world help. And he never said, 'Wait a minute, what's the price of this?' cause all he cared about was bein' the big cheese, makin' his mark."

It puffed on its cigar and continued, "So the boss says, 'Give him what he wants, it could work to our advantage,' and puts one of the top guys on the job.'

"Top guy?" Chesney said.

"Crocell, a full-weight *Dux Asinorum*."

Letitia's father had prided himself on his legal Latin. "A Duke of Fools," she translated. "A Duke of Hell."

One of the weasel eyes squinted in her direction, while the black lips spoke around the smoking Havana. "And Hardacre wasn't the only one thought the 'angel' was the cat's pajamas, was he?"

The woman's face fell. "Pride again. I thought myself special because I had a man who spoke with an angel of the Lord."

"Nuttin' special about it," said Xaphan. "Our standard product, right off the line. Foolin' fools. It's what we do."

Melda said, "But this wasn't a standard situation. The Devil wanted Hardacre as an option, in case he really did bring on the end of the world."

"If we're showin' our hands," Xaphan said, "the boss also wanted him to bring you-know-who back from that little place we visited. Figured he might come in handy, too." The fiend smiled. "Tricky business, too, not lettin' that demon-bustin' prophet catch on about Crocell's little act – the duke had to make sure never to touch the preacher or anythin' on the premises, or old Josh would have sniffed it out. He was supposeta think it was me he smelled. Guess it worked."

Chesney frowned. "Never mind the self-congratulation. The situation now is that the Devil's got a connection to Joshua – they're writing a book together – so Hardacre gets the chop. And so does my mother."

"We're innocent," Letitia said. "They tricked us."

"You could argue that in court," said the demon. "Course, it's our court." It puffed the cigar to a brighter glow. "Judge's name is Minos. He's kinda strict."

"But now he doesn't need the preacher," Melda said. "So he could let him and Letitia go."

"No can do," said the fiend. "Like the boss says, we don't make the rules."

"Enough!" said Chesney. "I need to think!"

"It's not your kind of problem," said Letitia. "Let me talk to Billy Lee–"

"No," said Melda, "he won't listen. Besides, Chesney can do this." She put a hand on the young man's arm. "Go on, sweetie, work it through."

Chesney went to the other side of the Tree of Life and sat down cross-legged on the thick, soft turf, his back against the warm, smooth-barked trunk. The light in the Garden of Eden was as pure as it had been that first morning, but it provided no clear pool of il-lumination for this problem. The nub of it, he posited, was to prevent Hardacre from bringing on the end of the world. Then he thought, no, that's not it. The problem is to keep Mother and Billy Lee out of Hell. Because, having accepted help from a demon, having taken the fruits of the underworld, that's where they were heading.

He remembered Nat Blowdell being whipped through the iron gates of Hell. He couldn't let that happen to his mother, for all the grief she had caused him. But the rules were the rules. Then his mind went to Joshua. Did he really have the authority to forgive sins, the way he was empowered to cast out demons? Or was that a quality that had been tacked on later, after the little man had been transfigured into a deity?

But Chesney couldn't approach the prophet while he was hobnobbing with Lucifer. Let the Devil get one whiff of what the young man wanted and he would do all he could to deny Chesney his wish. Satan had never forgiven – probably never could forgive – the blow that his pride had suffered when a mere human had thrown his kingdom into chaos.

We have to solve this ourselves, he thought. No, *I* have to solve it. He was one who had started it all, and having read a thousand comix, he knew enough about stories to know that the hero, however flawed a character he might be, has to step up when the situation is at its most perilous and do what needs to be done.

A petal from one of the great tree's blossoms spiraled down and landed on his knee. He could smell its perfume, strong and deeply pheremonic. He looked up and saw the light dappling through the foliage, the long, cylindrical fruit hanging from their stems. And in a moment, he knew. "Thank you," he said. Then he uncrossed his legs and rose, thinking, yes, the hero has to solve the problem – but sometimes the author gives him a little nudge in the right direction.

He reached up into the tree and plucked one of the fruit. It was heavy and warm in his hand, smooth and with the suggestion of veins under the silky, almost translucent skin. A pair of convoluted blossoms, like roses turned in on themselves, clustered at the base of the fruit, where it emerged from the stem.

He stepped around to where the others were waiting, his mother and Melda standing in identical postures, arms folded, heads down, but their bodies angled away from each other so that their gazes need not meet. Xaphan was hovering behind them, a fresh tumbler of rum in its hand.

"Let's go," Chesney told it, "all of us, right now."

The demon swallowed the liquor. "Where to?"

"Hardacre's place. The kitchen."

• • • •

Billy Lee was enjoying himself. He was seated at the desk in his study, where he had polished the new gospel to a high gloss before preparing another video clip of the prophet to upload to the internet, when the moment was right. That wasn't quite yet, although the disruptions were spreading rapidly. A growing fount of trouble in the streets were the tens of millions of Americans who had been assured that, come the time of tribulations, they would be raptured out of the line of fire, so they could watch from comfortable seats in Heaven as their fellow mortals reaped the wages of sin. Now that it appeared that the end of days was just around the corner, and yet here they still were, being jostled by rioters and buffeted by the panic-stricken. They were not taking the disappointment well. They were showing a tendency to set fires and smash windows.

Hardacre was reminded of Nero's burning of Rome, a slum-clearance program that the cithera-strumming emperor had blamed on Christians trying to hurry up the arrival of the Kingdom of Heaven. Maybe there had been some truth in the old Roman's allegations. On the flatscreen TV mounted on the wall he saw a middle-aged man in khaki pants and a well-pressed short-sleeve shirt hurl a brick through a plate-glass window – downtown Atlanta, said the crawl underneath the image – then a woman in a flower-print dress followed it with a molotov cocktail. The rioters were turning to shake fists at the sky as the scene cut to another gaggle of talking heads seated around a table in a newsroom.

"Cardinal Walenz," a silver-haired anchor asked an ancient man wearing a black cassock and a red skull-cap, "is this the end of the world as prophesied in the Book of Revelations?"

The churchman leaned back in his chair. His voice was papery thin. "That's 'Revelation,'" he said. "No ess."

The newsman thanked the cardinal for the correction though he didn't seem all that grateful for the information. "But what about it? Is this what's prophesied in the Bible?"

"Have you read the Book of Revelation?"

"I've been a little busy." He waved a piece of paper. "I have a summary here."

"Well," said the cleric, "the Book of Revelation specifies boiling seas, the moon turned to blood, Christ appearing in the Heavens on his throne, angels from one horizon to the other."

"We're not seeing that, are we?"

"We are not." The cardinal folded his hands together and looked grave. "I don't want to say too much before the Holy Father speaks, but I think it's safe to say that what we're seeing now is the Devil at work in the world."

"The Devil?" The silvery eyebrows climbed toward the silvery hairline.

"None other. And you'll notice that the worst of the disruptions are taking place in the non-Catholic countries."

The newsman checked the screen of a laptop beside him. "There have been serious riots in France and Italy," he said.

"Those hardly qualify as Catholic countries," the cardinal said. "But to return to the question, one thing we have not seen is the rise of the Antichrist – the world leader who leads the faithful astray."

"I thought Hall Bruster had confessed to that."

"Again," said the cleric, "a peak audience of three-and-a-half million viewers is hardly world leadership. Mr Bruster is clearly unbalanced."

"But you've seen the clip." The anchor spoke to someone out of shot, "Roll the Bruster clip again." A moment later a window appeared in the corner of Hardacre's television screen, and he saw for the umpteenth time the casting out of the two demons.

"The man with the beard," the newsman said, "is believed by," – he consulted his laptop screen again – "eighty-eight per cent of the American people to be Jesus Christ, returned to Earth."

"Well, he's not," said the cardinal. "He doesn't look like any of his pictures."

The interviewer let that one go by. "And almost eighty per cent believe that by casting two demons out of Hall Bruster, Jesus has vanquished the Antichrist. So the end can now come."

"God," said the cardinal, "does not pay much attention to public opinion polls."

Time, thought Billy Lee. He reached for the wireless computer mouse, moved it and clicked the left button. On the desktop monitor in front of him a blue bar went from left to right. Ten seconds later, the newsman put two fingers to the bud in his ear then interrupted the cardinal to say, "I'm being told that the

Reverend Billy Lee Hardacre has issued another video statement. Okay, roll it."

Hardacre was looking at himself as he had been fifteen minutes earlier, sitting behind this desk. The video camera that had captured the moment was still mounted on its tripod a few feet away. He had to admit that he looked pretty good.

"Brothers and sisters," his voice said from the television speakers, "the Lord has asked me to deliver unto you his new revelation. He himself has left us again – only temporarily, I can assure you – to do personal battle with Satan the deceiver. Out of that struggle will come a new day for humankind, and a renewal of the world."

He paused to let that sink in, then said, "In the meantime, he has asked me to be his representative on Earth. Together, he and I have written a new gospel – to be called the *Book of Jesus* – which I will shortly upload to the internet. It will, of course, be available for free.

"The new gospel spells out how the returned Jesus wishes the world to be prepared for his final coming, when he will rule over us for a thousand years. That millennium will be the time of perfecting. None shall die. None shall be prey to sickness, nor shall they want for sustenance or comfort."

He paused again, to offer a beatific smile. "Between now and the dawning of that millennium of peace, brothers and sisters, will be a time of building and re-organizing. The world must be made fit for his divine rule.

"We will need to institute new systems of government, new modes of economic life, new relations between man and man, between man and woman, and between man and God. The *Book of Jesus*, the only gospel authored by the messiah himself, will make plain how those ends are to be achieved."

On the screen, Hardacre folded his hands just the way the cardinal had. "Brothers and sisters," he said, "the new day is almost at hand. Let us join together to help our Lord in his struggle against the Evil One, by making the world a fit place for his victorious return.

"Watch for the *Book of Jesus*, read its message, and let the Lord's will be done." He gave them another smile of blessing, and the image faded. Then they were back in the newsroom, with the anchor and the cardinal.

"Well," said the prelate, "you were looking for your Antichrist. There he goes."

Hardacre laughed. Outside he could faintly hear a new hubbub among the reporters camped on his lawn. It was probably time to have the police remove them. He reached for the bottle of Scotch then thought better of it. "Shouldn't drink on an empty stomach," he said to himself. It was long past lunchtime. Letitia would have fixed one of his energy drinks for him. And maybe there would be time for a little connubial contact. He went looking for her.

The kitchen was unexpectedly crowded. Beside his wife, her son and the girlfriend were seated around the breakfast nook table. The presence of the weasel-headed demon, hovering over in a corner, explained how they had arrived without having to struggle through the crowds outside. The fiend was subsisting on rum and cigar smoke, as usual, but as Hardacre walked in, Letitia was just pouring all of them some kind of fruit concoction from a pitcher.

"Smoothie, dear?" she said. "There's plenty." He attributed the strained note in her voice to the necessity of having to raise it over the sound of a helicopter racketing low over the roof. Definitely time to have the cops shoo away the media, Hardacre thought.

The copter sounded not only loud but stationary, as if it had set down on the back lawn, but when he looked through the window, Hardacre saw it angling away over the trees at the rear of the property. Meanwhile, Letitia had risen from the table, her eyes bright, a glass of something thick and yellow-colored in her hand. "Here," she said.

He took the glass, sniffed the drink. It had a heady, almost womanly smell to it. He felt a sudden stirring in the front of his pants. "What's in it?"

She spoke in an off-hand tone. "Peaches, papaya, kiwi, ginkgo biloba, a nice ripe mango ..."

She knew he liked mango more than any other fruit. And, by God, Billy Lee knew, if ever a man deserved a taste of mango, it was himself, now in his moment of triumph. He raised the glass and took a mouthful. His tastebuds registered shock at a new taste that overpowered the familiar flavors. Then his whole gustatory apparatus gave itself over to ecstasy. He drank the whole thing down and gave a gasp of satisfaction as it settled in his stomach.

She was looking at him differently now. "…and a little something special," she finished.

"What do you mean?"

Chesney was on his feet and coming toward them, a glass full of the fruit concoction in his hand. He gave it to his mother and said, "You'd better drink some, too."

"I suppose I had," she said. She drained her glass. Hardacre saw the same look come over her face as she must be seeing in his. Then her eyes darkened in a way that, over the past few weeks, had become both familiar and welcome. The stirring in his groin became a whirlpool. He heard his own voice sounding thick in his ears. "Upstairs."

"Right away," she breathed, and took his offered hand.

They turned toward the door that led into the hallway. At that moment, they heard a crash from the back of the house. Hardacre had time to think that someone must have kicked in the back door, when Captain Denby appeared in the doorway, his face strained and pale, his eyes glittering.

In his hands was an automatic pistol, dark and angular, its muzzle like the mouth of a tunnel into blackest oblivion. Without a word, he raised it and Billy Lee Hardacre saw flame shoot toward him, twice.

FIFTEEN

The first bullet was like a train smashing into his chest, the second like the train's big brother piling on. Everything slowed down and Billy Lee felt himself floating backward under the double impact, his knees folding. His hand was torn free of Letitia's and he could see her face turning to follow him, the desire that had filled her eyes mutating into shock. He knew somehow that at least one of the bullets had torn his heart to pieces and that there would be no recovery. He would continue to drift backward and downward until he landed supine upon the kitchen floor. And then he would die.

He felt his buttocks hit the tiles, then his shoulders, then the back of his head. It seemed ridiculous to him that he felt the pain of the last impact over the incredible fire in his chest. All over the world, because of him, people were walking away from their daily routines to congregate in churches or public squares, or to loot and riot – yet Billy Lee Hardacre's own cranial nerves were staying on the job, faithfully reporting a now entirely irrelevant injury.

Sheesh, he thought, and waited for the blackness to come, followed by the light and the tunnel. Perhaps the Throne would be waiting to escort him into Heaven. He had no doubt that's where he was heading – had he not been doing Heaven's work all this time?

He closed his eyes. The surcease would be welcome. The pain in his chest was not fading. If anything, it was getting worse. He continued to breathe, and could not escape noticing that the shots had smashed through some of his ribs, turning them into sharp splinters that jabbed into his already torn and traumatized flesh.

But death did not come. Impossibly, the pain grew worse. He opened his eyes again, saw Letitia bending over him, the shock now changing to agony. Behind her, he saw her son leaping with blinding speed to seize the pistol from the policeman and knock him down. He even saw the surprise on Denby's face as the young man, his strength augmented by infernal powers, handled the captain as if he were a child.

Then he saw Chesney turn his gaze toward something that was behind and beyond his own field of vision and heard him say, "Xaphan! Fix Billy Lee!"

The demon floated into Hardacre's view now, hovering above him and looking down at him without interest. "Can't," it said. "This mug's off limits. Basic rule."

"Then take us back thirty seconds and put me in costume!"

"No can do."

Letitia said, "At least put him out! Or stop the pain."

The demon shrugged and tapped ash from its cigar. "Nope."

MATTHEW HUGHES363

"If you don't," said Chesney, "I'm asking for a new
assistant. My contract says 'assisted by a demon of my
free choice.'"

The weasel brows drew down. "You don't wanna do
that. Another demon might not work so well wid you."

"Last chance," the young man said.

The demon stuck the cigar in its mouth, just behind
one of the saber fangs. "Tell you what I'll do," it said.
"I'll put him to sleep, stop the bleedin', but anythin'
more, you got to take it up wid the boss."

"All right. Do it."

The demon looked down at Hardacre again. For
Billy Lee, everything went mercifully black.

For Captain Denby, things had become unmercifully
confusing. Shooting Hardacre had gone just the way
he'd envisioned it, though it had felt like a dream. But
the kid had been a surprise. The preacher was just hitting the tiles when suddenly the nerd, who'd been
sitting at the breakfast nook, was all the way across
the kitchen, yanking the gun out of his hands then
driving him down to the floor with the force of a four
hundred-pound linebacker. Then he had held Denby's
wrists together with one hand, in a grip that made the
small bones grind together.

And through all this, the kid was not paying any attention to his prisoner, nor to the other people in the
room. He was looking toward an empty corner of the
room and Denby could see the young man's jaw mus-
cles working, as if he was speaking emphatically,
though the policeman heard no sound.

Since the kid seemed distracted, Denby now tried to break free. His effort was fruitless. The kid glanced at him, then flicked the backs of his fingers across Denby's jaw, a motion like brushing away a bothersome fly. But the captain's head snapped back as if he had taken a solid punch. He didn't even have time to be surprised. His last thought before he slid under the covers was that somebody had not told him the truth about Chesney Arnstruther.

Chesney said to Xaphan, "Fetch some rope to tie Denby up." Instantly, the demon shimmered and offered him a length of clothesline. "And a gag," the young man said, and found one in his hand the moment he'd finished speaking. The threat of asking for a new assistant seemed to have motivated the fiend to raise its standard of job performance.

The young man sized up the situation. Denby was controlled. His mother was falling apart. He had often wondered what it would take to shake her confidence that she could surmount anything the world might throw at her. Now he knew that it would involve the sight of her husband bleeding heavily across the kitchen floor, his chest a ruin and his back probably even worse where the bullets had torn their way out of his torso.

Melda was on her knees beside Hardacre. She had torn open his bloodstained shirt and was pressing a towel to the frontal wounds. The young man felt a brief surge of pride in his girlfriend. When this was over, he was going to make sure that his mother understood that Melda McCann was a woman who deserved her respect.

But first this situation had to be resolved. Again, no obvious solution leapt into Chesney's mind, bathed in clear light. He could not simply order his assistant to break one of Hell's fundamental rules. True, Xaphan was capable of bending the statutes when it suited; the demon had even fought one of its own when Nat Blowdell's infernal handler, Melech, had attacked Chesney. But that was different: Melech had been the one breaking the rule, in the belief that all the rules would soon be changed. That was a far cry from asking Xaphan to intervene in a relationship between a damned soul – which Hardacre surely was – and an archduke of the netherworld.

So, he told himself, work it through. What would Malc Turner do? He would follow the trail, starting with what he knew and working his way toward where the facts led. Fact one: the Devil had been play-ing a duplicitous game, as ought to have been expected. Despite his continuing protestations that he was not a character in a book, he had clearly come around to that point of view some time ago.

So, knowing that he was part of a story, what would Lucifer do? He would try to use the knowledge to im-prove his role. And what was the best way to do that? In a moment, Chesney knew the answer: the thing that most chafed the Adversary was that he had to play a game in whose rules he had had no say. He would try to put himself in a position where he could rewrite the rules.

That meant working with the characters who al-ready knew the truth about the real underpinnings of the universe: Chesney, Hardacre, Letitia and Melda. The agreement that had settled the strike in Hell prevented Satan from attempting to manipulate Chesney. And that prohibition included indirect methods, so the Devil could not get at Chesney through his girlfriend.

That left Billy Lee and Chesney's mother. They had been attracted to each other. Lucifer had almost certainly intensified that bond by working on their libidos. But the real opportunity had been the couple's pride. Billy Lee was justifiably proud that he, and he alone, had figured out the meaning of existence – and more than that, he had had the insight to fix a plot problem when the divine story broke down.

Letitia was hugely proud to be the wife of someone who was, arguably, the most important man in the world, and one of the most significant figures in the history of humankind. And to add to his already singular accomplishment, Billy Lee regularly consulted with a high-ranking member of the angelic hierarchy; together, they were writing the book that would remake the world. What Hardacre didn't know was that he was not co-authoring a new gospel with an angel; he was being fooled by a *dux asinorum* of Hell.

That had been one of the strings to the Devil's bow. But once that strategy had been set in motion, Satan had developed another. Hardacre had reasoned out that the great book kept being rewritten as the story unfolded. That raised the question of what happened to the discarded drafts. Lucifer went looking for them and found them. And in one of them, living out one

endlessly repeated eternal day, he found an unexpected opportunity.

So the Devil canceled his first plan, stimulating
Denby to steal the book that Hardacre and the duke
had been composing. Once it was out of Billy Lee's
house, Satan made sure it could not complicate his
new, second strategy. It did not matter to Satan that
the preacher continued with his plan to bring about
the end of the world, closing down the present draft
of the great narrative, and starting a new one based
on his own new gospel, this one written without su-
pernatural assistance. The worst Hardacre's efforts
could do would be to cause some riots and perhaps
topple some governments or established churches –
none of which would have disturbed so much as a
whisker of the Devil's neatly shaped beard.

The original plan had mutated into the new one.
Chesney had gone to timeless Nazareth and brought
back Joshua bar Yusuf, the historical Jesus. And then
he had brought the prophet to where Lucifer sat waiting, so that the Devil could make a better offer than
the one he had originally put forward, when he had
taken the messiah up to that "high place" from where
it was possible to see all the kingdoms of the world.

The second offer, made in the Garden of Eden where
all of the drama had started, had now been made. The
last Chesney knew, the terms were being considered.
He could make a reasonable guess as to what Lucifer
wanted. He was not at all sure what Joshua's reply
would be, but as he thought about it, Chesney discovered an opportunity.

"Xaphan," he said, "we're taking Billy Lee back to Eden."

"Sez who?" The demon set its cigar at a pugnacious angle. "His nibs ain't gonna welcome me showin' up wid an archduke's handiwork. I ain't doin' it."

"You'll be showing up, "Chesney said, "with exactly what he needs, and probably just about the time he's coming to realize that he needs something he doesn't have."

Xaphan looked at him with the squint of a suspicious weasel. "You tryin' to pull a fast one on me?" it said.

"Nope," said Chesney. "But this could look pretty good on your employment record. And, chances are, there are going to be some interesting new jobs opening up in the next few years."

"What kinda jobs?"

"Who can say? But your boss is writing new rules for how the game is played. He's going to need demons that can handle new ideas." Chesney looked his assistant up and down. "Question is: are you that kind of demon?"

The oversized weasel eyes narrowed to slits. "When did you start doin' all this noodle-work? I liked you better when you was simple-minded."

Chesney knew the answer to that one, too, but now was not the time. "Get used to it," he said. "Now, are we going, or do I need to summon Hardacre's duke?" He smiled. "Who would then get all the credit."

They brought Denby with them. The time traveler story was not going to hold much longer and Chesney didn't want to take a chance on the policeman escaping if they didn't get back to the Hardacre mansion soon. Xaphan's recommendation that they "just rub the flat-foot out" was disregarded.

They laid Billy Lee beneath the Tree of Life – the location couldn't do him any harm and might even do some good – then left him there with Letitia to watch over him and the still unconscious captain. They made their way along the fragrant paths to the Tree of the Knowledge of Good and Evil, where they found Joshua and Lucifer deep in conversation. A black-maned lion was cropping the grass in the foreground, but the beast only purred as they passed by.

"Do you want me to help?" Melda said. "Or are you in a pool of light on this one?"

Chesney smiled. "I think the days of light and darkness are behind us," he said. "My head seems to be working differently now."

"Why? How?" she said.

He saw a look of concern on her face, and when he studied her more closely he realized that there was also a touch of fear in her eyes. "Don't worry," he said, "nothing is going to come between us."

"How can you be sure?"

He laughed. "I figured it out."

The prophet and the Devil had broken off their colloquy. Lucifer looked annoyed. "We're trying to work, here," he said. "I thought we were done with you."

Chesney had been thinking of what to say and now he used the gambit he had decided upon. "Not going well, is it?"

Joshua rolled his eyes in a silent *oy*, but the Devil said, "None of your business."

"Sure it is," the young man said. "I'm the one who started all of this."

Satan made a dismissive motion. "You're a plot device," he said. "You're nothing but a pivot on which to turn the story in a new direction."

Chesney nodded as if giving the idea consideration. "But then again, from my point of view, I'm the hero."

"Every mugwump and mutton-thumper has the same point of view. It's irrelevant."

Again, Chesney conceded the apparent reasonableness of the Devil's position, then said, "But that brings us back to your problem, doesn't it?"

Joshua interrupted. "How are you feeling?"

"I think you know the answer to that," Chesney said. "You did more, back in your day, than cast out demons and predict the end of the world, didn't you?"

Melda had been watching, with a small vertical line deepening above the bridge of her nose. "What's going on here?" she said.

The look the prophet gave her was almost bashful. "Your betrothed, he was not quite well when you met him, am I right?"

"There was nothing wrong with him!"

"No need to be the lioness defending her cub," said Joshua. "I'm sure he was a very fine young man, but…" He raised both hands in an equivocal gesture.

"High-functioning autism is what they called it when I was a kid," Chesney said.

"Did you like being that way?"

"I was used to it."

"You mean you found ways of coping."

Chesney shrugged. "I suppose."

"And now you don't have to."

Melda said, "Do you mind? What are you talking about?"

Chesney said, "He fixed me."

"What? How?"

"I don't know the details. I must've touched the hem of his garment or something. But that's why I can think my way through things I never could have handled before."

"It was when I poured the wine and gave it to you," Joshua said. "You've been gradually getting better?"

"Yes." said Chesney. "So it's not instantaneous?"

"What do you want, miracles?" said the prophet. "I made a blind man see again, once. Still, it took a while before he could throw a stone with any accuracy."

"That's what I figured," Chesney said.

"Well," said Joshua, "there you go."

"No more pools of light?" said Melda.

"Nor any more acres of darkness," said the bearded man. He looked at her kindly. "But he won't stop needing you. His abilities have changed, his soul hasn't."

"Told you," Chesney said.

Lucifer had been sitting through all this with signs of a growing impatience. "We have more important things to consider than the canoodlings of a pair of plot devices," he said.

Melda gave him a glare that should have scorched the Devil's whiskers, but Chesney put a calming hand on her shoulder and said, "Speaking of such matters, we've brought you exactly what you need."

Satan's pride wrestled with his curiosity. Before a winner could be established, Joshua said, "What?"

"A ringer," said the young man, "a seasoned professional. Better yet, one who already knows the story so far."

Lucifer frowned. "Hardacre? He's out of the picture."

"No," said Chesney. "He was, but we've put him back in."

"Can't be done. One of my dukes has him in thrall."

"You'll have to disenthrall him."

"Against the rules," said Satan. "Which, I remind you, I did not write."

Chesney turned to Joshua. "Can you forgive sins?" he said.

The bearded man shook his head. "That's the other fellow. I was never so presumptuous. Faith-healing, demon-routing, that was about it."

Chesney shrugged like a man who has tried something even though he didn't expect it to work. He turned back to Lucifer. "So Hardacre's been consorting with demons, even though he didn't know it—"

"And didn't want to know it," said the Devil.

"A valid point," said the young man. "Even so, he's not yours until he dies, right? Those are the rules?"

"Yes, so?"

"So he's not going to die."

The Devil's brows grew down to a vee, like a

slim-winged bird of prey hovering just before it struck. "What?"

"Tree of Life," Chesney said, "a little taste. He's got some wounds that need fixing, though. In fact, I think you arranged for him to be shot, once you'd moved on to this new project."

"Tough," said Lucifer. "The rules, you know."

"I could fix him," Joshua said. "It would take a little time, but if he has eaten of the Tree of Life, he's got time to spare." He looked at Lucifer. "Of course, not much work would get done in the meantime."

The Adversary's face had darkened. "Am I being made a fool of?" he said.

"No," Chesney said, "together, we're bending the rules, so that you two, with Billy Lee's help, can write new ones. Isn't that what you've always wanted?"

The Devil's expression flitted between moods before hardening again. "But I'm not the one who's making it happen."

Joshua said, "You're going to let your pride be your undoing? Again?"

"Wait," said Chesney. "Think it through. Everything that's been happening since the strike was settled – Hardacre and his new gospel, the almost end of the world, Joshua being rescued from his endless Nazareth – that was all because of your machinations, right?"

"Yes," said Lucifer.

"It's got you where you wanted to be, co-writing a new set of rules, a new gospel, with the messiah?"

"Yes."

"In fact, the whole story, from the incident right here with the fruit from the tree, actually started before that. It started when you decided you weren't going to go along to get along."

"So?" said the Devil, wariness coming into his tone.

"So why does the prime mover in all of this need a new rule before he can cooperate?" The Devil said nothing, his face busy with thoughts. Chesney pressed on. "Who says that you always have to let your pride work against your best interests? Is that a rule? Or is it up to you?"

"He's got a point," said Joshua. "We'd be making more progress if you didn't want to be in charge."

"It was my idea!" said Lucifer.

"Then you'll get top billing," said Chesney. "The thing is, if you bend this rule, now, for Hardacre, you'll be stepping out of the box, won't you?"

Again, the Devil's expression reflected the work going on behind the darkness of the eyes. And again Chesney pushed the stone a little farther up the hill. "And who put you in that box in the first place?"

And now the young man saw the dots becoming connected, as Lucifer's eyes narrowed in thought then opened. "Ah," said the Devil, and after a moment, "agreed." A slim finger stirred the air and Billy Lee Hardacre's ravaged body appeared before them on the grass beneath the great tree.

Simultaneously, from not far away, Chesney heard a cry of shock and despair. "If you don't mind," he said to the Devil. Satan shrugged and stirred the air again, and a moment later, Letitia and Captain Denby appeared.

The policeman's eyes fluttered; he was regaining consciousness.

Lucifer looked down at the blood-stained preacher, then made a shooing motion with one hand. Immediately, Hardacre's wounds closed, the pallor of his face was replaced by pink-cheeked health, and he opened his eyes. He sat up, looked into the faces gazing down at him and said, "Somebody want to tell me what's going on?"

Chesney did, succinctly and with a certain new-found authority. When he'd finished, the preacher said, "You want me to ghost-write the new gospel–"

Chesney amended the statement: "This time it will be the real one."

Hardacre accepted the redaction. He looked at his two co-authors. "Basically," he said, "we're talking a Manichean setup?"

"Basically, yes," said Joshua, "light and dark, balance of forces."

"Constantly at war?"

"Is night at war with day?" said the prophet.

Hardacre focused on Lucifer. "That the way you see it?"

There was a silence. Chesney sensed a struggle going on within the Adversary. Then, "Yes, balance. Yin and yang."

Hardacre looked around. "And I stay here, working with you until we get it written so that everybody's happy?"

"With your wife," said Joshua.

The preacher looked around. "I've had worse gigs," he said. "But suppose I don't want the job?"

"Then," said Lucifer, "you go back to the world, though without the assistance you've been getting from my resources."

Hardacre smiled wryly. "So it wasn't just my natural charisma?"

"No. I think you can count on being identified as a threat to the security of your country," said the Devil. "The proceedings would no doubt be informal and extra-judicial in nature. You'd be confined for the rest of your life to a small room that contained both your bed and your toilet."

"And," said Chesney, "the rest of your life would be a very, very, long time."

Hardacre smiled again. "It could be worse," he said. "Imagine if they kept trying to execute me." He shrugged. "And after the writing's done?"

Chesney said, "As the world works its way forward, under the new setup, differences between the partners" – he indicated the prophet and the Devil – "are bound to arise. They will probably need a good arbitrator – that used to be your line of work."

"Agreed," said Joshua. After a moment, Satan concurred.

"All right," said Billy Lee, "providing my wife agrees."

Letitia expressed general agreement, but suggested they work out the details, over in the vicinity of the Tree of Life.

"Then I suppose we're done," said Chesney. He felt a strong desire to be back in the world, before his mother and her husband got underneath the Tree of

Life and under its influence. Sound traveled extraordinarily well in Eden.

But Melda said, "Wait."

"What?" said several voices.

To Hardacre she said, "You've got a mansion and a lot of money, sitting there all on its own. Don't you think you'll need a reliable caretaker couple?"

The preacher smiled. "I told you you should have been a lawyer." He turned to Chesney. "Power of attorney suit you?"

Chesney looked at his betrothed. "If it's joint, between Melda and me."

The Devil motioned toward the blank pages on the table. One of them filled with printing then wafted over to Billy Lee's hands. He scanned the document. "Nice wording," he said. "Airtight. And back-dated."

Lucifer accepted the compliment. "Just to be sure," he said, "deeds and bank accounts have already been transferred into their names."

Hardacre looked at Chesney. "So now you're Bruce Wayne. And your buddy's going to be chief of police." He indicated the young woman. "Is she going to be your Robin?"

"Not a bad idea," said the Actionary.

"Here's something to think about," said the preacher. "What if all of that is part of somebody else's plan?" He cocked a head toward the dark entity at the table.

"I guess," said Chesney, "I'll just have to think it through and figure out what's best. Which may be part of somebody else's plan, too."

Letitia took Billy Lee's arm and began to draw him away. Then she paused and looked back at her son. "Come and visit us from time to time," she said. Now she turned to Melda. There was a brief struggle in the old woman's face, then it resolved and she added, "You, too, my dear."

Captain Denby was still gagged, but he was making noises around the ball of cloth. Chesney bent and loosened the ties and removed the obstruction. The policeman said, "What the Hell–"

"We'll explain it all back at the bat cave," Melda said. "With apologies."

"Xaphan," Chesney said, "we're out of here."

"'Bout time, too," said the demon, his oversized weasel eyes reflecting the earthly paradise around them. "This place gives me the heebie-jeebies."

ABOUT THE AUTHOR

Matt Hughes was born sixty years ago in Liverpool, England, but his family moved to Canada when he was five. He has made a living as a writer all of his adult life, first as a journalist, then as a staff speechwriter to the Canadian Ministers of Justice and Environment, and – from 1979 until a few years back – as a freelance corporate and political speechwriter in British Columbia. He is a former director of the Federation of British Columbia Writers and used to belong to Mensa Canada, but these days he's conserving his energies to write fiction.

He's been married to a very patient woman since the late 1960s, and he has three grown sons. Of late, Matt has taken up the secondary occupation of housesitter, so that he can afford to keep on writing fiction yet still eat every day. He's always interested to hear from people who've read his work.

archonate.com

"A GREAT READ. IT WILL FOREVER
CONTAIN THE MOST INTENSE GAME OF
POKER I HAVE EVER READ. 5 *****"
— CELEBRITY CAFÉ

Wake eat read sleep repeat.

Twitter @**angryrobotbooks**

ANGRY ROBOT

TOO MUCH IS NOT ENOUGH
Collect the entire Angry Robot catalog